BEYOND THE SHROUD

By Rick Hautala

WORLD OF DARKNESS
www.worldofdarkness.com

Copyright © 1995 by Paradox Interactive AB
ISBN 978-1-63789-197-1
Beyond the Shroud is a product of Paradox Interactive AB
First Printing 1995
Crossroad Press Edition published in Agreement with Paradox Interactive

Cover illustration by Drew Tucker

Crossroad Press Trade Edition

Dedication

To Bonnie and Jim Moore ... without whom ...

"I wear the chains I forged in life."

- Charles Dickens

"Oh, ye interminable gloomy realms
Of swimming shadows and enormous shapes,
Some fully shown, some indistinct, and all
Mighty and melancholy—what are ye?
Live ye, or have ye lived?"

- Lord Byron, *Cain*

Prologue

PORTLAND PRESS HERALD,
Wednesday, July 17 LONDON (UPI)

Investigators report no further leads in their investigation of the theft from London's Riverside Museum last week of three knives reputed to have belonged to the nineteenth century serial killer popularly known as "Jack the Ripper."

The antique surgical "post-mortem" knives with hard rubber handles and 24 cm. blades were reported missing after a routine check by security guards following closing time at the museum on the evening of July 11.

Investigators have determined that no other displays or objects, some of which are of much greater value than the knives, were tampered with or stolen. Police are baffled as to why the culprit or culprits would steal only those particular items. Unofficial speculation is that the theft was planned and executed by a Ripper enthusiast, or "Ripperologist," as they are known, who wanted to personally own a small piece of one of London's most notorious crime sprees.

Not many people in Portland, Maine—or the rest of the country, for that matter—noticed this small news article when it ran on the wires on July 17th.

If the year had been 1988, the centenary "celebration" of Jack the Ripper's ghastly murder spree, more people might have paid attention to it. It might even have garnered a brief mention on the CBS Evening News.

As it was, however, the five sentence squib on page three of the *Portland Press Herald* was either quickly read and forgotten, or else overlooked entirely by nearly everyone who read the newspaper that day.

Sarah Robinson never had much time for anything more than a cursory glance at the headlines on this or any other morning. Most mornings, she barely had time to gulp down her coffee and take a bite of toast or bagel before grabbing her purse and running out so she wouldn't be late for her job at the University of Maine Law Library. Ever since the divorce from her husband, David, had been finalized six months ago, she'd had a tough enough time pulling her life together—especially following the deeper and much longer lasting pain of losing her nine-year-old daughter, Karen, five years previous.

The last thing Sarah was inclined to notice or give even the slightest bit of thought to was a relatively petty theft in London, England.

That evening, after work and a Light supper, she folded the newspaper in half, not even noticing that the "Ripper" article was face up as she placed it underneath her cat Bingley's water bowl on the kitchen floor.

Over the next several days, the paper would wrinkle from spilled water and turn yellow in the hot summer sun as the printer's ink slowly faded to gray.

awakening.

Chapter One

Consciousness returned slowly… like dark, heavy drapes being pulled aside by unseen hands….

David Robinson could feel his face, chest, and belly pressing down against the uneven ground. His fingers were hooked, like claws, into the loose gravel. He could feel a groan gathering strength deep within him, but no matter how hard he tried, he couldn't release it.

It was as though he had forgotten how.

The dense air blanketed him, squeezing and pressing him mercilessly down against the unyielding earth, forcing the breath out of him. When he tried to breathe, he could not feel even the slightest movement of muscles and ribs expanding his chest… no cool rush of air in his throat and lungs.

A cold, stark fear stronger than any emotion he had experienced before gripped David as he stared into the darkness pulsing behind his eyes.

And then, after he had stared into that utter nothingness for a terrifying, timeless instant, patterns began to emerge.

Veined flashes of yellow and white-hot light split the purple, velvet darkness….

Hazy, flickering amorphous shapes like huge, glowing amoebae simultaneously advanced and receded in the darkness behind his eyes….

Faces, stained by impenetrable shadow, danced and whirled around him like vagrant breezes, pulling at him from all directions at once....

Vague thoughts and dull, echoing voices flitted like phantoms through his mind. When he tried to grasp any one particular thought, it would slip away from him like fine beach sand sifting between his fingers.

Gone...

Lost forever...

Just like I am, a tiny voice whispered like hissing, spitting water in his mind.

Memories and half-remembered words drifted past him like wind-tossed sheets and disappeared before he could catch any of them until—finally—one single image burned more strongly and clearly in his mind than the others....

Lights!

Yes, twin spinning whirlpools of light... like razor-edged cyclones, zooming straight at him from out of the darkness.

David felt his body tense, and he automatically ducked to one side as though braced for the impact.

Yes, impact!

The thought was as palpable as a stinging slap across his face.

There had been... IMPACT!

A sudden rush of sound, like the tearing of old, wet cloth, filled his ears, making him cringe inwardly. He remembered hearing a heavy, dull *thud* followed by a chorus of wailing voices.

And there had been something else... something about a... a river....

David struggled hard to sharpen his memory.

... Time moves like a river... and you can either sink or swim...

That's it!

He'd been looking down into the swirling depths of the Stroudwater River.

It had been night.

Late at night, maybe even almost dawn.

The sky had been overcast with no moon or stars overhead. A gray shroud seemed to envelop him where he had been standing, isolating him from the rest of the world.

In the darkness, the river had looked like slick oil, sliding with a faint, throaty gurgle under the cement pillars of the bridge. Whirlpools and eddies dimpled the river's surface, and something-a faint, trilling voice-had been calling his name.

David's hands had been hot and sticky against the thick metal railing that still radiated heat from the blistering summer day. The night air had been raw in his throat, thick and burning as he gulped it like water into his lungs.

Dark water… choking him…

In the distance, he remembered hearing a steady, hissing whisper. He eventually realized that it must have been traffic, passing by on the Interstate.

But there wasn't much traffic out here on East Bridge Street.

Not at this hour.

David often walked out here late at night… to think, he told himself, to work through story and character ideas, and to contemplate what the hell he was going to do with his life now that-once again-it had changed so drastically.

But tonight, he remembered, he had told himself that he had done all the thinking he was going to do.

Tonight he had determined-finally—to *do* something about it!

And why not? It was all over.

Just yesterday morning, his publisher had rejected his proposal for a new mystery novel. His editor had also informed him—as politely as he could—that he wouldn't be interested in seeing anything else from him.

With the divorce finalized more than six months ago, compounded with the grief of losing his only child five years before that, his rapidly shrinking income and increasing depression, after destroying whatever love his wife might have once had for him, had finally broken him, too.

Over the last six months, he had withdrawn more and more into a shell of total isolation punctuated only by outbursts of anger. He had directed most of his anger at his ex-wife, but he had known deep inside that the real anger—the *pure* anger—more properly should have been directed against himself.

But what was he supposed to do?

Pick up his life, at least what was left of it, and get on with it?

Just as, for the last five years, he was supposed to work through his grief and guilt and get on with living after Karen died.

Just as, with sales of his novels and his book advances steadily declining, he was supposed to get on with his life as a professional writer, or else find something else to do to earn a living. As if he could find anything better than pumping gas at the corner Sunoco or bagging groceries at Shop 'n Save!

No, it didn't work that way, at least not for him!

David had told himself many times that he had tried to make his life work out, but—ultimately—it hadn't.

He had failed.

So—finally—tonight, feeling as though he had absolutely nothing left—no options; no one to talk to; nowhere to turn— he had decided to *do* it.

He was going to kill himself.

His face was still pressing against the hard ground, but he was starting to remember more clearly now. Fragmented images and memories coalesced into bigger chunks that began to have content and meaning. Some parts of what he remembered almost made sense.

He'd been standing on the bridge, gazing down into the river and wishing—no, *praying* to God that he had the strength and courage to go through with what he had planned.

He knew that it could be easy.

All he had to do was clear the railing with a smooth, easy vault, and then let himself drop. Let gravity do all the work.

He tried to imagine what it would feel like, and that, perhaps, was one of the drawbacks of being a writer: He could imagine violent and deadly things much too easily and vividly.

Free-fall.

Arms and legs kicking in the air. Hands tearing at the overcast night sky until finally, with a sudden, cold shock, he would hit the water.

Standing there at the bridge railing, he could almost taste the thick, choking stench of the polluted river water gushing into his nose and mouth....

He had watched the dark river's current, strong and fast, channeling between the stone pilings, waiting to pull him under....

He could almost feel the burning need for air as his lungs collapsed inward, choking him...strangling him... like huge, unseen hands that had caught him and were wringing his body like the useless dishrag his marriage, his career—his entire *life* had become.

But I didn't have the courage to do it!

That single thought burned inside David like the white-hot flame of a welding torch. He experienced a misery and despair that he hadn't felt since Karen died.

He had *thought* about doing it, had planned it and imagined it in finite detail; but when it had finally come down to leaping off the bridge into the river, he hadn't had the fucking balls to do it!

But then... something else had happened.

Something had gone terribly wrong!

If only he could remember...

———

A telephone call in the middle of the night usually means one of two things—either someone has dialed the wrong number, or else there was bad news.

The sudden ringing of the telephone beside her bed, inches from her head, ripped Sarah from a deep, dreamless sleep. She uttered a strangled cry as she bolted upright, one hand reaching for the phone and the other supporting her as she shifted her eyes over to the blue digital numerals of the alarm clock and tried to focus.

4:08.

"Oh, *shit*," she muttered before snatching up the receiver in the middle of its third ring.

Her heart was thumping quick and hard in her neck. A sour taste flooded the back of her throat. The only semi-lucid thought she had was that it probably was David, pissed off again about something.

But maybe it wasn't so bad. Maybe the worst that had happened was that he'd been drinking and hadn't been paying attention to the time. Since the divorce, that had happened... more times than she cared to remember.

The telephone receiver was slick and cool in her hand as she pressed it to her ear. In a raw, rattling voice, she said, "Hello."

"Is this Mrs. David Robinson?"

This isn't David's voice was her only clear thought as she tried to force herself awake. *This could be bad!*

"Ahh-yeah, yeah," she said, her voice still ragged with sleep. "At least I used to be."

No matter how much she tried to swallow, the sour taste wouldn't leave the back of her mouth. Her stomach suddenly felt like it was full of acid.

"This is Officer Murray, down at the Westbrook Police station. Are you married to a Mr. David Robinson?"

"I *was*. We've been divorced a while now," Sarah said thickly.

She wiped her dry lips with the back of her hand, noticing how chapped they felt, and swallowed tightly. Tension gripped her with a cold pressure that centered in her chest.

She knew that whatever this policeman was going to say next, it wasn't going to be good.

In a flash, her mind registered that the only possible question was—*How bad is it going to be?*

"I'm afraid there's been an accident, ma'am. Your ex-husband was killed tonight."

"Oh, Jesus!" Sarah let her breath out in a shuddering groan. Her mind went blank for a moment. "Wha-what happened?"

The air seemed suddenly to have been sucked out of the room. The night was hot, and she had been sleeping in a thin nightgown outside the covers, but suddenly the room felt several degrees colder. Sarah shivered violently.

"Apparently he was taking a late-night walk—"

"Yeah, he's a writer," Sarah blurted out, grasping for something—anything to say, even though it sounded rather foolish. Her eyes brimmed with tears as they darted back and forth, scanning the darkened bedroom. "He—he takes a lot of late-night walks. To get ideas and stuff."

'Tm sorry to have to tell you like this, over the phone, ma'am. I would have sent someone directly to your place, but we've had some—uh, another situation to deal with tonight as well. Anyway, as your husband—your ex-husband was crossing East Street Bridge here in Westbrook, a trailer truck struck and killed him. The driver says he never even saw him until it was too late."

"Oh, Jesus... Oh, *Jesus!* Was he—? Did he—?"

"The M.E. says it looks like he was killed instantly, that he most likely didn't suffer," the officer said.

"Umm... I see," Sarah said, staring blankly ahead. She blinked her tear-filled eyes rapidly, making her view of the room go all gray and blurry. She looked around for something to ground her, and tried to focus on the rectangle of the window where slivers of light from the corner streetlight angled through the slats of the miniblinds, but her eyes kept twitching back and forth, making the whole room dance jerkily.

"I know it's terribly late," Officer Murray said mildly, "but if possible, we'd like you to come down to the hospital morgue to make a positive I.D."

"A what?"

"We need you to identify your husband's body," Officer Murray said. "Do you think you're up to doing that?"

"Oh, yeah... Sure."

"If you could be ready in a half hour, I'll have a squad car pick you up."

Sarah started to reply, but then her mind went suddenly blank. She had barely heard, much less understood, what the policeman had said. Her vision of the darkened bedroom was blurry and out of focus. For a brief, shattering instant, she thought she saw the dark silhouette of a man, standing between the foot of the bed and the window.

She gasped and sucked in her breath sharply.

"Mrs. Robinson? Are you all right?"

When Sarah blinked her eyes and looked again, the illusion was gone. It took her several seconds to recover. She cleared her throat and said into the telephone, "I–I'm sorry. What did you say?"

"I said I can have a squad car stop by to pick you up in fifteen minutes if you can be ready that fast."

"Yeah, I–I guess so," Sarah replied weakly, still staggered by the news. It all had an unreal cast, like this was still part of some terrible dream.

"You're at Sixteen Canal Street, correct?"

"Yes. I... I'll be ready in fifteen minutes," Sarah said, and then she cradled the phone.

For the next five minutes or so, she sat on the edge of the bed, all the while shaking her head and trying desperately to clear her mind. The ambient light in her bedroom was still shattered by the tears that filled her eyes, but as she looked more carefully at the softly glowing window, she could see that no one was there.

Of course there wasn't! How *could there be?*

She took a calming breath and held it for a moment. Without looking away from the spot at the foot of the bed, she reached over and snapped on the bedside light; but even with the warm, lemon glow bathing her small bedroom, she couldn't shake the thought that—for just an instant—there really *had* been someone there...

Someone who had been *looking* at her... holding his arms out to her as though pleading with her...

And she couldn't shake the feeling that—maybe—just maybe—he was still there...

Unseen... no matter how dark or light the room was.

David was still lying on the ground with his head turned to one side as he listened to the wind. It whipped and snapped like loose ropes in the darkness. The shrill whistle reminded him of a blizzard, sweeping across the land. He closed his eyes and tried to remember what had happened earlier tonight, if it was, in fact, still tonight. His mind was flooded with fragmentary images and memories which he still couldn't piece together into anything meaningful.

One of the sharpest images, though, and the one that made the least sense to him, was a hooded figure he thought he had seen leaning over him. His vision had been distorted, making everything look like he was underwater, looking up at the sky. Hazy blobs of light shimmered and shattered into warped curtains of glowing energy. The face inside the hood that had leaned close to him had been lost in a dense pool of darkness.

A darkness as deep as a moonless midnight.

He also remembered either this cloaked figure or someone else speaking to him, but he couldn't recall any of what had been said.

It took a great deal of effort, but David managed to roll over and sit up. Hugging his knees with both arms, he looked around, hoping to get his bearings. As he scanned up and down the street, he realized one thing that had been bothering him. Although the wind was blowing with a loud, flutelike whistle, he couldn't feel even the faintest trace of a breeze on his face or arms.

His sense of time seemed off, as well. He had no idea how long ago he had been standing on the bridge, looking down into the dark river. It could have been minutes or days ago... maybe even an entire lifetime ago.

Am I dead? he thought, but he quickly dismissed the idea.

His idea of what *death* was didn't include self-awareness.

He had always imagined death to be pure, total oblivion, and that's exactly what he had been seeking tonight.

Oblivion!

He recalled that the summer night had been warm. The air had been close and sticky with humidity, but right now he had absolutely no sensation of temperature. Everything—even the atmosphere surrounding him—felt strangely neutral and distant. He couldn't resist the odd sensation that he was somehow detached from reality, as if he were floating outside of it in a bubble and looking in.

"Jesus, what the hell's going on here?" David whispered hoarsely to himself as he slowly stood up and brushed his hands together. His palms made a faint clapping sound that echoed oddly in the close night.

David frowned as he looked down at his hands.

He could feel them touching each other, but even as simple a sensation as rubbing his hands together seemed strangely distorted. It felt as if he were touching everything through thick, padded gloves.

A deep, lonely ache filled David when he looked around and realized that he didn't know where he was. This *certainly* didn't look like anywhere near the bridge on East Bridge Street... at least, not as far as he could see.

It was night, that much he was sure of.

But he wasn't even sure if it was still the same night he had gone for a walk to the bridge.

The sky appeared too close and dense, like a low-hanging fog bank. Each streetlight lining the side of the road cast a dull glow that fragmented into deep blue and purple splinters of light that cast ink-wash-thin shadows across the stony ground. When David raised his hand to his forehead, the numerous shadows of his arm coiled at his feet on the ground like a tangled nest of snakes. He took several lurching steps forward, but the effect of his multiple shadows moving along with him was completely disorienting. He almost lost his balance.

Leaning forward with both hands on his knees, he braced himself as he looked around. He was standing in the middle of a debris-strewn road in what looked like an ancient, abandoned city.

He didn't recognize anything.

He was surrounded by tall buildings looming darkly against the pressing night sky. Their square hulks looked ancient and somehow threatening. Along the fronts of every building—most of them three or four stories tall—were dark windows gaping open like huge, hungry mouths. In many of the windows and shadowed doorways, David thought he caught subtle hints of motion—of people or possibly animals moving about; but when he looked directly at anything, he couldn't see what might have caused it.

A cold, clammy sensation traveled up his back to the base of his skull. He couldn't shake the sensation that numerous unseen eyes were watching him from the darkness, studying his every move.

He wanted to start moving, but he had no idea which way to go until he heard the soft scuffing sound of feet dragging in the dirt behind him.

Clenching both fists, David whirled around to see a dark, hunched figure, making its way slowly toward him.

The figure was stooped over. One leg—his left—dragged behind him as though partially paralyzed. Tension filled David as he cautiously watched. The light from the streetlights overlie the person's features, casting the hollows of his cheeks and neck into deep shadow.

David could see that it was a man—or at least what had once been a man. As he approached, David could see that his features were decomposing. Wide, white flaps of skin hung from his forehead and cheeks. They swayed with every halting step he took closer to David.

"Why don't you stop right there, friend?" David said, surprising even himself by the strength of his voice.

The old man jerked to a halt. Hunching over to one side, he glared at David.

"Friend?" he said in a high, cackling voice. "I like that! Friend, indeed!"

The streetlight's glare caught the old man's right eye, making it glow with a deep, eerie gleam.

"Why don't you just back off?" David said.

"I can do whatever I like," the old man replied. "I sure as shit don't need *you* telling *me* what to do!" The old man's voice sounded as ancient as the decrepit buildings that surrounded him and David.

A cold, clutching sensation of fear took hold of David's throat. It grew steadily stronger as he and the old man squared off, facing each other. Less than twenty feet separated them, but David had the unnerving impression that the man was somehow insubstantial… as if he might not really even be there.

"Who the fuck are you?" David finally asked, once he could stand the silence no longer. "Where am I? What the hell's going on here?"

The only response from the old man was a sniff of laughter; but then, as though reacting to a sound which David hadn't heard, he stiffened and cast a wary glance over his shoulder.

"It's not safe out here at night. I can tell you *that* much," the old man said.

"And just where the hell *are* we?" David made no attempt to disguise the nervous quaver in his voice.

The old man continued to look over his shoulder for a while. Then he turned around slowly to face David again.

"Maybe you'll see something you recognize come daylight," he said. "Although, to tell you the truth, it doesn't often get all that much lighter even when the sun's out."

David was filled with a sudden, violent urge to grab the old man by the throat and throttle him until he told him exactly where he was and what the hell was going on.

Instead, he clenched his fists tightly at his sides, barely managing to control the hot rush of anger that swept through him with surprising force. It was almost as if he experienced the pure essence of the emotion.

"Hey! No need to get all hostile about it," the old man said. "I'm just trying to help you… if that's what you want."

"I don't need your goddamned help," David snapped, his voice still tight with anger. "I just want you to tell me what's going on here."

"Why, you're in the Shadowlands," the old man said. "I'm surprised you didn't realize that. Are you that new here?"

Again, the old man glanced over his shoulder, and this time David could hear something—a distant, echoing, keening that sounded a bit like a pack of howling dogs.

"Barghests. I think they're headed this way," the old man said. Then he chuckled. "Maybe they smelled the new meat."

David was about to ask him what he meant by *new meat* but then realized he didn't have to. He looked past the old man, trying to see what might be making all that noise, but the night was too dense and dark. All he could see were the streetlights, disappearing like a string of Christmas tree lights into the distance.

"You can come along with me if you'd like," the old man said. "But whether you do or not, I'd suggest you don't want to be here when the barghests get here."

"What are they?"

The old man snorted again with laughter and said simply, "Trust me. You don't want to find out."

With that, he began walking slowly toward one of the dark buildings, moving much faster than he had when approaching David. His left leg dragged behind him, leaving a scalloped line in the thin dirt.

"The streets aren't safe at night, I tell yah that much," the old man called back over his shoulder just before he disappeared into the darkened doorway of one of the buildings. Like an apparition, he faded from sight, leaving David with the distinct impression that he might not ever have been there in the first place.

But the sound in the distance was definitely getting closer. It sounded like a pack of barking dogs, their angry yips, howls and growls filling the night.

David glanced toward the building where the old man had disappeared and almost ran over to it, but then decided not to follow him.

How did he know he could trust that old man?

He preferred taking his chances in one of the other buildings—alone. Once the sun was up, he'd take a look around and try to figure out where he was.

Off to his left, not more than a hundred feet up the street, David saw a darkened doorway. After casting a quick glance over his shoulder, he started running toward the building. His footsteps echoed like distant gunshots in the night.

Just before he ducked into the shadowed doorway, David looked back one last time to see—something.

At the far end of the street, huge, indistinguishable shapes appeared, black as holes in the night. Some of them ran on all fours. Others ambled on two legs, their arms dangling at their sides. The chorus of wails filled the night and was loud enough to hurt David's ears as he felt his way to the back of the building through the rubble littering the floor. When he bumped into the far wall, he turned around and slid to the floor, where he sat hunched up, his arms wrapped around his legs.

Lost as he was in the darkness, he realized that his only hope was that whatever those things out there were, they hadn't seen or smelled him and wouldn't know he was hiding in here.

deserted streets.

Chapter Two

Tony Ranieri smiled confidently to himself as he strode up the stairway of Bailey Hall, heading toward the University of Southern Maine's library. Through the large, plate-glass window, he could see that Sarah Robinson was alone at the checkout counter.

Okay, so maybe today will be my lucky day! he thought.

Or maybe it'll be HER lucky day....

His smile twisted into a lopsided smirk as he ducked behind a pillar and quickly raked his hands through his hair and zipped open the brown leather jacket he was wearing. He was going for that casual, wind-blown look. After adjusting the bookbag on his left shoulder, he undid the top three buttons of his shirt to expose his curly chest hair. Then, sucking in his breath, he wheeled around the pillar and approached the library door, consciously putting a brisk, causal bounce in his walk.

As he swung the heavy door open, he glanced at his reflection in the dark glass and smiled with approval.

How could she not be interested in him?

Sure, she was quite a bit older than he was, maybe even ten years older, but didn't most women like their men young and strong?

He was positive that Sarah wasn't married. At least she never wore a wedding band or engagement ring on her ring finger. In the eight months since he had first noticed her, they had never spoken except for passing comments now and then at the counter when he was checking out a book. In fact, he only knew her name because of the brass plate on her desk. As far as she was concerned, he was just another nameless face in an ocean of people.

But as confident and cool as he was trying to appear on the surface, Tony was shaking inwardly as he pushed through the swinging arm of the entrance gate.

He wasn't quite sure why.

Usually, he didn't feel the least bit intimidated about approaching a woman he intended to hit on. But those women generally were undergraduates. Maybe it was because Sarah was older and seemed more settled and secure in her life.

After a quick glance at her when she wasn't looking up, he strolled over to the array of computers located beside the old card catalog. The back of his neck was burning, and his hands felt clammy as he imagined—and hoped—that Sarah couldn't help but notice him, and that—even now—she was surreptitiously watching his every step and wanting him.

Whistling tunelessly under his breath, Tony casually slung his bookbag onto one of the desks, leaned over the computer, and began punching the keys on the keyboard, pretending to be entering a book search. By cocking his hip to one side and angling his body, he positioned himself so he could maintain a clear view of the front desk. After clacking on the keys for a few seconds, he glanced over at Sarah again.

His heart thudded heavily in his chest, and a thin sheen of sweat broke across his brow when he saw that she was looking straight at him.

As soon as they made eye contact, she raised her right hand and curled her index finger, signaling him over to the front desk.

Holy shit! A sudden tightening took hold of Tony's stomach and groin. *She wants me!*

Pretending confused surprise and struggling to stay in control, he tapped his chest with his forefinger and raised his eyebrows questioningly.

Sarah smiled and nodded, then reached under the desk and pulled out two hardbound books. Holding them up, she tapped the top book with her finger and mouthed what looked to Tony like she was saying: "Are these yours?"

Tony let his smile widen and nodded as he grabbed his bookbag and walked quickly over to the counter. The back of his neck was prickly with heat. Chilling trickles of sweat ran down the inside of his shirt from his armpits. His legs felt like they were filled with jelly.

"The books you wanted through interlibrary loan came in the other day," Sarah said, keeping her voice to a whisper as she glanced around the library. "I think the notice was mailed out yesterday."

Tony was disappointed to hear her speak to him with such an "all-business" tone of voice, but he continued to smile widely. He was satisfied that she, obviously, had recognized him. That was a good start.

"Oh, good. Thanks… thanks a lot," Tony said, nodding and feeling totally stupid for not thinking of anything more intriguing to say. "I-uh—" He glanced nervously over his shoulder at the reference desk. "I've got to check out a couple of other books, first. I'll pick 'em up when I leave."

"No problem. They'll be right here," Sarah said without the slightest bit of interest in her voice.

Tony continued to smile brightly at her, but he was disappointed to realize that his charm hadn't worked on her. Sarah scooched down and replaced the books on the shelf below the counter. Then, without another word to him, she walked back to her desk and resumed working.

Tony hesitated another few seconds, all the while trying desperately to think of *something* to say, but his mind drew a total blank.

After nodding his thanks, he backed away from the counter and walked back to the computer he'd been using.

Oh, real smooth, there, buddy! he thought. *That'll make her want to jump into the sack with you!*

Tony's hand trembled slightly as he fished the pen from his jacket pocket, took a sheet of scratch paper from the desk, and pretended to scan the screen while writing down titles and call numbers without paying any attention to what he was writing. He kept himself busy for another minute or two, all the while taking every opportunity to glance over at Sarah to see if she was looking at him, but she was involved with her work.

Tony was crestfallen.

Figuring it was time to leave, he slid the pen back into his jacket pocket and hefted his bookbag. When he looked at the sheet of paper and saw what he had written there, he snorted with surprise. A young woman, standing opposite him at another terminal, glanced at him and frowned.

On the sheet of paper were the words: *She's yours if you want her!*

For a dizzying instant, Tony stared at the message, not quite believing what he was seeing. This didn't even look like his own handwriting.

Did I write that? he wondered. *Or had someone else left this piece of scrap behind?*

Narrowing his gaze, he looked around the room to see if any of his friends might be close by, watching his confused reaction.

He didn't see anyone he knew.

But even as he cried to dismiss it, an uncontrollable shiver rippled up his back. He looked around at the wide expanse of the room, focusing, in turn, on the students and faculty members who were seated or standing around, studying or whispering to each other.

For an instant, Tony was acutely aware of how utterly strange everything appeared. He felt disoriented, as if he had somehow slipped outside of reality and was looking at everything through an inches-thick plate glass window. Dull afternoon sunlight filtered into the library through the windows between the slats of the blinds. Everything looked diffuse and dusty.

Every sound Tony could hear—even the hushed whispers of the two students closest to him—seemed oddly muffled and distant. The sound of someone turning the pages of a book was oddly magnified and sounded like tearing paper.

A quick thrill of alarm raced through Tony.

A moment later, a stronger, deeper tingle of fear gripped him.

Maybe he was getting paranoid because of the knife he was carrying in his bookbag. He had found it in the alleyway the night before, while he was taking a shortcut to his apartment after work. To help with his expenses, Tony was waiting tables at the Hollow Reed, an upscale, vegetarian restaurant on Commercial Street in Portland.

His throat felt suddenly hot and dry as he sucked in a shallow breath and rubbed one hand against the side of his canvas bookbag. He looked up but still didn't see anyone watching him. He could feel the handle of the knife through the thin material. It made him suddenly nervous to have the knife here with him.

What if the blade sets off the metal detector when I cry to leave?

A sickening rush of panic ran through his gut.

A knife with an almost six-inch-long blade certainly constituted a legal weapon.

Carrying it into the library had been a stupid thing to do. He could get nailed for carrying a concealed weapon!

How would he ever explain it to the campus cops?

Then again, how could he even explain where he had gotten the knife in the first place?

Would anyone believe the truth, that he had picked it up in an alleyway late last night?

He shuddered to remember what had happened.

It had been later than usual—a little past midnight when he had finally gotten off work. A large party of six rowdy couples, obviously on vacation, had been seated fifteen minutes before closing time. Because he had an eight o'clock class the next morning, and had already missed it too many times this session, he thought he could save a little time by cutting through the alleyway from Commercial to Fore Street. Tony was finding it tough enough just going to summer school, but working a full-time job while going to law school was wearing him down fast. And here it was, only the second week of July, with four more weeks of classes to go.

Still, he couldn't help but wonder how had he even noticed the knife in the first place, or why he had bothered to pick it up.

The alleyway had been darker than he'd expected, with only the faintest glow of light from the streetlight on Fore Street at the far end of the alley. He had taken this particular shortcut many times before, but usually during the day.

At night, Tony had a hard time feeling his way through the rubble and trash that clogged the narrow alley. But as he worked his way along, he had noticed a sliver of light as faint as moonlight, angling down the throat of the alleyway. Faint as it was, it had illuminated the knife blade like the hot center of a searchlight.

The blade had shined with an iridescent blue glow that he hadn't been able to ignore.

He had stopped and stared at the knife for a long time before finally picking it up. And he told himself he'd only picked it up because it had practically demanded his attention.

The instant he picked the knife up, it felt strange in his hand, as if it were charged with a current of energy. It was quite obviously old, maybe even an antique. Its hard rubber handle, narrow at the hilt and bulbous at the end, was cracked and worn. The blade was slim and symmetrically straight with no hilt guard. The most unusual feature Tony noticed was the small indentation on the metal sleeve in which the blade was fitted. As he gripped the rubber handle, he'd been struck by an odd sense of familiarity.

It was almost as if he had held this very knife before.

Automatically, he rested his thumb comfortably in the narrow indentation above the hilt. He realized that this must have been designed so the user—the cutter could apply some serious pressure when using it.

Tony had lost all sense of time, but he snapped back to attention when he realized how heavily he was panting as he hefted the knife.

He was surprised by how light the knife was for its size. Turning it over a few times, he smiled as the blade gleamed wickedly in the dim light of the alleyway. He braced himself and slashed the knife back and forth a few times, smiling as he listened to the loud *whick-whick* sound the blade made as it cut the air.

He had known instantly that he was going to keep the knife, so he slipped it into his back pocket, making sure to pull his jacket down so the knife wouldn't stick out as he continued his walk home.

It wasn't until he had arrived at his apartment on Congress Street and examined the knife under better light that he noticed what looked like a thin wash of rusty streaks at the base of the blade and on the handle. Although he tried to deny it, he realized that these could only be bloodstains.

A cold shock of surprise hit him when he opened his hand and saw on his palm a faint, red smudge.

He had gone to the kitchen sink and hadn't been able to stop his hands from trembling as he washed the knife under the faucet. For some reason, he kept looking furtively over his shoulder as though expecting to see someone watching him. He'd been careful to hide the knife in his bookbag so his roommate, Alexander, wouldn't discover it.

He had no idea how or why, but Tony knew that he couldn't let Alex or anyone else know that he had found this knife.

It seemed almost silly, he thought, feeling that way about it; but just knowing that he possessed it gave him a funny sensation, almost a new and different measure of security and power.

Yes, power!

Feeling like he was in a daze, Tony shook his head and squared his shoulders before walking back to the library checkout counter. It took him a minute to catch Sarah's attention, but she nodded as she got up from her desk and walked over to him. He took his library card from his wallet and, without a word, handed it to her. Sarah smiled pleasantly as she took the two books from the shelf and began processing them.

"So, did you find what you were looking for?" she said.

Her tone seemed warm and friendly, and Tony noticed that's he gave him a quick, intense look this time.

He smiled back at her, sensing that she might be interested in him after all, but he was too nervous to respond.

All he could think about was how he was going to get the knife through the security gate. For an instant, he was convinced that—somehow—Sarah knew what he was carrying in his bookbag. Cold panic gripped him, making it impossible for him to speak.

Finally, though, he managed to grunt and say, "Uhh—no, I—uh, I didn't."

Sarah bit down gently on her lower lip as she nodded and then stamped the due dates in the back of the books. Before handing them to him, she glanced at the titles. Her expression revealed her surprise.

"*Inside the Criminal Mind and Autopsy.*" She raised one eyebrow higher than the other. "What are you studying, anyway?"

Tony realized that this was his chance.

She had obviously noticed him before and had at least taken the trouble to remember his name. Now she was trying to initiate a conversation.

But Tony was feeling feverish and tense. All he wanted was to get outside and catch some fresh air.

"I'm—uh, I'm studying law. For the summer session, I–I'm taking Criminal Psych with—ah, with Professor Morgan."

He cringed, thinking how lame he must sound. He desperately wanted to say something—anything—to keep things going, but she seemed to pick up right away on his reaction. After handing him the books, she quickly started back to her desk.

"Uh—thanks," Tony said, mentally kicking himself in the seat of the pants.

Sarah barely turned to look at him as she waved one hand over her shoulder in farewell.

Jesus, what the fuck's the matter with me? Tony thought as he unzipped his bookbag, carefully shielding the knife inside, slipped the two books in between his notebooks and hurriedly zipped his bookbag shut.

For several seconds, he just stared at Sarah's back, wishing to God that he had responded to her a little more aggressively.

Why didn't he ask if she'd like to go out for a drink after work?

But he knew it wasn't talking to Sarah that had gotten him so wound up.

It was knowing that the next few steps were going to tell whether or not he would set off the alarm, and if he was going to have to open his bookbag for the campus security cop who was sitting by the exit.

He was trying his damnedest not to look guilty as he slung the bookbag onto his shoulder. Feeling like a condemned man, trudging slowly toward the scaffold, he sucked in a sharp breath and held it as he walked through the metal detector. He cringed, waiting to hear the high-pitched warning buzz, and almost fainted with relief when the alarm didn't go off. He felt so relieved that he looked back at Sarah and called out to her in as jaunty a voice as he could muster, "Hey, catch yah later."

He didn't wait to see if she had heard him.

A thin, gray wash of morning light seeped into the building, slowly washing away the shadows.

David was leaning against the wall, as far away from the door as he could get. At first, he barely noticed the change in light, but at some indistinguishable point he realized that he could see his pale, thin hands, clasped tightly together around his bent knees. The tendons in the backs of his hands looked like thin pencils just beneath the surface of the skin. It took him an indeterminate time to realize that something was wrong.

Then he suddenly got it.

His hands had never looked like this before! They looked thin and pale, like an old man's hands.

What the hell was going on here?

Maybe it was just a trick of the light, he told himself, but when he took a quick personal inventory, he realized that other things—*several* things were definitely wrong.

For one, he had the distinct and frightening sensation that he wasn't breathing.

No matter how long he sat there and thought about it, and no matter how much he tried to *do* it, he couldn't feel even the slightest hint of motion in his chest or throat. There was no steady intake and exhalation of air—no surge of warm breath through his nostrils.

"Jesus, this is fucking *weird*," he whispered to himself, but just as quickly he cut himself off when he heard the hollow echo of his voice in the gloomy silence. His words reminded him of the scraping, skittering sound rats made, scurrying for cover.

His eyes were wide open as he looked around and tried to pierce the inky gloom.

Something was *definitely* wrong!

He felt suddenly compelled to get up and start checking things out. It was time he figured out just where the hell he was.

If he could determine that, then maybe he could dredge up other memories about what had happened.

Fragments of thought flitted through his mind, but most of them didn't make sense. The most vivid memories—especially the one of a hooded figure leaning over him and whispering to him—were too terrifying to contemplate for long. He had a vague impression of a skeletal face peering at him from within the folds of a heavy hood, but dismissed that as just his overworked imagination.

He hoped that he would forget all about those disturbing thoughts if he got up and started moving around. If he didn't do *something*, he was going to go *nuts!*

But then he started thinking about the old man he'd met last night.

Who the hell was he?

What was his story?

And those hounds or whatever those things he'd heard baying were…

What had the old man called them?

Barghests?

Well, whatever they were, what if they were looking for him? What if they came back?

The old man with the crippled leg had obviously been afraid to be caught out in the open.

After finding his way into the building, David had crouched in the darkness and listened to them, their howls growing louder and louder until he was positive they were right outside the building where he was hiding. He had even heard one or more of them sniffing and snorting around the dark entrance of the building. He didn't doubt that they had caught his scent, but for some reason they had moved away from his hiding place. He guessed they must be hunting someone else.

David groaned as he stretched his arms over his head. His muscles felt as thin and dry as paper. His bones and tendons seemed ready to snap as he shifted his weight forward and shakily stood up. As he straightened his body out, something in the small of his back popped. He let out another low groan and sank back down and slumped against the wall as a surprisingly strong wave of nausea and dizziness swept over him.

Cupping both hands over his eyes, he stared into the perfect well of darkness behind his eyes until the feeling eventually faded away. He had no idea how long it took.

Once it was gone, it struck David as strange how the sensation of pain had been more like a memory of pain than the real thing.

Something was *definitely* wrong here!

After taking a few seconds to collect himself, David stood up and slowly picked his way through the debris toward the doorway. The closer he got to the door the more his eyes stung from the gradually brightening daylight outside. When he reached the doorway, he supported himself by leaning against the rotting doorjamb as he looked outside.

He was struck with utter amazement by what he saw.

The city—wherever the hell he was—looked like the bombed-out ruins he'd seen in World War II footage. The street was a mess of rubble and debris. Broken bricks and stones, piles of trash, uprooted trees, bent and rusted street signs and other litter were strewn everywhere. A few rusted hulks of abandoned cars and trucks lined both sides of the road. The sun, hanging low in the sky, looked bloated and red as it rose above the distant tree line. Its feeble light cast thin, jagged shadows across the street and buildings.

A steady, whistling wind was blowing around sheets of yellowed newspaper and other litter that flapped like broken bird wings until they fetched up against a building or rusted chainlink fence. David half-expected to see a pack of mongrel dogs rummaging through the garbage in the alleyways, but the street was strangely deserted, absolutely devoid of any people or animals. "Even birds," David whispered as he craned his neck back and scanned the sky beyond the bare branches of a few nearby trees.

Come to think of it, where were the leaves?

It was supposed to be July.

Shouldn't the trees be covered with leaves and filled with singing birds?

But as he looked around, all he could hear was the low, hollow whistle of the wind and the high hiss of dust being blown about.

David wanted to call out, to see if he could draw anyone's attention, but then he remembered the baying hounds he had heard the night before and, for now, decided to explore the area in silence. He wasn't sure he wanted to encounter the man with the bad leg again. There had been something about him that had bothered David. Talking to him had been like...

"—like talking to a corpse," David said.

His words were whisked away by the whistling wind like fine dust. The sound was almost like faint laughter.

David felt all but drained of energy as he started walking up the street, looking from side to side, trying to see anything familiar. It was only when he paused and looked back at the building where he had spent the night that a cold blade of panic sliced through him.

Above the arching doorway of the building was a sign.

The painted letters were chipped and faded, but by squinting he could still make out what was written there. He read the name out loud, then repeated it a few times before it finally sank into his awareness.

"Pine Knoll Elementary... Pine Knoll Elementary! *Jesus Christ!* That can't be *Pine Knoll Elementary!*"

For a dizzying instant, David felt completely disoriented. It had to be just coincidence that this building had the same name as the elementary school in Portland that he had attended when he was young.

But the longer he stared at the building, mentally trying to rescore it by ignoring the near total decay and deterioration, the more he realized that this, in fact, *had* to be the school he had attended.

Tension gripped him.

He couldn't fathom what had happened to the school since he had last seen it, but he could see now that this was the familiar building at the corner of Deering Avenue and Prospect Street.

"How the hell... ?" His voice trailed off as he tried to absorb the shock.

How had he ended up here?

The last thing he clearly remembered was standing on the East Bridge Street bridge in Westbrook sometime after midnight and looking down into the murky water. There were other, vaguer memories after that—some of them terribly frightening—but there was no *way* he could have gotten here!

And there was no way this could be Deering Avenue!

Granted, it had been a while since he had been out this way, but it had been a month or two at the most. There was no way this part of Portland could have deteriorated so quickly.

"What the hell is going on here?" he said, clenching his fists and bouncing them against the sides of his head.

"I might be able to explain it… some of it, anyway."

The voice, speaking so suddenly and so close behind him, startled David. He let out a shout of surprise that echoed from the derelict buildings as he wheeled around and saw the old man with the injured left leg, standing less than ten feet behind him.

David had no idea how the man could have gotten this close without him hearing his approach, especially with his bad leg, but there he was, smiling a grin that exposed a top row of yellowed, rotting teeth.

David was filled with a sudden burst of rage that made him want to grab the old man by the collar and throttle him until his few remaining teeth fell out of his head, but—somehow—he managed to control himself.

"That would be… yeah, I–I'd appreciate that," David finally said, once his initial shock and rage had passed, and he could speak again.

The old man smiled crookedly as he nodded to David and then turned. Looking back at David over his shoulder, he hooked his forefinger and beckoned for him to follow.

"Come with me, then, if you'd like," the old man said. His voice was as faint as the whickering whisper of the wind.

"Where are you going?" David called out, his voice sharp and demanding. He folded his arms across his chest, making it clear that he wasn't going anywhere until he got some straight answers.

"No, not out here… Not out here," the old man said, shaking his head as he cast a furtive glance up and down the street. "We don't want to be seen out here."

"Who will see us?" David asked, frowning as he looked around. "As far as I can tell, there isn't another living soul within miles."

The old man smiled and cocked his head back as he laughed out loud, but his laughter sounded more like a snarl as he shook his head from side to side. When he spoke again, his voice snapped at David like a whip.

"That's it! That's exactly it," he said with a high, wavering cackle. "Not another living soul! That's rich! Still, we don't want to be seen by anyone! I can tell you what's going on—some of it, anyway, but I doubt that you'll believe me."

"Try me," David said with a forcefulness that he didn't truly feel.

"Well, then..." the old man said. His eyes gleamed wickedly as he moved a few steps closer to David.

"For one thing—you're dead. You're a wraith now. But I'll bet you already figured that part of it out, didn't you?"

Sarah didn't take her eyes off Tony Ranieri as he left the building and walked away down the sidewalk.

She couldn't help but notice how uptight and nervous he had seemed, and that surprised her. Usually, he came across as totally confident and secure. That was one of the first things she had noticed about him, besides the fact that he was extremely handsome. She couldn't help but notice how many girls kept their eyes on him whenever he came into the library. Sarah had, in fact, first noticed him right around the time the divorce from David came through, and she was pretty sure that she had picked up that he was interested in her as well.

But after he was gone, Sarah chastised herself for even thinking about him. For one thing, he was much too young for her. Maybe not young enough to be her son, but still...

She had known before today that he was working on his law degree, so that meant he already had a bachelor's degree. That put him in his early twenties, at least. Sarah guessed around twenty-five or so.

So why was she—a thirty-six-year-old divorced woman—thinking about dating someone who was at least ten years younger than she?

The answer was simple enough.

She liked the way he looked, and the few times they had spoken, only at the book circulation desk, she had found herself attracted to his mild but confident manner.

He was a heart breaker all right, and Sarah told herself to forget him.

Granted, these days it was tough enough for a divorced, almost middle-aged woman to find a suitable date. What was it her friend Carol was always saying? "All the good ones are either married or gay." Although the divorce was only six months old, she had been separated from David for more than five years... pretty much ever since Karen died. It had been a while since she'd had any loving.

But thinking about Karen instantly cast a cloud over Sarah's attitude. If Karen had lived, Sarah thought, they would have celebrated her fourteenth birthday last May.

Fourteen years old!

It was such a tragedy that she had been robbed of those years!

The divorce had been hard enough on her, but Sarah knew that she'd eventually get over it. She was, in fact, pretty much *over it* already.

But the death of a child—her *only* child—was a loss that Sarah *knew* she would *never* recover from. It was also what had caused the minor stresses and strains in her and David's relationship to finally destroy their marriage.

And now—as of last night—Sarah had even lost her ex-husband.

She was alone and found herself wishing she had someone she could talk to, but—maybe from living so long with David—she had gotten used to bottling things up inside her.

Sarah was surprised that she wasn't feeling more upset about David's death. She guessed it was simply because—at least right now—she was still in shock about it. Going to the hospital early this morning to identify his body had seemed almost surreal. She was having a great deal of difficulty convincing herself that it had even happened.

Couldn't it have been some terrible nightmare?

She knew or at least sensed that, over the next few days, the true depth of her loss would finally sink in as she made David's funeral arrangements and settled his affairs.

She also knew that David's death, as terrible as it was, would never cue her to the core or shake her faith in *everything* the way Karen's death had.

The loss of a child was something she felt no one should ever have to face. There still weren't many nights when she didn't wake up crying, positive that she had heard the soft tread of footsteps or the gentle sound of breathing coming from Karen's empty bedroom.

It was the one loss she knew she could never reconcile unless she was willing to give up and accept the idea that the Universe was nothing but a meaningless, mindless machine that functioned purely on chance and that, in the great scheme of things, no one's life or death amounted to anything of any lasting importance.

But how else could she explain the death of a nine-year-old girl—a beautiful, bright nine-year-old girl who had her whole life ahead of her?

Sarah shook her head and straightened up, suddenly aware that she had been standing at the counter, staring out the window at the sidewalk where, quite some time ago, Tony Ranieri had walked away.

She could feel the slick tracks of her tears streaming down her cheeks. Sniffing loudly, she wiped them away with the heel of her hand. She noticed that her face was cool—almost cold to the couch.

Closing her eyes for a moment, she pinched the bridge of her nose and tried valiantly to collect herself; but surges of grief twisted like a nest of snakes in her stomach. She knew that things were only going to get much worse over the next few days and weeks.

Sarah jumped and uttered a high squeal when the phone on her desk began to ring. Her hand was trembling violently as she spun around, lifted the receiver, and pressed it to her ear.

"U.S.M. Library. Ms. Robinson speaking."

"Yeah, you were married to Dave Robinson, right?"

The man's voice over the phone sounded sharp with demand.

"Uh—yes. Yes, I was."

Sarah frowned suspiciously, wondering who this was. He obviously hadn't heard yet that David had died.

"This here's Sam Lowell, his landlord over on Brown Street," the man said, still sounding edgy and demanding.

Sarah felt a sudden wave of grief for David.

"I need you to help me out with something," Lowell said.

Sarah closed her eyes, took a steadying breath, and held it for a moment before speaking. Then she cleared her throat and, as calmly as she could, said, "I'm sorry, Mr. Lowell... I don't know if you've been notified yet, but David was in an accident last night. He was—"

"Yeah, yeah, I know. He died last night," Lowell snapped. "That's why I called. The end of the month's coming right up, and his rent's already a week past due. I know this probably ain't a good time for you and all, but if you can't pay up his rent,

I'm gonna have to ask you to have his place cleaned out by the end of the week."

Sarah covered her mouth with one hand and blinked her eyes rapidly to force back the sudden hot rush of tears. Another, stronger wave of grief washed through her, leaving her feeling cold and limp.

"You still there?" Lowell said, almost a growl.

"Yes, I–I'm still here. Just a minute, Mr. Lowell."

Sarah stared down at the floor and took another deep breath, struggling to control herself.

"To tell you the truth," Lowell went on, "he's bounced checks on me more times than Michael Jordan's bounced a friggin' basketball. You can understand my position here, can't you?"

Sarah cleared her throat and then, in a high, trembling voice, said, "Well, you know, David is—he was a writer, and you know how that is. Sometimes the money just doesn't come in fast enough."

"Look, I don't care if he wrote the friggin' Bible, as long as he pays his rent on time... which he almost never did. I ain't in this business as a friggin' charity, you know."

Anger and grief clashed inside Sarah like storm clouds. She wok another deep breath and said, "I'll have a check in the mail to you by tomorrow morning at the latest, Mr. Lowell. How much does David owe you?"

"Four-fifty, plus a late fee of another fifty dollars," Lowell said. "Five hunnert even. You can make the check out directly to me. Send it to 47 Brown Street in Westbrook. You know the zip?"

"I can look it up," Sarah said.

"It's 04092. Got that?"

Before she had to listen to one more word from Lowell, Sarah depressed the cutoff button with her thumb and hung up the phone. She was vaguely aware that someone was standing at the counter, waiting to check out some books; but without saying a word, Sarah turned and ran to the staff lounge out back where she collapsed into a chair, leaned forward with her face in both hands, and began to cry.

fetters.

Chapter Three

Gusts of wind buffeted the building like hammer blows. Wherever there was a crack or hole in the walls or windows, a steady breeze blew in with a high, shrill whistle that set David's nerves on edge.

For the last half hour or so, David had been pacing back and forth across the floor of a cavernous, dimly lit room, all the while keeping a wary eye on the old man who was seated cross-legged in the center of the floor. The ancient floorboards creaked horribly with every step he took. With every gust of wind, dust and fine grains of sand filtered down from between the planks of the ceiling overhead. Through the narrow windows at ground level, David could see that the sun was shining, but it had an odd, muted glow that made his view of the city street look like a sepia-tone photograph.

The old man had led David down a crumbling cement stairway into the basement of what appeared to be an abandoned factory or warehouse. The room was filled with ancient, rusted equipment. The grease and dust-laden hulks of huge lathes and drill presses, as well as radial arm saws and other machinery that David didn't recognize, were ranged in three rows, one against each long wall and one running straight down the center of the room to form two wide aisles along either side. The wooden floor, walls, and ceiling were caked with thick black rot. Especially in the corners and under the machinery, it looked like a spreading, cancerous growth.

"Does the wind always sound like that?" David asked.

He shivered involuntarily as he rubbed his hands together, unable to get rid of the odd, dissociated feeling he had whenever he couched anything, even his own body. Every sensation seemed so far away.

Muffled was the first word that sprang to mind.

"Oh, sometimes it's much worse," the old man replied softly. "But most times—hell, it ain't so bad. Eventually you get used to it and hardly notice it a'tall."

David nodded agreement as he cast a furtive glance around the huge room. Although he hadn't seen or heard anybody else, he had the distinct impression that he was being watched by someone—maybe several someones who were hidden in the deepest shadows. The hairs on the nape of his neck tingled as though charged with a current of electricity. Once or twice, when David turned his head quickly, he thought he caught a quick flutter of motion, but there was never anything there, at least as far as he could see.

"Do you mean to tell me I'm going to be *stuck* here? That this is it? This is what being dead's all about?"

The old man tossed his head back and laughed heartily, but the sound was deep and hollow, more chilling than humorous.

"Christ, no! No one knows what being dead's *all about.* You're a wraith in the Shadowlands. Far as I know, this is just the beginning."

"A wraith...?"

"Yeah," the old man said. "A ghost—a phantom. Remember? You're dead. You don't have a body anymore."

David extended his hand and waved it. "So then—what's this?"

"Your *corpus.* It's kinda different from your body. It's what's left after the physical part... sloughs away."

"Yeah, okay, but then tell me what—exactly—are these—these *Shadowlands?*" David arched his eyebrows. He wasn't sure why, but just saying the word *Shadowlands* filled him with a gnawing sense of loneliness and discomfort.

"Well, 's far as I can figure it," the old man said, "there are dozens of levels of existence. Hell, maybe there're hundreds or even thousands of 'em that you and I'll *never* understand—probably never *could* understand. I reckon you're here now because of something that's keeping you here."

"What do you mean, *keeping* me here?" David asked sharply. A sudden spark of anger flared inside him, but he gritted his teeth, trying hard to repress it.

"Look, I didn't ask for this, all right?" he said, his voice low and trembling. "And I *sure* as hell don't want to *stay* here!"

"Oh, but you see—you don't really have much choice about the matter. 'Least, not right away. Not unless you want to embrace Oblivion."

Without even knowing what the old man meant, David shook his head firmly. He didn't like the sound of that word. His first thought was that Oblivion sounded like *death* for the dead.

"But, hey," the old man continued, "as long as you're here, you might as well make the most of it. I'd suggest you consider hooking up with some of the other wraiths."

"The others? How many other wraiths are there? You're the only person—uh, wraith I've seen since I—"

He cut himself off sharply because he'd been about to say: since *I got here,* but then he realized what he really should say is: *since I died.*

"Sure. Of course there are others."

The old man seemed to be taking inordinate pleasure in David's confusion and surprise.

"There's plenty of folks who have 'passed on' but who remain here for—well, sometimes for quite some length of time. Take, for instance, them that were out hunting last night."

"You mean the dogs I heard barking?" David asked, trembling at the memory.

"Not dogs. They're called *bargliests*, and believe me, you don't wanna let them catch you. Of course, there were some other wraiths hanging around, too." The old man looked steadily at David, his eyes gleaming as if he were insane.

"Maybe you didn't see any of 'em, huh?"

"No, I–I didn't see anyone except you," David replied, shaking his head. He couldn't shake the memory of *feeling* like other people, unseen, were watching him even now.

Another, stronger flash of anger rushed through David. At first he thought it was directed at the old man, but he quickly realized what was really happening: he was having trouble processing everything that had happened to him so far.

And who could blame him?

How could he be expected simply to accept the fact that he was *dead?*

He wanted to believe that he *couldn't* be *dead*, that this all had to be some crazy dream or hallucination.

That's it! David grasped desperately at the thought. *Maybe I did finally jump, and I'm imagining all of this while I'm drowning.*

But all of his sensory impressions so far, while oddly distant, seemed much too real, much too immediate to be simply products of his imagination, dying or not.

He had to admit to himself that he had *wanted* to die. And he *would* have jumped off that bridge... if he'd had the balls! So on some level, maybe this was real.

He really was dead!

"Why should I hook up, as you say, with other wraiths?" he asked after a moment of silence, broken only by the fluting of the wind outside.

The old man didn't respond immediately. David watched as his eyes shifted like oiled beads first to one side, then to the other. He looked like he was keeping a watchful eye on someone that David couldn't see.

"Well... because the Shadowlands are a very dangerous place," he said at last.

"How can they be dangerous?" David said even as a coil of tension slithered through him. "We're already dead, for Christ's sake. What can possibly hurt us now?"

"Oh, plenty of things," the old man replied. "For one, there's the slavers. They'll take yah if you drop your guard. And there's lots of other wraiths who'd just as soon cart you off in chains and throw your corpus into the forges in Stygia."

Leaning forward, the old man cast another cautious glance back and forth, then in a low voice added, "And, of course, there's always the ... *Ferrymen*."

The old man whispered the last word so softly David wasn't quite sure he'd heard him correctly.

"Ferrymen?" he repeated, taking a step closer to the old man. He wanted to say something more, but his voice failed him.

In the silence that followed, he began to feel extremely uncomfortable. As if on cue, the wind outside suddenly gusted much louder. It shook the building's walls and caused something on one of the upper floors to fall with a loud crash.

David jumped, startled by the sound. He looked furtively around, expecting at any moment to be rushed from his blind side. He felt as though he should say or do something, but he had no idea what. If there was anyone else around here—any other wraiths—he'd probably be damned glad to join up with them. They certainly couldn't be half as loony as this old coot!

The old man nailed David with a long, piercing stare. Then, in a low, almost accusatory voice, he said, "As a matter of fact, I understand that you were seen talking to a Ferryman."

"Oh, no—no way." David shook his head in adamant denial. "That isn't possible. I haven't seen anyone here, much less spoken to them, before I met you last night. I was just—actually, I have no idea how I got here. All I can think is I was transported here or something. The last thing I remember was going out for a walk and then next thing I know, I wake upon the side of the road. I have no idea what happened."

The old man smiled at him grimly, exposing his bad teeth all the way to the gums. David shied away from him as if the old man were a rabid animal about to try to bite him.

"Well, now, maybe you don't remember it," the old man said, "but you were definitely seen with one. And I have to tell you—that ain't good. Not good a'tall."

"Why's that?"

The tension winding up inside David was almost unbearable. His chest ached as if he had been panting heavily, even though, no matter how hard he tried, he couldn't feel even the slightest motion in his ribs and chest. The fringes of his vision began to vibrate and blur, and for a single, shattering instant, he remembered—

He remembered looking up at a hooded figure leaning over him... and he remembered staring into the swirling black nothingness inside the heavy cowl... and he remembered hearing a grating, iron-hard voice whisper to him... whispering words that didn't quite make sense, but which, on some deep level, spoke directly to his soul.

"It ain't good because that ferryman may have put his mark on you," the old man replied, casting a fearful glance over his shoulder as though afraid they might be overheard. "If that's the case, that may have been him out last night, hunting for you, trying to collect his property."

"I'm not anyone's *property!*" David said with an angry snarl.

"That's just the thing." The old man shrugged, looking like he was enjoying this just a little too much. "That may not be for *you to* decide. Tell me—after I took off last night, where did you spend the night?"

David was about to respond, but something warned him that it might not be such a good idea to let anyone know where he'd been. He smiled thinly and shook his head, saying nothing.

"If they *were* looking for you, and you avoided them," the old man said, "then you must have found a haunt that has quite a bit of power. Usually, barghests can track down anyone pretty easily. But then again…"

The old man shrugged again and leaned back, trying to appear absolutely casual, but there was something in his manner that seemed entirely forced to David. A crazed, eager fire gleamed in the old man's eyes, and any second, David expected him to break out in maniacal laughter or to lunge at him.

"Maybe they weren't after you, after all," he said. "But you ought to tell me where you spent the night."

"Just… outside," David said with a shrug.

"Outside? Ha! Your first night in the Shadowlands, and you mean to tell me you spent it *outside?* By yourself?" He shook his head and clicked his tongue. "My goodness, you certainly *are* a brave little soul, aren't you?"

"I—ah, over the years, I've gotten used to being alone," David said, hoping that he could end the discussion. He was anxious to get outside and see if he might meet some of the other wraiths who were supposedly in the area.

"So—ah, what do you do here… in the Shadowlands, I mean? What's the point?"

The old man tipped his head back and roared with abrasive laughter.

"The point?" he said, hardly able to talk. "Shit, it's just like when you were alive. You have to *make* your own point!"

David considered this for a moment, then said, "Well then, can you give me some idea why I'm here? I sure as hell never wanted to end up here."

"It's your fetters."

David thought the old man looked more and more squirrelly with each passing minute.

"There's something—maybe *several* things from when you were alive that are keeping you here. Holding you from moving on. You know what they say: We wear the chains we forged in life."

"That was Marley's ghost, in A *Christmas Carol*," David said. "But look—as far as I'm concerned, I've got nothing to keep me here." He shook his head, thoroughly confused. "Just like I had nothing to keep me when I was... alive."

Even before he finished saying that, aching loneliness welled up within David, filling him with such deep misery that he almost cried out loud. He suddenly felt as though he were falling backward, spinning head over heels in an endless, black void. He'd felt like that before, when he was alive. Not as intensely, but now he realized with a hard jolt of fear that the endless void might be inside him.

He *had* lived an isolated life.

Even when he and Sarah were married, he had kept too much to himself, had bottled too much inside him. He had always told Sarah—and anyone else who would listen—that it was just part and parcel of being a writer and who he was. He maintained that he *had* to be self-involved to a large degree simply to create.

It was only after Karen had been born that he'd even begun to come out of his self-imposed isolation.

And then, after Karen died...

"After she... after my daughter... died..." David started to say. His voice broke on nearly every syllable until he finally fell silent.

"Yes-s-s-s?" the old man said, drawing the word out like a snake's hiss.

"I... I just couldn't see any... any reason to keep on living," David said, surprised by the suddenness of his confession. "It destroyed my marriage, my career... my whole fucking *life!*"

"You had a daughter, you say?"

The old man looked at David with eyes that glistened with interest. David barely had the strength to nod his head.

"So she might be here, too," the old man said, as much to himself as to David. "In fact, she might be one of your fetters — one of the things that brought you to this part of the Shadowlands. Maybe she's the reason you can't go on."

In the center of his chest, David could feel a feeble spark of hope flare up; but it was so small it quickly sputtered and faded.

Karen is dead, and that's all there is to it! But what if she's here?

He wanted desperately not to hope.

What if she has spent the last five years, wandering around alone in this dangerous, desolate place...?

An almost overwhelming feeling of parental concern surged inside of David. He had to close his eyes tightly and try to control the storm of emotion that raged in his heart.

"Maybe you should try to find her," the old man said in a voice so low that David almost mistook it for his own thoughts. He looked at the old man, wanting to ask him if he had any idea how he could find Karen.

Where could he start looking?

But then — suddenly — he knew. Just as, somehow without his knowing why he had ended up at Pine Knoll Elementary School — probably because of the attachment he must still feel for the place, at least as a haven of safety — he got an idea where to start looking for Karen.

He'd go out to Riverside Cemetery, where his daughter was buried.

"Is something the matter?" the old man asked,. arching his eyebrows. The flaps of skin hanging from his face fluttered when he spoke.

David almost said what was on his mind, but then stopped himself.

"I have to go outside," he said, and without waiting to hear if the old man had anything more to say to him, he turned and walked up the concrete stairs, back into the world of diffused sunlight.

The tires grumbled and spit up gravel, making the car's frame rattle as Sarah took the turn into Riverside Cemetery.

It was another hot and humid July day—the fifth in a row.

Interlacing trees—mostly maples mixed with a few pines—overshadowed the narrow, rutted dirt road. Their leaves and needles hung limply in the heavy heat. Like everything else along the side of the road, they were coated with a fine layer of gray dust. The cemetery lawn and shrubbery, the flowers, even the ordered rows of tombstones all looked like they were in desperate need of a cooling rain. Along the western horizon, a dark row of thunderheads outlined with bright, white light gave Sarah hope that relief might be coming later this afternoon. Right now, though, the summer air was as heavy and warm as a wee wool sweater.

It was early Friday morning, and Sarah didn't have to be at work until two o'clock. Usually she waited until Saturday or Sunday morning to visit Karen's grave, but for some reason—no doubt because of David's recent death—she felt compelled to come out here today. She told herself that it was just to water the potted flowers she'd placed on Karen's grave last Sunday, but she knew better.

Sarah often came out here to be alone to think… and remember.

Today more than most days, she needed to sort out some things mentally before she had to deal with them head on. The next few days were going to be tough, and she wasn't sure she had the necessary resources.

It had been more than five years since Karen had died, but the terrible, lonely ache of loss still filled Sarah whenever she came out here. The pain seemed absolutely undiminished by time and tears.

It was stronger, if anything.

As she negotiated the curves in the road, she noticed that her grip on the steering wheel was tight enough to make her knuckles turn white. She also realized that she was clenching her teeth and holding her breath. Her lungs ached. But just as she was mentally commanding herself to relax a little, she looked up ahead and saw the grassy slope where Karen's grave was located.

"Oh, *Christ,*" she whispered, blinking back the tears that instantly formed in her eyes.

Karen's grave and a few others were nestled at the top of a small hillock in a far corner of the cemetery. The site faced roughly east and was bordered on three sides by a dense wall of trees and shrubbery. Throughout most of the day, those trees shaded the whole area; but this early in the morning, a hazy wash of sunlight was lighting up the gravestones and grass with muted pastels.

Sarah considered this one of the loveliest spots in the entire cemetery, which lined the Stroudwater River for almost a mile. She always appreciated coming out here. The spot was so private she felt as though she could be completely alone with her thoughts. She often talked out loud to Karen, telling her what she'd been doing that week, and how much she missed having her around. All the while she would stand with her hands folded in front of her as she stared at the small, pink marble headstone until her vision blurred.

"What the—"

Sarah's voice choked off when she noticed something at the top of the rising slope of land.

For just an instant, she thought she caught a glimpse of what looked like a man, standing with his head bowed beside Karen's grave.

Sarah stepped down hard on the brakes. The tires skidded in the dirt with a raw, tearing sound. The car heaved to one side, and then stopped short. Sarah was thrown forward and would have bumped against the steering wheel if she hadn't been wearing her seat belt. Panting heavily, she jammed the shift into *park* and, leaning across the passenger's seat, stared up the rise.

No. There's no one there.

At least not now.

She looked up and down the road just to make sure the person—if there really had been someone up there—hadn't walked away from the grave while she wasn't looking.

The grassy slope rippled with dense heat waves that distorted her view of the trees beyond. The sky to the west looked like hammered pewter. Sarah's stomach clenched like a fist with anxiety as she rolled down the window, cocked her ear, and listened, but the only sounds she could hear were the distant trilling of a robin and the rhythmic, flickering hiss of the cemetery sprinkler system.

Maybe he wandered back into the woods behind the cemetery.

Sarah knew that the land dropped off steeply to the riverbank not more than fifty feet beyond Karen's grave. The slope was covered with dense brush and trees where people threw old flower arrangements and other trash.

No, if someone was there, he couldn't have gone that way. So who the hell could it have been?

And how could he have disappeared so quickly?

Sarah's body was wire-tight with tension as she switched off the ignition, undid her seat belt, stepped out of the car, and slammed the car door shut. The sound echoed dully, like a gunshot in the dense air. Her legs felt as stiff as wooden spindles as she started up the hill toward her daughter's grave. All the while, she kept scanning the area for any sign of the person she was sure she had seen there just a moment ago.

No, it must have been just a shadow or something, she told herself, but the thought gave her little comfort.

Maybe she was so upset she was imagining things.

She paused beside Karen's grave and lowered her head. Sucking in a sharp breath, she stared at the tiny headstone until the name and dates started to blur. All around the plot, the grass was wilted and yellowed from the heat. It was too dry to leave any clear tracks to determine if someone had been standing here.

Sarah wanted to believe otherwise, but she couldn't shake the feeling that she *had* seen *someone!*

Usually she found the cemetery so peaceful, but right now it filled her with a surging sense of apprehension and foreboding.

She looked up at the sky again.

The thunderstorm was blowing up faster than she had expected. The horizon was purple with haze that might be falling rain. The air had the sharp sting of ozone. The leaves at the tops of the trees fluttered wildly, but Sarah couldn't feel even the slightest trace of the breeze at ground level. The hairs on the back of her arms tingled as though the air were charged with static electricity.

She shivered violently when she glanced over at the empty plot beside Karen's grave and realized that very soon—tomorrow or the next day at the latest—workmen would come out here with a backhoe and excavate a hole for David's coffin.

"Jesus, Jesus, oh, Jesus!"

Her voice suddenly choked off and was followed by a high, strangled moan that simultaneously seemed to be coming from the surrounding woods as well as from deep inside her. Sarah clutched her head tightly with both hands and shook it from side to side.

Unable to stand up any longer, she collapsed onto her knees and slumped forward, her face buried in her hands as powerful sobs wracked her body. The cups of her palms filled with her tears as the sun beat down mercilessly on her back. A deep grumble of thunder that sounded like tumbling boulders vibrated the dense air and made the hair on the back of her neck stir.

When did everything go so terribly wrong? she wondered as her body shook with pent-up emotions.

She'd had such a good start in life—a fun childhood and four good years of high school followed by a challenging but still rewarding four years at the University of Maine and then generally decent library jobs, doing work that she enjoyed.

But somehow, somewhere along the line, it had all gone sour.

It had happened so gradually that she couldn't really pinpoint when it had started or when she had first noticed it.

When she did notice it, it was already too late to fix.

Even during the first few years of her marriage, though, right after college, she'd begun to think that something essential was missing in her relationship with David. She thought there might be something wrong with her, but she blamed a lot of it on what seemed like his negative attitude. As much as she had tried to resist it, over the years she had found herself drifting further and further away from her husband. She found the depth she needed from relationships with her close friends and coworkers instead of her spouse. After Karen had been born, she had thought, briefly, that this might pull her and David back together.

For a while it had.

But then came that terrible day in February....

Karen had started fourth grade that September. It was February school vacation, and David, who still maintained that he felt guilty having the house all to himself every day, said that he wanted to cake Karen and Sarah skiing. Because college was still in session that week, Sarah hadn't been able to arrange for the time off from work, but David and Karen had gone without her to Mt. Rainey, just outside of Augusta.

Then, late that afternoon, just around the time Sarah was expecting a phone call from David, telling her that they were back home after having a total *blast* on the slopes, he called her from the hospital in Augusta....

There had been an accident, David had told her, his voice breaking with sobs.

How bad? she'd asked.

Realty bad!

Karen had been coming down a slope that was maybe a little too difficult for her level of ability. In fact, the slope was much steeper than either she or David had expected, but she had said that she wanted to give it a cry.

She did fine until the first, sharp cum.

David said he had seen her have trouble negotiating the cum, and he had watched—helplessly—as she plowed into a stand of pines.

Over the years, David had told her—too many times, in exacting detail—what had happened.

The impact had been hard enough to knock one of Karen's ski boots clean off her foot. Both skis were shattered. The poles bent like corkscrews. Karen's face was smashed and flattened. As she lay on the snow, taking shallow, raw gasps of the cold mountain air, ribbons of blood had bubbled up and run from her mouth and nostrils.

David said he had shouted out for her to slow down. Sarah had heard it so many times, she thought she *had* actually witnessed it, watching it all happen and unable to do anything to stop it.

He had kicked off his skis and, tears streaming down his face, run over to her and knelt down in the snow to cradle her head in his lap as he told her how much he loved her and that everything was going to be all right.

But everything didn't turn out all right.

Sarah couldn't help but cry whenever she imagined her daughter's eyelids fluttering and then closing as she faded away with a final, shuddering groan. Worse of all, she couldn't bear the thought that her daughter had died, and she—the person who had brought her into the world—hadn't been there with her!

That had been almost five and a half years ago, but Sarah's memories of that terrible day, and the stinging, numbed memories of the funeral that followed, were as sharp and painful as if they had happened just yesterday.

"I miss you, sugar," Sarah whispered in a broken voice as hot tears coursed down her cheeks.

Suddenly she shivered and straightened up.

Even with the sun beating down warmly on her back, she felt a sudden rush of chills tingle up her back. She had the distinct, almost overpowering impression that someone had just touched her.

Someone had tugged at her shoulder with the faintest of touches.

Sarah's throat closed off, and her eyes were wide with fear as she turned around, expecting to see the person she had seen earlier standing there behind her. She let out a long, pained moan and almost fainted when she saw that she was alone. The cemetery was deserted.

When she looked down at her car, parked at the foot of the slope, it looked impossibly far away, almost lost in the hazy distance. The tops of the trees surrounding the cemetery were tossing back and forth wildly in the wind, but the air around her was absolutely motionless.

Sarah had the impression that she had somehow been transported outside of the world and was watching it like a passive observer. The air was charged with subtle currents of electricity that were gathering strength. Sarah was suddenly fearful that, with the thunderstorm approaching so rapidly, being up on a hill might put her in danger.

C'mon! Get your butt out of here! she thought, but she was too frightened to move.

She knew that she should sit in her car and wait out the storm. Usually storms that came up this fast blew over just as fast.

Or maybe she should go back home and come out here another day — sometime when she could handle it a little better.

No matter what she decided, she knew with a dull, dread certainty that she'd be back out here in another few days for David's funeral; but as she looked around the cemetery, she couldn't shake the feeling that the touch on her shoulder had been real — more than a static charge in the air and more than her imagination.

She could easily imagine that invisible hands had reached out to her and had tried to touch her.

Maybe it was Karen! she thought.

"Jesus," Sarah muttered as she stood up slowly. She could feel every muscle and bone in her body creak like she was eighty years old. Her stomach felt like hollow pit. The world seemed to be spinning crazily around her, and she had to struggle to maintain her balance.

The keen sense of loss she felt was suddenly too much to bear.

As she started back down the hill, heading to her car, she took halting, choppy steps and looked all around as though she wanted to start running, but had no idea which way to go. Emotions welled up from deep inside her, and she was vaguely aware that she was crying...

Crying for Karen... for David... and for herself.

At the moment, there was only one thing she knew with any certainty—that no matter how long she lived, her feelings of grief and loss, of guilt and despair, would never, *never* be dulled, much less go away.

As if watching her in a dream, David stared at Sarah as she walked up the hill toward their daughter's grave. Her hands were clasped in front of her, and her head was bowed.

He had no idea how he had gotten out to the cemetery, or how long it had taken him to get here. He had only a hazy memory of walking down Deering Avenue and along outer Congress Street to the cemetery. He had experienced an odd sensation of time passing and of distances being crossed, but he couldn't remember anything about it very clearly. Time and distance seemed to be much more tenuous, less well-ordered and defined than they had ever been when he was alive.

Along the way he remembered noticing several other people.

Some of them seemed to have taken notice of him, and others had ignored him completely, either on purpose or because, he assumed, they were living and *couldn't* see him.

In either event, he had decided that it would be futile, possibly even dangerous, to attempt to speak to any of them. The old man had told him that the Shadowlands were dangerous, and whether he wanted to believe him or not, David could *feel* the danger like a palpable presence in the air. If he ignored everyone he met, then maybe they'd all ignore him and leave him alone.

It didn't take David very long to realize that it was relatively easy to distinguish the living from the dead.

The living, even those who looked like they might be harboring some deep-seated sickness inside them, all seemed to vibrate with a sparkling, healthy glow of energy. Some of them even appeared to be almost translucent, like "ghosts" dwelling in the dead world.

All of the dead, on the other hand, appeared to have a dull, gray pallor about them that was far more than the lifeless tone of their skin. Their "essences," maybe what New Agers would call their "auras," appeared to be wilted and faint, as though tainted by the corrupting touch of Death. Their eyes looked hollow and blank, like poorly polished marble.

Whatever the case, somehow David found himself at Karen's grave when Sarah arrived. Standing at the top of the hill, he watched as his ex-wife moved toward him in slow-motion. She looked as though she were battling her way through an invisible barrier.

David felt no exhaustion from the effort of walking all the way to the cemetery, even though he knew it was better than four miles from Pine Knoll Elementary to Riverside; but once he was at his daughter's gravesite, he felt drained both emotionally and physically.

How can I feel drained physically when I don't even have a body anymore? he wondered.

He was almost amused by the concept of actually being dead.

He assumed that everything he was thinking and feeling was his own thoughts and emotions; but being dead, now that he was free of any physical reactions or restrictions, seemed to heighten such intense feelings.

Standing beside his daughter's grave, David trembled as he watched, half-frightened and half-amazed, as he clasped his fingers together tightly. No matter how hard he tried to squeeze his own hand, he couldn't get rid of the uncanny dissociative feeling that there was almost no feeling in his hands. It was like watching someone else move.

Powerful, conflicting emotions almost overwhelmed him as he watched Sarah kneel down beside Karen's grave, bow her head, and start to cry.

David could experience grief, too, but no matter how strong it surged inside him, tears wouldn't spill from his eyes. The emotions felt bottled up inside him, with no way to find release.

It was pure torture.

His corpus shuddered horribly as he looked at Sarah and called out to her.

"Sarah... Sarah."

He forced his voice to rise louder and louder as he moved closer to her and reached out with one hand. He could barely stop himself from shaking as he touched her on the shoulder, but then he watched in stunned horror as his hand passed like a whiff of smoke through Sarah.

His entire being was filled with knife-sharp pangs of dread and agony when he saw Sarah suddenly startle and look around.

Her lips moved as she said something, but the air seemed too dense, and the sound was too distorted for David to hear her clearly.

"Yes!... Yes, Sarah! I'm right here!" he shouted. "It's me, David! I'm standing right beside you!"

David was convinced that she could neither hear nor see him, but he felt a slim ray of hope when he saw Sarah tense, seeming almost to respond to his voice. She stood up slowly, frowning as she looked around.

David lunged forward, seeming to move in slow-motion as he grabbed at her with both hands, trying to embrace her and shake her; but it was like watching everything through a thick, dirt-filmed pane of glass. Dimensions and distances seemed oddly warped. A dark, tugging swell of vertigo surged through him, and inside his head he felt as though he were falling backward, spinning crazily, head over heels.

"Please, Sarah!… Listen to me… Look at me…" he wailed.

She was so close… so close, yet so far away!

"Please, Sarah! I'm right here beside you!" he shouted with all his strength, but even to his own ears, his voice sounded no stronger than a whisper of wind, not even strong enough to blow out a candle.

Tormented beyond belief, David watched as Sarah glanced around the cemetery. Then, wiping the tears from her eyes with both hands, she started down the slope, back to her car.

David followed after her, still pulling at her, trying to touch her, but it was useless. After one last, tearful glance at Karen's grave, Sarah got into her car, started it up, and drove away. A plume of dust rose up like yellow smoke in the wake of her car.

David was left standing in the dappled shade of the trees, feeling more alone and desolate that he had ever felt before. The receding sound of the car reverberated in the dense air like the fading patter of distant drumbeats.

As soon as her car was out of sight, he was filled with such a deep, lonely ache that he wished he could simply will himself to dissolve into nothingness.

The old man's words echoed in his memory, mixing with the dull, distant roll of thunder….

"*Not unless you want to embrace Oblivion.*"

Standing there alone in the cemetery, watching as the fine dust settled to the ground like gently falling snow, David would have cried if he could have.

the storm breaks.

Chapter Four

A s he walked away from Riverside Cemetery, not really knowing or caring where he was headed, the sky rapidly darkened. Mountainous clouds the deep purple color of bruises shifted from the west across the hazy gray arc of sky. The air seemed charged with static electricity.

Because all of his perceptions, even his senses of time and distance, were severely altered David thought that night must be coming on much faster than usual. After a moment, however, he realized that a thunderstorm was blowing in from the west.

David was mesmerized by the energy and power he could feel in the approaching storm. About a mile away from the cemetery, he stopped on the roadside and listened as the wind gathered strength. A deep-throated, hollow whistle sounded from the sky as strong gusts rippled like gushes of water over the trees and grass. Dust and debris blew in tiny tornadoes down the street. David found it slightly bothersome at first, then almost fascinating that he couldn't feel even the slightest puff of wind on his face. It wasn't until the rain began beating against the sidewalk, leaving wee splotches the size of half dollars, that a wave of sadness came over him.

He couldn't feel the rain hitting him!

Most people, if not actually *afraid* of thunderstorms, at least didn't *enjoy* them; but David always had—especially at night, when brilliant flashes of lightning flickered like blue strobe lights across the dark land, and the breeze was tinged with the sharp, fresh aroma of ozone and damp earth.

And now, here he was—*dead*—and it was raining hard enough to make the pavement look like it was dancing with energy, and he couldn't even *feel* it.

Infuriating!

The sky steadily darkened as the storm clouds, moving like closing drapes, clashed together. Thin veins of lightning forked across the purple sky. The ground trembled with the low, steady rumble of approaching thunder.

David was surprised to notice how everything around him seemed to be glowing with a diaphanous haze of static electricity. Trees, passing cars, road signs... everything he looked at was surrounded by shifting halos of light. He extended his hands and looked at them, amazed to see tiny curling tendrils of blue light caught like spider webs between his fingers.

Any sense of time vanished as David tilted his head back and watched the storm unleash its fury all around him.

The trees tossed violently back and forth, and the loud patter of rain on the road was almost deafening. All of the cars passing by had their headlights and wipers on. Their tires threw up fantails of spray from the wee pavement that hissed like angry serpents. Thin, angry rivulets of runoff water washed down into the weed and litter-clogged roadside ditches. Blankets of steam rose like twisting ghosts from the sunbaked asphalt as the cool rain washed the world.

The only other person David saw outside was an elderly woman, who was muttering to herself as she walked toward him on the same side of the road. Her "aura" looked absolutely neutral, and David wasn't able to decide if she looked alive or dead.

Not that it mattered.

When she was beside him, he greeted her with a smile and a curt nod. She glanced at him and scowled angrily.

"Hey, have a nice day, ma'am," he said.

The old woman's scowl deepened. She waved her hand once, dismissively, in his direction and continued on her way without a backward glance.

"Must be a dead one," David muttered to himself, shaking his head.

Even though he couldn't feel the chill in the air, David shivered. He still wasn't reconciled to the idea of being dead. He didn't like the way his perceptions seemed so distorted. It was disconcerting, at best. He couldn't stop wondering if he would eventually adjust to this, or if he would have to exist indefinitely in this odd state of distorted—and sometimes frightening—awareness.

But the most pressing problem on his mind was simply—*How long is this going to last?*

If he was already dead, when or how would it ever end? He couldn't very well exist like this forever—

Could he?

If everyone who had ever died was still walking the earth, trapped here in the Shadowlands, then even a small city like Portland, Maine, should be swarming with wraiths. The old man had told him that there were other wraiths in the Shadowlands, but how many? They couldn't *all* still be here. He would have seen more of them by now.

So where did all the other wraiths go?

It was possible, he supposed, that many of chem had passed on to Heaven or some other kind of paradise in the afterlife that the ministers and priests and yogis were always talking about. If the old man hadn't struck him as a potentially dangerous lunatic, David might consider seeking him out and asking him more about this. He decided not to, though, figuring that he'd eventually encounter other wraiths he could question about it all.

But the big question that he still didn't have an answer for was simply *Why am I here?*

What was the word the old man had used? *Fetters?*

So what *fetters* were keeping him here?

As the storm raged around him, David pondered this question for a while, but he concluded that he wouldn't come to any final answers on his own. After a last glance at the sky, he continued on his way. Because he wasn't able to feel the rain pelting his face or back, he felt isolated from it all, as if he were encased in a transparent, protective bubble.

Maybe he was even invincible.

Even if the Shadowlands were as dangerous as the old man had told him they were, David figured, since he was already dead, there wasn't much that could harm him. He was confident that eventually he would figure out what was going on here and, more importantly, he'd get some idea how he was going to get the hell out of here!

He continued to walk, not really paying any attention to the direction he was headed, hardly even aware of the activity because he no longer had a physical body that could become exhausted. Suddenly he drew to a halt and looked up, amazed to see where he had arrived.

Although it didn't look very much like it had five years ago, when he and his family used to come here regularly to picnic and play, he instantly recognized the Brighton Avenue park.

A shock of pure, unalloyed surprise shot through David as he looked around.

The area appeared to be much larger than he remembered it, and starker, more desolate.

Maybe sometime during the last five years the city of Portland had expanded the park, he thought; but if they had, they also had allowed it to decline into near ruins.

The grassy field where he and Sarah and Karen used to throw Frisbees was now clotted with clumps of crabgrass and yellowing weeds. The ball field where, in the evenings, they would watch Little League teams play now looked like a washed-out dust bowl. The rain had turned the depressions along the baselines into long, narrow quagmires of brown water. Even the trees that surrounded the park, what had once been beautiful stands of oak and birch mixed with pine and cedar, now looked scraggly, old, and diseased. The playground equipment—the swing set, slides, and climbing bars where Karen used to play with such delight—were all rusted and broken. The wooden supports were black with rot. Fitful gusts of wind caught the swings and tossed chem back and forth. The sound of rusted chains scraping against each other grated on David's ears.

He couldn't believe that the park had deteriorated this much in such a short time—just like Pine Knoll Elementary, he thought.

But how could everything have fallen into decay so fast?

The longer David stared at the park, the more he became aware of how distorted his perceptions were. He wondered why some sensations seemed so distant and dull, while others, things which he might not have even noticed when he was alive, were now loud and irritating. The more he focused on any particular sound, the more it seemed to work on his nerves. The hiss of rain sweeping across the field and trees was almost maddeningly loud. The sound of traffic passing by on Brighton Avenue approached and receded with warbling, hollow *whooshing* sounds. And everywhere he looked, the world—at least here in the park—appeared to be gray, drab and desolate, as if it had all been touched by the hand of death.

Out of habit rather than necessity, David stood in the shelter of the trees and watched, enthralled as gray curtains of rain shifted across the field. A flock of small, black birds darted across the lowering sky like wind-tossed leaves. David had the quick impression that they looked skeletal against the sky.

The sense of loneliness and loss that filled him was almost too much to tolerate. Thinking that he'd rather be *anywhere* except here, he was just about to turn and leave when he noticed a small, frail figure, standing hunched against the storm over by the swing set.

Instant recognition hit David like a thunderclap.

"Karen?"

As soon as he whispered her name, it was swept away by the wind. A hollow ache of despair and regret filled him as he stared across the field at the solitary figure, not quite able to trust his senses.

She was standing no more than a hundred yards away, her head bowed to the rain as though she could actually feel it. The features of her face were lost beneath the thin, gray shadow of her hooded raincoat.

"*Karen!*" David called out again, louder. He winced at the almost frantic tremolo he heard in his voice.

Either she couldn't hear him, or else she chose to ignore him. She just stood there, as still as a statue beside the bowl-shaped depression in the ground underneath one of the swings. Her face was downcast as though she was hypnotized by the plump drops of rain hitting the muddy surface of the puddle.

Shivering inside, David took a halting step forward. He didn't even dare to blink because he was afraid that she would vanish the instant he did.

Jesus! Can this really be her?

He was trying hard to contain the chilled rushes of excitement. A dull glimmer of hope flared up inside him when he started across the field at a brisk walk. After a few steps, he broke into a run.

Of COURSE it's her!... Yes, if she's alone and afraid, she might come here! ... We used to come here all the time... ever since she was a little baby!

David cupped one hand to his mouth and shouted as he waved his other arm wildly over his head.

"Karen! It's me! It's Daddy!"

When he was more than halfway to her, the little girl looked up, shifting her head slowly, almost mechanically.

David still couldn't clearly see her face beneath her hood, but he thought—no, he *knew* that he recognized Karen's red, rubber raincoat—the one with the emblem of a yellow duck holding an umbrella sewn above the breast pocket. She was wearing the faded blue jeans she always preferred and her favorite white sneakers with purple laces.

By Jesus, it *is* her!... It *has* to be her!

Rain and mist swirled across the field like the smoke of battle. The sky pressed down like a coffin lid as he ran toward her. But as he was running, for the first time since he had realized he was dead, David was suddenly gripped by complete and utter exhaustion. His arms and legs felt like they were being weighed down by iron shackles. He continued running toward the swing set, but every step he took was increasingly difficult until he was overcome with the sensation that he wasn't getting any closer to her. It felt like he was sliding backward with every step in the rain-slick grass.

Then, in a blinding flash, David's vision suddenly exploded with a bright flash of white light. For a single, terrifying instant, he felt as though he'd been swept up by a powerful current of wind, and his body was being tossed around like a handful of dust. All around him the air was filled with flashing lines of blue and white light that ripped through him like a buzz saw. After a dizzying, timeless moment, there came the deafening concussion of an explosion that knocked David to the ground.

He hit the ground hard but was disoriented only for a moment.

Shaking his head to clear it, he leapt to his feet and looked over at the swing set. Somehow, he wasn't surprised to see that there was no one there.

She was gone!

He darted his glance back and forth, scanning the expansive field, trying to see where she could have gone. At first glance, he didn't notice her; but then, far across the field, at the border of the trees, he saw the small, red-hooded figure.

"No..." David's voice was lost within the fury of the storm.

Absolute despair wrung him out. He dropped onto his hands and knees in the wet grass, knowing that he didn't have the strength to follow. He was positive that, whoever it was, even if it was Karen, she would disappear again as soon as he got close to her.

"Oh, Karen..."

He held his arms out to her in desperation.

The solitary figure tilted her head up and looked up at him. David could feel her penetrating gaze focusing on him. Then, like a column of smoke whisked away by the wind, she disappeared, blending into the gray fingers of mist that swirled like rivers among the rain-blackened trunks of trees.

At least fifty or sixty people were crowded onto the small dance floor. They seemed to be happy, packed shoulder to shoulder and hip to hip as they moved about in languid, random gyrations. The room was filled with a cacophony of shrill laughter and shouted conversation that struggled to be heard above the bone-jarring music, if that's what you could call it, of the band on stage. The singer's voice was buried in a bad sound mix that pushed the bass guitar and drums up much too loud.

The only time she could be heard clearly was between every song, when she mumbled what sounded like a very insincere "thank you very much" to the audience.

Thick, blue rafts of cigarette smoke swirled like ghostly strata. Thin, flickering lines of green laser light pierced the darkness above the dancers, turning everyone into an indistinguishable mass of dark, twisting bodies. Sarah's first impression when she and Tony entered the club was that they looked like tormented souls, writhing in Hell.

It didn't take long for the noise of the crowd to get on Sarah's nerves. She felt at least ten years too old for a scene like this, and she couldn't help but notice the numerous quizzical glances she'd gotten when she and Tony arrived. But she smiled broadly as she and Tony went out onto the floor and started to dance. She smiled, wanting Tony to think she was having fun.

She had to admit that she enjoyed watching Tony move. His arms, head, and hips shifted and waved in time with the hard-edged beat. Although she had hesitated at first, she was glad she had finally accepted when Tony called her at the library and asked her out. She had almost admitted to him that her ex-husband had died the other day, and that she needed some time alone to absorb what had happened; but after feeling the way she had out at the cemetery this morning, and now that a thunder shower had cut the humidity—at least for the evening—she had quickly decided that being alone was exactly what she *didn't* need.

The best thing for her tonight would be to get out, maybe have a few drinks and conversation, and then stroll around the Exchange Street area for an hour or two before...

Well, she wasn't quite sure what would happen next, but she had some ideas. If she and Tony ended up at his or her place later on, and if they made love—well then, all the better. It had been too long since she'd had sex with *anyone*. It'd be nice to feel a man hold her once again and enter her—especially a man as young and strong as Tony.

The only problem was, she hadn't been counting on something like *this!*

The song the band was playing sounded identical to every other one they had played so far. It ended with a crash of cymbals, and then the singer announced that they would be taking a short break.

Sarah leaned forward to say something to Tony, but before she got half a sentence out, the music system in the club kicked in, blasting recorded music even louder than the band had been playing. Tony took Sarah by the hand and led her through the crowd over to the bar.

"Would you like something to drink?" he asked. He had to lean close to her ear and shout to be heard above the thundering music.

Sarah considered for a moment, then shook her head. The noise was hurting her ears. Putting her mouth so close to Tony's ear that she could feel his body heat radiating off him, she yelled, "Maybe we could find someplace a little quieter."

"Quieter?" Tony repeated, his eyebrows rising like dark commas. "You mean *this* place isn't *quiet* enough for you?"

Sarah laughed and shook her head, then motioned as if to stick her fingers in her ears.

"What did you have in mind?" Tony asked, leaning closer to her.

Sarah was pretty sure she picked up the message he was communicating by the glint in his eyes. She told herself that she might be going too fast, that it was still too early in the evening to be thinking about having sex; but she couldn't deny the strong attraction she felt for him—an attraction she had, in fact, felt for him since the first time she had noticed him in the library.

"I dunno... Maybe some other place," she said, cupping her hands over his ear and bringing her mouth so close to his ear lobe that she could have licked it. She had to resist the temptation. "Someplace we can talk."

Tony looked at her and smiled as he cast a quick glance around the room. Then, gripping her hand tightly, he led her through the crowd to the front door.

The instant they stepped outside, and the barroom door swung shut behind them, the noise level dropped, becoming almost bearable. Sarah's ears were still ringing as she closed her eyes, leaned her head back, and took a deep breath. Her face and arms were slick with sweat, and she shivered from the chill of the night air.

"I didn't realize so many young people still smoked cigarettes," she said, wrinkling her nose.

Tony smiled at her, then looked up and down the street as though unable to choose which way to go. Sarah squeezed Tony's hand tightly and he started up Exchange Street, heading toward Federal Street.

"I'd rather not go past where I work," Tony said, smiling tightly. "I see enough of that damned place during the day."

Sarah nodded her agreement and walked along slowly beside him, pausing every now and again to look at the displays in the lighted score windows. Their conversation was friendly and casual. Tony told her about his law studies, his frustrations with his job at the Hollow Reed, and his intention eventually — to establish his own law practice. He hadn't yet decided on a specialty, but he told her that he thought he might like to do something to help protect abused children. Sarah found that admirable.

Sarah skirted around the details of her own life, talking mostly about how much she enjoyed her work at the university library. Feeling the way she did tonight, she figured she'd let Tony do most of the talking. It was best if she just avoided revealing any details about her marriage, divorce, and—especially—Karen's and David's deaths.

"So how come you're not married or anything?" Tony asked when they were standing outside the Painted Horse, gazing at the assortment of painted wooden toys and puzzles in the window.

Sarah felt a twinge of remorse, remembering how she and David had bought Karen a rocking horse from here for her second birthday. She stiffened slightly and looked away, momentarily flustered by the sudden rush of emotion. She considered not telling the truth, but then decided that it would probably do more harm than good not to.

"I was married... for a while," she said, hoping Tony wouldn't notice the dry tightness in her voice. "But—well, actually, the divorce just came through a couple of months ago."

"Umm, I see. Sorry to hear that," Tony said. Smiling, he squeezed her hand and added, "Well, not really."

Blinking back the tears that were forming in her eyes, Sarah looked at him and smiled.

"I—I've been kind of—you know, just starting to pick myself up, trying to find a new social life and all," she said. "It isn't easy for a woman my age."

"I wouldn't think so. Not for someone as beautiful as you," Tony said as he gently caressed her cheek.

Sarah looked at him for a moment and then, feeling as though the moment was perfectly right, she leaned forward until their lips met. At first they merely brushed their lips against each other, but then Tony shifted forward and pulled her close. He started kissing her with rapidly increasing warmth and passion.

Sarah closed her eyes and let herself melt into the kiss. She shivered when she felt his hands let go of hers and slide around her waist and then down to her hips. His hands felt big and strong. A wave of dizziness almost swept her away, but then she broke off the kiss, pulled back, and smiled at him.

"I sure do hope your plans include continuing to date young law students," he said. His heated breath washed like water across her face.

Sarah tossed her head back and laughed nervously. "Well, we'll just have to see what kind of case this young law student can make for himself," she said.

Hand in hand, they started up the street again, leaning close to each other, Sarah's head resting on his shoulder.

This feels good, she told herself. *Good* and *natural.*

They passed other couples and small groups of people out enjoying the gorgeous summer night. High over the buildings, a nearly full moon hung suspended like a white spotlight in the deep blue sky. The rain had passed a little after sunset, leaving the air with a clean, fresh tang. She could smell the ocean not far away.

"So—ah, were you happy—being married, I mean?" Tony asked after a while.

Sarah shrugged and didn't look at him as she bit down on her lower lip and shook her head. She felt even more compelled to tell him about what had happened to David, but right now the last thing she wanted to do was cast a pall over their time together.

She told herself to be careful. Tony was quite a bit younger than she, and getting involved with anybody this fast—and so soon after the divorce—could only complicate things. Tomorrow morning, she had to start facing the harsh realities of settling David's affairs and arranging his funeral.

Right now wasn't the time to mention any of that.

She couldn't deny the strong attraction she felt for Tony. She told herself that it wasn't just his good looks. There was something about him—his presence… something in his eyes, and in the way he carried himself that she found irresistibly attractive. She kept warning herself that this might just be because it had been so long since she'd had sex, but it felt deeper, much deeper than that.

"We wouldn't have gotten divorced if we'd been happy, now, would **we?**" she finally said.

Tony laughed nervously. Their footsteps clicked on the cobblestone sidewalk.

"No, I suppose not," Tony said as he gave her hand a gentle squeeze. He seemed to sense that it would be a good idea to leave it at that, and fell silent.

He looked up the street and smiled as he pointed to the yellow and white striped awning of a TCBY score.

"Hey, you wanna indulge a little?"

Happy for the moment to put any morbid thoughts about David's death out of her mind, Sarah nodded.

"Why not?" she said, laughing a little too loud, she thought, as they picked up their pace.

As they walked up to the shop, Sarah couldn't get over how instantly comfortable she felt being with Tony. The thought crossed her mind—as it had already several times this evening—that she wouldn't mind... in fact, she was rather anxious to see if they ended up in bed together tonight.

That would be nice.

When they paused outside the TCBY store, Tony opened the door with an exaggerated flourish and held it for her.

In the sudden glare of light from inside the shop, Sarah got another good look at his dark, handsome face. Then and there, she decided that if they didn't spend the night together tonight, she was going to be disappointed. And she mentally vowed to do everything she could to keep this thing going until they did end up in bed together.

The storm ended just before sunset, and the sun came out blazing, shining with a molten glow on the undersides of the storm clouds as they raced to the east and out to sea. The puddles that had formed along the rutted baselines and under the swings flashed like polished mirrors that reflected the angled sunlight and clouds scudding by overhead. Raindrops hung from the tips of almost every leaf and blade of grass. They glowed like fat drops of mercury. The wooden playground equipment looked slick and black from the rain.

David, filled with near total despair, stood rooted to the spot in the middle of the playing field, just staring blankly ahead into the fringe *of* woods where the small figure had disappeared.

He was *positive* that it had been Karen, so he couldn't understand why she had avoided him.

She *must* have heard him call out to her.

Why had she run away?

The flash of lightning and clap of thunder had momentarily blinded him and left him shaken. He wasn't sure how she could have gotten away from him so fast, unless he'd been unconscious for at least several seconds.

The only possible answer was that, if she had spent the last five years alone in the Shadowlands, she must be afraid of everyone and everything here. She had been only nine years old when she died. Maybe she hadn't even recognized him. Or maybe she hadn't heard him, even though he'd been yelling as loud as he could. David had no idea how sound traveled here.

It was more likely, though, that she was too frightened to trust *anyone* who spoke to or approached her.

But I'm her father, for Christ's sake! Anger and the hurt of rejection coiled inside David like a python. *She should trust me!*

David felt an almost overwhelming compulsion to follow after her into the woods, but he knew that he'd never catch up with her or find her if she wanted to avoid him.

Besides, with evening rapidly approaching, he wanted to make sure to get back to Pine Knoll Elementary in case the *barghests* returned. The old man had said the Shadowlands were dangerous, especially at night. He'd also hinted to David that wherever it was he had spent the previous night, it must offer some kind of protection. David wasn't very keen about "joining up" with the old man or any of the other wraiths he'd seen thus far. The thought of spending the night in the old man's warehouse, his "haunt," as he called it, filled David with an ill-defined dread. Even in the daylight, the place had struck him as really creepy. If he hadn't been so upset about seeing Karen and not being able to talk with her, David would have found the idea that a ghost could be frightened almost amusing.

"But—*dammit!*—! *will* find her!"

He stared off into the woods, all the while helplessly wringing his hands together.

Now that the rain was over, the evening looked mild and pleasant, even though David couldn't feel any difference in the air. All of his senses still felt maddeningly distant and neutral.

Some kids, obviously relieved at the break in the heat, showed up at the park with baseball gloves, balls, and bats, ready for a scratch game. They vocally expressed their disappointment when they saw the washed out playing field, but they started the game anyway.

Needle-sharp pangs of loneliness and loss stabbed at David's heart as he watched a young mother who couldn't have been more than twenty years old wheel a newborn baby in a stroller across the still damp field. Her large breasts bounced heavily beneath her thin T-shirt, and David felt a stirring of sexual attraction made all the worse because he knew he could no longer satisfy it.

The young mother and her baby looked so happy, so...

"So *alive!* David whispered.

His words sounded like the wind, whisking over the rain-trampled grass.

He felt almost overwhelmed by an immense, aching sadness when he thought about what had happened to him and Karen, and he couldn't get rid of the gnawing thought that someday even this young woman and her child — so happy and full of life on this glorious, summer afternoon — were eventually going to die.

Die and end up here, lost and alone in the gray, lifeless desolation of the Shadowlands!

Jesus, what's the fucking point?

David hung his head as he turned slowly and began to walk away. He tried to forget or at least ignore the infinite sadness he sensed was at the heart of everything.

Life — existence — it all seemed so pointless.

He started up the sidewalk along Brighton Avenue with the vague intention of heading back into Portland. A nearly unbroken line of late afternoon rush hour traffic was streaming out of the city and back to the suburbs, but David paid only the slightest attention to it. He walked slowly with his head bowed. His footsteps dragged on the ground with a dull, scuffing sound.

Tall, desolate buildings lined both sides of the avenue. David knew that, in the living world, most of these buildings hadn't been — and probably still weren't — as run-down as they appeared now. Everywhere he looked, all he could see were decaying storefronts and apartment buildings with shadowed alleyways, broken windows, faded and peeling doorways, and derelict cars and trucks parked along the street. The trees and shrubs were stripped of leaves, looking like they had been blasted by a strong November gale. Wet leaves stripped from the trees by the wind and rain were pasted to the street and sidewalk like bloated, black leeches.

David realized that he would have to accept that just about everything in the Shadowlands was just a pale, decrepit reflection of what he had known in the "real" world—if that's what he could call it. After all, this existence was just as *real*, and much more unnerving than his previous life had been.

And by the looks of things, being here might last a hell of a lot longer than his life had.

Along the way, David encountered several other beings which he guessed must be wraiths. He chose to ignore all of them, even the few who hailed him with loud, friendly greetings.

Just as he had done when he was alive, David preferred to be alone. He repeated to himself something he had always said, half in jest to Sarah and his few friends:

"Just because I'm alone doesn't mean I'm lonely."

At the intersection of Brighton and Deering Avenue, he knew that he should turn left in order to go back to Pine Knoll Elementary, but without making a clear, conscious decision or even knowing quite where he intended to go, he kept walking straight on Brighton.

When he approached the Brighton Medical Center, he stopped suddenly in his cracks and stared up at the building in amazement.

The hospital where Karen had been born was not at all the way he remembered it in real life.

On the site of the building, instead of the modern brick, steel, and glass structure he recalled, was a sprawling, eight-story Victorian mausoleum that looked like it had been built more than a hundred years ago. Dark and brooding, it perched like a vulture on the crest of a desolate hill. A cower with a corroded green copper-roofed cupola pierced the sky from the center of the building. Badly deteriorating cement gargoyles lined all of the cornices, their blank eyes staring ahead into nothingness. The front doors were heavy wood that had been weather-beaten to a dull, black sheen.

In the dying rays of the setting sun, the hospital's imposing brick facade glowed the color of dried blood. Row upon row of long, narrow windows blankly reflected the gathering night sky from glass that looked like slabs of polished black marble. Through the grimy panes of the windows, many of chem broken, David caught fleeting glimpses of motion—faces and gauzy white figures that shifted in and out of sight like wind-blown swirls of dust. On the upper floor of the cower, more than eight stories above the street, an old woman whose face was as pale and wrinkled as death was leaning out through a jagged, circular hole in the glass. After staring coldly down at David, she motioned with a faint flutter of her pallid, clawlike hand.

A cold shock of fear ripped through David when he realized that she was signaling to him.

He quickly looked away and picked up his pace as he continued down the street.

Just before the building disappeared from sight behind him, he turned around to look back. Stark terror hit him when he saw that the old woman was still leaning out of the window, still watching him and beckoning to him. Even after he had started down the hill, and the hospital was no longer in sight, he held in his memory an image of that old woman's steady, unblinking gaze. He could almost feel it boring like a heated drill into the back of his head.

David wasn't consciously aware of where he was going until sometime later, when he arrived at the intersection of Brighton and Forest Avenue. Across the street, no more thana block or two away, was Canal Street, where Sarah lived.

"Shit, yes," David whispered. "Of course!"

His voice rasped, sounding like someone dragging their feet in looses and.

Why *not* go visit Sarah?

She definitely was one of the *fetters* the old man had said were keeping him in the Shadowlands. Probably the only one.

At the cemetery this morning, when he had tried to touch her and speak to her, he felt certain that she had sensed his presence, however briefly. He had seen her react to his touch with a violent shiver.

So maybe it was as simple as that. Maybe all he had to do was contact Sarah before he could move along to the next level, whatever it was.

She already knew where he kept his life insurance policy and other important papers, and he didn't have any other bank accounts or stocks hidden that she didn't know about, so it wasn't a matter of him having to settle any unfinished business he'd left behind.

True, there was *Fallen Angels*, the novel he'd been working on; but he accepted that he would never complete it now. Besides, his publisher had turned down the proposal. According to his agent, because of the dismal sales of his last two novels, no one in New York wanted his next book. That particular book wasn't going ta be the one that finally blasted him out of the mid-list ghetto where his career had been floundering for the last ten years or more.

Maybe—someday—he might have written that ever-elusive "breakout" novel, but he was positive *Fallen Angels* wasn't going ta be the one to do it. In fact, for the last couple of years he'd begun to doubt that he even *had* a breakout novel in him.

No, his failed writing career wasn't keeping him connected to his old life, so maybe that's all he had to do—say a final goodbye to Sarah.

He had already tried once this morning, but maybe he'd do better if he visited her at night—the time when ghosts were supposed to haunt the living.

Maybe daylight was what had kept him from touching her.

The sun slowly dropped below the horizon, and night settled down on the city like a soft cushion. In the gathering gloom, streetlights silently winked on, casting distorted ovals of orange light onto the darkening sidewalk and street.

David experienced a vague inner tension as he walked down to the corner of Canal Street. Sarah's house—the house where all three of them had lived before the divorce and before Karen had died—was the third one on the right.

A dark tremor of sadness went through David, and if he could have cried, he would have when he stopped beneath the shadow of the maple tree in the front yard and looked up at the dark windows.

Here in the Shadowlands, even Sarah's house looked like it had fallen into serious disrepair. David hadn't been over to visit in several months because he wanted to avoid any unpleasant memories the house might stir in him, but he knew for certain that Sarah hadn't let the place fall apart *this* badly.

David realized with a sudden jolt that, ever since he discovered that he was dead, he hadn't entered a building other than the schoolhouse last night. Last night, the schoolhouse door had been open. The door there was hanging to one side as if someone had ripped it *off* its hinges.

David wasn't sure he'd even be able to enter a building. If his hand was going to pass through the doorknob, how was he going to open a door?

Just because he was transparent, and no one in the living world could see him, that didn't necessarily mean that he could simply walk through one of the walls to enter, did it?

He hadn't done anything like that yet, and he wasn't so sure he wanted to try.

The fact that, as a wraith, he could walk down the street without falling through the asphalt indicated *something*, but he wasn't sure what. Although he was still experiencing that curious deadening of his senses, when he stomped his feet on the ground the sidewalk felt perfectly solid and real beneath him.

So what was keeping him here in the Shadowlands? Why didn't he just fall through reality into… something else?

Why would a simple wall stop him? It couldn't be that much of a barrier, could it?

Was existence here just as real to him now as "reality" had been when he was alive, or was he limited only because he *thought* he was limited?

He lost track of the time as he stood outside the house, thinking about such things.

He was distantly aware of the night sky deepening until it fairly vibrated with darkness. The small sprinkling of stars that he could see through the ambient light of the surrounding city looked like diamond dust spread against a drape of gray velvet. The bone-white moon had risen over the buildings, looking huge and bloated. It seemed to leave behind a trailing blue afterimage as it streaked across the sky. A few people passed by on the street, but none of them acknowledged David's presence.

Some time later, David heard the steady rumble of a car as it turned off Brighton Avenue. Out of habit, he ducked behind the maple tree and watched as a sleek, red Corvette turned onto Canal Street and pulled to a stop in Sarah's driveway. The glare of headlights illuminated the peeling paint of the garage door before winking out. David heard the car doors click open, and then watched as Sarah and a young man David had never seen before got out of the car. They were laughing about something. The sound of their laughter reverberated with an odd distortion in the eerily silent night.

"I *do* have to meet with my Crim. Psych. professor first thing tomorrow morning," the young man said, "so I really can't stay very long."

Slow anger began to simmer in David when he saw his ex-wife take the stranger by the hand and pull him close to her.

Their arms encircled each other's waist, and then they kissed, long and passionately. David could hear the low moaning his ex-wife was making deep in her throat. The sound she made when they made love.

Sudden fury shifted like scarlet curtains behind David's eyes. He clenched his fists and took a threatening seep forward, more than ready to pummel this man.

"Are you sure about that?" Sarah asked, looking up into the young man's eyes when they broke off the kiss.

They stared at each other for what seemed to David to be entirely too long. Cold jealousy and blazing anger surged inside him. He was ready to explode with anger as he watched Sarah lead the young man up the side seeps onto the porch. She paused long enough to fish her keys from her purse, then unlocked the side door and, stepping to one side, waved her hand for the young man to enter.

"Welcome," she said with a short, breathy laugh.

Just as the young man was about to step across the threshold, a blur of motion streaked from the darkened corner of the porch and zipped like ball lightning between his legs and into the house. He let out a shout of surprise and jumped backward. Sarah chuckled softly to herself as she reached inside the house and snapped on the overhead light in the kitchen.

"Oh, don't worry," she said. "That was just Bingley, my cat."

The young man's face was bathed by the glow of yellow light that highlighted the hollowness under his cheekbones as he looked at Sarah and smiled tightly.

"I... don't really like cats very much," he said, sounding more than a little annoyed.

"You don't have to worry about Bingley," Sarah said, still snickering. "He'll avoid you more than you'll avoid him. He's a loner, just like my ex used to be."

"Umm," the young man said, nodding and looking grim.

As they were about to enter the house, David suddenly realized that he didn't want to test whether or not he could open the door or walk through walls. As Sarah followed the young man inside, David leaped up onto the porch, hoping to get inside before she closed the door. Even if he wasn't able to communicate with her, the least he could do was keep an eye on her.

But Sarah went inside and swung the door shut, locking it shut before David could follow her, and he was left standing outside, looking in through the door window. His view of the kitchen was horribly distorted, as if the glass were fogged. Moving about inside, Sarah and the man looked like rippling figures swimming underwater.

David was fuming with anger as he watched Sarah open the refrigerator and take out a bottle of white wine. At her direction, the young man fetched two wine glasses from the cupboard above the sink and placed them on the counter. He took the wine bottle from Sarah, worked the cork out of the bottle neck, and poured them each a generous amount. David watched as they walked off into the living room.

Feeling sad and angry and frustrated, David turned and walked slowly down the porch steps. It pained him to think that, here it was, only six months after their divorce, and already she was bringing a new man home with her.

But it didn't really surprise him.

One of the many wedges that had split them apart was the conflict between Sarah's passionate, sociable nature and what she always referred to as his "stick-in-the-mud" attitude.

With a hollow, sinking feeling deep inside him, David realized that no matter what he tried to do now, no matter how hard he tried, he would never be able to feel or regain that kind of passion.

It was only for the living.

He bowed his head, unable to stop himself from dwelling on all the things that he had missed simply because he had let them slip away from him.

And now they were gone…

Forever.

His footsteps echoed softly in the night as he walked slowly back to Brighton Avenue, heading back to Pine Knoll Elementary.

a taste of oblivion.

Chapter Five

"My mommy needs help. She's in a lot of trouble."

The fragile voice—a little girl's—came to David from out of the spinning well of darkness that surrounded him. It echoed softly, sounding like the powdery flutter of a moth's wings against the night.

After a moment of disorientation, David realized that he was sitting up, his body rigid, his eyes wide open.

He had no idea if he had been asleep or awake or somewhere in between.

All he knew was that the night had been long and dark, and filled with a penetrating cold that seemed to originate inside him. Throughout the night, the silence of the schoolhouse had often been punctuated by faint, echoing groans, low laughter, soft whisperings, and dull clanking sounds. All night long, the floorboards creaked loudly, as though possessed by tormented souls. Less frequently, from outside, David heard distant screaming and animal-sounding howls that throbbed in the night.

David lost track of time and even a sense of himself as he huddled in the darkness, leaning against the cold, plaster wall with his knees bent and pressed hard against his chest.

After wandering the streets of Portland, not even caring if he encountered any of the dangers the old man had spoken about, he'd returned to Pine Knoll Elementary. After making sure that he wasn't being watched by any wandering wraiths, he'd entered the old schoolhouse and felt his way in the darkness across the floor to the same spot where he had spent the previous night.

He hadn't thought to check out the school during the day, and in the dark it was hard to tell exactly where he was. He thought he might be in the janitor's closet, or maybe in the old supply storage closet underneath the wide stairway. If there was someone here in the dark with him, he had no idea where they might be lurking.

"What?" David tensed as he spoke the word out loud, fighting against the powerfully unnerving feeling of dissociation. He had the strong impression that he had imagined hearing that little girl speak to him. "What did you say?"

Even though he carefully pronounced each word, his voice seemed to be no more than a meaningless groan. If he were speaking out loud, and not just thinking this, he didn't want to frighten whoever might be here.

But there's no one there!... How could there be?

His first and most powerful impression was that the little girl had sounded quite a bit like Karen.

Quite a bit?... No, *exactly like* her!

David stared ahead into the darkness but could see nothing. He wanted to believe he had heard her speak to him, that it wasn't just his imagination. There had been a sullen dullness in the voice—a bleak emptiness, as though whoever it was had long since given up hope.

And who could blame her, being in a place like this?

A deep shudder ran through David.

"It's my... my mommy," the little girl said. Every word warbled up and down the scale in the darkness, as though she were trembling with fear.

David jumped and almost screamed out loud when he heard the voice, more clearly this time. He shook his head, trying to convince himself he wasn't dreaming this.

"I... I saw you there... tonight... at the—the house tonight... and she was there, too... she was with that man... that really *bad* man."

What she was saying bothered David, but he was still trying to decide if this voice was even real... and if it was, if it could really be Karen.

He hardly dared to hope, even though he wanted so badly for it to be her!

"Wha–what's your name?" he finally managed to ask. He struggled to keep his voice hushed and controlled, but even to his own ears it sounded like someone hammering on metal.

"My... name?"

"Yeah. You have a name, don't you?"

David shifted forward as if about to stand up. The scraping sound his feet made on the ancient wooden floor was loud and abrasive, like a long, deep sigh. As far as he could tell, this was really happening, and he wanted to be ready to react to anything. Staring straight ahead, he tried to pierce the darkness; but, other than the faint glowing gray light in the doorway on the opposite side of the room, he couldn't see a thing.

Not even a shadow within a shadow.

"I don't... I don't use my name much anymore," the girl said, sounding defeated.

"But you do *have* a name—" A cold flash of worry shot through David. "Do you remember your name?"

"Are you my... my daddy?" The little girl's voice broke with desperate pleading. "You sound a little like my daddy."

"I–Idon't know," David said, trembling terribly inside. "I might be, but I— Why don't you tell me your name, so I can be sure?"

"If you're really my daddy, you'd know my name."

"I know what it is… *Karen.*"

The instant he said her name out loud, it felt like a sharp, metal blade had carved a deep trench through his mind and soul.

"What? What are you doing here, Daddy?" Karen asked, sounding stunned with disbelief.

David could hear her voice, hitching with anguish and fear.

"I've been here… all alone… for s-o-o long. Why didn't you come with me? You were there with me, weren't you?"

"Where's that, sugar?"

"With me… when I… when I got hurt. I got hurt really bad, didn't I, Daddy?"

"Is it… Is that really you, Karen?" David asked. His voice was high and tight, barely a whisper in the darkness.

He didn't dare hope.

From the heaviness he felt in his chest, he knew that the Shadowlands wasn't the kind of place where anyone could feel *hope.*

Leaning forward and reaching out into the darkness, he groped desperately with both hands, but didn't connect with anything substantial. His fingers clawed at the night like it was a sheer curtain he could tear away. All the while, he couldn't stop thinking that he had to be imagining all of this.

It isn't possible! This has to be something I'm hallucinating! None of this is real! How can it be?

"Daddy…?"

Karen's voice still sounded flat and empty, like she was talking in her sleep, but the high, frantic edge in it tore through David like a searing knife.

"I–I'm scared, Daddy… really scared."

"Don't worry, Karen. I'm right here," he whispered, even though he couldn't see her in the dark.

"Will you… hug me?"

"Oh, my God! *Karen!*"

He felt a terrible wrenching deep inside his chest as he shifted forward on his knees and flailed around with both hands like a blind man who had fallen down. He was trying not to think that, if she was dead, too, they might not be able to touch.

Weren't they both wraiths?

If they were both dead, how could the dead embrace?

A powerful chill raced up his arms to the base of his neck when his hand brushed against something that wasn't a wall. He let out a low moan as he felt her arm, just above the elbow. He ran his hand up to her shoulder and grabbed her with the other hand and pulled her to him in a tight, desperate embrace. "Oh, my God!"

His voice was little more than a tormented sigh.

Raw emotions, pure and blinding, seethed in his mind. He wished he was able to cry, if only to relieve the terrible pressure that was building up in the center of his soul. Karen was trembling like a terrified bird in his arms.

"I'm right here with you, sugar," David whispered.

He rubbed the back of her head with one hand, surprised by the solid feel of her. His sense of touch still felt weirdly distant, but just holding his daughter tightly against his chest filled him—for the first time—with the slimmest ray of hope that, even though they *were* both dead, things might turn out all right after all.

Tony Ranieri's back was slick with sweat that stung where it ran into the shallow scratches Sarah had made.

The night air was cool. Both bedroom windows were wide open, and the lacy window curtains were bellowing in and out with every vagrant puff of wind. A thin glaze of blue light from the nearby streetlight cast soft shadows across the floor and up onto a corner of the bed.

Lying beside him in bed, Sarah slept with one leg draped over Tony's thigh. Her breathing was deep and even, as peaceful as a baby's. The light entering the bedroom was just strong enough for him to see the gentle swelling of her large breasts beneath the sweat-soaked sheet. He felt a strong, almost painful stirring in his groin as he rolled over and started to reach for her, but then he stopped himself.

No!

He licked his lips and rolled his eyes as the tension in his groin spread to his lower stomach, like a pang of hunger.

Maybe I'll try something else....

He was glad that Sarah hadn't seen him pick up the knife from the floor of the car where he'd put it, and slip it into the back pocket of his jeans. As they walked into the house, he'd been afraid she would notice the bulge it made under his summer-weight polo shirt, but she hadn't.

After sharing most of a bottle of white wine while sitting side by side on the couch in the living room, they had started kissing.

And one thing led to another, just as Tony had hoped it would from the moment he'd first seen her.

But as strongly attracted to her as he was, Tony hadn't really wanted to do anything.

Not tonight.

It wasn't that he didn't feel a powerful sexual charge coming from her. The first thing he'd ever noticed about her was the size of her breasts. Large, round, and firm—just the way he liked them. Although she was considerably older than he was, she also had a look of experience that attracted him to her.

But tonight he'd been too afraid that she would discover the knife he was carrying. If she had, he wasn't sure what he would have said or done about it.

The plain truth was, he had no idea what to think about it.

Ever since finding the knife the other night, he hadn't been able to think about much of anything else. Simply possessing it bothered him, yet it also made him feel strangely attracted to it, compelled to look at it… and hold it.

And use it! a voice deep inside his mind whispered.

Yes, he liked the way it fit his hand, almost as if it had been sculpted for his grip. When he squeezed the hard rubber handle and placed his thumb on the small metal indentation just below the blade, he could vividly imagine using it to cut upward with a long, steady pressure.

The knife filled him with a sense of power and control.

"Jesus," he whispered into the darkness as the thought of using the knife to cut Sarah filled his mind. "What the fuck's the matter with me?"

He tensed and squeezed his eyes tightly closed, but that only made the violent thoughts intensify.

He could almost hear the raw, wet ripping sound the blade would make as it sliced her throat.

He could practically smell the hot copper scent of fresh blood, gushing from her throat and down over her breasts.

And even with his eyes tightly shut, he could picture the wild, panic-filled gleam that would fill her eyes as he plunged the knife deeper into her, and he watched the life slowly seep out of her.

But no! Jesus! I don't want to hurt her!

He wedged his eyes open and stared at her until the hazy image began to blur.

Reaching out with one hand, he gently caressed the sheet-covered curve of her breast. The pain in his groin got suddenly more intense, and he was filled with a violent urge to rip the sheet away from her and force himself on her...

To fuck her until it hurt...

Yes, until it hurt so bad it fucking *killed* her!

"Fuck... *fuck!*" Tony whispered into the darkness as the violent images grew steadily sharper in his mind with every heavy throb of his pulse.

The darkness in the bedroom seemed almost alive with shifting red curtains of light.

The knife was still on the floor beside the bed, sticking out of the back pocket of his jeans. He'd been careful to hide it while they were undressing, but he knew exactly where it was.

Sighing heavily, he rolled over and let his hand hang down over the edge of the bed. An electric tingle sparked his fingertips as they brushed lightly against the knife's handle. Cold, numbing waves seemed to paralyze his arm muscles so he couldn't take his hand away.

In some crazy way, he felt as if the knife were a horrible extension of his arm, a necessary part of his hand. Something without which he wasn't complete.

When his fingers unlocked enough so he could move them, he stretched them out and took hold of the rubber handle and squeezed it so tightly spinning blue dots of light exploded in front of his eyes.

No! Jesus! You don't want to do this!

The knife blade made a long, slow scraping sound as he slowly withdrew it from the back pocket of his pants.

Rolling over onto his back, he held the knife up close to his face. Framed by the soft glow of the streetlight shining through the windows, the blade seemed to glow with a pale, silver fire.

Tony reached out and flicked his thumb against the edge of the blade. He grunted with satisfaction at the razor sharpness of the honed edge.

Yeah, it'd do the job, all right! Quickly and cleanly.

It would slice through her skin and muscles and tendons and veins with little or no effort.

Hell, the knife would do all the work for him! All he had to do was hold onto it, and it would do the rest.

He lay there in the dark, hardly breathing as he stared at the blade. The crazy thought occurred to him that the knife might even have a mind of its own.

Yeah, that was it!

How else could he explain the way he had found it?

It had seemed almost as if the *knife* had found *him* — as if it had been there *waiting* for him and him alone to come through the alleyway that night and find it.

It was almost as if the knife had *wanted* to be found!

Tony didn't doubt that if he even brought it close to Sarah's neck, the blade would dart forward on its own, like a striking snake. It would seek out her carotid artery and sever it before he could even think to stop it.

And if he allowed that, the blade would thank him afterward.

Yes, *thank* him for bathing it in the wash of her hot, vital blood.

Christ! What the fuck am I thinking?

Tony's body was rigid with tension as he twisted the knife back and forth, and stared at the blade until it seemed to be sparkling with blue fingers of energy.

You're not a killer! a voice in his mind screeched. *Get rid of that damn thing now, and stop thinking like that!*

But he couldn't stop wondering what it would be like to feel the gathering pressure in his hand, and then feel the sudden release as he drove the blade into Sarah's warm, living flesh and ripped deeper and deeper into her.

He couldn't stop wondering what it would be like to stare into the eyes of his first victim as her body slumped in his embrace, and all strength and vitality ebbed out of her like a rushing red tide.

"No, goddammit," Tony whispered into the night.

He was panting, his breath hissing like water being splashed onto a hot stove. His hand was vibrating as though he were being electrocuted as he reached down beside the bed and then, forcing his fingers to open, let the knife drop.

It hit the carpeted floor with a dull *thunk.*

"What was that?" Sarah said, startling awake and sitting up in the bed. Her voice, speaking so suddenly and so close to him, made Tony jump.

"Jesus!" he cried out. "I didn't know you were awake!"

"I–I wasn't," Sarah said sleepily. "I thought I heard something—sounded like a door closing downstairs, or footsteps or something."

Tony could see her, sitting up and scanning the room.

"Uh—no. No," he said, trying to slow his rapidly pounding heart. "I was still awake, and I didn't hear anything."

Tony was bathed in sweat. He shivered as a cool breeze wafted over his body.

"Hey, is something the matter?" Sarah whispered, leaning forward and bringing her mouth close to his ear. "Maybe I was too much for you, huh?" She laughed deep in her throat. "Did I give you a little too much to think about? Is that it?"

She placed one hand on his chest and began to rub ever-widening circles as she nibbled on his ear lobe.

"No, I–I was just—uh, I'm usually a pretty light sleeper, is all," he said.

Sarah slid her hand down across his belly and then, moving her fingers in delicate, lingering circles, traced a spiral path down his crotch. She took hold of him lightly at first, and then squeezed. In spite of himself, Tony felt himself getting a rock-solid erection.

"Umm..." Sarah cooed as she licked his ear passionately. "Feels to me like the little rascal might be ready for round two."

Tony was all set to tell her that he didn't feel at *all* like making love again, but before he could say a thing, Sarah shifted down and took him into her mouth. The sucking pressure of her lips and the soft cushion of her tongue sent waves of ecstasy surging through him. He shifted up onto his elbows and looked down at the top of her head as it bobbed up and down. The sheets made soft rustling sounds, like faint voices whispering to him. He could hear the soft grunting noises she made as she slid him deeper and deeper into her mouth with each stroke.

In spite of himself, Tony couldn't resist.

Reaching down with one hand, he wound his fingers in her dark hair like reins and guided her, up and down, up and down, letting the tingling thrill of desire roar throughout his body.

His legs stiffened and locked at the knees. His back arched. After letting her work on him a while longer, he shifted around and rolled her onto her back. Spreading her legs wide with his knees, he entered her with a sudden, violent thrust forward. As their bodies merged, and they began pumping in unison, Tony couldn't get rid of the single, sharp image that burned like white-hot metal in his mind.

He was imagining that his penis, that his entire body was gleaming like the honed edge of a knife that was ripping into Sarah, shredding her to bloody ribbons.

———

David had no idea what to do next.

He spent what seemed like hours, maybe even whole days and nights, trying to comfort Karen; and after a while, she did seem to settle in his arms, curling up tightly so her face was pressed against his chest. Her trembling gradually subsided and then stopped. She lay still and silent in his embrace—not even breathing—but still, David felt no relief from the pressing sadness that engulfed him.

She's not even breathing!

He couldn't escape the memory of kneeling in the snow and hugging her lifeless body to him, feeling her shudder as she exhaled her final breath that turned to steam in the cold mountain air and then was whisked away.

As he held her now and stared vacantly into the twisting black shadows of night, he found himself wishing that he could cry, even if it were only a single teardrop.

He brushed his hand lightly against his daughter's cold cheek, but his sense of touch still seemed so dull that the feeling of dissociation grew almost unbearably strong. A deep, yearning ache filled him with fear when he realized how utterly *lifeless* she felt in his arms.

His mind was suddenly filled with the painful memory of her funeral, five years ago.

As if it were only yesterday, he remembered looking down at her as she lay in the small, white coffin he and Sarah had picked out for her. She was wearing a yellow late dress, and her hands, looking so small, like tiny birds, were folded across her thin, motionless chest.

Since he couldn't see her now, in the darkness, David wondered if she was wearing the same dress she had been buried in. When he reached down and felt her clothing, rubbing his fingers over her back, his sense of touch was too distorted for him to tell with any certainty. All he could be sure of was that this wasn't a rubber raincoat, red or any other color.

In spite of the damage to her face, the funeral director had successfully restored and arranged her features in an expression David knew was supposed to look relaxed and at peace. To him, though, she had looked like she was grimacing in misery. He wondered if, in the dreary tinted daylight of the Shadowlands, her face would still show signs of the damage, or if somehow her corpus had been healed. So far, he hadn't seen her face, other than within the shadow of her hood.

With a sharp sting of memory, David recalled how both before and during the funeral, he had leaned down to kiss her on the forehead, his lips brushing against skin that felt as lifeless and cool as marble.

That's how she felt now.

Her body was as unyielding as stone.

That's because she's dead! The thought made him tremble inwardly. *We're BOTH dead!*

Beyond the sinking sadness of that thought, David also felt... something else—a deep-seated worry that gnawed at the core of his heart because of what Karen had said to him.

"My mommy's in trouble... She's with that really bad man."

The memory of her words filled David with dread. Staring into the darkness until his vision seemed to collapse, he found that he couldn't stop thinking about—and *worrying* about—Sarah.

He had no idea who the man in the red car might have been, but there was *something* about him that David had found deeply disturbing.

He didn't think it was simply the fact that the man was so much younger than Sarah.

It hadn't been any single thing he had seen or sensed about the man. It was more like there was a... a dark taint to him... some slight but undefinable indication in the way he moved or spoke or acted that set off a warning.

And Karen was worried about her, too.

David shifted uneasily, not sure if his daughter was asleep or awake. In fact, the more he thought about it, the more confused he became.

Had he slept at all last night or earlier tonight?

He wasn't sure, but he felt as though he had been in *some* kind of altered state.

But why would the dead need to sleep?

Was it merely habit, based on a lifetime of conditioning?

Or did he, even as a wraith, need a certain amount of rest?

Once again, David thought he might ask the old man about this—if he ever saw him again—but he was grateful that he hadn't seen him since this morning. He figured that, eventually, just like in life, when problems and questions arose, he'd either figure chem out for himself or else make up the rules as he went.

"Should I go over to the house and check on her?" David asked. His voice sounded like a lingering sigh in the close darkness.

"Uh-huh."

The reply wasn't much more than the echo of a gasp.

"'Cause you think she's in trouble?"

"Uh-huh."

"How do you know she's even there at the house, much less in some kind of danger?"

"I was *there*, and I saw you there, too," Karen said. "Didn't you see it in the man's aura? It was as red as... as blood!"

"No, I didn't see anything. I just—I'm not used to... to being like this."

David was hesitant to use the word *dead*. Something inside him rebelled at the idea. He wanted to believe that this was all just a dream or hallucination he was having while lying face-down beside the road after the truck or car or whatever it was hit him.

He hoped to God that he was imagining all of this; and if he was dying, he wished earnestly that he would hurry up and get it over with so the bleak agony of this experience would be over.

Yes, dear God, I want it all to be OVER!

The instant he formed that idea clearly in his mind, he felt a sudden, frigid sinking sensation in the pit of his stomach.

For a dizzying, timeless instant, a huge, black vacuum seemed to open up inside him. He could feel himself being pulled toward it like a leaf being swept away by hurricane winds.

No!... Jesus! ... NO!

His mind was screaming, but the floating, tumbling feeling grew steadily stronger, tugging at him, sucking him into itself. He could feel himself expanding and dissolving, thinning out into something thinner than air, soaking into the bottomless, empty void that swirled like a tornado in the center of his being.

He toyed with the idea of giving over to the feeling... of letting go and losing himself in the eternal darkness of Oblivion that was threatening to engulf him.

And why not? That's what death is all about, isn't it? A final release... total dissolution.

But then he heard a faint voice that didn't seem like his own thoughts. The voice gently tugged him back from the edge of infinity.

"*... you have to try... you have to do something to help her...*"

Somehow, David found his way out of the impenetrable blackness that filled him.

After a few more terrifying moments, each of which seemed like an eternity, the dark, crashing waves of vertigo began to subside.

Once again, he could see the faint, gray glowing rectangle of the doorway. He could feel the dead weight of his daughter in his arms, pressing against him.

Moaning softly, he slumped back against the wall, wishing that he could take a deep breath.

He very well may have, but he had absolutely no sensation of his chest moving or his lungs filling with air.

"I–I don't think you should come with me," David whispered as he raked his fingers through her hair. He wished he could find some measure of reassurance in the touch, but he still felt terribly alone.

"Will you be all right, staying here alone?"

Distantly, he felt Karen nod her agreement.

He wanted to ask her where she had been spending the nights, and how she had gotten along in the Shadowlands for the last five years, but the sudden need to go back to Sarah's house and check on her was far more compelling.

He shifted away from Karen, kissed her gently on the forehead, then stood up and felt his way across the floor to the exit.

Outside, the night was dense and dark, as though the sky were filled with churning coils of black smoke. Weird, ghostly pale lights flickered in the deepest shadows all around him, but then, just as quickly, they winked out of sight. Bracing himself for any of the unknown dangers the old man had said stalked the Shadowlands, he left the schoolhouse and started walking.

The walk to Sarah's house along the desolate streets was even more unnerving than he could have imagined. Several times he caught fleeting glimpses of other wraiths—or maybe living people—wandering alone or in small groups. He avoided contact with any of them, hiding from them when he felt he had to. He was intent on only one thing—getting back to his ex-wife's house as quickly as possible, and making sure that she was safe.

Safe from what... or whom?

The gathering fear that thought generated seemed to make time and distance pass with excruciating slowness, but somehow, he eventually arrived at the house on Canal Street. The house seemed to glow in the night with an odd, shimmering purple light that was stronger than the reflected light from the nearby streetlight. David felt a dull current of dread as he looked up at the darkened bedroom windows.

"Yeah, and how the hell do I get inside?" he whispered. His voice hissed like a gentle breath of wind in the night.

Sensations of tension and gathering fear grew steadily stronger inside him as he trudged slowly up the steps to the kitchen door and looked in through the window.

The interior was filled with inky darkness, but David thought he caught a shifting motion of dark against dark, moving through the doorway into the living room.

His body was vibrating like a tuning fork as he raised both hands to the door and pressed them against the wood. All he could feel was that same muffled dullness, as though he were wearing heavy work gloves.

"Come on. *Come on!*" he whispered to himself as he stared at the door and concentrated on it.

"You're nothing. You're dead. You don't exist, so this door is nothing. It can't stop you!"

Gritting his teeth, he pushed harder against the door, but it still didn't yield. Despair and worry blossomed inside David like dark and deadly flowers.

How the hell could he affect anything in the living world if he was a wraith?

This is *useless… absolutely useless!* he thought.

But as he continued to press against the door, he got a flash of insight.

Instead of pressing harder, and thus acknowledging that the door was a solid barrier, maybe he should do the exact opposite.

Maybe he should concentrate on making that numbed sensation of touch get stronger.

Maybe he could only pass through the door if he convinced himself that it was even less solid than he was.

Closing his eyes, David allowed the deadened sensation in his hands to travel up his wrists and arms. The feeling was similar to a severe case of pins-'n-needles, but he focused on letting it get worse instead of better. It wasn't long before he lost all sense of touch. His hands felt as though they no longer existed—that his arms ended in blunt stumps just above the wrists.

Wedging his eyes open, David was amazed to see that his hands had passed through the door.

A wave of excitement flashed through him, almost breaking his concentration, but he focused all the harder on making it feel as though his whole body didn't exist. He watched, amazed, as he pushed himself further through the door.

Holy shit, I'm doing it!

The thought filled him with a sudden rush of discovery, the closest thing to joy he had experienced since arriving in the Shadowlands.

He closed his eyes again and tried to eliminate any sense of his body.

A thin shiver of panic ran through him when he was suddenly afraid that he might also lose complete sense of his own identity and be swallowed up by the Oblivion inside him, but—dammit!—he had to try!

Once again, David closed his eyes and concentrated on only one thing—moving forward without paying the slightest bit of attention to the supposed barrier of the door.

If he ended up winking out of existence… if he plummeted into the eternal blackness in the center of his soul and was lost forever, then so be it.

Strange, disturbing sensations that he couldn't even begin to describe gripped him like iron hands. He felt simultaneously as though he were immersed in frigid water and walking through a dense wall of flame.

A tiny corner of his mind was screaming that this was the end—that he was truly going to cease to exist—but he forced himself to keep moving forward.

And then, as though he had stepped instantaneously from the sweltering heat of a mid-August afternoon into the Arctic cool of an air-conditioned building, he was through.

David stumbled and almost fell when he opened his eyes and looked around to see that he was standing in the middle of Sarah's kitchen.

"Jesus Christ," he whispered.

The darkness surrounding him split his voice into dozens of echoing whispers that repeated until they gradually faded away.

David felt totally drained by the experience, and he guessed that perhaps that's why wraiths—even though they were no longer alive—needed to sleep. They needed to restore the energy they used to *do* things.

But he didn't have time to ponder this too deeply.

All he wanted to do was get upstairs and make sure Sarah was safe.

A stone-cold heaviness filled his chest as he trudged up the stairs.

He didn't dare consider for long why he didn't fall through the steps. As strange and altered as existence in the Shadowlands was, he feared that, if he let go of *some* sense of reality, he would plunge into the endless, black void of Oblivion.

His feet made light scuffing noises on the carpet as he walked down the short hallway to the bedroom that he and Sarah had shared until less than a year ago. He realized that he hadn't been up here since the day he packed up and moved to his apartment in Westbrook.

The pain of loss he felt was almost palpable.

His whole being was shaking as he approached the door and saw that it was open halfway. He stepped up close to it and looked inside.

"Oh, Jesus!" he murmured when he saw what Sarah and the young man were doing.

Deep within his chest, he could feel an agonized groan gathering strength, threatening to burst out of him. Shifting soundlessly to one side, he entered the bedroom, unable to look away as he watched the young man making love to his ex-wife.

"Sarah... Oh, no, Sarah," he said, moaning as though in pain.

The light coming through the bedroom windows illuminated the young man's muscular back as he braced himself with one hand on either side of Sarah and drove his hips repeatedly forward. David could hear the dull echoes of their passionate grunts and groans. The sound of creaking bedsprings fell like hammer blows on his ears. Rage and the sharp sting of regret and loss filled him until he thought he was going to explode with fury.

"Stop it, Sarah! Jesus Christ! Stop it right now!" he shouted as loud as he could, but even to his own ears, his voice sounded flat, as though lost in the distance.

It pained him to think about how many times he and Sarah had made love in this bed. It was the bed in which they had made love on the night they conceived Karen. David imagined that he could almost see a ghostly reflection of himself and Sarah writhing in ecstasy on the bed.

"Ohh... *ohhh!*" Sarah moaned.

She gripped the man's back and buried her face into the curve of his neck. She trembled as her pleasure rose, wave after wave. David caught glimpses of shimmering sheets of colored light that curled around them—subtle, shifting shades of green and blue and red that twisted and intermingled like oil and water.

He moved closer to the bed. With trembling hands, he reached out to touch Sarah, but his hands passed through her effortlessly. Agony filled him like he had never experienced before. He desperately wanted to turn and leave, but something made him stay and watch.

Was it his anger and misery? Or was it something else…

Something more?

A hint of dark motion down by his feet drew David's attention. He saw Bingley—their old cat—standing by the closet door, staring straight at him. His back was up, and his tail was puffed.

"Go on! Get outta here!" David shouted, stepping forward and waving his hands at the cat.

But Bingley did just the opposite.

Bingley's eyes widened, reflecting green in the eerie light as he hissed at David.

"What the—" the young man said, suddenly stopping and turning to look over at the half-opened bedroom door.

Raising both arms, David lunged forward and swatted at the cat while stamping his foot on the floor.

Bingley jumped into the air and took off like lightning. With a loud, trailing yowl, he leaped onto the bed and landed squarely on the young man's back.

The young man let out a piercing yell as he rolled away from Sarah and swatted with both hands at his back. In a flurry of fur and claws, Bingley hit the floor, tumbled over once, scrambled to gain traction on the carpet, and then darted out the door. The last thing David saw was Bingley's rail, puffed up to twice its size as he scurried down the stairs.

"*Jesus Christ!*" the young man shouted. "That fucking cat scratched the shit out of me!"

Sarah fumbled in the darkness until she found the switch for the bedside light. When she snapped it on, at least as far as David could tell, the additional light did little to dispel the murky gloom of the bedroom.

"Now, now," Sarah said, her voice low and soothing as she leaned forward and looked at the wounds. "Let's take a look at that."

The young man swung his feet to the floor. It looked to David as though he purposely kicked his discarded jeans under the bed before he sat perfectly still and angled his back to the light. Sarah grimaced as she carefully inspected the wounds. David was happy to see him cringe when she gingerly touched him on the back.

"It's not all that bad," she said, "but I should probably put some hydrogen peroxide on it."

Moving slowly, as though chains were dragging at his feet, David walked around to the other side of the bed. He laughed out loud when he saw the deep, red gashes that raked down the man's back. A couple of them looked quite deep. The blood glowed like scarlet ribbons as it flowed down to the man's ass and soaked into the bed sheets.

Sarah suddenly stiffened and glanced over her shoulder toward where David was standing.

"What was that?" she asked, frowning as she looked around.

"The damned cat!" the man said with a snarl.

"No, I thought I heard something else," Sarah said, looking mystified.

David thought for a moment that she could see him, and he almost ducked for cover until he remembered that there was no way she could see him. He glanced over his shoulder, but all he saw was the window curtains, drifting in and out on the gentle night breeze.

"Are you gonna do something about this or not?" the young man said, scowling.

"Yeah, sure," Sarah said.

She scrambled off the bed. Still naked, she hurried out into the hallway.

Feeling a deep ache in his soul, David watched her go, wishing that there was some way he could speak to her and make her see him. He still hadn't forgotten what Karen had said about her being in danger, and he couldn't help but think that this man was the source of it.

While Sarah was out of the room, David watched the young man carefully, trying to see the "red aura" Karen had mentioned, but he couldn't see anything unusual about him.

After a moment, the young man slipped off the bed and reached down to the floor for his pants. David's first thought was that he was going to get dressed and leave, but then he saw the young man adjust something that was wrapped up inside the pants.

David moved forward, trying to see what it was.

An icy wave swept over him when he saw the black handle of a knife and a small portion of the blade.

Jesus! he whispered, and as soon as he said it, the young man tensed and looked around furtively. He stared at exactly the spot where David was standing.

David couldn't take his gaze away from the knife. It was unlike any knife he had even seen in his life.

The handle was dark and black, as if it had been dipped in oil. The blade seemed to glow with a sickly purple light. Even the glare of the bedroom light hardly dispelled the glow. The edge of the blade, all the way from the tip to the handle, was stained with a thick, black substance. It took David a moment to realize that this must be blood-ancient, dried blood that was still dripping in thick clots from the knife.

He watched in mute fascination as globs of the black liquid fell to the floor where they sizzled and smoked before dissolving away to nothing.

It struck him as odd that the young man seemed not to notice this as he gripped the handle and swung his arm back and forth, slicing the air with several quick slashes.

Sarah's footsteps sounded in the hall, and the young man hurriedly folded his pants back up, making sure the knife was hidden underneath chem before pushing the bundle back under the bed. He straightened up on the edge of the bed and waited patiently.

Sarah entered the room with a wet washcloth in one hand and a boccie of hydrogen peroxide in the other.

Smiling, she approached the bed, looking somewhat wary of the young man.

"You know, you ought to get rid of that fucking cat," the young man said. His voice was a low, vibrating growl.

"Bingley? Oh, he's a good cat," Sarah said. "Something must've spooked him."

Sarah glanced around the bedroom again, then out into the hallway, but Bingley was nowhere to be seen. She looked like she was forcing a smile as she motioned for the young man to turn around so she could tend to his wound.

"This may sting a little," she said.

She unscrewed the bottle cap and splashed the washcloth with peroxide. The man sucked in his breath and clenched his teeth as he braced himself.

"Yeow!" he shouted, pulling away from her touch. He turned and glared at Sarah. For a flickering instant, David thought he saw a shimmering red glow surround the young man, as if his body were radiating heat; but just as fast, the light faded away, and David was left not even sure if he had seen it or not.

"Don't be such a big baby," Sarah said, chuckling softly as she gripped him by the shoulder with one hand and applied the washcloth to his back with quick dabs.

David laughed out loud again when he saw the thin streams of blood running down the young man's back turn pink.

Not dark enough, he thought, mildly surprised by the sudden violence of his thought.

He wondered if it was just because he had caught this man fucking his ex-wife, or if it was something else.

Right now, though, he didn't want to take the time to try to figure it out. He felt a need to get back to Pine Knoll Elementary and check on Karen. For now, he was content that—at least tonight—Sarah was not in any imminent danger.

Moving like wind-blown smoke, he left the bedroom and walked down the stairs. He passed through the kitchen door with must less difficulty this time, and was outside.

Without a backward glance at the house, he started walking slowly up the street. By the time he arrived back at the school, the sky was brightening with the first hint of dawn. In the thin wash of gray light, he saw to his horror that Karen was gone.

preparations.

Chapter Six

Sarah figured that it was all for the best when she awoke shortly before dawn and saw that Tony was gone.

She groaned softly as she rolled over onto her back, laced her hands together behind her head, and stared up at the blank ceiling. She couldn't help but wonder if she would ever see him again, and—at least right now—she wasn't so sure she wanted to.

But then she remembered how he had made her feel last night… at least until Bingley screwed things up.

Shivering slightly, she raised her head and looked around the silent bedroom. A gauzy, gray glow was beginning to suffuse everything. A lazy, sweet-smelling breeze shifted the lacy curtains, which made faint scraping sounds as they brushed against the windowsill. Through the open window, Sarah could hear the morning chorus of birds. From somewhere far down the street, she heard footsteps and then a car door open and slam shut. The car started up and drove off, sputtering as it faded away. Then the silence fell again.

Already, the events of only a few hours ago seemed distant and strangely unreal to Sarah, as if they hadn't really happened or had been part of a dream.

A feeling of loneliness filled her, and she found herself crying as her thoughts turned to David.

She sniffed and wiped her eyes, but more tears came. She realized she'd been doing a lot of crying lately—certainly a lot more than she had after their separation. The tragedy of his death seemed to weigh down her heart like a heavy stone, rekindling the deeper grief of losing her daughter.

Sarah sighed heavily and swung her feet to the floor. When she stood up, something in her lower back popped. Stretching her arms back, she took a deep breath and twisted from side to side to loosen up. Still naked, she started down the hallway toward the bathroom; but halfway there, she stopped in her tracks.

Bingley was curled up into a tight ball on the carpeted floor at the top of the stairs. The cat narrowed his eyes to slits and shifted his head like a mechanical toy as he tracked Sarah. The cat's cool, unblinking glance made Sarah feel uncomfortable, but she forced a smile as she knelt down beside him and started scratching him behind his ears.

"So what's up with you, huh?" Sarah asked softly.

The cat started purring as he pressed his head into the warm cup of Sarah's hand. His eyes glinted like gold coins in the semi-darkness.

"Were you crying to tell me that you didn't like him? Is that it?"

Sarah tossed her head back, shook her hair, and laughed softly.

"Well, you had fair warning," she said, her voice tightening slightly as the cat's golden-eyed stare sent a tingle of fear racing through her.

"He *said* that he didn't like cats. What's the matter, did you take it personally?"

Sarah continued to scratch Bingley's head until she realized that she probably should get moving. Even though it was Saturday and she didn't have to work, she had a lot to accomplish. As far as she could see, none of it was going to be either pleasant or easy.

After showering, Sarah put on her favorite faded jeans and a yellow, sleeveless T-shirt, and went downstairs to fix a light breakfast of low-fat cereal, half a poppyseed bagel and a small glass of grapefruit juice.

Sitting at the counter, she took a pen and clean sheet of paper from the counter drawer. She intended to jot down her plan for the day as she ate, but she knew there were only two things she *had to* get done.

First, she had to drive over to David's place in Westbrook and at least take a look around so she could start thinking about what she was going to do with everything. She had to decide which possessions to keep, and what she'd either sell, throw away or donate to charity.

That was going to be tough enough as it was, but nowhere near as tough as going over to the Oaks Funeral Home this afternoon and meeting with Morris Green to arrange for David's funeral service and burial.

Even after five years, the memories of doing the same thing for Karen were still much too sharp and painful for Sarah to face. As she ate, tears kept welling up in her eyes. She soaked several napkins, dabbing them away. She wondered if she should call Cindy or Ruth or another of her friends and ask them to come with her, just in case things got too emotional; but she decided against it, telling herself that she could handle it. After you bury your only child, you pretty much should be able to face anything else.

By the time she left the house, the sun was up and blazing. It looked like a swollen, red ball, suspended above the heat-hazed city skyline. Back Bay looked as flat as beaten pewter. A few early morning joggers were out, obviously hoping to beat the worst of the heat, but the morning sky was already dense with humidity. Across the narrow bay, the Casco Bank building flashed the time and temperature. Any relief the thunderstorm may have brought last night was gone.

Sarah found the heat oppressive just walking down to her car. It didn't take long before her armpits were damp with sweat. Morning dew speckled the car's windshield like beads of mercury. Sarah started her car up and turned on her windshield wipers to wipe the moisture away before backing out of the driveway. She clicked on the car's air conditioner, hoping to God it would kick in fast.

There wasn't much traffic this early in the morning, and Sarah caught mostly green lights as she headed out Forest Avenue, so the drive to Westbrook took less than fifteen minutes. The chimney stacks of the paper mill in Westbrook were spewing white funnel-shaped columns of exhaust into the air, but the heavy atmospheric inversion held the vapors down. The stench of rotten eggs and sour milk was almost overpowering. Across from the mill, Sarah turned left onto Brown Street, rounded the corner past St. Mark's Cathedral and pulled to a stop at the curb in front of David's apartment building.

A wave of sadness swept through her when she looked up at the building where David had been living for the several months since they separated. The building was painted a sickly yellow that David always described as "baby-shit gold." It looked sticky "and wet in the morning light. A rolled-up newspaper, drenched with dew, lay on the walk halfway to the front steps. Remembering what David had told her about this neighborhood, Sarah made sure she locked the car after she got out.

Gripping her key ring tightly in her fist, she started up to the front door, carefully stepping over the rolled-up newspaper as if it were a sleeping dog. All the while, she had the discomforting feeling that someone was watching her, but when she looked around, she couldn't see anyone peering out of any windows at her. The entire neighborhood seemed depressed and drowsy in the thick humidity.

Sarah hadn't been to David's apartment very often—only two or three times that she could remember. After she had initiated divorce proceedings, she and David hadn't been able to spend any amount of time together without ending up in a shouting match. Mostly, she thought he started the arguments, but she had never hesitated to jump in and defend herself. Even their occasional telephone calls quickly turned hostile. She did have a key to his apartment, though. He'd always said that she would need it, in case he got hurt or died.

Well, by Jesus, I guess that's how it turned out!

That thought made her eyes fill with warm tears.

She might have gotten used to not having any more romance in her life, but still—the realization that the man she had loved once upon a time, the man who had fathered her only child, was now dead was almost overwhelming.

Wiping her eyes with the heels of her hands, she braced herself before letting herself in through the front door.

As soon as she stepped across the threshold and closed the heavy door behind her, she let out a loud gasp. The building reeked of an indescribable stench that seemed to be a mixture of three-day-old fish, stale cigarette smoke, boiled cabbage and something else—something wet and rotting.

As she started cautiously up the narrow, rickety flight of seeps to the second-floor landing, the sound of creaking floorboards set her teeth on edge. She tried to tip-toe down the dim hallway to David's door.

His name was written on a cracked and fading embossed red plastic label, which was stuck to the door marked 2-B with tarnished brass numerals.

"Two-B or not two-B."

Sarah chuckled grimly to herself as she recalled the joke David used to make about his apartment number, about how it was *perfect* for a writer!

She fit the key into the tarnished door lock, but before opening it, she sighed heavily and leaned her head against the door panel. It was cool, almost cold to the touch.

"Well, Davy," she whispered under her breath. "I guess *you* chose not to be, huh?"

She turned the key slowly and, with some effort, the door lock clicked. Gritting her teeth, she twisted the doorknob.

The door hinges chattered like a braying mule, setting her teeth on edge as she pushed the door open and entered.

The instant she stepped into the apartment, a sudden rush of shivers ran through her. Sarah hugged herself as if she were outside on a January morning. After taking a moment to collect herself, she shut the front door, making sure the lock clicked shut. Just to be on the safe side, she also slid the safety chain into position.

The apartment was cool and dark and, not surprisingly, very clean. David had always been a much better housekeeper than she had been. It had turned into something of a joke among their friends. The furniture, most of which was older pieces he had salvaged from their attic, was dusted and neatly arranged. The floor and threadbare carpet looked as though they had been vacuumed just this morning. All of his published books and every collection and magazine in which he had a short story were neatly arranged on the mantle.

In the kitchen, there were no dirty dishes in the sink. All the plates, glasses, cups, and silverware had been washed and neatly stacked in the plastic dish drainer.

He must have done that sometime before going out for his late-night walk.

Sadness tightened like a hand around Sarah's heart.

Trembling inside, she left the kitchen and walked down the short hallway to David's bedroom.

The bed was made, and all of David's clothes were neatly folded and put away. The only thing that might constitute a mess was the stack of books and magazines on the small table beside the bed.

Sarah glanced at a few of the titles, not at all surprised to see that David's reading habits hadn't changed much in the last few months. There were several mystery and suspense novels, including the latest books by James Let Burke, E Paul Wilson and Dean Koontz, along with tattered copies of *Scientific American*, *Playboy*, *Ellery Queen* and *Cemetery Dance*. Sarah cringed when she looked at the cover of *Cemetery Dance*, which depicted a rotting corpse strung with barbed wire, crucifixion-style, to a fence post in the middle of a vast, yellowing com field.

David's desk was over by the window that looked out over a shadowed back alley. The desk was barely large enough to hold the computer keyboard and monitor. A small laser printer covered by a plastic dust cover was on a rickety card table beside the desk. Paper scrolled into the printer, but there was nothing coming out of it.

A chill gripped Sarah's insides as she walked over to the keyboard and stared at the monitor's blank screen. After a while, her eyes began to shift in and out of focus. She couldn't help but wonder what—if anything—David had been working on before he died. She was tempted to switch on the machine to see, but stopped herself, feeling as though that would somehow be an invasion of privacy.

"Not that it matters anymore," she whispered.

It would be just as well if anything he'd been working on was left alone.

The cold, gnawing sensation in her stomach grew steadily stronger as she brushed her fingertips lightly across the keyboard. Suddenly a loud *snap* followed by a high, crackling sound made her jump back. A soft, electronic hum grew louder as the fan inside the computer began to whirl. A few seconds later, the monitor lit up. After running through the initial setup, the computer screen displayed an opening menu.

Sarah's heart was beating fast and high as she backed away from the machine, all the while staring at it in amazement.

She was sure she hadn't pressed the power button.

Maybe David had the machine rigged to turn on automatically or something.

"What the hell?" she whispered when she noticed the message flashing at the top of the screen:

... YOU HAVE 1 E-MAIL LETTER(S) WAITING...

The temperature in the apartment instantly seemed to drop several degrees.

Sarah glanced out the window above the desk and noted that, at least at this time of day, this side of the building was shaded, but that didn't account for the sudden decrease in temperature she felt.

There wasn't a fan running, and the air conditioner wasn't on; nevertheless, a cool breeze was gently wafting over her back, making the hairs at the nape of her neck stir.

Covering her mouth with one hand and nibbling nervously on the knuckle of her forefinger, Sarah shook her head as though trying to clear water from her ear.

Suddenly curious, she approached the desk. Her hand was shaking as she reached out and quickly switched off the machine. The screen crackled as it went blank. The computer's internal fan slowed down with a soft *whir* and then stopped.

Maybe the fan inside the machine was making that breeze, she thought, but she wasn't convinced.

For several seconds, she just stood there, holding her breath, nibbling her knuckle and staring at the computer. She had no idea how the machine could have switched on by itself.

Maybe there had been a sudden power surge, or there might be a defect in wiring or in the power switch.

She wondered if she should unplug the computer so it wouldn't get damaged if it turned on by itself again after she was gone, but she was too afraid to touch the computer again.

"Jesus, don't be ridiculous," she whispered to herself. "It's just a goddamned machine!"

But that didn't do any good. Her courage failed her.

Backing up slowly, her hand still covering her mouth so she wouldn't scream, Sarah left David's bedroom.

Once outside the bedroom door, she walked quickly through the living room to the front door. Her hands felt cold and clammy as she fumbled to unlock the door. She was just about to leave when she turned for one last look around.

She couldn't account for the sudden nervous feeling that had gripped her. It might just be that the sadness she felt for David was starting to sink in. Seeing his apartment and his workspace, and knowing that he'd never come back here to live and work again filled her with the pain of regret and loss.

But—somehow—it seemed more than that.

The sense of imminent danger in the apartment was almost palpable. Sarah could practically see it floating like a gray haze of smoke in the air all around her.

Besides, she didn't need to stay here long.

She had a pretty good idea what she would do with everything. All of David's clothes and most of his household items would go to the Salvation Army and Goodwill. She didn't need or want any of the old furniture, even the portable color TV and the VCR he had set up in the living room. She might take a quick look through his books and magazines, but her and David's reading tastes had always been dissimilar. Whenever she found time to read, which hadn't been very often lately, she preferred romances and historical novels.

The only real concern she had was what to do with David's computer.

She knew that it was less than a year old. It was much too valuable simply to throw or give away. She might be able to use it at home, but she had no idea what she should do about all of David's files that still must be on the hard drive.

It would be a pity simply to erase them all, especially without reading through them first.

David's writing had pretty much been his whole life—his *only* real involvement, it seemed to her, at least before Karen was born. After encouraging him through the first two or three novels, Sarah had admitted to him one day that she never really liked any of his books or stories because they were all so dark and violent, particularly the four he'd written following Karen's death.

She was sure she wasn't up to the task of reading through any of his old files. Then again, she didn't know anyone she could ask—or trust—to do it for her, either.

She just wasn't up to doing it, at least not yet.

"I'll deal with it later," she muttered as she stepped out into the hallway and yanked the door shut.

She jiggled the doorknob, making sure the door was securely locked before she walked away.

She'd already sent Sam Lowell a check for this month's rent, so the place was covered at least until the end of July. If she had to pay rent for another month or two until she found the time and courage to clean it out, she was pretty sure Lowell wouldn't mind—as long as her checks didn't bounce.

All she had to remember to do on Monday or Tuesday, depending on which day she chose for David's funeral, was call the electric and water companies and tell them to switch off service to the apartment and send her a final bill.

Sarah's footsteps echoed in the stairwell as she walked down to the first floor, and once again she had the feeling that someone was watching her.

She sighed when she stepped outside into the blistering heat of the day. The sun was still lost in a gray heat haze that made the world appear to be underwater. The instant blast of warmth chased away the bone-deep chill she'd felt in David's apartment, but she still felt as though something wasn't quite right... as if she were forgetting or missing something that was so obvious.

In the church parking lot across the street, several boys, most of chem shirtless and wearing shorts, were playing stickball, using scraps of cardboard and wood for bases. On the corner next to a small "mom and pop" store, some older kids, teenagers with skateboards, were hanging out, smoking cigarettes and swearing loudly with every other word as they joked around. Several of them eyed Sarah suspiciously as she hurried down the walkway to her car. With fretful glances down the street to make sure they weren't moving toward her, she unlocked the car door, got in and started it up.

As she drove away she decided that the next time she came over here she would ask one of her male friends to come along with her.

Maybe she'd even ask Tony... if she ever saw him again.

David was filled with powerful, conflicting emotions.

Cold, black agony clashed with sudden surges of terrible anger as he watched Sarah leave his apartment, practically running down the stairs and out to her car.

He was tormented, wondering if she had in any way sensed his presence, and he wondered if she was now afraid of the place.

As soon as she slammed the door shut behind her and he listened to her jiggle the lock back and forth, he knew that he could have followed after her, but he chose not to. He wondered whether he actually could have ridden in the car with her if he had gotten down to the street before she drove off, but he was too exhausted to follow after her. What he needed was to stay here for a while and rest.

After arriving back at Pine Knoll Elementary last night and seeing that Karen was missing, he'd been nearly frantic with fear. He wasn't sure why, but he had felt compelled to come back to his apartment.

He didn't know how to find his daughter. He had no idea where to start looking or what to do.

He was positive that he had told Karen to stay where she was and wait for him, so all he could assume was that she was in some kind of danger.

Maybe serious danger.

What if someone—perhaps that old man with the bad left leg or one of the other wraiths lurking nearby—had found her alone in the schoolhouse and had kidnapped her?

David had no doubt that the dangers in the Shadowlands were very real; but he'd lost his daughter once before, and he was determined not to let that happen again!

Before he could think of a plan of action, though, as the sun was rising in the east, turning the sky gunmetal gray and pushing the shadows back into the farthest corners of the school, he had been filled with the sudden, almost overwhelming compulsion to return to his apartment in Westbrook.

He couldn't explain it.

It was almost as if someone—or something—had been calling him back, luring him.

The deep sense of loss he was feeling for his old life and his work as a writer was almost too much to bear, but this felt like it was more than that. It was much too powerful to ignore.

It was several miles from Pine Knoll Elementary to the apartment building on Brown Street, but David had already noticed how time and distance could play tricks on him. At times it seemed as though the more anxious he was to get somewhere or do something, the longer it seemed to take.

That was the important word.

Seem.

Everything he had experienced since regaining consciousness in the Shadowlands had all *seemed* so subjective.

There weren't any rules, at least as far as he could tell. Whatever rules applied to the living world certainly didn't work here. He wondered if it was simply a matter of learning the new rules... or if he could make up his own rules.

The sky was gray with haze when he started out for Westbrook. The leaves on the trees hung lifelessly from the branches. The air seemed dense, almost like being underwater. What few sounds David heard were muffled and distant. He could tell, just by the way things looked, that the day was hot and humid, but he had no physical sensation of it.

As he walked, he forced himself to remain as calm as possible. He wasn't sure how long the walk to Westbrook had taken, but when he arrived at his apartment, the sun, which had broken through the haze, seemed only fractionally higher in the sky than when he had started.

He was inside his apartment, simply standing there, lost in his own thoughts as he looked around, enjoying the soft gray silence, when Sarah arrived.

Passing through doors and walls was no longer a problem. All it seemed to require was a strong effort of will and an intense focus, and before he knew it he was through whatever barrier he wanted to pass. It was a little like using a part of his mind or maybe even parts of his body in a way he had never thought possible. He felt a slight stirring of elation at the discovery of this new talent, but that feeling was quickly replaced by surprise, anger, and a painful twinge of envy for the living when he saw the apartment door open and Sarah entered.

He had watched silently, walking along beside her as she moved through the apartment, looking around. He guessed she was taking inventory of his possessions before cleaning everything out. It was only when she went into his bedroom and walked over to his computer that he decided that he had to try to contact her.

"Sarah," he called out.

His voice had less substance than the sputtering sound a candle makes when it is blown out.

"Please, Sarah... Why can't you hear me?... I'm standing right here beside you."

He grabbed for at her, but his hands passed through her with no resistance. He wondered why it was so difficult to touch a living person when the rest of reality, even the pale reflection of the living world he could see, seemed so substantial.

Shivering inside, he watched as Sarah idly brushed her fingers across the computer keyboard. The faint clicking sounds the keys made rang like heavy hammer blows in David's ears.

As he watched her, he could tell that she was thinking about him. It was more than her expression or body posture. There seemed to be a direct electrical charge coming from her and filling him with subtle, unseen energy. Strong jolts of pure emotion and vitality zipped through him, but these quickly shifted to bleak desperation when he reached out again and tried to touch her.

Once again, he called her name, but she didn't respond.

He wanted so badly to touch her, but she seemed totally unaware of his presence.

Then he got an idea.

If there was electricity passing between them, then maybe he could alter the flow of electricity in the living world. Maybe that's what his corpus was made of.

Reaching past her, he focused every bit of mental energy into the tip of his forefinger. He almost laughed with joy when he reached out and actually felt the slight but very solid resistance of the power button under his finger.

Staring inwardly at the eternal blackness that swirled in the center of his heart, he concentrated and tried to push the button.

It seemed to take forever, and the effort was absolutely exhausting him, but—finally—he heard the button click. The computer switched on with a low, vibrating hum.

David watched with a mixture of amazed satisfaction and hopelessness as Sarah jerked back and stared at the computer as it ran through its opening menu screens. Sudden fear gripped him when she frowned.

"*No!*" David shouted as loud as he could when he saw her reaching for the power button.

He thought he detected a slight shiver run through Sarah, but he couldn't tell for sure. The energy he had felt pouring into him from her suddenly shut off. A shimmering black curtain like a cloud seemed to hover around her.

"No, please!… Please don't turn it off!… I'll write you a message!… Wait!… *Please!*"

David made a desperate grab for her hand, hoping to stop her, but Sarah snapped the power button, and the computer screen winked off. The crackle of diminishing energy in the air was as loud as a roll of thunder. He felt it prickle his corpus like pins-and-needles.

Filled with sudden frustration and waves of rage, David tried once again to focus his energy to turn the machine back on, but he knew it was futile.

He was much too exhausted from the effort of turning it on the first time. He watched, sighing helplessly as Sarah backed out of the bedroom, walked to the front door and left, locking the door behind her.

David would have followed, but he was completely drained of strength. The night had long since passed, but there had been no rest for him. Even knowing that Karen was missing, and wanting desperately to find her again, he could hardly move.

Besides, it was restful, here in the shadowed gloom of his apartment.

Restful and as quiet as a tomb.

David moaned softly to himself as he leaned against the wall and slid into a huddled heap on the floor. Closing his eyes didn't do any good. It didn't matter if they were open or closed; he still saw the same thing. He watched, entranced as thoughts and emotions took shape in his mind and exploded with frightening visual effects.

It's too late... too late for anything!

Turmoil raged like a beast inside his mind.

My life... my work... anyone I've ever loved ... anything and everything I ever could have done is gone... gone forever...

Once again, the cold void of impenetrable darkness churned inside him, threatening to claim him.

Filled with utter despair, David let himself slip closer and closer into the darkness behind his eyes. He would have let himself be carried away if it hadn't been for one single, simple, pure thought that burned with the brightness of an acetylene torch. A voice that didn't even sound like his own kept whispering in his mind—*Before you go... You have to see Karen... just one last time...*

Tony had never really liked night and darkness, but right now darkness served his purposes.

Since leaving Sarah's house sometime in the predawn stillness, he'd been alternately filled with rage, frustration, and jealousy.

The rage was perhaps the easiest for him to understand.

His back still stung from the claw marks Sarah's cat had left. They sliced at an angle from the top of his left shoulder to the middle center of his back. It had hurt like hell when Sarah cleaned the cuts with hydrogen peroxide and bandaged them. Tony was positive that he could feel the infection spreading like a brush fire, inflaming every nerve in his back, neck, and shoulders.

But he told himself to bottle up all of the pain and rage because he wasn't going to let matters just sit there the way they were.

Oh, no.

He was going to do something about that, by Jesus!

That's why, about an hour after sunset, he'd left his car parked in a restaurant's parking lot on Forest Avenue and walked the mile or so down the street to Sarah's house.

The frustration he felt was the result of other, more complex things, particularly his embarrassment at his own sexual performance last night.

True, Sarah had *seemed* satisfied, and she had told him repeatedly that he made her feel things she hadn't felt in a *long* time and, in fact, had begun to wonder if she would ever feel again.

But Tony prided himself on his sexual staying power, and last night... he wasn't so sure about last night.

Maybe it had been too much wine before getting down to business.

Or maybe his own nervousness that he was actually in bed with Sarah had gotten in the way of his performance. Maybe he'd been intimidated because she was so much older than he was.

Or maybe there were other, less definable things.

Whatever it was, Tony didn't think he had performed the way he should have even before that goddamned cat screwed things up. He wished Sarah was home right now so he could go in there and *show* her.

But there would be time for that, too.

He'd show her what kind of lover he really was!

The jealousy was probably the most difficult thing for Tony to understand.

Although he was a bright and very personable man, he wasn't exactly introspective. Long ago, through the trials of his own childhood and adolescence, he had convinced himself that *feelings* only got in the way of success, particularly for anyone who wanted to be a successful lawyer.

But something last night had filled him with an aching sense of his own lack of worth or ability. He'd thought about it all day while working at the restaurant, but he couldn't pin it down.

Maybe it was as simple as feeling jealous because Sarah had been married before he met her.

It wasn't as though Tony hadn't fucked a married woman or two in the past, but last night had seemed... *different*, somehow.

He wasn't sure how or what it was, and he wasn't sure he cared to know, as long as what he *did* about it got *rid* of it!

In fact, the more he thought about it, the more he felt as though there had been another person in bed with him and Sarah.

While they'd been drinking wine in the living room, before they went to the bedroom, she had told him that her ex-husband had died recently. She didn't specify *exactly* how recently or how he had died, but that had put a blanket over everything. The entire time they were fucking and, especially, afterward, once she had bandaged his wounds and he was getting dressed to go home, he'd had the distinct impression that she was still emotionally attached to her ex-husband and that she had been completely shattered by his death.

There weren't many things Tony knew for sure, but one of them was that he could never... *never* compete with a dead person for someone's affections.

He'd already cried that once before with his mother when he was thirteen, and his father was killed on an air mission over

Vietnam. Once his father died — a hero, defending his country — there was no time or emotion left for little Tony.

So now, as he clung to the shadows outside Sarah's house on this humid summer evening, Tony was more bothered than confused by the conflicting thoughts and emotions inside him.

He knew that he had to *do* something. He had to strike out, and maybe not just at Sarah, but at the whole fucking world!

Swirls of darkness filled his vision whenever he squeezed his eyes shut and tried to force himself to stop thinking and feeling.

But it had never worked for him in the past, even when he was thirteen years old, and he didn't expect it to work for him now.

The only thing that made him feel even marginally better was when he reached under his shirt to his hip pocket and felt the hard rubber handle of the knife. Even the slightest brushing touch against the knife's handle filled him with an indescribable energy and a feeling of purpose that he couldn't even begin to understand or explain.

Not that he wanted co.

The knife made him feel powerful, and he had a pretty good idea he knew why.

If life is a mystery, and death is the doorway, then the long-bladed knife he had found in the alley the other night was the key to unlocking the door.

And he intended to try it out.

Tonight!

The blade was practically crying out for blood!

Ever since he had found it, Tony couldn't understand why he felt so good when he held it. He received an almost electric charge when he pressed his thumb against the metal thumb rest and slashed the air with the blade. He reveled in the rush of scarlet images that filled his mind and imagined the power of life and death that it wielded.

The key to the doorway between life and death.

Chuckling softly to himself, Tony stepped out of the shadows. As he was starting up the side steps, a car rounded the corner onto Canal Street. For a blinding instant, the pale wash of headlights froze him in mid-step, like a deer caught in the sudden glare.

If that's Sarah, I'm fucked! he thought, shivering in spite of the humid night.

But the headlights swept over him, and the car passed down the street without any hesitation.

Tony stared after the car to make sure it was gone. Chances were that the driver, whoever it was, hadn't noticed him.

And even if he had, so what?

Tony reached under his shirt and slowly withdrew the knife, squeezing the handle so tightly the palm of his hand began to ache.

But he smiled.

This was a *good* ache...

A *comforting* ache.

It was the kind of ache that he knew could only be satiated when he saw the blade slice into warm flesh and release a gush of hot, vital lifeblood.

And he knew just where he was going to start.

With his other hand, Tony took a small plastic bag from his shirt pocket and shook it open. He wrinkled his nose at the rank smell of the fish fillet he had stolen from the restaurant earlier today. He laughed softly as he knelt down in the shadow of the porch and clicked his tongue several times.

"Here, Bingley. Com'on, kitty, kitty," he called out into the night.

The hand holding the knife was trembling terribly, as though a steady electric current were tickling through him.

"Here kitty, kitty, kitty..."

As Tony glanced around into the surrounding darkness, he thought he caught a reflection of bright blue light glancing from the long blade. His smile widened until it started to hurt his cheeks.

The moon was lost behind the haze. Not even the slightest breeze stirred the humid night. Tony listened to the sounds of traffic passing in the distance. Closer to the house, but lost in the darkness, he could hear crickets buzzing and the soft rustle of insect wings, like short, breathy whispers against his ear. He realized with a start that he had a rock-hard erection.

Still kneeling and looking around, he opened the plastic bag wider and waved it about, fanning the strong aroma into the night.

"Com'on kitty, kitty," he called softly. "I have a special treat for you."

A sudden shifting of motion at the end of the porch caught his attention. He felt his body tense as he squeezed the knife handle. Spinning white dots of light tracked like comets across his vision, so Tony couldn't see very well, but he knew that it *had* to be Bingley.

Clicking his tongue softly as he wrinkled his nose against the strong stench, he carefully dumped the fish onto the porch floor.

Still using a high-pitched, pleasant-sounding voice, he called out, "Come on, Bingley. Come and get it, you furry little fuck."

burial.

Chapter Seven

Two days later, David felt a sudden, urgent need to go back out to Riverside Cemetery. Until he found out otherwise, he desperately hoped that it was because Karen was there, waiting for him.

After spending close to twenty-four hours at his old apartment, recuperating and losing himself in the pure, unbroken silence, he had spent the next two days—Sunday and Monday—and most of the nights searching the Shadowlands for Karen. More times than he cared to count or could remember, he searched the area around Pine Knoll Elementary, Riverside Cemetery, Sarah's house, and the Brighton Avenue Park where he had first seen her.

All to no avail.

He had no idea where else she might go.

Although he encountered numerous other wraiths, many of them in small groups that he approached and questioned about Karen, none of them would say if they had seen her.

At least none of them would *admit* to it.

David got the distinct impression from several of them that they weren't being entirely honest with him. He couldn't help but notice how most of the wraiths he encountered acted extremely furtive or skittish around him. A few even appeared to be genuinely afraid when he approached them. One wraith— a young man with a horribly mutilated face—muttered something about the "death-mark" David carried on him, but David had no idea what he was talking about.

David spent at least part of each night huddled in Pine Knoll Elementary, alone and afraid. He couldn't help but be frightened—more for Karen than for himself.

He couldn't stop thinking about how, when he was alive, he had contemplated suicide—almost daily, in fact—following his daughter's death.

He wished he was able to cry as he took a quick mental tally of his failed life.

He'd destroyed his marriage, for one.

He'd lost his daughter through what he saw as largely his own negligence, for another.

And he had been trying with steadily diminishing success to patch together a writing career that had been floundering ever since it had started.

He had no friends to speak of, at least locally, so there was no one he could have talked to about what he'd been going through.

How many areas of his life did he have to fuck up before he finally lost the will to live and found the courage to cash in his chips?

Three strikes and you're out, buddy!

He had wanted to die, and he had gotten his wish.

He was beginning to think—or at least hope—that here in the Shadowlands he might be able to accomplish the same thing.

If only he dared to let himself slip into the endless void that he could feel at the core of his being—that cold, limitless black nothingness that called to him, continually pulled at him, dragging him down... deeper and deeper... into...

Oblivion!

"No!" David said in a harsh whisper that joined the chorus of voices and laughter inside the schoolhouse.

He wasn't going to give in to it.

Not yet.

Not until he found Karen or at least learned what had happened to her.

On Tuesday morning, when he awoke shortly before dawn and felt a strong impulse to go out to Riverside Cemetery, he decided to follow his instinct and go there immediately.

Maybe Karen's there... Maybe she's haunting her own grave... Maybe she's trying to reach out to her mother... or find me....

It was almost too much to hope for, but he couldn't stand the thought of his daughter being alone and afraid in this terrifying realm of existence.

The anxiety he felt made his journey out to the cemetery seem to take forever.

The sun was just coming up over the city when he started out. The day looked to be much brighter and cooler than it had been for the last few days, but David couldn't feel a thing. His last memory of any physical sensation was how sticky and humid the night air had been the night he died. But now the sun was high and strong. It lit the world with a vibrant yellow glare that made it appear as though he were wearing yellow-tinted sunglasses. The leaves of the trees, while still looking pallid and gray, fluttered in a gusting wind that David wished to God he could feel on his face.

As he walked along the roadside, contemplating how much he missed the warmth of the sun on his face and the sweet smell of growing things, he was filled with a deep, inexpressible sadness. He decided that being deprived of any sensations — even the physical aspects of the emotions he was feeling — was a perfect definition of "Hell."

David was so involved with his own thoughts that he barely noticed the solid line of cars that streamed past him as he approached the cemetery. All of the cars had their headlights on and were moving in a slow, stately procession. He finally took note of them when they pulled in at the cemetery gate, slithering around the curve in the road like a huge, black snake. Thin dust that glittered like flecks of gold in the slanting rays of the sun rose in their wake.

"Must be a funeral," David muttered to himself, but he barely spared a thought for the poor person who had died and was being buried today.

Without even thinking about it, he passed easily through the stone wall that surrounded the cemetery. It was only when he was cutting across the cemetery lawn, passing like a wisp of gray smoke between the trees and marble headstones, that he looked up and saw that the funeral procession had stopped at the base of the hill where Karen was buried.

"Oh, shit," he whispered.

He was gripped by a fear that he didn't dare name.

A cold uneasiness filled him as he drew to a halt beneath the shade of a tall maple tree and watched the mourners park their cars and get out. The sound of car doors opening and slamming shut was like the dull popping of distant gunfire in the still morning.

The mourners, looking like ghosts themselves, moved silently up to the crest of the hill. Some walked hand in hand. Most bowed their heads, and all of them spoke in hushed tones. A group of young men wearing black suits, none of whom David recognized, opened the back door of the hearse and pulled out the long, dark mahogany box. Their knees buckled and their shoulders sagged as they hefted the weight.

The gnawing fear inside David grew steadily stronger, but he tried to keep the stark, terrifying realization at bay.

No! That can't be ME in there!

There were mostly young to middle-aged men and women attending. Some of them were alone; some were in couples. A few had one or more children. Even in the summer heat, almost everyone was wearing dark suits or dresses. As David watched the people scream up the rise to the area next to Karen's grave, he had the distinct impression that some of those attending were wraiths, moving about unseen by the living mourners. Like ghouls, they seemed to be enjoying the spectacle of another funeral—another member joining their ranks. Several times one or more of the people looked down the hill to where David was standing in the sun-dappled shadows. One of them—an old woman David thought he recognized but wasn't sure from where—waved a thin hand at him, signaling for him to approach.

Filled with caution, and feeling a cold darkness grip the center of his chest, David stepped out into the sunlight and started up the hill. His body looked insubstantial in the blazing summer sun. He felt both wary and tense, realizing now for certain that this was *his* funeral!

When he was halfway up the hill, he stopped short in his tracks as if he had walked into a solid, invisible wall. He finally recognized the old woman who was beckoning to him.

It was Mrs. Burke, his second-grade teacher. She had died more than fifteen years ago!

Shaking his head, he took a step backward in spite of the angry glare Mrs. Burke gave him.

David let out a loud tortured moan, when he saw Sarah. She was wearing a black ankle-length dress and was standing close to Karen's tombstone. The fingers of her left hand were brushing lightly against the polished pink marble, as if she didn't quite know what to do with her hands.

As the men carrying the coffin approached, she bowed her head slightly and clasped her hands tightly in from of her. David could see, beneath the black veil she was wearing, that her face was slick with tears, but he had the distinct impression that she was thinking just as much about Karen as she was about him. He could no longer feel that subtle, invisible charge of energy coming from her that he had felt a few days ago in his old apartment.

If he could have cried, he would have.

Avoiding Mrs. Burke, he slowly approached the group, certain that some of them, at least, could see him. He got close enough to the hole in the ground to look down into it. The gaping, rectangular hole looked flat and black, like a doorway leading… someplace else. A pile of dirt and thick clumps of sod covered by a tarp were stacked neatly over to one side. At the head of the hole were several arrangements of white and red flowers adorned with ribbons that fluttered in the gentle breeze.

"Oh, Jesus," David muttered. "Oh, *Jesus!*"

In the pressing silence, his voice sounded with a hollow echo, like a sudden rush of cold wind. Several of the mourners closest to him turned and looked around, frowning curiously. Mrs. Burke clicked her tongue and shook her head, making him feel once again like an unruly schoolboy. Another one of the mourners looked steadily at him while nodding his head in silent acknowledgment.

The minister—Reverend Harry Grant, from the Lutheran church in Portland that Sarah and Karen attended—was reading from the open Bible in his hands. His voice was lost in the high-pitched rushing sound that swirled like tugging hands all around David.

It took a long time for the impact of what was happening to sink in as David glanced at the faces of the people who had gathered.

He recognized most of them, but not all.

There were friends and relatives, many of whom he hadn't seen or spoken to in years. He saw a few local writers and other "book people" he knew from around town. Mrs. Abbiati from the Warren Library, who had always been so supportive of his books, was there. Her eyes were swollen and her cheeks were flushed red from crying. The biggest surprise was that Bill

Relling, his literary agent, had actually bothered to fly up from New York. David figured he had to be on vacation, because the commission from his last novel sale certainly wouldn't have covered airfare.

David's insides wrenched with sadness, but he also found it slightly amusing that all of these people, many of whom seemed not to have given him a second thought when he was alive, were now gathered to see him buried.

Oily, black waves of fear and grief and anger washed through him when he finally found the courage to look squarely at the coffin, that was resting on cloth-draped supports next to the open grave. Sunlight glinted like white fire from the brass handles and fixtures, leaving trailing afterimages behind. He could hear the wood creaking and snapping as it heated up in the sun.

Jesus! How can I really be the one who's shut up inside that box?

The thought made the blackness inside him surge with almost unbearable strength. For a dizzying instant, David imagined that—right now—he *really was* inside that closed box, staring up with lifeless eyes at the solid wall of eternal darkness that surrounded him. No matter how much he tried to resist, he could feel himself being sucked into the bottomless well of darkness inside him.

Maybe that's it after all!

A tight thrill of terror filled him.

Maybe as soon as my coffin's lowered into the ground and covered with dirt, I'll just fade away... dissolve into nothingness.

Maybe I'm only hanging around like these other wraiths I've seen until I'm six feet under, and then I'll move on to the next level... whatever it may be.

Feeling both fascination and dread throb through him, he watched as the pallbearers shifted the coffin onto the lowering mechanism. The minister took a handful of dirt and sprinkled it onto the coffin. Once again, David had the distinct impression that he was lying inside the coffin, listening to the dirt rattle on the wood like rain on a metal roof.

Then they began to lower the coffin into the ground.

Each *click* of the ratchet felt like a hot spike being driven into David's head. His vision blurred and then shattered into a million hazy fragments that merged and separated like a kaleidoscope as he watched the wooden box containing his last mortal remains lowered slowly out of sight.

click...

Click...

CLICK!...

Down into the pure, impenetrable darkness of eternity!

The fear was too much to bear.

David slouched forward and covered his face with both hands as he let out a long, agonized wail that warbled crazily up and down the scale. Even with his hands shielding his eyes, he was able to see the faces of the mourners floating like pale, bloated balloons in the darkness behind his eyes. Their eyes were open wide and unblinking, spearing him with their lifeless stares. Their mouths gaped open. Their thin lips moved as though they were trying to tell him something, but their voices were so low, and the words they spoke came so slowly that whatever they were saying was lost in an incomprehensible babble of noise.

Strong, trembling surges of darkness passed through David like earthquakes. The whole world—inside and outside his head—was spinning out of control. It no longer mattered if his eyes were opened or closed—he knew he would be staring into the same eternal blackness...

Forever!

David had the sudden feeling that his body was lighter than a feather and was spreading out, thinning until he was less substantial than the air.

Powerful, irresistible forces took hold of his soul and stretched him out in all directions at once.

"...trusting in the strength of the Lord... assured that David is now at peace with the Lord... so as we commit his earthly remains to the ground... believing in the resurrection of the body and the life everlasting..."

These words, which he barely heard, much less understood, echoed all around him and — somehow — cut through the raging confusion he was feeling and drew him back, screaming, from the edge of the void.

Clenching waves of nausea gripped him, but he knew that these were not physical sensations. His mind was trying desperately to process and accept the pure emotion of this ultimate loss.

He *was dead! ... Forever!*

Vibrating pulses of red and violet light throbbed in his vision when he opened his eyes to look at the gathered mourners.

A cold shock hit him when he saw that he was alone on the hill.

The cemetery was entirely deserted.

He found himself standing alone beside his and Karen's graves.

A rounded mound of fresh-turned earth and sod covered the place where, mere moments ago, it seemed, he had watched as his coffin was lowered into the ground. The wind sighed like someone in agony as it swirled among the headstones. Long, knife-edged slashes of shadow streaked across the neatly trimmed cemetery lawn. The sky was the dense color of lead and looked just as heavy as it pressed down on him.

They're gone!

The thought left him with a deep chill.

They're all gone now, and before long I'll be forgotten.

Less than a memory.

The shadows visibly lengthened and deepened as he stood there staring at his own grave.

He knew that he wasn't crying, but his vision was distorted as though he were looking at the world through the wrong end of a telescope. Everything appeared distant and blurred.

It's all for nothing!

David tried to block out the thought as wave after wave of misery washed through him.

It's all absolutely useless!

But then a single, burning spark flared up in the darkness inside him.

...but I'm still here...

The thought was the merest whisper in the back of his mind.

...It was close, but I didn't fade away...

For the second time, now, he had felt the chilling embrace, the seductive lure of Oblivion; and he had almost yielded to it, but ultimately he had resisted.

And he knew why!

Karen!

Before he let go entirely, he *had* to find her!

He had no idea how, but—somehow—he was going to figure out exactly what realm of the afterlife they were trapped in, and he was going to do anything and everything he could to help his daughter find some measure of peace.

He told himself he didn't care if he never found it for himself.

That didn't matter!

Even if he had to spend the rest of eternity in this gray, hallucinatory state of being, he didn't care as long as he could find his daughter and do everything—absolutely *everything* to help her find release!

David braced himself, suddenly filled with purpose.

The funeral was over.

Good!

Let the mourners go back home. Let the living return to their daily lives. Apparently death *wasn't* the end of it. In due time, they'll find themselves here.

All of them!

And they'll deal with whatever they encounter in their own way. He had his own problems to deal with.

As a new sense of courage and purpose filled him, his vision gradually cleared. David saw to his amazement that time had passed, and evening was already falling.

Could a whole day have passed that quickly?

He looked around the cemetery and knew that he was ready to begin his search for his daughter. But as he started down the hill, he noticed a dark figure standing in the shadows at the fringe of woods.

David drew to a halt and stared at it.

It was so silent and motionless David couldn't be sure it was really there.

When he first saw the hooded face and slouched shoulders, a feeble spark of hope that this might be Karen filled him, but he quickly realized that the figure was too thin and too tall. Even in the dying daylight, he could see that the person—whoever it was—wore a long, dark cloak. The hood was pulled forward like a monk's cowl, creating a long, narrow tube that hid the person's face from sight; but David could sense cold, unblinking eyes staring at him within the shadow of the cowl.

He had no idea what to do.

He wanted to call out to the figure, to determine first of all if it was even real. Chances were it was just another wandering wraith that had come out to where its body was buried.

But the sight of it filled David with unreasonable fear as well as a vague sense of recognition.

For a flashing instant, he had a memory of acute, physical pain—the sensation of something iron hard slamming into his body.

The darkness around the figure seemed to swell and pulsate with subtle energy as the memory teased David's mind. He moaned softly, filled with fear when he saw the figure raise one arm and, extending a bony finger, beckon to him.

"No... no, I—"

David shook his head and took a step backward as the figure continued to motion to him. Deep within the blackness under the figure's cowl, he was sure he could see a dull red glow of eyes, burning like angry embers.

"I... I have to find her first," David said in a high, trembling voice no louder than the wind, swirling among the tombstones.

He was suddenly sure, now, that this had to be Death, come at last to claim him.

"Just... just give me a... a little more time," he pleaded, his voice stammering and breaking on nearly every syllable. "Let me... let me find her first. That's all I ask. Let me... I have to—to find her and... and help her before I... before I go."

The figure shook its head ever so slightly from side to side. David thought he could hear the rough scratching sound of heavy cloth and something that sounded like a deep rumble of laughter.

"Please... please, just let me find her."

And then, having no idea what the figure might do, David turned away from it and started walking toward the cemetery gate. With each step, he expected to hear a dark rushing sound of wings behind him and feel a chilling tap on his shoulder, but he kept walking.

He left the cemetery, moving as fast as he could, even though his feet were dragging like heavy chains. His footsteps echoed dully in the still night air.

Sarah had a vague sense that she was dreaming, but she couldn't shake the feeling that it was all somehow very real too.

She was in David's bedroom, kneeling on the floor beside his bed and searching through the teetering stacks of magazines and books that were stacked up on the floor. The light through the small window was pale and gray, hardly strong enough to see by. The air in the room seemed dense. Motes of dust swirled around her like a heavy suspension in liquid.

A feeling of desperation verging on panic filled her.

She knew that she was looking for something very specific, but she wasn't sure exactly what. Her hands moved with agonizing slowness, and every book she lifted seemed thicker and heavier than the last. The piles of books seemed to be growing continually taller, pushing up toward the ceiling like a slow-motion gush from an oil well.

"I'll know it when I see it… I'll know it when I see it," she kept chanting to herself as she worked feverishly, shifting arm-breaking stacks of books and magazines from one side to the other.

One stack of magazines beside her fell over and fanned out across the floor like a spread-out deck of cards. She imagined hearing a man's voice, low and sonorous, like a magician's, say, "Pick a magazine… any magazine"

"Shit, shit, oh, *shit!*" she muttered as she leaned forward on her hands and knees, and scooped the magazines back into a stack.

Once again, she began chanting, "I'll know it when I see it I'll know it when I see it."

A thrill of discovery went through her when she looked down and realized she could see her own hands.

She remembered reading that you weren't supposed to be able to see your own hands in a dream, but there they were, pawing and shuffling through the books and magazines. Her fingers looked too pale and thin, almost skeletal. She was filled with the sudden unnerving idea that these might not even be her own hands. She had the distinctly disconcerting impression that someone else was reaching around from behind her, moving things around.

Cold, prickling waves of panic filled her.

She groaned out loud, wishing to God that she dared to turn around to see who was standing there behind her.

Instead, she just watched, feeling oddly disembodied as her hands rifled through the magazines at the top of the stack. She picked one up and held it at arm's length.

It was an issue of *Cemetery Dance*—the one depicting the rotting, crucified corpse. Only now the cover painting looked as though it had been done in rich sepia tones, and the face of the corpse looked frighteningly familiar.

It was David's face, staring back at her, his mouth open in silent, frozen agony.

She tried to look away but couldn't as the corpse's head in the illustration began to toss slowly from side to side. David's lipless mouth was moving as his body writhed in agony.

The illusion was so real Sarah thought she could hear the rattle of dried bones and the stretching of desiccated muscles and tendons. Craning her head forward, she listened, positive that she could hear the creaking, breathy rustle as the skeleton that had once been her husband tried to speak.

No! Wait just a goddamned second! This can't be happening! This is too vivid to be just a dream!

She was mildly surprised that she could be consciously aware that she was dreaming and still not wake up.

Almost against her will, as if her hands were no longer under her conscious control, she placed the issue of *Cemetery Dance* down and then continued to shuffle through the stacks of books.

Looking from side to side, but not quite daring to glance over her shoulder, she saw the piles of books looming higher and higher above her head until they teetered back and forth like buildings swaying in an earthquake.

"It's in this pile, here, someplace," a low voice whispered softly, close to her ear.

"I'll know it when I see it. I'll know it when I see it," she answered automatically, but she still didn't have the courage to turn to see who was behind her.

It had been a man's voice, she knew that much. The tone and pitch had sounded vaguely familiar, but Sarah couldn't quite place it.

Or maybe she didn't *want* to place it.

She had no idea which pile he might have meant; but her hand, moving as if it had a will of its own, reached out and touched one of the stacks to her left. The fingernail of her forefinger clicked like a ratchet as she ran it down along the spines of the books.

None of the titles seemed to make any sense. The words were strung together in meaningless *non sequiturs*.

"I'll know it when I see it... I'll know it when I see it..."

Her finger hesitated, pressing against the side of one book so hard she almost pushed the whole stack over.

James... Moore's... Complete... Encyclopedia... of ... Mass... Murderers ...

She had the distinct feeling that these words were somehow connected, but, at least in the dream, they didn't seem to make any sense whatsoever.

"Yes, that's the one," the man's voice whispered from behind her, so close that Sarah thought she could feel the cold draft of his breath against her neck.

She shivered and felt a mild shock of recognition.

It could be David's voice, she thought, but he usually didn't sound even half as mellow as this voice sounded.

166 / Rick Hautala

Especially during the last few years they'd lived together, there always seemed to be a hard, almost frantic edge in his voice—a sharp timbre that grated on her nerves.

"This one?" Sarah asked, still not daring to look behind her.

She had the impression that, as she moved her head, the person behind her also moved, always keeping out of sight.

Tingling with steadily rising terror, Sarah watched as a thin hand and bone-white arm reached around from behind her and tapped the spine of the book. The curled, yellowed fingernail clicked like an insect's wings against the ragged paper cover.

Convinced that she wouldn't see whoever this was if she turned around and looked, she watched as her own hands reached out and touched the spine of the thick, green book. The dust jacket was frayed from use, and she could barely read the title.

"Page one hundred and thirty-seven," a voice that sounded uncannily like David's whispered inside her head. "I just thought you might like to know."

Why? she thought, but didn't dare ask out loud. *What's on page one thirty-seven?*

The steadily tightening pressure twisting inside her suddenly spiked sharp enough to make her cry out as she jerked backward.

She knew that she wouldn't be able to get the book out without toppling over the stack, but she had to try. There was something on page one thirty-seven. Grabbing the top and bottom edges of the book, she tried to wiggle the book out, but the stack started swaying heavily from side to side. Before she got the book, everything started to collapse in slow-motion, like a house of cards.

Sarah lurched forward, hoping to stop it, but falling books started raining down all around her. Like tumbling dominoes, stack after stack fell with a prolonged, thunderous roar. The book she had been trying to get was lost in the sudden avalanche.

Sarah clapped both hands over her mouth to stifle the scream inside her as her body snapped into an upright, sitting position.

Her eyes were wide open when she found herself staring wide-eyed at the soft, gray glow of light that was filtering through her bedroom windows. The air in the room was dense and hot, but she was left with the vivid impression that David's bedroom in her dream had been as cold as a refrigerator. Her throat felt hot and raw as she inhaled sharply and shook her head, trying desperately to clear it.

It *was just a dream.... * It *was all just a dream*, she told herself, but that didn't make the cold, slithery feeling inside her go away.

With bated breath, she looked around the room, waiting anxiously for her eyes to adjust to the darkness. When she saw the mounded lump on the bed beside her, she jumped and uttered a soft cry. Once the initial surprise passed, she let out her breath in a long, soft *whoosh.*

It was just Tony, asleep beside her. It was a miracle she hadn't awakened him.

After another moment or two, she remembered everything that had happened earlier that evening.

On Monday, Tony had called her at work. After apologizing for the way he had acted the other night, he had asked her out for a movie that night.

Sarah hadn't wanted to tell him that she had to attend visiting hours at the funeral home for her ex-husband, so she had graciously declined.

When Tony called on Tuesday afternoon shortly after she returned home from David's funeral and asked her out again, she decided with some hesitation to accept. She told herself that she needed to do something to get her mind off the sad events of the day. David's funeral had stirred up too many dark remembrances about Karen's death, and she was finding it difficult, if not impossible, to shake them.

Even though she had vowed not to let it happen again, after going to a movie, they had ended up back at her house. After a drink and casual conversation in the living room, they had gone up to her bedroom.

Sarah glanced at the alarm clock beside her bed.

It was almost three o'clock. She and Tony had been asleep for at least a couple of hours.

She rubbed her face and let out another long sigh as she crossed her legs and shifted forward.

The memory of the dream was already dissolving like cotton candy in the rain. She tried to catch a few wispy fragments before they disappeared entirely, but all she could remember was a number:

137.

It didn't make any sense.

She had no idea why that number would pop into her mind.

Squinting, she glanced around the darkened bedroom and shook her head in wonder.

"I'll know it when I see it," she whispered into the darkness.

"What the hell are you talking about?" Tony asked.

His deep-pitched voice, speaking so suddenly in the darkness, made Sarah jump. Her breath caught in her throat with an audible click.

"Huh—? Oh, oh, nothing... I was just having a—it must've been a dream."

"Umm... a dream," Tony said, smacking his lips sleepily.

Rolling over to face her, he shifted up onto one elbow. The mattress creaked beneath his weight. "You wanna tell me about it?"

Sarah considered for a moment, then shook her head even though she knew the motion was wasted in the darkness.

Reaching out with one hand, she touched him lightly on the left shoulder. The memory of their love-making earlier that night filled her with a warm glow that almost—but not quite—dispelled the chills the dream had left inside her.

Tony shifted closer to her, then flopped onto his back again and reached for her with both hands. He gripped her shoulders tightly as he pulled her down to him. His lips made soft clicking sounds as he kissed her passionately on the mouth, neck and shoulders.

"Sounds like it was a doozy," Tony said between kisses.

His breath was hot in the shallow of her shoulder as his tongue flicked out like a snake's and started tracing a warm, wet line across her collarbone and down to the tips of her breasts. He began to lap and suck greedily on her nipples.

Sarah couldn't answer him.

She tilted her head back and moaned softly as she clutched his head with both hands. Wave after burning wave of passion swept through her, making her whole body tremble.

"Yeah, it… it was," she gasped.

Rushes of heat swept like a brushfire through her, radiating outward from her stomach when she felt Tony's hands start rubbing against the small of her back, applying pressure as he pulled her closer to him.

"Think you can handle round two?" he asked. His voice was muffled against her flesh.

Almost swooning, Sarah was about to say *yes;* but then in a sudden flash she remembered at least one part of her dream.

She tensed, almost overwhelmed by the sudden certainty that she and Tony weren't alone… that someone else was in the bedroom with them, watching them… silent and unseen.

Her body was as stiff and unyielding as wood. She pulled away from Tony and clenched her fists, poised to hit him if he didn't let her go.

"Hey," he said, grabbing playfully at her.

"No!" Sarah shouted as the fear inside her spiked stronger.

The darkness in the bedroom seemed to be pressing in on her from every direction at once. She found it difficult, almost impossible, to take a deep enough breath. A cold sheen of sweat broke out over her body.

"What the fuck?" Tony said.

Sarah couldn't help but notice the angry edge in his voice.

"I said no," she said. "It–it's just that I–I don't really feel like it. That's all."

"Why the hell not?"

In the darkness, Tony's voice sounded like flint striking iron. She expected to see sparks fly.

Tony shifted closer and reached for her, but she swatted his hand away.

The tension inside her was becoming almost unbearable. She had the distinct feeling that someone was standing behind her, watching them; and that no matter where she looked, she would never be able to see who it was. Sitting naked on the bed, she felt suddenly weak and vulnerable.

Totally exposed.

"Hey, you need to relax a little. Take the edge off," Tony said, softening his voice. "You're probably just stressed out from work. Come on, lie down. Let me give you a massage."

Sarah was in no mood for a massage, but she relented after a moment and laydown on the bed, flat on her stomach. Tony shifted around to straddle her. She could feel the hot pressure of his balls against the soft mound of her butt. The way she was feeling, that sensation was the farthest thing from sexual.

"Hey, wait just a second," Tony said. "I got something for you."

Sarah felt him lean forward and heard him feeling around for something down on the floor beside the bed, close to where he had dropped his clothes.

The tension inside her wasn't letting up. She was filled with a strong urge to leap up off the bed and run through the house, turning on all the lights. It took a great deal of effort just to lie there and wait.

Once again Tony straddled her, and then Sarah felt a light touch on her back. For an instant, she was confused; then she realized that he was massaging her with something soft—a glove of some kind.

"There, now is that better?" Tony asked. He was moving his hand in wide circles that swept from the base of her neck to the tip of her spine.

Against her will, Sarah allowed his touch soothe her. It was almost ticklish, but she focused on letting it make her feel languid and sensuous. A cascade of warmth and well-being flooded her, pushing away all the frightening thoughts and images that had gripped her. With her head cocked to one side, she took a long, shuddering breath and then let it out slowly as Tony's touch drew the tension out of her body.

"Umm… That feels *really* good," she said in a breathy whisper. "What's that you're using?"

"Huh? Oh, nothing," Tony said.

For just a second, Sarah thought she detected a slight chuckle in his voice, but she chose to ignore it.

"Just a little piece of fur I picked up. I think it's—ah, rabbit fur or something."

"Oh, yeah… That feels unbelievable," Sarah said. She moaned softly, telling herself she had to unwind.

Her body felt like it was turning to mush as Tony continued to rub the swatch of fur up and down the length of her back. He shifted to one side and ran it all the way down her thighs to the bottoms of her feet, and then back up to her shoulders and neck.

"If you keep this up much longer," she whispered, "I'll be sound asleep in no time."

"Well, I was kinda hoping for something else," Tony whispered.

This time he did laugh out loud, but Sarah was feeling much too relaxed to notice.

The night vibrated with unseen dangers as David walked along strangely deserted streets, heading back to Pine Knoll Elementary. His footsteps clicked softly on the pavement, sounding like the steady ticking of a clock as he crossed the bridge over the Stroudwater River where it joined the Fore River before entering Casco Bay. The dark water below gurgled a soft, sad song beneath the pilings. It reminded David of another night—a night which now seemed like an eternity ago, when he'd been poised on a bridge some distance upriver, trying to find the necessary courage to jump.

If he'd had the courage to end his life that way, he thought, his drowned body might have floated all the way downstream to this bridge before finally being discovered… if it ever would have been discovered. Maybe he would have floated all the way out to sea.

But that was idle speculation and, like everything else in his past life, long past repair.

Time and distance were still playing tricks on him, and it seemed to be taking much longer than he thought it should to walk the few miles back to the schoolhouse.

Along the way, as he passed deserted storefronts, vacant apartment buildings, and what looked like abandoned houses, he could hear faint echoes and voices from the surrounding darkness. Sometimes piercing screams and anguished wailing sounds rose in the night and were punctuated by deeper, wrenching moans that sounded like souls groaning in misery.

David remembered the warnings the old man had given him about the dangers of the Shadowlands, but he couldn't decide if it was his own fearful mindset, or if there was something he didn't know anything about, something terrible and dangerous that was gathering strength in the Shadowlands.

The night was a deep, pulsating purple energy that seemed about to rip the sky open at any moment. The line of streetlights cast ghostly blue ovals onto the sidewalk at the base of each telephone pole. As David walked from one small pool of light to the next, he could feel distinct temperature fluctuations that made him shiver inwardly.

Just as he was cresting the hill at the turn onto Deering Avenue, he heard a rising chorus off in the distance that sounded like barking hounds. The baying sounds echoed hollowly in the night, seeming both far away and much too close.

A ripple of fear raced through David as he looked around, hoping to find someplace to hide, but the shadowed doorways and windows seemed even more threatening than the surrounding night.

After listening for what seemed like much too long a time, David realized that—thankfully—the sound was moving away from him. The howling cries reverberated in the darkness as they gradually faded. David's body was tingling with apprehension as he continued on his way, all the while poised and ready either to run or fight to defend himself, if he had to.

He crossed Capisic Street and was no more than half a mile from Pine Knoll Elementary when, off to his left, a sudden flurry of activity in the shadows beside one of the derelict buildings caught his attention. Wheeling around with his fists clenched, he stared into the dense shadows inside the ruined buildings.

There was nothing there... nothing that he could see, anyway.

But then something much darker than the shadows moved so fast that he had no time to react to it. With a high peel of laughter, it rushed out of a darkened doorway and slammed into David.

Even though he experienced the impact only as a distant shock, it knocked him off his feet. His body felt like a useless sack of grain as it hit the ground. He felt oddly detached from reality as he tumbled over backward, and the person or creature or whatever it was leaped into the air and landed on top of his chest.

The world was spinning crazily out of control.

David felt a strong jolt of fear when he realized that he was flat on his back, and that someone—a creature with rotting tatters of flesh hanging from its face and hollow, wide-set eyes that blazed with a savage red glow in the sullen light of the night—had him pinned to the ground. Its bony knees were grinding painfully into his upper arms.

"You're *mine* now," the creature whispered as it leaned close to David's ear. Its voice crackled and snapped like cold water splashed onto a hot stove.

There was no way David could think of this thing as ever having been human. Thin strings of dark hair hung in loose clumps from its head. Wide, ragged patches mottled its face where the rotting skin had pulled away, exposing grayish yellow bone that was decayed and crawling with worms. The creature's lips peeled back, exposing teeth and gums that were black with rot.

Nearly insane with fear, David struggled to free himself, but it was useless.

The creature straddled his chest, pinning him down firmly to the hard ground. Bony fingers dug like spikes into the sides of David's head as the creature gripped him and, leaning forward, brought its face so close to David's that they almost touched noses. Thick, looping strings of drool ran from the creature's mouth as it cackled with deep, rattling laughter. An insane light shined deep within the creature's eyes.

Unable to believe that this was really happening, David tried to resist, but the creature was much too strong for him. He cringed inwardly when he felt the creature shift its weight, and then heard a loud, clanking sound. Glancing down, he saw that the creature was holding a coiled length of chain with metal clamps on the ends that looked like leg irons. The rings of the chain flickered with a curious light that made them appear dull yellow.

With a quick flick of its wrists, the creature snapped open one of the cuffs and started to force David's wrist into it.

The pain David felt the instant the metal touched his forearm and the cuff snapped shut was indescribable. Searing hot flames and powerful surges of numbing cold ripped through his body and mind. He listened to the shrill chorus of agonized screams that seemed to be coming from inside the chain links.

The creature tossed its head back. Glaring up at the thick night sky, it let loose another gale of insane laughter.

"Mine! Mine! You're all *mine* now!" it howled, its voice warbling higher and higher until it finally cracked. This was followed by another burst of maniacal laughter as the creature snapped open another cuff and shackled David's other arm.

For a moment, David was immobilized by his fear, but he quickly discovered that he couldn't resist even if he wanted to. The mere touch of the strange metal—so cold that it burned white hot against his body—drained him of all strength and resolve. The weight of the chains pinned him to the ground with a crushing heaviness that was like nothing he had ever experienced before, either in life or in the Shadowlands. His body felt as though it were encased in molten iron. Every fiber of his being shrieked with pain and anguish, but no matter how hard he tried, he couldn't move.

"Wha–what do you—"

"Shut up, slave!" the creature squealed.

Sitting back on its haunches, it hauled back and slapped David across the mouth. The impact was dull and nowhere close to the intense agony of the chains, but it knocked David's head back against the ground hard enough to daze him. Explosions of brightly colored light flashed across his vision. His view of the night sky shattered into a thousand mirrored fragments.

The creature swung off David's chest and then, reaching down, snapped open the two remaining cuffs. It was just about to clamp them shut on David's ankles when a sudden rush of dark motion against the night sky drew David's attention. He tried to life his head enough to see what it was, convinced that it must be one of the creature's accomplices, but he couldn't move.

A hopeless, sinking sensation filled him when he saw —and recognized—the hooded figure that he had seen earlier this evening at the cemetery. The long, dark cowl masked its face in shadow, but David could feel its cold, savage scare boring into him with almost unbearable intensity.

The creature had its back to the hooded figure and seemed completely oblivious to its presence.

"Oh, I'll get a good price for this one, I'll bet. Yes, sir, I will," it babbled to itself between cackling laughter as it forced one of David's legs into the cuff and snapped it shut. "This here's a good, strong corpus, it is. And he's all mine! *All mine!*"

"Release him at once." The hooded figure's voice boomed in the night like a cannon shot that echoed from the empty buildings across the street.

The creature froze instantly, its expression fixed in a startled, horrified grimace. The fiery glow in its eyes seemed to die instantly. If such a terrifying creature could itself be scared, this one was. It cringed like a whipped animal as it turned around slowly and looked at whoever—or whatever—was standing behind it.

"Right *now!*" the hooded figure commanded, slowly raising one hand and pointing a forefinger at the creature.

"But I... I caught him, fair and square, Ferryman," the creature said. There wasn't very much strength or conviction in its voice. "He's... mine!"

"No, he's *mine!* I removed his caul. My mark is upon him," the hooded figure replied in a deep, sonorous voice that seemed to come from several directions at once, as if the night itself had found a voice.

"Release him *immediately,* or be prepared to suffer the consequences."

"But I... I *want* him," the creature said, its voice rising an octave or two. "I *deserve* him! I *tracked* him here. I found out where he stays, and I *caught* him. By all rights, Ferryman, he should be mine."

"*I'm* his reaper!" The hooded figure said nothing more as it stared at the cringing creature. After a long, tense silence, he extended both hands above his head and clapped chem once. The sound was like a crack of thunder that split the night sky.

The creature kneeling beside David was trembling horribly. It glanced furtively from side to side, as though looking for help that obviously wasn't going to arrive. After another long, tense moment, the creature slumped forward. Reaching into the back pocket of its tattered clothes, it produced a key. Its hands were trembling horribly as it leaned forward and began to unlock the leg and wrist cuffs.

David couldn't describe the sudden, intense relief he felt the instant the heavy chains fell away. The searing pain immediately dissolved, and the faint chorus of screams slowly faded away to nothing.

The chains clanked heavily together, and the light seemed to bleed out of them as the creature hastily gathered them together. With head bowed as though it didn't dare glance at the hooded figure, the creature stood up shakily. Hunching over as though withered with age, it scuttled off into the night. The last David heard of it was the distant clank of its chains.

Then silence settled down, thick and solid.

David was too stunned to move.

The surprise attack had caught him completely off guard. His body still felt drained of all strength. He realized that those chains must be forged of some magical material to have affected him so dramatically. He wasn't sure he could move, much less stand up.

The hooded figure regarded David with a long, steady stare.

Once again, David felt the cold intensity boring into him. He wanted to say something—to thank his deliverer, if nothing else, but he wasn't at all convinced that his situation had improved.

He tried to speak, but the only sound he could manage was a stammering "Thank you."

Without a word, the hooded figure reached out and silently flicked his fingers, urging David to take hold of his hand.

David wasn't sure he wanted or dared to touch this person, whoever he was, but he reached up and grasped the mysterious figure's hand. The touch wasn't nearly as cold as he'd expected. In fact, he felt a mild charge of rejuvenating energy infuse his being as their hands touched.

"Come with me," the figure said after David stood up.

David still felt oddly disoriented. It took him a moment or two to regain his balance. He glanced at the darkened buildings on either side of the street, convinced that he could see numerous pale faces watching them from the shadows. A deep, trembling fear gripped him.

"Who... who are you?" he asked. "What do you want with me?"

His voice sounded faint and raw, but David was amazed that he could speak at all. A steadily tightening pressure clutched his chest like huge, unseen hands.

"We have much to talk about," the cowled figure said in a deep voice that reverberated in the night. "You already have a safe place to stay. Let's go there."

ferryman.

Chapter Eight

After making love for a second time that night—something Sarah told Tony she hadn't done with David or anyone else in *years*—*Sarah* drifted off to sleep; but here it was, well past two o'clock in the morning, and Tony was still wide awake.

He was naked, lying flat on his back on top of the sheets which were still damp with the sweat of their lovemaking. With his hands clenched tightly at his sides, he stared up at the ceiling as a cool breeze wafted through the open bedroom windows and washed over his body like a refreshing mountain stream.

But it did little to calm Tony down.

His mind was whirling with disturbing thoughts, some of them even crazy, and all of them were centered around the knife.

What the hell was he going to do about that goddamned knife?

Better yet, what the hell was he going to do *with* it?

It seemed as though, ever since he found it that night in the alleyway, he hadn't been able to stop thinking about it.

It was like a sickness—a fever that burned deep inside his brain.

He carried the knife with him wherever he went, and it seemed as though every few seconds or minutes he was compelled to feel for it underneath his shirt or in his jacket pocket, if only to reassure himself that it was still there.

That it was still his.

So what was the problem with that?

So what if he liked the way it felt?

It made him feel confident, more secure.

He liked the smooth touch of the hard rubber handle. He liked flicking his thumb along the razor-sharp edge.

There was nothing wrong with that, was there?

Every time he touched it or even thought about it, the image of the knife seemed to infuse his body and mind with hot, coursing energy that generated strange, powerful thoughts and emotions. Whenever he gripped the knife, squeezing the rubber handle so tight that the palm of his hand hurt, violent images too fleeting and insubstantial to grasp would fill his mind and make him shudder with pleasure and expectation.

Especially at night, when he lay in bed, trying to drift off to sleep. Rage...

Anger...

Fear...

And hatred.

But all of these words were too mild, too mundane even to begin to express how the knife made him feel. He wasn't sure there were words in English or any language adequate to capture how the knife made him feel. Sometimes he would even imagine that he could hear soft voices whispering to him in the dark.

And these voices, whether they were in the room or inside his head, would grow louder and more insistent the more firmly he gripped the knife's handle. Some of the voices sounded desperate, wracked with grief and pain. He listened to their shrill shrieking and bubbly gasps, and tried to imagine the horrible images that accompanied them.

But there was one voice in particular that Tony heard, and this one he listened to.

This was the voice that he had come to think of as the *true* voice of the knife.

It urged him to do things.

Terrible things!

Tony had no idea how the knife could be influencing him like this. He didn't want to know, but especially at night, he listened intently to its secret urgings. Up until the time he had found the knife, he had never entertained such thoughts, and he had certainly never given in to any violent impulses.

But that seemed to be what the knife wanted!

It was telling him that it wanted to be used... it *needed* to be used! As if it had a mind or a will or a purpose of its own, it whispered to him that its one, clear purpose was to slice into living flesh and feel the hot gush of blood bathe its metal edge as, like a fleeing vapor, life drained away.

Tony tried to convince himself that using the knife once, as he had on Bingley last night, would satisfy the blade; but even then something told him that he was kidding himself.

As he lay in the darkness of Sarah's bedroom and listened to the deep, steady rhythm of her breathing, he knew that wasn't the case at all.

The blade had tasted blood again after a long time, and now, after such a long period of abstinence, it wanted more.

Much more!

Only this time, it wanted a different *kind* of blood.

It wanted *human* blood!

At least subconsciously, Tony knew what the knife was asking, was *demanding* of him, but he struggled against the savage impulses that seemed to radiate from the knife.

Christ, no! I can't kill anyone!

Powerful emotions coiled like snakes inside him, making him shiver as though in the grip of a fever.

He wasn't a cold-blooded killer!

What he had done to Bingley had been just a... just an experiment. That was all. He had simply wanted to try out the blade to see how well it worked.

If he *ever* thought—even for a moment—that he might use the knife on someone else—on Sarah, for instance—then he would have to get rid of it.

That would be simple enough, wouldn't it?

Just throw it away.

Toss it back into the alleyway where he'd found it.

Let some other asshole come along and find it.

Let someone else deal with it.

He had more than enough problems in his life as it was. He sure as hell didn't need this kind of shit!

A cold sweat had broken out over his body. Rolling his head from side to side, he grit his teeth and clenched his fists, trying to stop himself from thinking like this.

He didn't want to hurt Sarah or anyone else!

He would *have* to get rid of the knife before it made him do something he'd regret.

Or even if he didn't actually get rid of the knife, he was determined that he could control the bloody impulses it stirred inside him.

He would have to!

He was studying to be a lawyer, for Christ's sake! As far as he was concerned, he was a law-abiding citizen who valued the law above everything else... everything, that is, except success and maybe a nice piece of pussy every now and then.

He was *never* going to *use* the knife on anyone or anything!

Killing Bingley had been a mistake, he now realized, and he deeply regretted that he had ever given in to the impulse.

But the knife was as much to blame as he was.

Maybe *more!*

Tony imagined that he could see things as he stared into the darkness. Gauzy figures rose up like smoke and swirled in the gentle breeze that blew through the room. He watched in amazement as faces formed in the darkness—mostly women's faces. Their eyes looked hollow and gaunt, their faces pale and stretched in the throes of agony. The dark ovals of their mouths opened wide in silent screams. Hands as white as bone reached out for him... grasping... clawing....

Tony covered his face with both hands as a deep, wrenching sob shook him, but even then the images didn't vanish.

"Jesus, make it stop," he whispered into the cup formed by his hands. "I didn't have anything to do with it... I just couldn't... couldn't control it!"

But as much as he tried to deny it, Tony knew that killing Bingley hadn't been totally on impulse. He had carefully planned the whole damned thing. He had, in fact, actually been looking forward to it with a great deal of anticipation.

How impulsive could it have been if he had hidden outside Sarah's house and waited until he saw her leave?

How spontaneous could it have been if he had stolen a piece of fish from the restaurant the night before to use as bait?

Yes, bait... to catch that little bastard!

And then, the most calculated thing of all—how could he excuse or explain skinning the cat and using its pelt to massage Sarah before making love to her?

Tony couldn't help but chuckle in the darkness as he thought about it. The sound of his laughter was so close to him that it sounded like someone else leaning near his ear and snickering. He had to admit that it had been pretty goddamned funny, almost inspired.

And it had worked, too.

Sarah had gotten so horny they had screwed for almost an hour solid before he finally couldn't hold back any longer. Now she'd gone back to sleep like a goddamned baby, and he was wide awake.

Wide awake and thinking.

But maybe—in the long run—what he had done to Bingley had been all for the best. It had let him try out the knife, and it had given the knife a taste of blood.

He couldn't feel much regret for Bingley. He owed the little motherfucker a big payback for clawing his back the other night. The wounds on Tony's back still stung.

So Tony decided that the bottom line was, he didn't feel the least bit of guile or remorse for what he had done.

And he had no intention of ever getting rid of the knife.

He *liked* the way it made him feel, even when the thoughts that filled his mind seemed so out-of-control compared to how he usually thought and felt.

And he liked knowing that if anyone else messed with him—anyone at all—even Sarah—he wouldn't have to put up with any shit.

No shit from *anyone*, anymore!

And he wouldn't hesitate to use the knife again, either.

After all, the knife would like it!

It would *enjoy* it!

He could use it for what *it* wanted just as much if not more than for what h*e* wanted!

Again, Tony chuckled softly to himself as he rolled over onto his side.

He felt better, more relaxed.

He lazily draped one hand over the edge of the bed, letting his fingertips brush against the rubber handle of the knife.

Instantly, he felt reassured.

Everything would be all right, he told himself, as long as he never lost possession of the knife.

Owning it made him feel good… almost like it was something he had owned once before… long ago… and now, after so many years, they had been reunited. He had never realized how incomplete his hand had felt until that first night when he held the knife and had *used* it!

David was filled with a cold, twisting apprehension as he and the hooded figure silently entered the darkness within Pine Knoll Elementary School. They hadn't spoken another word to each other throughout the walk to the schoolhouse. David had hardly dared even to look at the mysterious figure. If this person—or whatever it was—had been carrying a long, curved scythe, he would have been a perfect incarnation of Death.

David guessed that's exactly who he must be.

Without exchanging a word between them, they made their way through the pitch darkness to the far wall. Their feet scuffed softly on the wood. The floorboards groaned like something in pain.

David still couldn't figure out how he could be feeling so nervous and exhausted without a living body. No matter what the reason, he knew he was close to collapsing. The darkness around him was vibrating with a raw, dangerous energy. He could almost imagine two huge, dark arms reaching out of the dark, eager to enfold him.

Groping blindly in front of him, he felt around until he found the rough plaster wall, then turned and, leaning his back against the wall, slowly slid down into a sitting position with his knees pressed up against his chest. He had no idea where the hooded figure might be or what it might be doing, but he hardly cared.

Here in near total darkness, he couldn't see anything except the dull, gray rectangle that was the door leading outside. It was faint and looked impossibly far away.

The silence was so thick it seemed to ring like a deep-throated bell in the night. If it hadn't been for the low, whispering voices he heard coming from somewhere upstairs, David would have been absolutely convinced that he was alone.

And that's how he wanted to be.

All alone.

Just him with his own thoughts.

Shivering deep inside, he crouched in the darkness and waited. He wished he could rest, but his mind was whirling with too many disturbing thoughts and emotions.

He couldn't stop thinking about the verbal exchange between the hooded figure and the creature that had attacked him. The creature had called him "Ferryman." David wondered if that was this individual's name or his title.

He also couldn't stop wondering what the Ferryman had meant when he'd told the creature that he was David's "reaper," and that his "mark" was on him.

Could he really be the Grim Reaper, come to collect his soul?

David sensed that there were too many things going on here in the Shadowlands—too many dynamics that he couldn't even begin to understand.

He sensed that this person—this Ferryman—certainly should be able to explain many things about existence in the Shadowlands, but he didn't dare ask. He wanted desperately to know what was going on, but near total exhaustion was weighing him down. All he could think about was rest, so he closed his eyes—at least he thought he did; it seemed not to make the slightest bit of difference in the darkness if his eyes were open or closed—and leaned his head back against the rough wall.

A deep shudder ran through him as the memory of how powerless those chains had made him feel stirred uneasily within him. He experienced stark flashes of fear filled him that he might slip and lose himself in the void of darkness in the center of his soul, but he couldn't stop himself from drifting further and further away.

"So why did you help me?" The question sounded like the soft rustle of coarse cloth in the darkness. David wasn't even sure if he or someone else had spoken. The darkness behind his eyes throbbed, dense and impenetrable.

"I think we might be able to help each other," came the reply in a voice so deep David knew instantly that it wasn't his own.

"Help… each other?" He was trembling inside, unable to dispel the impression that he was simply listening to himself speak, and that his voice was coming from a great distance away. "But I–I have no idea what's going on. I don't even know where I am."

"You've already been told that. You're a wraith in the Shadowlands." The reply was barely above the threshold of sound.

"Yeah, but… but *how* did *I get here?* And what's *keeping* me here? If I'm already dead—"

"Your fetters are what's keeping you here."

"Fetters?" A soul-deep chill ran through David as he spoke the word, and his memory stirred. "You mean like… like those chains that creature put on me?"

He was dimly aware that he was rubbing his left wrist with one hand as though trying to massage away the pain, but he could still feel the dull, burning collar of pain where the metal clasps had touched him.

A soft, sniffing laughter filled the darkness.

"No," the Ferryman said, "the chains that reaper had were forged in Stygia. That's another matter entirely."

"So what the hell are these… these fetters you say are keeping me here?"

"There are more fetters than there are people who have died," the voice said soothingly, almost laughing. "Generally, they're unfinished business you have in the land of the living or attachments to someone who is still alive.

Then again, they could be as simple a thing as that it just wasn't your time to die yet."

"My time to—"

David's voice choked off as the memory returned of seeing his ex-wife, relatives, friends, and acquaintances gathered at Riverside Cemetery to watch as his coffin was lowered into the ground. The emotions that single memory stirred were terrifying in their purity and power. They almost overwhelmed him, but he clung desperately to his awareness.

"—Die," the voice from the darkness finished for him.

The word echoed in the darkness, seeming for several seconds to intensify before it finally faded away.

"So that creature—you called it a—a reaper," David said, almost too frightened to speak. "He referred to you as Ferryman. Is that your name?"

Again, a low rumble of laughter filled the darkness.

"No, that's my... my function here."

"You mean like in ancient Greek mythology, how—what was his name? Charon. How Charon ferried dead souls across the River Styx?"

David didn't know how, but the darkness suddenly seemed to change. He could feel a stirring energy, like the subtle static charge just before a thunderstorm breaks loose. Even the voices whispering in the schoolhouse fell silent.

"Be *very* careful about when and where you speak that name!" The Ferryman's voice ripped like a blade through the darkness. "What, you mean Char—?"

"Be advised! It's not wise to speak of things about which you have no knowledge."

David was burning to ask the Ferryman what he meant, but he didn't dare speak. The dark silence lengthened, closing in around David with a steadily rising pressure.

"So what about my daughter?" he finally managed to ask after what seemed like too long a time. "Do you know anything about her? Why is she here?"

For a long time, no reply came out of the darkness. David was almost convinced that he was alone—that he had been alone all this time and had imagined the entire conversation. Maybe he'd even imagined everything he had experienced since coming to the Shadowlands. Cold fear slithered like a large black snake inside him.

"Can you… tell me why she's still here?" he finally asked.

"It's not for me to say," the Ferryman replied. His voice echoed with a hollow reverberation that made it sound like several voices combined.

A sudden desperation filled David. He was worried about Karen and couldn't stop wondering where she had gone and if she was in some kind of danger. He wanted desperately to see her again and decided that, if seeing her again was one of his fetters, he would gladly embrace it if only it meant that he *would* see her … at least just once more before death claimed him.

"Do you know where I can find her?" he asked, his voice twisted with emotion. "I *have* to find her! I have to *help* her if I can!"

"As I said," the low, resonant voice replied from out of the darkness, "perhaps we can help each other."

"Help… *How?*"

David found it almost impossible not to shout, but his voice—the faintest of whispers—echoed as softly as a flutter of wings in the close darkness.

"There's someone you're connected co, someone who is still in the land of the living—what we call the *Skinlands*—who has something that I want. Something that I need."

"Oh, yeah? And what's that?"

"A very valuable relic," the voice answered.

"A relic? What kind of relic? I don't know what the hell you're talking about, so what makes you think I can help you get it?"

"I *did* say *perhaps*," the Ferryman said simply.

Red, blazing anger filled David as his fear for his daughter's safety grew sharper.

"Don't start talking riddles with me!" he shouted. "Tell me straight out what you want! Are you saying, if I do something for you—"

"—then perhaps in return I'll be able to do something for you. *Perhaps.* It's that simple. Even here in the afterlife, that's how things work."

The sound of the low laughter filled the darkness, but David wasn't entirely sure from which direction it was coming.

"So what is this... this relic you want so badly?" he asked.

For a long time, no reply came; and once again he began to feel as though he were utterly alone in the dark—that he always had been and always would be alone. But he could sense if not actually see that the Ferryman was close by. David was surprised that he didn't feel the creature's cold breath against his skin.

But we're all dead here, he thought. *No one here has any breath!*

"There is a knife... a knife that is—how can I put it?—invested with great power. I need your help to obtain it."

A sudden and inexplicable anger flashed like lightning inside David's mind. He wanted to reach out into the darkness, grab the Ferryman by the throat and throttle him.

All he cared about—all he could think about—was Karen's safety. He remembered seeing the knife the young man had hidden beneath his clothes at Sarah's house. That had to be what the Ferryman was talking about. But all that mattered to David right now was finding Karen and helping her in any way he could.

He didn't have time for bullshit like this!

"I don't know anything about any goddamned knife!" he wailed, filled with frustration. He was lying, and he was positive that the Ferryman could tell that he was lying because of the warbling edge in his voice.

"And even if I did, I wouldn't know how to go about *getting* it for you or for anyone else. I don't know how it is for you or anyone else here, but I'm finding it just about impossible to touch anything in the real world—the... the *skinlands*, as you call them! I can't talk to anyone. I can't touch anything. I can't make anyone see me because I'm dead! Get it? I'm not part of that world anymore!"

"Oh, but your fetters keep you in contact with the skinlands," the Ferryman said softly. "That's what I've been trying to explain to you."

"Maybe, but still—all I can do is watch it like... like it's some kind of sideshow or movie or something!"

"Oh, it's difficult to reach through the Shroud, I'll grant you that, but it's not impossible. There are *always* ways." The voice was low and soothing, but it did little to calm David.

"There are many skills you can learn here," the Ferryman went on. "Unfortunately, most of these skills take time and practice, and I'm afraid that you—and I—don't have much of either in this matter."

"Why?" David said, trying hard to shout but hearing his voice only as a whisper. "What's so important about this knife?"

David still couldn't entirely rid himself of the impression that this entire conversation was going on inside his own head, but he struggled to understand what the Ferryman was saying to him.

"This knife is... very special," the Ferryman said. "It's a relic of awesome power that once belonged to a man you may have heard of. His name was Jack the Ripper."

"Jack the—"

"Does that name mean anything to you?"

David couldn't help but laugh out loud even though the sound was as faint as the flutter of a moth's wings.

"What the fuck are you talking about? Jack the Ripper lived in London, England, over a hundred years ago. What the hell has he got to do with anything here in Portland?"

"For almost a century, now, that knife and two others of its kind were in safekeeping, but recently all three of them have been stolen. The person who first took them has already used them again, too, as others have. Quite against their will, you understand, but there have been several wraiths seen wandering in the Shadowlands that have the death mark of those blades on their souls."

The mention of the mark on their souls made David think to ask the Ferryman about the mark he had said was on him, but he stopped himself and let the Ferryman continue.

"I haven't yet learned where the other two knives are, but I'm sure they'll show up eventually. They have a way of making their presence known. I *do* know that someone who lives near here has one of them and has already used it."

"Jesus, you're right," David said as a dim memory sparked within him. "A couple of months ago, there was something on the news about a young woman who was murdered here in Portland. I think they said it was with a knife."

"What you have to understand," the Ferryman said, "is that whoever it was didn't really do it. It was the *knife*. I've already found the man responsible for that particular woman's death. He's a wraith here, but he no longer possesses the knife. Someone else has it now. Someone who has a connection with you, and the knife's power is beginning to influence him."

"Influence him? How?" David asked, already dreading the answer before he finished asking the question.

"Whoever possesses any one of those knives is also possessed *by* it. Eventually he'll do whatever the knife wants.

Make no mistake about it. He'll use it soon—if he hasn't already. No matter how hard he tries to resist, eventually he will have to use it."

"To kill," David said, his voice almost breaking, "like Jack the Ripper."

"Exactly!" The Ferryman clapped his hands together. "All three of those knives are strong instruments of puppetry."

"Puppetry?" David echoed weakly. This was all too much. He was finding it almost impossible to process any of it.

"Look, I don't like you talking circles around me like this, okay?" he said. "Just tell me straight out what it is you want from me."

"I want your help to obtain that knife," the Ferryman said from the darkness. "Haven't I already made that perfectly clear?"

"Sure you have," David said. "But how?" He wished he could protest more forcefully, but he was in the grip of total exhaustion that was dragging him down, deeper and deeper. He could feel himself fading away like a whisper into the night.

"For now, you need rest," the Ferryman's deep voice said almost soothingly. "Close your eyes and relax. The touch of those Stygian chains has drained more out of your corpus than you realize. You need to restore yourself."

David groaned softly, wanting to say more, but he couldn't. He settled his head against the wall and rolled it back and forth, all the while groaning softly. The sound created a steady vibration inside his head that he found soothing. A light touch caressed his forehead, but rather than frightening him, it sent waves of calmness washing through him.

"Relax now. Just relax."

"Yeah, but I… what about my daughter?" David could hear his own voice echoing in the darkness. "You said that you could… that you would help me if I helped you."

"I said I will… if I can."

"Then can you help me find her... my daughter?" David asked.

"I'm sorry," the Ferryman's voice replied, sounding faint and lost in the distance, "You'll have to find her yourself—"

A mild spark of anger filled David, but he was much too exhausted to react. He could feel himself drifting further and further away... dissolving into nothing... fading like a gossamer dream into the dense, vibrating darkness that surrounded him. He imagined that his whole existence was little more than a tiny candle flame, sputtering until it finally burned itself out.

"—and after you find her," said the Ferryman's sonorous voice from an even greater distance, "if you get that knife for me, I promise that I'll do whatever I can to help you... and her."

––––––––

Leaning out the kitchen door with one hand braced against the door jamb, Sarah frowned as she looked up and down the side porch. Already the day was heavy with humidity.

"Hey! What'cha doing?"

Sarah squealed when Tony spoke so suddenly behind her. Spinning around, she stared at him for a moment, her breath caught like a hoc coal in the center of her chest. Her hands were clenched into tight fists.

"*Jesus*, you scared the *shit* out of me!"

A vague sense of danger filled her as she watched Tony saunter past the kitchen table toward her. All he was wearing were his boxer shorts. He was smiling broadly, but Sarah could sense that something wasn't quite right.

Clutching the collar of her thin bathrobe to her throat, she came back into the house. The screen door swung shut behind her, slamming loud enough to make her jump again.

"I was just calling Bingley," she said tightly. "He's usually at the door, first thing in the morning. You know, now that I think about it, I don't remember seeing him yesterday afternoon either."

"Hmm," Tony said, cocking his hip to one side and stroking his cheek. He covered his mouth with his hand, but Sarah thought she caught a glimpse of a faint smile. Her frown deepened as she stared at him, wondering what the hell was up.

There was definitely something, but she couldn't quite put her finger on it.

A slanting ray of sunlight shot through the window above the kitchen sink and illuminated Tony's bare legs. The curling black hairs on his thighs made his skin look pale. She wondered why he didn't get out in the sun more often, but figured, between work at the restaurant and studying at law school, he was probably too busy to indulge in much recreation.

"I–I've been calling him for more than ten minutes," she said, feeling tight and trembling inside. "I'm afraid something might've happened to him."

She kept staring at Tony, all the while thinking, *Jesus, something* is *really wrong here!*

"Aww, he's gotta be around somewhere," Tony said.

This time there was no mistaking it. A big smile was playing at the corners of his mouth as he came close to Sarah and wrapped his arms around her, pulling her close.

When he tried to kiss her, she turned away. She wasn't feeling very cuddly right now. Her body was ramrod stiff, unyielding in his arms.

What the hell's wrong? she thought. *What is it about him that's giving me the creeps?*

"So what do you have on cap for today?" Tony asked casually as he nuzzled his mouth against her neck. His kisses were wet and cool on her skin. They made her shiver.

"I have to go to work at—" She glanced past him to the clock on the kitchen wall and saw that it was a little past eight. "At nine o'clock."

"Really? I thought the library didn't open until ten o'clock during the summer session."

"Yeah, it doesn't, but I–I'm supposed to get there early today. I've got a lot of computer entries to make."

She hoped the lie wasn't *too* obvious. Blinking her eyes rapidly, she stared up at the ceiling and nibbled nervously on her lower lip, not even sure herself why she had lied to Tony. She really wasn't due at work until one o'clock; but for some reason, she wanted to be alone this morning. In fact, she regretted letting Tony spend the night.

But then again, why not spend the morning with him?

She couldn't deny how great it felt to have a man in her bed again, ready and willing to give her pleasure.

"You probably don't have the time for a little quickie, then, huh?"

Tony grunted as he thrust his hips forward, bumping against her. The solid lump of his erection pressed like a roll of quarters against her thigh, but the thought of making love to him right now almost nauseated her. She tried to convince herself that it had to be because she was still upset about what had happened to David; but for some reason, that didn't exactly strike her as what was wrong.

She still hadn't even told Tony that David's funeral had been yesterday.

Why was she keeping it such a big secret?

He was a great lover, and he seemed genuinely interested in a relationship with her; but there was something else about him, something in the way he was acting this morning that bothered her deeply. Now that she had slept with him a few times and was getting to know him, he seemed almost like a different person—like someone she didn't know in the least, and she found it a little bit scary.

She wished she could put her finger on *exactly* what it was.

Tony continued to kiss her neck passionately as his hands slid up and down her back, massaging the stiff muscles. She felt a warm, pleasant gush of blood in her lower abdomen and wished she could just give in to the feeling, but it was no good.

She was too worried, and it wasn't just about Bingley. Something was different....

Something was very wrong!

rip her.

Chapter Nine

The touch was light, almost feathery.

For a timeless moment, David thought it must be the Ferryman, still gently massaging his forehead as he drifted deeper and deeper into sleep.

But do the dead really sleep? he wondered vaguely.

He found the thought almost amusing, but then another, more frightening thought intruded.

And if they do dream... what do they dream about?

He was seized by a deep, sad longing for the life he'd lost. It amazed him how much he missed such simple things as being able to open a door, feeling the wind and rain on his face, smelling the strong, damp earth after a rainstorm or feeling his daughter's kisses on his cheek.

Knowing that he would *never* experience any of these things again filled him with intense, almost unbearable agony.

But after another indeterminate length of time, as such thoughts swirled in his mind, David realized that the touch was no longer tracing light circles across his brow.

Someone was holding him by his shoulders and shaking him roughly. Very distantly, he could feel his head, lolling back and forth and grinding against the pitted surface of the plaster wall. Numbing cold radiating from the wall immobilized him.

For what seemed like an agonizingly long time, David struggled to pull himself out of the dream — if it was a dream — and back to consciousness. He vaguely hoped he would discover that everything he had experienced in the Shadowlands had been a dream.

Maybe I'm still alive ... Maybe I'm back home in bed, sleeping and dreaming that I took a late-night walk and was hit by an oncoming truck ... Maybe I never really wanted to die! ... Maybe... Just maybe...

A shallow, desperate hope filled him with emotion. He would have cried if he could have.

Besides, how can I be dead and still be aware of what's going on in the world?

No, I can't be dead! I have to be alive! This isn't what it's supposed to be like to be dead!

As these and other frantic thoughts crowded his mind, the touch grew stronger, more urgent and demanding.

Either that, or he was coming to.

As he struggled back toward consciousness, David felt oddly detached from his own body, as though it were nothing more than a useless dust rag being shaken out. It took an immense effort, but he focused his attention into a narrow beam and concentrated only on trying to figure out who was shaking his shoulder like this.

He had no idea when—or *if*—he opened his eyes.

The solid wall of darkness in front of him looked like it was no more than an inch from his face. But slowly, gradually, his mind cleared.

Shifting shadows whispered as they separated like heavy drapes.

Memories of what had happened earlier that evening started to come back in sharper detail. One predominate image was of a hooded figure, leaning over him. He recalled looking up into the darkness inside the hood—into a darkness that was deeper and colder than anything he had ever experienced before.

"Who—?"

His voice made a choking sound deep inside his chest, and he could say no more. That single word echoed and then faded away as if someone were gradually turning the volume control down to zero.

"I need you," came a faint, quavering voice that sounded impossibly far away. "I need you to help me."

"But I—"

Consciousness was returning, but the process was still maddeningly slow. Fleeting images and vague memories flapped like wind-blown sheets through his mind.

The hideously decaying face of the creature that had attacked him loomed at him out of the darkness. The peal of the creature's insane laughter rang sharply in his ears. The clank of heavy chains rang in his ears. Their freezing touch felt like nails being driven into his arms and legs. He imagined that the chains pinned him as though he had been crucified.

David struggled to move his body, but it was like trying to flex a hand that was padded in a thick glove. He was totally paralyzed.

With returning consciousness there also came jolting red currents of fear and hot spikes of anxiety.

What if this isn't all a dream?

The fear inside him was growing steadily stronger.

Or maybe—even if it is a dream—what if it hasn't ended yet?... What if it will never end?

Suddenly the darkness both inside and outside of him seemed to open up. He experienced a moment of rushing vertigo.

Total panic swept through him.

He cried out and made wild, frantic grabs with both hands, but there was nothing to hold on to. The whole universe was spinning insanely out of control, and he was at the center of it all.

Icy rushes of fear roared like demons inside his head, and he knew that his sanity would snap like a dry twig if he allowed the fear to take over.

No! ... *NO!* he screamed inside his head as he tried desperately to resist the gathering fear, clinging to the few shreds of personal identity and sanity he still had left.

Dead or alive, there were things he had to do.

He had fetters that bound him to the Shadowlands, and he was more than willing to embrace them.

"Where have you *been?*" the faint voice called out.

It echoed all around him as if he were inside a huge metal cube.

"I've been looking all *over* for you."

David tried to focus his attention, concentrating hard on keeping the fear at bay and resisting the inexorable pull of Oblivion.

He thought he recognized the voice, but it was too much to hope for. It couldn't possibly be—

"Karen?"

In the roaring darkness, his own voice had the harsh sound of tearing paper. His panicky thoughts screamed louder than his voice.

"Please! Daddy! Please wake up! I need you to help me!"

The shaking grew more intense, more insistent; but at the same time, it also seemed to become somehow more muted, as though the more he concentrated on it, and the closer he got to it, the further away it moved.

"*Karen!*"

When his eyes suddenly snapped open, he couldn't believe what he was seeing. Everything was all gauzy and vague, like in a dream. Dull, diffused gray light that bled the life out of any colors was seeping like smoke into the old schoolhouse. All dimensions seemed oddly distorted. The perspective of the room was totally wrong. Walls and ceiling met at crazy angles that didn't make sense, like an Escher drawing.

David shook his head as though dazed and groaned loudly when he saw Karen kneeling on the floor in front of him. She was wearing a long, rumpled gray dress. Her pale face floated in and out of his view like a sad, wrinkled balloon. Her facial features appeared strangely flat and dimensionless. The dark hollows of her blank, staring eyes drew him in like sucking whirlpools. The expression on her face was emotionless, absolutely lifeless as she leaned forward, planted her hands firmly on his shoulders, and shook him with all her strength.

"I was afraid you were going to leave me again, Daddy!" Karen said.

Her voice was high-pitched and nervous-sounding, and seemed out of synch with her blank facial expression.

"I... You know I'd never do that," David managed to reply with a gasp. He couldn't decide if he was speaking out loud or just thinking the words.

"I... couldn't find you," he said. "I was afraid that I—that I'd lost you again."

"Don't ever leave me again, Daddy. Please, Daddy! Don't!" Karen pleaded.

David wanted to convince himself that he could see a deep sadness in her eyes, but it was disconcerting that she wasn't crying. She sounded frightened enough to be crying, so why wasn't she? He still couldn't get over the impression that none of this was really happening.

It couldn't be!

Karen looked much too thin and pale. Her skin was almost transparent. For the briefest instant, David thought he could actually see the dark plaster wall directly behind her, as if she were a movie projection on the wall.

"I won't leave you ever again, Sugar!" he said. "I promise you!"

The false hope that everything so far had all been a dream was quickly extinguished when he looked around, and the dank ruins of the old schoolhouse came into sharper focus. Shifting shadows clung like dark clots to the floor, ceiling and walls. Slanting shafts of diffused sunlight, looking like sickly gray columns of smoke, caught and illuminated the dense, dust-filled air. The silence of the room was so total it made David's ears ring.

There's something really wrong with her! David couldn't help but think as he stared into his daughter's vacant eyes.

He knew that he couldn't expect to see even a hint of life there.

She was dead... just as he was dead!

But the glazed coldness in Karen's eyes seemed to be more than the dull glaze of a dead person's eyes. There was an infinite distance inside her, a lifeless void that, for the first time, David realized with a shudder he could never breath or even begin to fathom.

He wondered if his own dead eyes looked as frightening to her as hers did to him.

"Did you see her?" Karen asked. "Did you talk to her yet?"

Although he thought he should hear at least a hint of desperation in her voice, David noticed that her tone sounded curiously flat. He nodded his head slowly, unable—or not daring—to break eye contact with her.

"Yeah, I–I did."

His voice sounded raw.

"I... I saw her and I tried to talk to her."

"Did you warn her? Did you tell her about the man with the knife?"

A sudden surge of panic made David reach out and grab his daughter's arms tightly. His sense of touch was still deadened, but her shoulders felt as fragile as dried bones in his grasp. He had the brief impression that there was nothing to her—no body at all inside her rumpled dress.

"How do you know about the knife?" he asked, unable to mask the tension that was winding up inside him.

For a long time, Karen didn't reply.

She just knelt there in front of him and stared at him with those dark, hollow eyes that looked like two bottomless pits. Her mouth hung open, exposing her small, flat teeth. It made her look somewhat feral. Against his will, David realized that he found her face and expression unnerving, almost repulsive.

"I... I saw it," Karen finally replied in a shattered whisper. "I was there... at the house... last night... and I saw that he had a knife and was... he was gonna use it on her!"

She has to mean *the knife the* Ferryman *was* talking *to me about,* David thought with a deep, internal shudder, *the same knife I saw that* night in *Sarah's bedroom.*

"You have to stop him, Daddy!" Karen pleaded. "He wants to *hurt* her! He wants to *kill* Mommy! I know he does!"

David almost told her everything he knew about the knife, but then decided it was probably better not to mention anything about it or his conversation with the Ferryman. She was afraid enough as it was for her mother's safety. He saw no reason to add to her distress.

"Don't you worry, Sugar," he said, his voice softer than a hushed whisper in the eerie silence of the room. "I'm gonna do everything I can to help her. I promise you."

David wished that he believed that himself. He wished earnestly in his heart that there *was* something he could do... *anything* to help Sarah, but he had no idea what. The Ferryman had told him that there were powers he could master in the Shadowlands, but he didn't have time for that.

"Have you ever tried to talk to her?" he asked Karen, peering intently into her dull eyes and trying to ignore the lifeless expression he saw there. It pained him not to see even the slightest hint of the young, vibrant person she had once been. It tore his heart to realize that all of those youthful, passionate qualities that he had so much loved and admired in his daughter had been ripped out of her—destroyed by Death.

"*Me?*" Karen said, sounding astounded. She shook her head slowly from side to side, continuing as she back away from him.

David released his grip on her. His hands fell uselessly to his sides.

"But I–I can't," Karen said in a trembling whisper that seemed to be echoed by other, fainter voices from upstairs.

"I tried. Lots of times I tried, but I–I don't know how to do it."

All the while, she continued to shake her head.

"Besides, I–I'm just a kid. I'm not strong enough. But I know you are, Daddy. You'll get through to her and tell her about that bad man with the knife, won't you?"

"I sure as hell intend to try," David said. "You can count on it!"

And then, for the first time, Karen's expression changed.

Her lips pulled back in what David supposed was a grin; but her expression looked like nothing except the silent, horrible grimace of Death.

———

The steady clacking of the computer keys was starting to get on Sarah's nerves.

Then again, *everything* today seemed to be getting on her nerves!

After she and Tony had eaten a light breakfast together— just orange juice and toast with jam—Tony had gotten dressed and left with a promise to call her at work later that afternoon.

Sarah wasn't sure she knew how she felt about that.

After he was gone, Sarah, still dressed in her bathrobe, spent the next half hour or so walking around outside the house and yard, clicking her tongue and calling to Bingley.

He never showed up.

This wasn't at all like him, and as much as she didn't want to admit it, she knew deep in her heart that something must have happened to him. She tried not to imagine him getting hit by a car while crossing the street last night and crawling off into the bushes somewhere to die.

If that was the case, all she could hope was that he had died quickly, without much suffering. She checked in the garage and peered underneath the porch, but there was no sign of him anywhere.

On the drive to work, tears kept filling her eyes as she couldn't stop wondering if she would ever see Bingley again. Even then, she realized that she was crying more for David and Karen and herself than she was for her poor, old cat.

She hadn't been lying to Tony about the data entries she had to make at work, so as soon as she got to the library, even though she was more than an hour early, she sat down at her desk, switched on the computer terminal, and started typing.

As she worked, the steady click-clicking of the keys quickly started to wear on her nerves.

She found it difficult, almost impossible to concentrate on her work. As her mind drifted, she found herself continually thinking back to David's funeral yesterday... and Karen's funeral five years before that.

Her vision blurred with tears that made the terminal screen look fuzzy green. Her eyes stung, and her cheeks were slick with tears. Every now and then she would glance down at her hands and marvel at how slim and pale they looked. The tendons shifting beneath her skin as she typed looked like chin pencils that could break with only the slightest amount of pressure.

This is no damn good!... This is no damn good!

She kept repeating this to herself, unable to stop thinking about the life she and David and Karen used to have together before it had been so horribly and tragically ripped apart.

She fought hard to control her emotions, but she knew that she was losing.

Earlier that day, Elizabeth McDonald, her boss, had offered for her to take a few days off; but Sarah had refused, saying that probably the best thing for her would be to keep working, to stick with some part of the regular routine of her life.

But now she was starting to think that that might not have been such a good idea.

Maybe what she really needed was a complete break from everything. She had some vacation time due in August. Maybe Elizabeth would let her take it now. A trip somewhere—anywhere—might be just what she needed, if only to get away from Tony for a while so she could try to sort out exactly what she thought about him.

But other things were bothering her as well—deeper things, like grief and despair and guilt, and she knew they weren't simply going to fly away.

She realized she should probably start cleaning out David's apartment soon. There was no sense paying another month's rent for an unoccupied apartment. That was something she wasn't exactly looking forward to. She wondered who she might call to ask to help her with it.

A wild shiver suddenly gripped her, shaking her so badly that she glanced nervously over her shoulder to see if anyone had noticed.

The library was almost deserted. A few students were slumped over their books in the study carrels and at the tables. One young couple, sitting on a couch in the periodicals section, seemed to be spending a lot more time gazing at each other and kissing than they did looking at their textbooks. Three people were using the card catalog computers, and Marilyn Crosby was busy reshelving books. Elizabeth was in her office with her head bowed as she concentrated on the sheaf of papers that was spread across her desk.

No one had noticed her, but Sarah frowned as she craned her neck to look around, unable to dispel the discomforting feeling that someone *was* watching her.

Maybe Tony was lurking nearby, watching her. He hadn't seemed the slightest bit mistrustful of her when she'd told him she had to work today, but maybe he was the jealous, suspicious kind who would follow her to work and spy on her anyway. She couldn't deny that there had been *something* weird about him this morning—something that she couldn't quite define but which she felt nonetheless.

As soon as she turned back to her work, another, stronger shiver raced through her veins like a surge of icy water.

Covering her face with both hands, she leaned forward with her elbows on the desk, closed her eyes, and took a deep breath. The air rushing between her cupped fingers whistled like a blustery winter wind. Cold, prickly sensations raced up and down her back as she stared into the darkness behind her eyes and calmly started counting to ten.

One… two… three…

She stared into the darkness that pulsated with two inward turning spirals of yellow and gray zigzag patterns. She found the whistling sound of her breathing almost soothing.

Almost…

Tension coiled like a tightening spring deep within her stomach.

Four… five…

Amorphous blobs of deep purple and radiant blue light appeared in her field of vision, seeming to advance and retreat at the same time, keeping time with her breathing.

Six… seven… eight…

The sounds in the library were muted and distant. Sarah had the momentary impression that she was listening to them from a great distance away. She kept breathing steadily, noticing the faint stinging smell of ozone. As she pulled the air deeper into her lungs, the smell got stronger.

Nine...

A shiver flickered like cold lightning through her. Her body instantly tensed when she heard a soft *click that* sounded a bit like one of the keys of the keyboard being depressed.

Ten ...

Her insides were trembling terribly as she slowly opened her eyes, but she didn't quite dare take her hands away from her face.

Not yet.

Then another *click* sounded close to her—a short, sharp *pop.* Cold sweat broke out over her forehead and neck. Her whole body went rigid. The muscles in her legs and arms felt like they had hardened into knots as she slowly pulled her hands away from her face and looked down at the computer keyboard.

She watched in utter amazement as another key—the letter P—clicked down as though being pressed by an invisible finger. She would have screamed if she'd had the air in her lungs. Something popped in her neck as she slowly raised her head and looked at the computer screen. She couldn't believe what she saw written there.

RIP

Her breath felt like a hot lead weight in the center of her chest. She wanted desperately to get up from the desk, but she couldn't move a muscle—she couldn't even blink as she watched and heard more keys click in rapid succession.

PER

The world around her suddenly went all hazy and out of focus. She could hear herself whimpering softly, but she found it impossible to get enough air deep into her lungs to make any other sound. Faster now, the keys continued to clack, and letters spilled across the screen.

R-I-P-P-E-R-R-I-P-P-E-R-R-I-P-P-E-R-R-I-P-
P-E-R-R-I-P-P-E-R-R-I-P-P-E-R-R-I-P-P-E-R
R-I-P-P-E-R-R-I-P-P-E-R-R-I-P-P-E-R-R-I-P-

Wave after wave of sour nausea swept through her. Sarah wanted to stand up, to get away from her desk, but everything in the room seemed so distant, so otherworldly. Strong, icy gusts of wind swirled around her, snatching her breath away and making her shiver wildly. All she could do was watch the glowing square of the computer screen and the letters as they appeared there.

RIPPER RIPPER RIPPER RIPPER RIPPER RIPPER RIP
PER RIPHER RIPHER RIPPER RIPPER RIPHER RIPHER
RIPHER RIPHER RIPHER RIPHER RIPHER RIPHER RIP

Sarah forced herself to look down at her hands, if only to reassure herself that she wasn't doing this. Her fingers were laced together and clenched tightly in her lap. The clicking sounds of the keyboard were so rapid now it sounded like a string of firecrackers going off inside her head.

RIP HER RIP HER RIP PER RIP PER RIP HER RIP
PER RIP PER RIP PER RIP HER RIP HER RIP HER
RIP PER RIP HER RIP PER RIP HER RIP HER RIP
HER RIP PER RIP PER RIP PER RIP HER RIP HER

"No… no… oh, sweet Jesus, no!" Her voice was low and strangled and sounded completely detached from her body.

Panic and confusion raged through her. She moaned softly, only distantly aware that she was rocking back and forth in her chair.

She wished she could find the strength to get away from the desk, but every muscle in her body felt unstrung, every nerve was wire-hot and tingling. She unclasped her fingers, raised her hands, and placed them on the edge of the desk. When she did finally manage to push herself back, she felt something *pop* in her lower back.

Thick, salty pressure was rapidly building up inside her head, and she was suddenly afraid that she was going to burst a blood vessel in her brain.

Maybe it's already burst! Maybe I'm dying right now!

Her eyes moved spasmodically as she scanned the computer screen, finding it impossible to make any sense out of the jumble of words and letters. Her lips moved slowly, like she had been drugged, as she sounded out the combinations of words until—finally—the meaning hit her like the blast of a shotgun.

"Ripper... Rip her," she whispered hoarsely. "What the hell does—"

"Everything okay here?"

Sarah spun around so quickly to see who had spoken that she almost blacked out. The room seemed to slip to one side like the deck of a storm-tossed ship. It took her a moment to realize that Elizabeth was standing close behind her. Feeling embarrassed and absolutely flustered, Sarah tried to say something but found she couldn't. Instead, she just stared blankly up at her boss and shrugged as she bit her lower lip and shook her head.

"Problem with the computer, huh?" Elizabeth said, frowning as she planted both hands on the desk in front of Sarah and leaned forward to look at the screen.

The hard coldness in Sarah's stomach tightened as she turned back around to face the terminal. She gasped when she saw that the screen was blank except for the blinking green rectangle of the cursor in the upper left corner of the screen.

"What was scrolling by there a second ago?" Elizabeth asked, her frown deepening.

All Sarah could do was shrug as she inhaled sharply. It didn't feel like she got anywhere near enough air into her lungs. Her throat felt dry and scratchy, as if she had just swallowed a handful of hot sand. She wanted to say something, but was afraid even to try to speak because of the sound she might make.

"Damn computers!" Elizabeth said, gently swatting the monitor with one hand. "I hope you didn't lose any of the work you'd already done?"

"Maybe a bit of it," Sarah said, shaking her head numbly.

She almost didn't understand what her boss was saying to her, and she couldn't stop wondering what had happened to the words that had been scrolling across the screen. They were gone now as if they had never been there.

"That's too bad," Elizabeth said.

She tapped the *Enter* key several times, but nothing happened.

"Maybe the hard drive's fried. I have no idea. I hope you had it all backed up?"

Tight-lipped, Sarah nodded and managed to say, "Yeah, I got most of it saved... I think." To her own ears, her voice sounded like a croaking frog.

Elizabeth tapped rapidly on the keys a few times. The clicking sound was like hot spikes to Sarah's nerves, but she tried her best to ignore it.

"Well, I have no idea what the hell's wrong with it," Elizabeth said.

She reached over and pressed the *power* button. The screen winked off with a crackle of static, and the computer powered down. Sarah half-expected to see the words GAME OVER appear on the blank screen.

"I'll have Janice take a look at it tomorrow," Elizabeth said, standing back and brushing her hands together as though dismissing it. When she looked at Sarah, her perplexed expression softened.

"You know, you don't look so good, Sarah," she said in a mild, understanding voice.

"No, I–I'm all right," Sarah replied tightly.

"Think you could use the rest of the day off?"

Sarah started to protest, but before she could say anything, Elizabeth waved her hand and pointed at the front door.

"Go on," she said. "This has got to be a really tough time for you, and—" Hands on her hips, she glanced around the nearly deserted library and smiled. "We're not exactly swamped here today."

Sarah wasn't at all sure that she had the strength even to stand up, much less walk all the way to the front door, but she managed to get up from her chair while nodding her thanks.

"Yeah, I–I think I'll go home and take a nap or something," she said dazedly.

"You do that," Elizabeth replied.

Sarah put the papers away, grabbed her purse from the bottom desk drawer, and walked to the door and out into the blistering heat of the day.

But as it turned out, she didn't go straight home.

Without knowing why, she drove out to David's apartment in Westbrook.

Still feeling all wound up and tense inside, she parked her car at the curb, made sure to lock it, and walked up to the apartment. Her hands were shaking as she unlocked the door and entered.

Although she had no specific idea of what she was doing, she sensed on some deep level that she had come here for a definite purpose. At times, it seemed almost as if she could hear a voice, whispering to her, telling her what to do; but it was always too faint for her to make out exactly what it was saying.

She told herself that it was just her imagination—her intuition or something. So maybe it was her intuition that directed her into David's bedroom. For a long time, she just stood there in the doorway, leaning against the door jamb as she tried to orient herself. The heat inside the small, closed apartment was stifling, but she could feel numbing chills deep inside her.

Try as she might, she still couldn't accept the fact that David really was dead forever. How could he be?

The drab, cramped rooms of his apartment still seemed imbued with his presence. She closed her eyes and inhaled deeply, almost catching a lingering trace of his aftershave.

A pang of loneliness and loss filled her, and she realized that, in spite of the problems they'd had and the divorce, in many ways she still loved him. For a silent, fragile moment, she could almost imagine that he was standing close beside her, and she found the thought comforting; but when she tried to imagine his voice, the only sound she could hear was the soft hiss of traffic passing by outside.

When she opened her eyes, the lighting in the room seemed to have changed subtly. A muted yellow glow filled the bedroom. The air seemed heavy and dense.

Sarah gasped out loud when her vision cleared, and she realized that she was staring straight ahead at the books and magazines that were stacked on the table beside David's bed. There was something about them... something that struck her as vaguely familiar.

What the hell was it?

A vague memory... or possibly something from a dream.

For some reason, she thought of the irritating clicking sound the keyboard at work had made, and that reminded her of something else... another sound that was very similar.

What the hell is it?

Feeling as if she were moving in a dream, she walked over to David's bed and sat down on the edge. The bedsprings sagged and creaked beneath her weight. A wave of tiredness swept over her, and she was tempted to lie down and fall asleep. She had the unnerving feeling that she might be dreaming all of this as she watched her hand reach out, as if it had a will of its own, toward the drawer of the bedside table.

The metal latch was cold to the touch as she hooked it with her forefinger and snapped it up. When she pulled it open, the rough scraping sound the drawer made set her teeth on edge.

She gasped again, louder this time, when she looked down and saw the small revolver inside the drawer. Without even thinking, she picked it up and hefted it.

The gun was compact and surprisingly heavy for its size. She didn't know the first thing about guns, so she had no idea what kind it was or even if it was loaded, but feeling it in her hand made her suddenly feel... different, somehow.

"Safer," she whispered as if in answer to an unasked question.

Squinting one eye shut, she raised the gun with a trembling hand and sighted along the shore barrel as if aiming to shoot. She let out a sharp gasp when her focus shifted from the tip of the revolver to what she was aiming at-

The faded, torn spine of a book.

Once again, the feeling came over her of knowing something but not consciously realizing what it was. Chills skittered like tiny hands up her back as she read the title out loud.

"James Moore's Complete Encyclopedia of Mass Murderers."

The gun suddenly felt too heavy to hold. It weighed down her hand and made it drop.

"Oh, Jesus," she whispered.

What is it about that title? she wondered. It rang a distant bell in her memory, but she couldn't say why or how.

She didn't think it was simply that she had noticed the book from when she and David were married. Always casting about for plots and backgrounds for his novels, David often bought and read books like this.

No, it was more than that.

Much more.

Her stomach tightened like a fist. Her hand was shaking as she slowly placed the gun on the bed beside her. She found it almost impossible to swallow or even breathe as she reached out to the stack of books. When she ran the tip of her finger down along the book spines, the faint clicking sound it made filled her with a discomforting feeling.

"One," she whispered softly. She listened to her voice as if it were someone else, speaking to her from another room.

"One thirty."

Cold, eight pressure filled her chest as she tried to grasp the thought that was dancing elusively in her mind, just out of reach.

"One thirty-seven."

She couldn't keep her hands from shaking as she shifted the book out from the middle of the stack and hefted it. Grunting, she placed it in her lap. Her fingers were tingling as she opened the book and idly rifled through the pages. Her vision of the room blurred when she cast a nervous glance over her shoulder, then stared back at the book and flipped pages until she got to page 137.

"Is this it?... Yes, this is it," she whispered raggedly.

There was a small block of text at the cop of the page, but what instantly drew her attention was the grainy black and white photograph of a knife that rook up the bottom half of the page. Beside the knife was a metric ruler which indicated that the blade was slightly more than twenty centimeters long. Sarah wasn't sure what the equivalent was in inches, but the thin blade with what looked like a rounded rubber handle looked absolutely wicked. The caption identified the knife as one of the surgical postmortem instruments from the Victorian Era. This particular knife was reputed to have been used by Jack the Ripper.

"Jack the—" Sarah whispered as a searing spark of panic leaped inside her.

"—Ripper..."

She moaned softly and closed her eyes. Instantly, her mind filled with the mental image of her computer screen scrolling the words *RIPPER... RIP-PER... RIP HER.*

"*Jesus, what's going on here?*" she muttered.

With a sudden surge of energy, she slammed the book shut and threw it to the floor. It hit with a *thud* that seemed as loud as a gunshot.

Shivering wildly inside, Sarah squeezed her head tightly with both hands as though trying to contain an imminent explosion. The salty pressure pounding like hammers behind her eyes was intolerable, and it seemed only to get worse when she opened her eyes again and looked around the room.

The weird yellow glow in the room seemed to intensify, making everything appear as though she were looking through a thick, transparent barrier like a plate glass window. Feeling as if she were watching herself in a movie, she once again reached out and picked up David's revolver. She grunted with satisfaction as she hefted it, but the sound seemed to come not from inside her, but from far away.

Knives aren't anything against a gun!

The sudden violence of her thought surprised her. Although she had never liked guns, and had always hoped that

David would get rid of his, for some reason it now felt good to hold.

It felt *right!*

Knowing that she possessed a gun made her feel a bit safer, but every muscle in her body was still wire-tight as she snapped open her purse and slid the gun underneath her wallet to hide it.

It made her feel like a thief, but she cold herself that David sure as hell didn't need it any longer...

And she might!

She didn't even want to try to explain it.

It just seemed like the right thing to do.

It was late in the afternoon. Golden bars of sunlight shot through the living room windows and cast thin, gray washes of shadow across the carpet and furniture. The air in the room was dense and quiet, a lot like being underwater. David felt drained with exhaustion as he leaned back against the wall and slowly lowered himself to the floor. His back made an abrasive hissing sound as it rubbed against the plaster. With no better idea of what to do, he had decided to wait here until Sarah came home.

Early that morning, he had left Karen at the schoolhouse with strict instructions not to go anywhere or do anything until he came back. He had guessed that Sarah would be at the university library, and had gone there to wait until she showed up. He had watched her reaction while he tried to type a message to her on the computer, but he knew that he had screwed it up.

His fingers had fumbled with the keys, sometimes passing clear through the keyboard and desk top as he concentrated, trying to focus all of his energy so he could type. Under different circumstances, he might have even found it amusing that he, a professional writer, was having so damned much trouble pressing even a single key, much less forming complete words or sentences.

After he'd gotten the first few letters on the screen, though, he had either hit the wrong key or else his presence was somehow messing up the electrical signals inside the computer. Whatever the reason, he hadn't been able to stop the words once they'd started scrolling crazily across the screen.

Sarah had, understandably, been frightened, and David had watched helplessly as she and her boss tried to figure out what was going wrong with the computer. The static charge that filled the air when Elizabeth switched off the power had given him a mild shock, and he was left feeling absolutely drained and hollow.

A mere ghost of my former self, he thought, and almost found the notion amusing.

David was most upset because he hadn't intended to scare Sarah. He wanted to find some way to warn her about the man she was seeing… and the knife that he owned. The danger that knife presented to Sarah seemed so real and immediate that it was almost palpable in the air.

The memory of watching that man make love to his ex-wife left traces of bitter jealousy in his heart and soul. He knew that he could neither forget nor forgive.

And it filled him with sadness to realize something else.

He realized, now that it was much too late, that he still loved Sarah. He loved her and he knew he always would, even beyond death.

And worse than watching the woman he loved make love to another man was knowing that he had seen the knife that night.

It *had* to be the knife the Ferryman wanted. David was irritated that he hadn't recognized its power. He might have done something about it then.

He had watched the young man take hold of the knife and swing it back and forth quickly several times, as if warming up, preparing to use it. When Sarah had returned to the bedroom, the man had hidden the knife beneath his clothes; but now David knew — or at least sensed — what the man intended to do with it.

He was going to kill Sarah!

Maybe he didn't want to.

Maybe, as the Ferryman had said, the knife was controlling him as much as he was controlling it.

Maybe it was something else, but David really didn't care.

The important thing was, it was just a matter of time before the man worked up his courage or rage or whatever it was going to take for him to use the knife on another human being. For more than ten years, in fourteen novels, David had made up stories about murderous passions and twisted minds. It was terribly unnerving to be confronted by such forces in real life.

If you can call this real life, he thought bitterly, *but I guess I really can't if I'm already dead!*

It was too bad he hadn't seen the danger of the knife that night… too bad he hadn't tried to do something about it when he had the chance.

But what could he have done? Even if he had tried, how was he going to gain possession of something that he couldn't even touch, much less pick up?

When Sarah left the library that afternoon, David had felt much too drained to follow after her immediately, so he had made his way back to Pine Knoll Elementary. After checking to make sure that Karen was all right, he walked over to Sarah's house.

He'd expected to see that she was already home when he got there, and was surprised to find that her car wasn't parked either in the driveway or in the garage.

Something was wrong.

He could feel a sense of impending danger like a subtle electrical charge in the air. His worry blossomed into stark fear when he passed through the closed door and walked into the kitchen.

The house was empty and as silent as a tomb—except for a faint scratching sound just at the threshold of hearing. David couldn't identify it. He wasn't even sure where the sound was coming from, but he chose to ignore it as he walked into the living room and sat down on the floor beside the TV to wait for Sarah to return home.

She would eventually.

He watched the sun slide smoothly across the floor, edging the furniture with a fine line of yellow fire. He leaned against the wall with his knees tucked up tightly against his chest and watched tiny dust motes drifting in the air. Like minuscule planets, they were illuminated for a few seconds by the narrow shafts of light, and then they winked out of existence and were gone.

Forever.

Just like our lives, David thought, transfixed by the barely perceptible fall of dust. It must have been his imagination, but he thought he could actually hear the dust hit the floor.

As he sat there, letting his thoughts drift like the dust, sad, poignant memories of the few short, happy years he had spent living here with Sarah and Karen filled him. At the time, those years hadn't seemed all that happy. He'd been struggling so damned hard to get his writing career going that he'd been fairly miserable to live with most of the time. He knew and acknowledged that at the time, but Sarah had made no bones about telling him so, anyway.

His frustration and anger at not making it big as an author was probably the single biggest factor contributing to their marriage falling apart. Karen's death had been the final straw.

In retrospect, however, maybe his life back then hadn't been all that bad.

It certainly wasn't as bad as things were now, and—at least as far as he could tell—this existence was never going to end!

Mired in his own depressing thoughts and wallowing in useless regret, David lost track of the time.

He suddenly jolted to alertness when he realized that the sun had long since set. A hushed, expectant darkness filled the room. Deep shadows stretched like groping hands across the floor, and Sarah still wasn't home.

David listened to the snapping and creaking sounds the house made as it cooled from the heat of the day. He hadn't heard any voices whispering in the dark, so he felt slightly reassured that there were no other unseen presences—no other wraiths haunting the house. The only other sound he heard was that faint scratching which seemed now to be coming from underneath the floor in the kitchen... or maybe it was coming from upstairs....

David couldn't get a direction on it, but he didn't spend much time worrying about it. He was much more concerned about Sarah's safety.

As he sat there in the gathering gloom and waited, a deep sense of futility and frustration mixed with an ineffable sadness. These feelings built up inside him and almost tore him apart. He could feel the dark, eternal emptiness in the center of his being swelling larger, reaching out for him as he wondered what had gone so terribly wrong with his life that it had come to this.

Sometime later—he had no idea when—the sound of footsteps and the doorknob turning drew his attention.

"Sarah," he called out, even though he knew that she wouldn't be able to hear him.

Moving like a raft of thin smoke, he got up and walked into the kitchen, where he saw a shadow shift across the closed window shade.

Then the door began to open slowly.

A brilliant flash of rage filled David when he saw that it wasn't Sarah. It was the young man she had been dating!

Moving cautiously, the man stepped into the house and then carefully eased the door shut behind him, locking it before glancing around. He didn't turn on any lights as he moved stealthily into the kitchen. David heard him swear softly under his breath when he bumped into the kitchen table on his way to the living room. Moving close behind him, David noticed the slight bulge under the man's shirt just above his back pocket and realized with a sudden jolt that it was the knife.

Jesus! He's come back to hurt her!

Sudden, desperate fury gripped him. He lunged forward and swung his arms around the man, hoping to tackle him, but his hands passed through his form like fleeting shadows.

The young man shivered at David's touch, stopped short in his tracks, looked around furtively, and shook his head. When he spoke, his voice sounded so low and distorted that David found it almost impossible to make out what he was saying.

"Place gives me the fucking creeps."

Frustrated, David watched the man walk through the living room and start up the stairs. He was moving a little more boldly now that he seemed assured that Sarah wasn't home.

David stayed close behind him even though he knew that he would not be able to stop him from whatever he was planning to do.

When the man was halfway up the stairs, he paused. Shivering again, he reached up under the back of his shirt. He licked his lips, and a strange glow filled his eyes as he slowly withdrew the knife and stared at it. The exposed blade shimmered in the darkness with a weird, flickering purple glow that cast fuzzy, swaying shadows on the steps and walls when the man moved the knife back and forth.

He's going to use it! By Jesus! He's going to kill Sarah!

The man's footsteps clumped heavily on the stairs as he started moving again. Beneath that sound, though, David could hear something else—that same faint scratching. He was crying to figure out where the sound was coming from and what it might be when he caught a hint of dark motion at the cop of the stairs. He cried out in surprise when he saw a small, dark, deformed shape, standing directly in Tony's path.

At first, David had no idea what this thing was.

It looked like an animal of some kind, but instead of fur its body was composed of a network of stringy pink and red muscle and white tendons that made it look like an anatomical diagram. Glistening white knobs of bone stuck out through the flesh, and a coiled piece of meat that looked like an intestine was hanging from underneath it. The wrinkled flesh made the animal look like a large, freshly peeled rat, but after a moment, David realized that it was—or at least it had been—a cat. Its round eyes reflected the night with a wicked green glare as it curled back its raw upper lip, exposing needle-sharp teeth.

"Jesus! *Bingley?*" David said in a hushed whisper.

The cat turned its head mechanically and glared down at him, but only for a moment before it shifted its unblinking gaze back to Tony, who was still making his way slowly up the stairs.

The man seemed totally oblivious to the cat waiting for him at the top.

David watched, both sickened and amused, as the monstrosity that had once been Sarah's pet hunched up its back and hissed loudly. The sound was harsh, like the hiss of escaping steam, but the man didn't seem to hear it. His step faltered, and he stumbled and might have fallen if he hadn't reached out quickly and caught the banister with one hand. He looked up and down the stairs as though momentarily confused by something, but then continued. Hunching up, the cat hissed again-a wild, piercing squeal. Then it scampered off, disappearing into the darkness of the hallway.

Jesus, he must have killed Bingley... and now he's coming after Sarah!

David was frantic with helpless fear. He knew that he either had to stop the man or else warn Sarah, but he had no idea how to do that.

He watched as Tony walked past where the cat had been and down the corridor to Sarah's bedroom. He entered the room and closed the door quietly behind him.

A sudden, loud rumbling sound from outside drew David's attention. He looked down the stairs as the harsh glare of headlights rippled across the living room walls. A car was pulling into the driveway.

Jesus, she's home!

Frozen for a moment, David was unable to decide which way to turn.

Could he warn Sarah somehow, or should he follow the man into the bedroom and try to stop him from what he was preparing to do?

Panic as clean and sharp as a stainless steel blade ripped through him when he heard Sarah's key rattle loudly in the lock.

Then the door opened, and he heard her enter. She sighed heavily before slamming the door shut behind her. A flood of warm, yellow light came on downstairs.

Standing poised halfway up the stairs, David watched and listened as Sarah walked into the living room, turning on lights as she went. She was whistling a tune under her breath, but David could sense that she was tense, nervous.

Finally, without any better idea of what to do, he moved as fast as he could down the hallway to the bedroom. The hall suddenly seemed to telescope outward as he moved; he had the unnerving impression that he walked past dozens, maybe hundreds of doors before he finally arrived at Sarah's bedroom. Trembling wildly, he entered the room by walking through the door.

The young man was naked and sitting on the edge of the bed in the dark. In his right hand, he was holding the knife and smiling sickly to himself as he twisted it back and forth, flicking it with quick snaps of his wrist. The blade made sharp whickering sounds as it cut the air, and this seemed to please the man to no end. The strange purple glow emanating from the knife blade lit the man's eyes. His tight, lopsided grin made him look positively insane.

"Get the hell out of here! Right now!" David shouted, but his words seemed to fade away to nothing before they left his mouth.

He lurched forward and tried to grab the man again, but his hands passed through him. David knew that no matter how hard he tried, he wasn't going to be able to touch him.

But there had to be something he could do!

The Ferryman had said that he wanted David to get the knife for him, so there must be some power or talent that he could draw upon to do it. If he only had the time to figure it out...

But *now* wasn't the time to try to figure *anything* out.

With a cold, dread certainty that settled like a lead weight in the center of his chest, David knew that if he didn't stop this man right now, Sarah was going to die tonight!

a dead man's dreams.

Chapter Ten

"Shitty day… Jesus, what a *shitty* day," Sarah muttered as she walked back into the kitchen.

She hesitated a moment before taking a glass and the bottle of burgundy down from the cupboard and pouring herself more than she thought she probably should have, but she told herself it was okay.

She probably needed it. After a day like today, she was going to need a *lot of* something to numb herself if she was ever going to get to sleep.

Heaving a deep sigh, she pulled a chair away from the kitchen table and sat down heavily. Grasping the glass with both hands to keep it steady, she took a big gulp and swallowed noisily.

Warm and rich, the burgundy exploded on the back of her tongue and tickled the back of her throat as it went down. After a second or two, it hit her stomach like a hard, warm fist. She gasped and nodded her approval before taking another sip. Then she leaned back in her chair and stared up at the ceiling, letting her vision go fuzzy.

"Jesus, what a day!"

After a long silence, she sat up and let her gaze drift to the kitchen counter, over by the door where she had left her purse as soon as she had entered the house. The small blue and white canvas bag looked slightly ominous to her, and she knew exactly why.

It was because of the gun she had stashed inside.

A *real gun!* She shivered. Something designed *specifically* to kill people!

She took another sip of burgundy and rolled it around in her mouth before swallowing. She kept asking herself why she had taken the gun, but she couldn't really say.

She certainly had no use for a gun. She didn't have any idea how to check to see if it was loaded, much less how to use it. If she seriously thought she needed some kind of protection, then she should find a firing range where she could learn how to use a gun properly. Better yet, she should get a dog. Now that Bingley was gone, that might not be such a bad idea.

If she ever really needed a gun for self-defense, she wasn't even sure she would dare to aim it at someone, much less actually pull the trigger and shoot.

Not at another human being!

All her life, she had despised the idea of owning guns, even if people maintained it was solely to protect themselves. More often than not, those same people ended up killing their relatives or friends during arguments... or worse, sometimes they took out an innocent bystander.

What she should do, she told herself, is get rid of the damned thing...

Right now!

Tomorrow at the latest.

Before she hurt someone.

Or herself.

What kind of danger was she in, anyway?

Sure, she'd been feeling tense lately, maybe a little more on edge than usual, but it had to be because she was imagining things. The sadness and grief she was feeling about David's death was working on her nerves.

Yes, David's death was sad, but their marriage had been over for years before she had finally found the courage to leave him. Dealing with his funeral arrangements and attending the burial had only opened up the older, deeper wounds of Karen's death-wounds that Sarah knew and accepted were *never* going to heal.

And now even Bingley was gone! The house seemed so empty without him. She already missed him rubbing against her ankles and meowing demands for food and attention.

A hot, salty taste flooded the back of Sarah's throat. She knew that it was something the burgundy, much less self-pity and regret, would never wash away. Her view of the kitchen blurred as tears flooded her eyes, shattering the glow of the overhead light into hundreds of tiny yellow fragments.

She raised her glass to take another sip, but the thought of the taste of burgundy nauseated her. A cold, fluttery trembling clutched her stomach. The air in the kitchen suddenly seemed too thin to breathe as wave after wave of dizziness rushed through her. Pinpoints of bright light drifted across her vision.

Sarah knew that it wasn't just the burgundy that was hitting her so hard.

It had to be the accumulated stress and pressure of the last few days finally catching up with her.

She sighed, wishing that she was already lying down in bed, but now she wasn't even sure she had the strength to stand up.

When the telephone suddenly rang, she squealed and spun around, almost falling out of her chair. Hot, sharp pain lanced the center of her chest.

Her first impulse was to get up and answer the phone, but then she thought to let the answering machine take it— especially if it was Tony. She wasn't exactly in the mood to talk to him or anyone else tonight.

By the third ring, though, she couldn't stand the nerve-rattling electronic beeping any longer, so she heaved herself to her feet and went over to the counter. Her hand was slick with sweat as she grabbed the phone from its base in the middle of the fourth ring.

"Hello," she said, her voice tight and strangled-sounding.

She was prepared to hear Tony at the other end of the line and was surprised when she heard a familiar woman's voice instead.

"Sarah. Hi. So, you're finally home, huh?"

"Hi, Mom," Sarah replied, hearing the funny, hollow echo in her own voice. The muscles in the back of her neck instantly knotted into rock-hard lumps. She let her head sag forward and her shoulders slump, hoping to relieve the tension.

"So how are you doing? Okay, I hope," her mother said.

Without waiting for Sarah to reply, she kept right on talking.

"I'm sorry Dad and I couldn't make it to the funeral, but—well, you know how we haven't been feeling exactly tip-top lately."

"I know, Mom," Sarah replied in a low, twisted voice.

"So how'd it all go?"

"Okay, I guess. About as well as you can expect. But—yeah, I'm doing okay."

"I can't tell you how terrible Dad and I feel about all of this," her mother went on as if she wasn't even listening to what Sarah said. "You know how we had always hoped that the two of you would work things out and eventually get back together."

"That wasn't going to happen, Mom, but you can definitely stop hoping for it now." Sarah cringed, regretting saying that even before the words were out of her mouth.

"Is—uh, is Dad around?" she asked, trying quickly to cover.

"He's asleep in front of the TV, as usual," her mother replied. "I was just a little bit worried about you and wanted to call to see how you were doing, that's all. I tried calling a couple of times earlier today, but I guess you weren't in. Don't you even listen to your phone messages?"

"I–I just walked in a minute ago," Sarah said, knowing that her mother wouldn't catch her in the lie.

"Well, I'm sure you have friends you can visit and talk to if you need to. I just wanted to let you know that you're not alone in all of this. You know you're always welcome here at home. That's another reason I was calling—to see if you'd think about flying down here and spending a few days with us. Maybe even a whole week. What do you say?"

"Thanks, Mom, but—I don't think so. Not right now, anyway."

"Why not? It's been hot as the dickens down here, but you could sit in the swimming pool up to your neck all day if you like. And we could go out to eat at—"

"Thanks, Mom," Sarah said quickly. "I really appreciate the offer, but I think I'll stick around here for now. Maybe sometime next month."

Sarah's head was spinning. For some reason, her mother's voice sounded oddly muffled in her ear. She eyed the more than half full glass of burgundy on the table and wondered if it really could be hitting her this hard this fast.

"Well, don't hesitate to call if you need to talk," her mother said. "After what you've been through—after everything that's happened, you'll only make yourself sick if you bottle it up inside."

Sarah couldn't help but notice that, even after five years, her mother still couldn't quite bring herself to mention Karen's death directly. She was suddenly quite sure that she didn't need her mother's help to deal with the current situation.

"I'm doing just fine, Mom—honest," she said. "Thanks for calling. I'll give you a buzz sometime next week, okay?"

"Or before that if you need to talk," her mother piped in, sounding almost cheerful.

"Yeah, sure. Talk to you soon, Mom."

"I love you, darling."

"Love you, too, Mom. Say hi to Dad for me, 'kay?"

"I sure will. Bye-bye for now."

And with that, her mother cut the connection, leaving Sarah with a loud, droning buzz in her ear.

Sarah was feeling all twisted up inside as she stared at the phone for several seconds, wishing earnestly that she could have felt a genuine connection with her mother. But ever since she could remember, there had always been an odd, unspoken awkwardness between them. Sure she *loved* her mother, but she wasn't positive that she *liked* her.

Fighting back her tears, she flicked the on/off switch with her thumb, cutting off the buzzing sound before replacing the receiver on its base.

"Jesus, Jesus, Jesus!"

She squeezed her head tightly with both hands. Tears gathered in her eyes and flowed, leaving warm streaks on her cheeks. She sniffed loudly and then, bracing herself, walked over to the sink and dumped the rest of her burgundy down the drain. It made a funny little gurgling noise as it went down.

As she turned away, she chanced to look down at the floor and saw Bingley's food and water bowl. The rounded mound of kibbles she'd dumped into it this morning still hadn't been touched. The water was still up to the brim of the bowl. The sight of it made the cold emptiness inside Sarah spike even more.

"Oh, Bing. What are we gonna do?" she said, no more than a whisper.

Razor-sharp misery twisted inside her like coils of barbed wire as she walked over to the door, opened it and stuck her head outside.

The night air was warm and rich with the smell of green growing things. Above the dark line of trees in the distance, she could see a faint sprinkling of scars. Not even the tiniest puff of breeze blew in off the ocean to cool her face.

"Bingley. Here, fella," she called out, but the only sounds she heard were the steady chirring of crickets and the hissing rush of traffic in the distance.

"Where the hell are you, you damned foolish cat?" she said in a voice that sounded as fragile as crystal.

Sniffing loudly and wiping her eyes with the heels of her hands, she looked out into the back yard, but there was no sign of him. Her tears were flowing steadily as she walked back into the house, being careful to close and lock the door behind her. Once again, she looked down at the bowl full of cat food and was overwhelmed with sadness.

Bingley was gone… just like David and Karen were gone… and none of them were ever coming back!

Pounding, hot pressure filled her head when she bent down to pick up the bowl. Her hands trembled, and her body was racked with sobs as she dumped its contents into the sink, then turned on the faucet and switched on the garbage disposal.

The whirring, grinding sound instantly got on her nerves.

After filling the bowl with hot water and detergent, she bent down to pick up the wrinkled, yellowed newspaper she had put on the floor underneath the bowl a few weeks ago. She was set to ball up the paper and throw it into the trash under the sink when a headline on the front page caught her attention.

POLICE HAVE NO NEW LEADS IN SEARCH FOR MURDERER

Stunned, Sarah looked at the date at the top of the page and saw that it was over a month old. She hadn't noticed this before. She remembered hearing something about a murder in downtown Portland several weeks ago, but she had dismissed it, assuming it was related to a drug or prostitution deal that had gone wrong—something that would never affect her.

Her hands wouldn't stop shaking as she sat down at the kitchen table and read the article. As she read, the tight nervousness in her stomach grew steadily worse. Chills played up and down her back, and she found it increasingly difficult even to breathe.

According to the article, the police were still investigating the murder of Margaret Harkness, a twenty-five-year-old woman who had worked as receptionist at Dixon Brothers Oil Company. She had been found dead in her Danforth Street apartment. A wave of dizziness hit Sarah, and she felt like she almost blacked out when she read further down in the article that Margaret had been stabbed to death.

"*Jesus...* Stabbed!"

Her hands went suddenly clammy and were too weak to hold the newspaper. Whimpering softly, she let go of the paper. It fluttered gently to the floor as she stood up and staggered backward, feeling blindly behind her for something — anything — to support her. She kept backing up until she bumped into the kitchen wall, and almost had the wind knocked out of her.

A low, strangled sound was gathering deep in her throat as she shook her head back and forth as though refusing to believe what she had just read. She had no idea why this was upsetting her so much, but she was filled with sudden, almost desperate panic.

You're just over-stressed, whispered a tiny voice in the back of her mind. *That's all there is to it. You're in overload.*

"No, no," she muttered as she turned and staggered into the living room, her hands clawing the air in front of her like it was a curtain she was trying to tear through.

She banged her left knee on the edge of the coffee table but, in her panic, hardly noticed the pain.

With a deep, shuddering groan, she collapsed face-first onto the couch and lay there trembling with her eyes closed. The whole world was spinning wildly out of control, like she was on a carousel and barely had the strength to hang on. Wrenching sobs shook her body as she pressed her face against the couch cushion and cried to stop the flood of thoughts that filled her mind.

Please... Stop it!... Someone! ... Make it stop!

David couldn't even begin to sort through all of the emotions that were raging inside him as he watched the naked man pull back the bed covers, climb into Sarah's bed and drape the sheet over his waist as he lay down flat on his back. The bulge of his erection tented the chin sheet. The man chuckled softly as he clutched the handle of the knife with both hands in front of his chest. He looked like a priest holding a crucifix.

The man's eyes were shining like those of an animal that had been caught in the sudden glare of the headlights of an oncoming car. His upper body was slick with sweat and highlighted by the dull purple glow the radiated from the blade. His breathing came in sharp, ragged gulps that filled the bedroom like the sounds of someone making violent, passionate love.

The thought that this man had made love to Sarah filled David with an unspeakable rage.

The man was still chuckling softly to himself when he raised the blade up in front of his face and turned it back and forth, admiring it in the darkness of the room. David wondered if he could see the subtle glow that emanated from it.

Jesus, he's gonna do it! he thought with a soul-deep shudder. *He's working up his courage, and he'll do it if I don't find some way to stop him!*

David moved closer to the bed and, leaning forward, stared deeply into the man's eyes. He concentrated as hard as he could to project his own thoughts into the man's mind.

Get out of here! … Now! … Before I rip your soul apart! I swear on my daughter's grave, if you hurt Sarah, I'll make you suffer in ways you can't even begin to imagine!

I mean it, you lousy bastard! I'll make you die a thousand deaths if you so much as touch her!

The rage boiling up inside David made the dark bedroom appear to be flashing with bursts of bright red light. He clenched his fists, squeezing them as hard as he could and wishing that—just once—if he swung at the man, he would be able to connect solidly with living flesh. David's sense of touch was still deadened, but he could feel a strong current of energy fill his being. It made him vibrate subtly, like a tuning fork.

With a sudden, anguished cry of rage and frustration, David cocked back his fist and swung it at the man's chest with every ounce of energy he could muster.

The effect was amazing!

The young man let out a sudden, loud grunt. His body snapped up into a sitting position. His chest was heaving, and his breath rattled in the dark. His eyes were wide open and staring as he looked all around the darkened bedroom, trying to figure out what the hell had just happened. He placed one hand on his chest, then put two fingers on the inside of his wrist to check his pulse.

Good! David thought when he saw that the man was shivering.

For a single instant, the man stared directly into David's eyes, and David was positive that the stranger was able to see him; but the man's gaze quickly shifted over to the closed bedroom door. Still looking tense and frightened, he threw aside the bed covers and stood up. Crouching low and moving stealthily, he went to the bedroom door, opened it and looked out into the hallway. A faint glow of light from downstairs illuminated the hard features of his face.

"Sarah!" David shouted, even though he knew it was useless. No one still living could hear him.

"Please, Sarah! Listen to me! Get out of the house!"

David was moving slowly toward the door, wondering how he could stop this man, but then he looked back at the bed and saw that the young man had left the knife on the bed. It lay there in the damp tangle of sheets, glowing dully, beckoning to David like a beacon.

Without thinking about it, David made a grab for the knife with both hands. Willing every bit of mental energy he could muster, he tried to imagine that his hands once again had real substance, and that he could touch the knife. He visualized his fingers curling around the handle and lifting the knife, trying desperately to remember how it felt to touch things.

But the memory was too distant, too hazy.

David glanced at the young man, who was still crouching by the door and peering out into the hall. He had never wanted anything more that he wanted — right now — to hold that knife, even if only for a few seconds — just long enough to slash and stab this son of a bitch!

And it was almost working!

For a tantalizing, fleeting instant, David thought he could actually feel the smooth texture of the rubber handle. The memory of touching and holding things when he had been alive grew sharper, filling him with a trembling excitement. A dark, dizzying, backward rush swept over him as he raised his hands and saw that the knife had risen an inch or two off the bed.

Jesus, it's working! I'm doing it!

A blinding rush of excitement filled David, but he cautioned himself not to get too excited; he couldn't break his concentration.

David stared intensely at the knife, moving it more by an effort of will than by physical means. He watched in amazement as the blade turned like the needle of a compass pointing north. It was aimed straight at the young man's naked back.

The knife knows what I want it to do, David thought with a shivering rush. *What IT wants to do!*

The words of the Ferryman came back to David, filling him with dread.

"Whoever possesses those knives is also possessed by them. Eventually he'll do what the knife wants. Make no mistake. No matter how hard he tries to resist it, he will use it."

Just like I want to use it now! David screamed inside his mind as he focused all of his energy into moving the gleaming knife closer to the man's back.

David's corpus was trembling violently as he strained with the effort of keeping the knife in his hands and not letting it slip out. It was like trying to clasp a stream of water or hold onto a ray of sunshine. The terrifying feeling of his own insubstantiality was overpowering. As he held the knife and stared at it in his hand, David couldn't even begin to determine which had less substance—him or the knife.

All I want to *do is use it!* he thought frantically.

Just once!

Only for a few seconds!

That's all I ask!

Please!

If there is a God... or an angel... or some spirit who really wants Good to triumph out over Evil, then let me do this!

Let *me kill him!*

NOW!

From somewhere far away, David heard a low, agonized wailing that grew steadily louder until it throbbed in the darkness like rolling thunder.

For the longest time, he didn't have the slightest inkling that the sound was coming from him. He focused his total attention on moving the knife, willing it to come closer... and closer to the man's naked back.

In the dim light, David could see the raw scabs of Bingley's claw marks that striped the man's back. He tried to imagine each of those wounds suddenly splitting open and gaping like raw, screaming mouths as they gushed fresh blood. The blade of the knife seemed to be glowing steadily brighter and vibrating wildly as it moved closer to its mark.

David imagined as clearly as he could the dazed look of surprise and terror he would see in the man's eyes when he felt the blade jab into his back and plunge through his lungs toward his heart.

He *wanted* it... He *willed* it....

Witha sudden, high-pitched scream, David thrust forward with every bit of energy he had left.

The knife whistled shrilly in the air.

For a terrifying instant, David imagined that the blade had actually screamed.

The stranger suddenly wheeled around as if he had heard or sensed something. With a surprised grunt, he dropped to the floor as the knife whizzed past his ear and buried the first inch or two of its blade into the wood of the door frame. It stuck there with a vibrating hum, mere inches from the top of the man's head.

"*Jesus!*" the man muttered, looking around, confused. He kept turning his head back and forth, staring at the blade and then at the pressing darkness around him.

"Where the *fuck* did *that* come from?"

"You bastard!" David wailed.

His voice echoed with a dull, muffled reverberation. The pit of frustration inside him was too much to take. David reached out for the knife again, but he knew that he could no longer maintain total concentration. He wished he could cry as he watched his hand pass through the hard rubber handle without the slightest bit of resistance.

No! … Please!… It's not fair!

The young man's eyes were wide with terror and confusion. His hand was shaking terribly as he took hold of the knife and wiggled it from the door jamb. Holding the blade close to his face, he checked for any damage. He smiled, his eyes glowing like lanterns as he thumbed the edge, making sure it was still razor-sharp. Then, moving quickly and silently, he got himself dressed and left the bedroom with the knife clutched tightly in his right hand.

David's panic rose as he watched the man stride down the hall to the stairs. He walked with his shoulders hunched, looking like a primitive savage on the hunt. Moving silently to the head of the stairs, he peered down over the railing at the glow of light that spilled into the hallway from the living room.

David followed along, no more than two or three steps behind as he crept silently down the stairs and into the living room. He wanted to shout out another warning when he saw the man crane his head forward, looking and listening for Sarah. His nostrils flared as though he were sniffing the air for a trace of her. He looked wild, feral.

If he sees her, he'll kill her!

Pure panic gripped David when he saw Sarah, lying face down on the couch. For a shimmering instant, he thought she looked as though she were already dead, but then he caught the slight shifting of her back as she breached steadily.

David knew that the young man must be able to see her, too, but the man didn't hesitate for even a second. Buttoning his shirt and zipping his fly as he went, the stranger hurried through the living room and into the kitchen, pausing only long enough to unlock the door before dashing out onto the porch. He was already halfway down the steps when the screen door slammed shut behind him.

The sound instantly woke Sarah. With a startled cry, she rolled off the couch and awkwardly scrambled to her feet. Her body was tense, her eyes wide with fear and her fists clenched in front of her as she looked around the room, crying to figure out what had happened.

David felt only a slight measure of relief when he followed her out into the kitchen and saw that the young man was gone.

"Bingley?" Sarah called out softly.

Her voice was a light, fluttering sound that was difficult for David to hear.

She looked around, confused and a little bit concerned, when she noticed that the kitchen door was unlocked. She threw the bolt again and then, casting a suspicious glance around the kitchen, walked slowly back into the living room. She turned out all of the lights except one, and then, rubbing her face and muttering softly to herself, she went upstairs.

David felt an aching twinge of sadness as he watched her go.

She was safe, he thought, at least for tonight; but he knew that young man would be back. He was still going to have to figure out a way to warn Sarah of the danger that was stalking her.

Somehow...

―――――

"What the hell?" Sarah whispered when she entered her bedroom, turned on the light, and saw the unmade bed.

It had been so hot over the last week or so that she had gotten rid of the blanket and bedspread, and just had a top and bottom sheet. But she was absolutely positive that she had pulled up the bed covers this morning, just as she did every morning.

But maybe, she thought, because she'd been so upset and nervous lately, she only *thought* she had done it this morning. Little personal rituals can easily become so much second-nature that sometimes you think you've done them when actually you haven't.

Leaning down, she grabbed the cop edge of the sheet, shook it out and pulled it up over the pillows. As she folded it down and smooched it out, she suddenly jumped in surprise, noticing that there was a warm spot on the bed.

As though someone's been sleeping here, she thought, suddenly tensing. She looked around the room, not having any idea what she expected to see.

Has Bingley been sleeping here? Maybe he's still alive somewhere in *the house!*

It was a futile hope, she knew, because his food and water hadn't been couched all day, but she got down on her hands and knees and looked under the bed.

Other than a few clots of dust, the only thing she found was what turned out to be a rolled up sock that was turned inside-out. She grabbed it and, standing up, shook it out with a quick snap of the wrist.

It was obviously a man's sock.

Tony must have left it there by mistake last night, she guessed.

Shaking her head with confusion, she tossed the sock out into the hallway where she collected her dirty laundry.

"Bingley?" she called out again, surprised by the high quaver in her voice.

"Com'on, boy. Come here, Bing." She clicked her tongue a few times, then held her breath and waited; but she neither saw nor heard any sign of her cat.

Her stomach felt all tight and fluttery with apprehension when she walked down the hall to the bathroom and washed up for bed. Once she was back in the bedroom, she undressed, put on her lightweight nightgown, and slipped in between the cool sheets. After years of marriage, she still favored sleeping on the left side of the bed. Without even consciously thinking about it, she reached over to feel the warm spot on the mattress again.

It no longer felt quite as warm as before, but it *did* feel slightly damp, as if someone had been lying there recently.

"Jesus," Sarah whispered, wondering who or what else it could have been if it hadn't been Bingley. "Someone's been sleeping in my bed," she said softly, using a "Three Little Bears" voice.

She almost chuckled, but the tension in her stomach wasn't going away.

It was getting worse.

With a heavy sigh, she rolled over onto her side away from the warm spot and closed her eyes, feeling much too emotionally wrung out to worry about it right now.

Besides, it was nothing... nothing at all...

Staring deeply into the darkness behind her eyelids, she took several long, even breaths and commanded herself to let her mind wander.

The weight of the last few days felt like it was crushing down on her, but soon enough she started to drift off to sleep.

It wasn't a very deep sleep, and before long she slipped into a dream. For the longest time, she had a soft, mildly disorienting sensation of floating effortlessly in that hazy borderland between sleep and wakefulness. Not long after that, vague images and fragments of thoughts began to rake shape. A small part of her mind was aware that she was dreaming, but she found this relaxing, so she snuggled her head into the pillow and let herself go with the gentle, cushiony flow.

After a long, timeless moment, she realized that she was no longer floating.

She was standing in a vast, dark room. The darkness all around her was so dense it was almost tangible. She listened to the faint echoes of dripping water and a soft, ruffling sound that might have been her pulse throbbing in her ear against the pillow.

A mild current of apprehension tickled her mind, but she pushed it aside as she stared into the swelling darkness.

As her vision sharpened, she realized that the darkness was seething with shifting, vaguely perceived figures.

After another indefinite time, faces began to materialize and dissolve, looming at her and then receding like wisps of smoke back into the darkness. She thought she could hear faint voices whispering to her from all directions at once, but she couldn't make out anything that was being said.

She realized with a sudden start that two faces—both pale, lifeless—were resolving much more clearly. They stared at her with blank, sightless eyes.

At first Sarah was only mildly curious, but then she became a bit uneasy.

Finally, with a violent jolt, she recognized both of them.

"No..." she whispered.

Her voice echoed weirdly in her dream, warbling up and down the register like someone was playing with the volume control.

She watched as the two faces resolved out of the darkness like slowly developing photographs. She was transfixed by the unblinking eyes that stared at her, cold and emotionless.

"David? Karen?"

She wasn't sure if she said their names out loud or not, but it didn't seem to matter. Neither one of them responded to her voice.

They just kept staring at her, their steady gazes drilling into her.

Sarah realized that the light around her was growing steadily brighter. The darkness was thinning like the gradually intensifying light of dawn. She could see that her ex-husband and daughter were standing side by side. Their hands were clasped tightly together. Sarah couldn't tell what kind of room they were in. It looked like some kind of large, deserted place — maybe an abandoned factory or schoolroom that had fallen into disrepair.

With mounting horror, Sarah realized that David and Karen appeared as stiff and pale as they had looked in their coffins. Stinging grief ripped through her like a silver blade.

When she tried to turn away, she realized with a tremendous jolt of fear that she was looking down at her own hands.

She was holding a gun!

She recognized it immediately. It was the small revolver she had stolen from David's apartment!

Icy panic surged inside her like a tidal wave as she watched, feeling detached from her own body and absolutely unable to control it as she slowly raised the gun to eye level and aimed it squarely at her daughter's face.

No!... Stop this!... I don't want to do this!

Sarah had no idea if she said this out loud or simply thought it, but it didn't matter. There was no way she could force her arm to turn the gun away. A deep, steady, trembling pressure was building up in her hand. She could feel her forefinger steadily tightening... pressing back against the trigger.

No!... Please! ... Make this stop right now!

But she couldn't resist or stop the tension in her hand, and she couldn't make herself look away.

A sudden, ear-shattering explosion and a brilliant flash of white light split the darkness.

Sarah screamed and tried to turn away, but she couldn't help but watch as her daughter's face exploded in front of her in vivid slow-motion. Bright red gouts of blood along with clumps of tangled, pink flesh, gray brain matter and shattered bone splashed into the air. Karen's left eye vanished instantly, as if it had been vaporized, but her right eye kept staring at Sarah from the bleeding hole that had appeared in the middle of her face. A wide sheet of blood was gushing down over her chest. It fell to the floor with sickening, plopping sounds.

Sarah watched as Karen's body slowly twisted to one side and then began to crumple like a marionette whose strings had been cut. Uttering a long, agonized groan, Karen collapsed into a shapeless heap on the ground, and then, in horrifying slow motion, the darkness swallowed her up.

David still stood there, his hand still extended, but now empty. He seemed not to react in the slightest to what had just happened. He continued to stare blankly at Sarah, his cold gaze piercing her like skewers. The dead-looking gleam in his eyes riveted Sarah, and she found it impossible to resist as her hand holding the gun swung around and took aim straight at David's face.

No!... Don't make me do this!

Her voice was screaming inside her head, warbling and echoing weirdly all around her. But the gun in her hand was the only thing that was real to her now. She sighted along its barrel, drawing a steady bead on her ex-husband's face.

Please! ... I don't want to do this!... Make it stop!

But she couldn't stop it. Her trigger finger twitched in a quick spasm, and the gun jumped in her hand.

Another flash and deafening explosion ripped the air. This time, Sarah managed to turn away before she had to see the effect the gunshot had on David.

She was trembling as though in the grip of a seizure as she stared into the swelling darkness. A wild, winding apprehension clutched her as she held her breath and waited... waited for something to happen next.

She didn't dare look up. She didn't dare move.

She cringed when she felt *something* moving closer to her.

A dark, menacing presence.

She jumped and screamed when a hand suddenly clamped down hard on her shoulder and started to squeeze.

The fringes of her vision dissolved into thick, vibrating black swirls as she slowly looked and saw—not David, but Tony. He was grinning at her like a madman. An insane glow blazed in his eyes. It took Sarah a heartbeat or two to realize that there was a small, black hole about the size of a quarter in the middle of Tony's forehead.

She stared at it for a moment, struck dumb with fear.

She imagined that the hole was an eye that was going to open and gaze into her heart and soul; but as she watched, a thin ribbon of bright, red blood began to trickle out of it. It ran down David's face, parting into two streams at the bridge of his nose.

"Why'd you go and do something like that?" Tony asked, his voice whiny.

Sarah started shaking her head from side to side and cried to back away from him, but his grip on her tightened all the more, holding her there.

I didn't want to! ... I couldn't help it!

Sarah wanted to scream this at him, but her voice was locked deep in her chest.

"The hell you couldn't!" Tony snarled.

His tongue flicked our of the corner of his mouth and lapped at the blood that was flowing down both sides of his face. His smile widened until it looked like it was going to split his face. The wild intensity in his eyes was almost blinding.

With a sudden, violent surge of strength, Sarah jerked forward and broke Tony's grip on her. The scream that had been building up inside her finally found its way out, and she let loose with a long, trailing shriek.

When she opened her eyes and looked around, she was surprised to see that she was sitting up in bed. Her body was slick with sweat. When she took a deep breath, it burned like acid in her throat and lungs. Her right shoulder hurt terribly, as if she had wrenched it.

Or as if someone had been holding me there... hurting me, she thought.

Covering her face with both hands, Sarah slumped forward on the bed and began to cry.

the shadow whispers.

Chapter Eleven

"**S**he has to kill him! Don't you understand that? And she's got to do it right away!"

David grunted and shook his head, unable to believe that he was hearing Karen correctly. Her voice maintained that flat, dead tone that bothered him so much, and he wondered if his own voice sounded as lifeless to her as hers did to him.

He wasn't sure he really wanted to know.

They were alone in Pine Knoll Elementary—at least as alone as they *could be.* Soft scraping sounds, faint voices, high laughter, and the distant opening and closing of doors echoed throughout the dark hallways. From down in the basement there came deep, reverberating groans and what sounded like the clanking of machinery or heavy chains. David felt a slight measure of relief that, at least so far, they hadn't encountered any other wraiths in the school. For now, the schoolhouse seemed about as safe a place as they were going to find.

Outside, the night was dense and pressing. A heavy overcast sky hid the moon and stars, and dulled the cold, blue glare of the streetlights. The air was charged with static electricity. Low clouds pulsated with a rippling purple light, like heat lightning that edged everything with an eerie glow.

Through the open doorway, David could catch glimpses every now and then of faint lights, shining like candles seen through dense fog, moving from one window to another in the buildings across the street. Closer, he could hear the rustling sound of unseen wings in the dark. He wondered if it was an owl, a bat, or something else. Just once, a shrill, rising scream tore through the night like the keening wail of a siren. It lasted for only a few seconds before fading away, but it was more than enough to remind David of the numerous dangers outside his haven.

He was sitting on the floor in the darkness and staring up at his daughter, who was standing a short distance away from him. He couldn't see her very well. She was no more than a dark splotch against the shadowy background of the far wall.

He was trying his best to make sense of what she had just said to him, but it didn't register.

He couldn't get rid of the unnerving thought that this didn't sound at all like Karen—not the tone of her voice or what she had said.

"For crying out loud, Karen," he said, hearing the desperate edge in his own voice. "Listen to yourself! Listen to what you're saying!"

"I know *exactly* what I'm saying," Karen replied with a hard edge to her voice. "He's going to *hurt* her. He *wants* to hurt her, and *he'll do it soon* unless someone stops him!"

A deep, twisting sense of frustration stirred within David.

"But I tried to," he said, feeling regret like a cold, iron ball in the center of his chest. "I tried as hard as I could, but I couldn't get through to her. I don't know how to, and I don't have any idea what else I can do."

"You have to try harder then, because he *has* to *die!*"

The torment David felt when he heard his daughter say this was nearly unbearable.

For just an instant, he thought that one of the voices he heard whispering upstairs was now inside his head, teasing him, taunting him, urging him to *do* something. He tried, but couldn't quite make out what it was saying.

He most definitely worried about Sarah and what might happen to her, but he was just as concerned about Karen and what seemed to be happening to her in the Shadowlands.

There was something more than a little "not right" about her.

There was something plain *wrong* with her.

He wished he knew of a truly safe place where he could take her, where she could be happy and content. He didn't like the tense, empty shell she appeared to be.

Isn't there such a thing as "heaven" where the dead can dwell in eternal peace and bliss? he wondered. *This can't be all there is to the afterlife!*

He kept trying to convince himself that what was wrong with Karen was simply the result of the new state of being in which she had found herself. Just like him, she was confused and frightened. He still found it difficult, if not impossible, to admit-even to himself-that, unless this was some kind of prolonged hallucination or nightmare, he and she were both *dead.*

At least for now, he knew that he *had* to accept that fact at face value.

They *were* dead! If, as the song said, life is just a dream, then death was turning out to be a real nightmare.

How else could he expect Karen to act? She wasn't old enough to understand what had happened to her. He had no idea where she had been or what she had done during the five long years she had been here—alone—in the Shadowlands.

It pained him to remember the vivacious, fun-loving child she had once been. No matter what the situation—even when his and Sarah's marriage was at its worst—Karen had always been ready and eager to embrace life and enjoy it to its fullest. In the deep recesses of his memory, David could still hear echoes of the high, sweet ring of her childish laughter.

And where's that laughter now?

An ever-deepening sense of sadness and loss embraced him like the dark arms of night.

Maybe—somehow—she had known subconsciously that she was going to die young. The Ferryman had said that a fetter could be simply that the person had died before his or her time. Maybe something in Karen's spirit had pushed her to grab and enjoy life as much as she could in the nine short years she had been given because she had always known that she didn't have any more time than that.

But somehow it seemed to David that it had to be more than that.

The changes in her, the qualities she had lost, seemed too dramatic, too drastic.

He had lost her once before when she died in his arms on the ski slope, and he dreaded the thought that he might be losing her again. It was all too much to bear, but there was no other way to look at it.

He had to admit that his daughter wasn't at all the same person or the same soul she had once been in life.

David had found existence in the Shadowlands extremely disorienting. He had tried many times to analyze himself, to determine if he, too, had changed as drastically as Karen appeared to have. At least as far as he could tell, he didn't think or feel or act that much differently from the way he had thought, felt and acted when he was alive.

True, he experienced emotions and physical sensations very differently now, but he told himself that this was simply because he no longer had a physical body that had biological reactions to what he felt and thought. His emotions were no longer complicated or enhanced by the physical. He experienced emotions and ideas in a purer, more essential, spiritual way.

He had no idea what his corpus, as the Ferryman had called it, was made of, but he found it incredibly disorienting the way his senses of hearing, touch and sight were distorted.

Maybe what he thought of now as his body was just an illusion—a visual echo of the form he'd once had. It had no reality to it other than as a memory. That was the only way he could explain the way his senses seemed so warped.

He'd lost accurate track of the time, but if his funeral had been just today—or was it yesterday?—he couldn't have been dead for very long. But no matter how long it had been, he wasn't getting any more used to it.

He wondered if he ever would.

He especially didn't like the curious loss of sensation whenever he physically touched something—even his own daughter.

Without the physical restrictions of his body, he experienced existence differently from when he was alive. He was still amazed and excited that he could do things that he had only been able to imagine before—things like walking through walls with no more effort than walking through a dense fog and walking great distances without any sense of fatigue.

And there were other powers and talents he might discover as well. The Ferryman had mentioned them, but David was afraid that he didn't have enough time to learn any of them. Certainly not soon enough to help Sarah.

A premonition of impending doom filled David with a sharp sense of urgency. He knew that he had to act swiftly and decisively. The problem was, he had no idea *what* to do!

And it pained him to see Karen here. Shouldn't someone who had died so young and innocent end up in something at least a bit closer to the religious concepts of Heaven, Nirvana, or Paradise?

It broke his heart to hear Karen say such hateful, vengeful things.

It tore him apart to sense such utter despair, hatred and fear in her. Where was inner peace and tranquility?

Even given their unique situation, he couldn't understand or account for the bizarre changes he had noticed in her personality.

Could five years in the Shadowlands literally have drained the life and spirit out of her so completely?

Was the same thing going to happen to him?

"Listen to me, Karen," he said, his voice low and controlled. "I–I know that we didn't have much time together when you were—when we were both alive, but one thing I think your mother and I both wanted to teach you, even though maybe you were too young to fully understand it, was that we have to respect life. We *have* to!" David listened to his own voice, hearing it as nothing more than a rattling whisper in the dark.

"And even though you and I aren't alive anymore, I think we *still* have to respect life."

"But *someone's* going to die!" Karen said, her voice resonating with a deep hollowness. "And *you* have a chance to choose who it's going to be—either my... my mother, or else that scumbag she's been fucking!"

"*Karen!*"

David was horrified to hear his sweet, innocent daughter speak like that. How much did she know? What had she seen and experienced in the time she had been alone in the Shadowlands?

"I'm serious, Daddy," Karen said. Coming to him out of the darkness, her voice sounded almost threatening. "When he has that knife—when he's holding it in his hand and is going to use it on her—that's when someone has to *kill* him!"

"*Stop* it, Karen! Please! I don't want to hear you talk like that! I don't want you even *thinking* like that!"

"But she *has* to do it! Don't you understand? She *has* to kill him while he's holding the knife!"

A sudden bolt of anger ripped through David. He leaped to his feet and began pacing back and forth in the darkness. His footsteps, dragging on the ancient floorboards, echoed weirdly in the dense darkness.

It's all for nothing, a voice whispered inside his head.

A deep chill sliced through David like the honed edge of a knife.

All of it... It's absolutely worthless! ... A useless waste of time and energy! ... So why not just give up? ... Karen's dead ... You're dead ... Why should you care if Sarah or anyone else lives or dies.... They're all going to die eventually, anyway ... Everyone you ever loved will die! ... And in the end, everything will fade away ... People, the world, the whole damned universe—EVERYTHING will be destroyed eventually... It will all fall into the bottomless pit... the endless void of Oblivion!

Against his will, David listened as the voice spoke deep inside his head. It terrified him. He had the distinct impression that someone was standing close beside him in the dark and whispering these terrible things into his ear.

"No," he said in a low, grating whisper as he clapped his hands over his ears and shook his head in adamant denial. "It's not like that. It can't be."

Oh, but it is, the voice inside his mind continued. *And you've always known it... Oh, yeah! ... Deep down in your heart, you've always understood the utter futility of it al... So why pretend anymore?... Why not just give in to it?... Why not embrace the darkness fully!... Let yourself go?... There's ultimate peace there, isn't it?... All of your suffering will end in the dark, eternal embrace of... Oblivion...*

"No, stop it. Damn it! *Stop it!*" David shouted between clenched teeth as he pounded the sides of his head with his fists.

"No, I won't stop it."

For a terrifying instant, David thought he had said that, but then he realized that Karen had spoken. Her voice sounded so far away, it was lost in the internal confusion that threatened to rip him apart. David was sure that, if he said anything right now, no matter how loud he yelled, she wouldn't be able to hear him.

"I won't stop it because *you* have to *do* it!" Karen said firmly. "You *have to* get her to *kill* him!"

"But... I... can't..."

His own voice sounded fainter than the grating voice that was taunting him inside his mind: *Give in to it, then! ... There's nothing else anyway*

... Eventually everything—even the Shadowlands and the entire universe—is going to fade away into nothing... into a vast... eternal... NOTHING!... You've known all along that existence is nothing but a terminal blip in the blank, meaningless, endless void.

"No ... it isn't." David's throat felt as though it were burning. "That can't be all there is! There *has* to be *some* kind of meaning or hope or... or otherwise—"

Otherwise ... what?

A cold ache filled David's chest, choking off his reply.

He was dimly aware that, if he still possessed a physical body, he would have been wracked with tears as he tried to stifle the voice that was whispering inside his head. He couldn't bear to think about what it was saying.

"No, there isn't," Karen said. She sounded impossibly far away, lost to him forever. "There's no hope at all unless she kills him. And he has to be holding that knife when she does it."

Finally, listening to the horrible things Karen was saying and hearing that low, hissing voice inside his head, David couldn't take it any longer. Shaking his fists in total frustration, he focused his full attention as he struggled to ground himself as firmly as he could in the reality in which he had found himself.

He looked around at the dim recesses of the schoolhouse, at the hazy gray and purple light that filtered in through the opened door and broken windows. The distant sounds of the night faded into the background, and he concentrated only on being aware of himself, standing there, facing his dead daughter.

"I–I'm going out," he said in a low, shattered voice.

Karen started to reply, but he already knew what she would say. He hushed her angrily.

"No! You listen to me! I want you to stay right here. Do you understand? I don't want you going *anywhere* or doing *anything* until I get back."

"Are you going co—"

"Be *quiet!* Just stay here. I'll be back as soon as I can."

Without another word, he turned and left the schoolhouse, but once he was outside in the night, he didn't feel even the slightest measure of relief. He couldn't shake the dreadful feeling that somewhere in the night, somewhere in the Shadowlands or maybe on some other level of existence, a dark menace was gathering strength and moving steadily closer to him.

And Karen!

Although he tried not to think about it, he knew that, when it arrived, if it hadn't already destroyed Karen and him, it would drag both of chem into a realm of terror that he couldn't even begin to fathom.

———

"You have to kill her! Don't you understand that? And you *have* to do it right away!"

The soft voice came to Tony like the hissing wind from out of the darkness, but it was loud enough to yank him out *of* a deep, dreamless sleep. He thought it sounded a little bit like a girl's voice, but for some reason, Tony found it neither odd nor threatening that there might be a little girl in his bedroom, talking to him in the middle of the night.

He must have been dreaming. It's just that he didn't remember it.

Sighing heavily, he opened his eyes and rubbed them. He grunted softly as he sat straight up in bed and scanned the dark bedroom.

There was a small, dark silhouette standing motionless at the foot of his bed. It certainly looked like a person standing there, but he figured that it had to be a trick of the darkness and his being half asleep.

Tony leaned forward, trying to see more clearly, but he still couldn't be sure.

All the shades in the bedroom were drawn. The only illumination was the thin glowing wedge of lemon light that slipped in from the hallway underneath his closed door.

It was impossible to see anything clearly.

Whenever he tried to look directly at her, trying to decided if there really could be a little girl in his bedroom, she wavered out of sight and shifted from one side of the bed to the other. Only by focusing on a spot a little off to one side of her was he able to see...

Something.

He caught the vaguest hint of a smoke-thin shadow against the darker background of the wall. But the shadow had eyes, and he realized with a deep shudder that the eyes were staring straight at him. They glowed with a steady, dull blue radiance that seemed to rear into him like claws that ripped him open, exposing the deepest secrets at the center of his soul.

"Who-who *are* you?" Tony whispered, painfully aware of the wire-tight tension in his voice.

This didn't make any sense at all.

He *had* to be dreaming!

There couldn't be anyone else here. His roommate was asleep in the next room, and Tony had made sure the apartment door had been locked before coming to bed.

"My name's Karen," the little girl replied. Her voice had a sweet, innocent quality, but it also sounded curiously flat.

"Do I... know you?" Tony asked.

She didn't answer right away, and Tony began to think that he must be alone in the room. She was nothing more than a lingering trace of a dream.

But then he caught another glimpse of her, standing at the foot of the bed. She appeared to be shaking her head slowly from side to side, and he thought he could hear her clicking her tongue as though scolding him.

"So what... what do you want from me?" Tony asked edgily. He certainly *felt* wide awake now. His scalp was crawling as though it were infested with worms. His breath caught like a hook in his throat.

"How did you—What the hell are you *doing* here?"

"You know she deserves it," the little girl said in a soft, hissing voice.

"Huh? *Who* deserves *what*?"

"She deserves to *die*. I hope you realize that you're going to have to *kill* her."

"Kill who? What the fuck are you talking—"

"Sarah Robinson, of course," came the reply in a voice so low it sounded almost masculine. "After all, she really does deserve it."

"And why's that?" Tony asked, trying to repress the wave of chills that raced through him.

"Oh, I don't think I have to tell you that," the little girl said, snickering softly. "I think you already know."

In the dark, she sounded like she was standing much too close to him. Tony shifted forward on his bed, tensed and ready to swing a fist at her if she proved threatening. A small corner of his mind was telling him this was impossible. It didn't make any sense.

How could it be happening?

How could anyone be here in his bedroom at this time of night?

And why would he be afraid of a little girl?

"She doesn't love you. She never did. Not in the least," the little girl whispered. "But I suspect you already knew that she was using you."

Her voice was starting to grate on Tony's nerves, and he didn't like what she had to say, but he had no choice but to believe her. One of his deepest fears was that Sarah—just like every other woman he had ever slept with over the years—didn't really like him, much less love him. Ever since he had first realized back in high school that he was quite good looking, and that girls were attracted to him, he had used his good looks to get whatever he wanted. Usually, at least for Tony, that meant sex without the added encumbrance of love. Over the years, it had become almost second nature for him to use women purely for his own sexual pleasure.

But his deep and abiding fear was that the joke was all on him.

All of them—every single woman he had ever screwed—had been doing the same thing to him.

Using him!

"She hasn't gotten fucked in a long time, you know," the little girl said, her voice high and taunting. "Not since she got divorced. And that's all you are for her—a good lay. She's gonna use you only for as long as she needs to, and then you're gonna be out the door on your ass like yesterday's trash."

"No, I... I don't think so," Tony whispered, shaking his head in denial. He craned forward, trying to see the little girl better, but her shadow kept shifting around the room, never standing still for very long. Her voice seemed to be coming from a great distance away and, simultaneously, so close he could almost feel the puff of her breath against his ear.

"Oh, she's using you, all right," the little girl said. "I know it because I know her. That's the way she is. She can't really help it, you know."

Tony cringed, realizing that this was one of the ways he had always justified his treatment of women. It was just the way he was.

"Oh, yeah?" he said shakily. "Well, even if she *is* using me, what's the harm? That's certainly no reason to—to *kill* her!"

Tony's chest was aching so badly he winced as he stared into the darkness. Realizing he'd been holding his breath, he let it out in a long, slow whistle.

"I know you'll do it," the little girl said, lowering her voice to a deep rumble, "because that's what it wants."

Tony opened his mouth, about to ask her what she meant by "it," but he suddenly stopped himself.

He knew the answer to that. He knew it as clearly as if she had already said the words.

The knife!

That's what the knife wants!

Tony uttered a low, tortured moan as he reached out, gripped the bed sheets with both hands, and balled them up in his fists. Cold sweat broke out like fine dew over his skin. A chill gripped his heart and quickly spread like poison throughout his body.

He had known this all along, but to hear someone else say it out loud filled him with an almost unbearable sense of apprehension, danger, and excitement.

Yes, excitement!

He *did* want to use the knife again.

He didn't stop to question who this little girl was or how she had gotten here or how she knew anything about the knife. On a deep, subconscious level, this all made sense.

"Yes," he whispered.

His eyes were wide open as he stared into the darkness until it started to throb with innumerable shifting figures that moved around him like wafting smoke. He could hear the faint rustle of their motion, like unseen wings in the night.

"Oh, you'll do it all right," the little girl said in a low, flat voice. "You'll do it because you don't really have any other choice in the matter, do you?" Tony tried to speak but couldn't. His lips felt like they were glued tight.

"*Do you?*" the little girl repeated, her voice as hard as iron.

Tony's heart was slamming like a trapped animal against the cage of his ribs. Trailing spirals of light exploded in front of his eyes, and he lost any sense of who he was, where he was or what was happening. The single clear thought in his mind was that he *had* the knife, and that he was going to *have* to use it… on Sarah.

"No, I… I don't have any choice," Tony replied, bowing his head submissively to the whispering darkness.

He's going w kill her! Don't you understand that? And he's going to do it right away!

That was the single, clearest thought David had as he walked along the dark desolation of Deering Avenue, away from the schoolhouse. No matter how hard he tried, he couldn't force that thought out of his mind.

The night sky was overcast and flickered with subtle energy as thin strings of lightning played like hot wires back and forth between the earth and clouds. Everything was lit up with blue flashes that left jagged traces of afterimages across David's vision. The distant, dull rumble of thunder shook the air, drowning out the dragging, scuffing sound of his footsteps that echoed from the empty buildings on either side of the street.

From out of the darkness all around him, he heard faint whisperings and deep hissing sounds that might have been the wind blowing through the alleyways... or something else.

David knew that it was dangerous, and maybe even foolhardy to be out alone at night in the Shadowlands, but he was so distraught that he no longer cared if anything happened to him.

He couldn't stop worrying about Sarah and the man who he was now convinced intended to kill her. The terrible thing was, he knew that there was *nothing* he could do to stop him.

He also couldn't stop thinking about the hard, cruel edge he had heard in Karen's voice when she insisted that her mother had to kill the man with the knife.

Karen's not herself... not anymore, anyway!

That thought filled David with the sharp bitterness of loss. He wished to God he could cry, if only to release the pent-up emotions that were building inside him, ripping him apart.

It was bad enough that five years ago he had to watch his daughter die in his arms. Now it seemed absolutely unimaginable that he could be losing her again, and in such a terrifying, horrible way.

She was losing—or had lost—the core of her humanity. It pained him to see that his daughter had become nothing more than an empty husk of the person she had been. Five years in the Shadowlands had drained away all of her gentle goodness, her sweetness, her bright sense of humor, and her love of life. Emotionally, she was as cold and rigid and empty as the corpse lying in her coffin on the hill in Riverside Cemetery.

Is that what's going to happen to me?

A tremor of despair ran through him at the thought.

The harsh cruelty of what Karen had said to him burned in his memory, weaving through his mind like an endless mantra.

She has to kill him! Don't you understand that? And she's got to do it right away!

He knew that if he didn't stop thinking about it, this would drive him insane before very long! The only way to stop it seemed to be if he could—somehow—warn Sarah about the danger that was stalking her.

But how do I do that? I've tried everything I can think of, and I've failed!

Once again, the teasing voice deep within his mind spoke, this time loud enough to startle him.

That's right, you HAVE failed! it whispered harshly. *So you might as well just give up!... You know, in the long run, that it's all useless, anyway! ... Everything's useless! ... Sarah's going to die. If not now, eventually Everyone you've ever known and loved is going to die, not that there were all that many people you could say you loved And in the end, none of this is going w make the slightest difference! ... All existence is an illusion that's going to fade away like a dream into eternal... Nothingness...*

David halted in his tracks and looked around, suddenly convinced that someone was close and speaking those words to him. He tensed as he scanned the shadows, but only in the corner of his eye could he detect even the slightest hint of motion within them. The weirdly lit street and flickering night sky seemed to waver and blur like heat mirages that were going to vanish at any instant.

"It... it may be that way," he whispered hoarsely, "but I at least have to try."

He cringed at the sound of his own voice, echoing in the night.

But why even try? the voice whispered. *You've done everything you can, and it won't do you a damned bit of good in the end, anyway! ... It's all just wasted effort! ... Wasted agony! ... You should give in to Oblivion now so it will all be over... You'll be gone, and with you goes all of your suffering...*

The void of darkness in the center of his soul seemed suddenly to open up like a hungry mouth inside him. A rush of chills raced through his corpus. He could feel himself being sucked closer to that cold, eternal embrace.

The voice is right. What good will it do for me or anyone else to resist? he thought.

Yes, that's absolutely right! said the hollow, rasping voice. *Just let go!... Let it all go!...*

David distantly realized that he was whimpering softly to himself. He closed his eyes and, with a deep, wrenching sob, covered his face with both hands and groaned. The feeling of his hands, pressed against his face, seemed strangely deadened.

Just let it all go! ... the voice rasped.

David's eyes were wide as he stared into the swelling darkness inside his hands. He was suddenly terrified, wondering if he had his eyes open or closed.

It didn't matter. The same eternal, black void was inside him and outside him, and it would never change.

He could feel himself being pulled inexorably into it.

"No," David whispered, his voice so faint it was almost lost inside his head.

Sudden, terrible panic seized him. He was vaguely aware that he was moving—either stepping backward or falling, but he had no sense of direction. He felt suddenly weightless... adrift in an eternal vacuum. He stretched out his arms in a vain attempt to orient himself, but he felt nothing and continued to tumble in freefall.

A strange-sounding wind was shrieking in his ears, and he had an internal sense of moving at a great speed. Strong, irresistible forces were tearing at him like cold, grasping hands, tossing him around. The darkness before him seemed impenetrable.

That's it! ... The ride of a lifetime! ... Just let go! the voice in his head wailed.

But then another, stronger voice—one that felt more centered inside him—suddenly spoke up.

No! ... You can't let go!... You can't give up!

David had the brief mental image that his corpus was nothing more than a piece of cork that had been held under water and now had suddenly been let go to pop up to the surface. Powerful waves of nausea gripped him as he struggled to clear his mind and force the chattering voice inside him to shut up.

I'm still me! That single, simple thought resounded like a cannon shot inside his mind. *I'm still me, and I can't give up! Not when Sarah and Karen still need me!*

He let loose a wild, warbling scream that seemed to originate in the soles of his feet. It tore through the night like a silver blade slashing through a sheer curtain.

The darkness in front of him coalesced into a dim, oval shape that was framed by the swirling glow of the night sky. White lines of lighting danced among the clouds.

With a jolt, David realized that he was flat on his back, looking up into the darkness inside the hood of the Ferryman. He couldn't see a trace of the Ferryman's features, but he could feel his eyes boring into him like heated pokers.

"You're strong," the Ferryman said. His voice was deep and resonant, and David found it somehow reassuring. "I knew you wouldn't give in that easily to the temptations of your shadow."

"My... shadow?"

David listened to himself talk as if he were someone else.

"You're new here, and there are many things you don't know," the Ferryman continued. "But you do seem to have a strong sense of yourself. That's good. Ultimately, it can only help."

David was feeling much too drained to reply—worse, even, than when the reaper had clamped Stygian chains on his arms and legs. The Ferryman leaned over him with one hand extended. David felt a numbing touch brush against his forehead.

"But he—he's going to... to kill her," David finally managed to say. It took an immense effort to think clearly, much less speak. "He's going to use that knife on her. I know he is, and there's nothing I can do to stop him!"

A low, chuffing sound like twisted laughter filled the night.

"Oh, there are things you can do," the Ferryman said in a deep, sonorous voice. "You have more abilities than you realize."

David still found it almost impossible to focus his thoughts. The sheer terror of what had just happened to him was too much to contemplate.

"You... you told me that there were skills, certain powers that I could use co... to help me," he said. "Can you teach them to me? Right now?"

For several seconds, the hooded figure remained perfectly immobile. Then, slowly, the Ferryman shook his head from side to side. The coarse cloth of his hood made a low rustling sound that seemed oddly magnified in the stillness of the night.

"I'm afraid I can't do that," the Ferryman replied after a long moment.

"Why the hell not?" David shouted, unable any longer to contain his agitation and anger. "My wife's in serious trouble. I know what I have to do to save her, but I—I can't unless you help me."

"You've already done what you can," the Ferryman said. "The best you can do is to keep trying, and see what happens. You haven't even begun to learn the basic skills of skin riding, much less puppetry, embodying, or keening. But even so, without knowing any of these skills, you *have* gotten through to her. You've contacted her."

"How? I've been watching her, but I've never seen her do anything that would indicate that I'm getting through to her. Besides trying to speak to her, the only thing I could think to do was try to manipulate the computer to type her a message. But it didn't work. Something messed it up."

"There is a skill we call Phantasm," the Ferryman said. "It's the ability a wraith can develop—with effort—to influence a mortal's dreams. I know for a fact that you invaded her dreams and brought her sleeping soul here to the Shadowlands"

Frowning, David shook his head in firm denial.

"I never did," he said, feeling almost overwhelmed by confusion and doubt. "I don't have any idea what you're talking about."

"She was here," the Ferryman replied in a solemn voice. "I saw her with you and the wraith that looks like your daughter."

"No, you have to be mistaken," David said, unable to shut off the sudden rush of discomforting thoughts that flooded his mind. "I was never—"

"Well, it was either you or else that other wraith who brought her here," the Ferryman said.

"What, do you mean Karen?"

A deep chill ran through David when he pictured the cold, blank expression on his daughter's face. A desperate yearning filled him.

"No. That's not your daughter," the Ferryman replied.

His voice resonated with a deep echo. For several seconds, David stared at the Ferryman, wishing and hoping that he hadn't heard him correctly. When David was finally able to speak, his voice was so weak he could hardly hear himself.

"What do you mean?"

"That wraith—it's not Karen," the Ferryman replied simply. "Your daughter was here a long while ago. I remember seeing her, but she hasn't been in the Shadowlands for... I can't remember how long. It's been a very long time. As I recall, she disappeared not long after she first showed up here."

"What the hell are you—That's impossible! I've seen her! I've spoken with her! Don't you think I'd recognize my own daughter?"

Anger surged inside David like an electrical overload, but he also felt a sharp edge of panic because, on some deep level, he knew that the Ferryman was right.

Karen hadn't been acting like herself because she *wasn't* herself!

"I saw him take her into the Tempest himself," the Ferryman said.

"Someone took her? Who? Where did he take her?"

The Ferryman shook his head slowly, making the cloth of his hood rustle with a harsh, scraping sound.

"A reaper working for the Hierarchy took your daughter," the Ferryman said. "He has… many names, but none of them would mean anything to you. There is one way you can recognize him, though. He walks with a limp."

"A limp… ?"

David heard his own voice as no more than a faint echo of the Ferryman.

"Yes, a limp. He has a bad left leg that makes him walk with a limp, at least whenever he's in his true form. I would guess that he's using the skill of imitation to appear to you in the form of your daughter. I wouldn't be surprised if he has your daughter imprisoned in his haunt. Perhaps it's somewhere inside the Tempest."

"Can you help me? Can you take me there?"

"I already told you," the Ferryman said. "You'll have to find her on your own. After that—" He shrugged and shook his head slowly.

"After that, I'll do whatever I can to help both of you."

the deception ends.

Chapter Twelve

Even though she thought she was ready for it, the sound of the gun going off six times in rapid succession made Sarah jump. She was glad that she was wearing protectors that deadened the sound at least enough so it didn't hurt her ears.

She glanced over at the man with close-cropped hair who was standing on the firing line. His name was Sy Warner. He was wearing black wraparound sunglasses, a tight-fitting, dark blue T-shirt tucked into the top of his dark jeans, and black sneakers. He had the body of a weightlifter. His thick, tanned arms rippled with knotted muscles and pencil-thick veins. His stomach was as flat and ridged as a washboard. Sarah thought the dark-colored ear protectors he wore made him look a bit like a comical, muscle-bound mouse.

A thin ribbon of blue smoke curled from the muzzle of his gun as he slowly lowered it and leaned forward to study the target. He glanced over his shoulder at Sarah, cocked a smile, and nodded with satisfaction.

About a hundred feet in front of him, backed by the scooped-out wall of a sand pit, the paper target of a life-sized human torso dangled from a thin, metal wire. Six holes—each of them the size of a quarter—peppered the inner white circle that marked the center of the figure's chest. The paper made a faint crinkling sound as it rustled in the hot, light breeze.

Sarah had found Sy's North Windham firing range listed in the Nynex Yellow Pages and had called him earlier that morning to ask about taking some shooting lessons. She couldn't help but wonder how he could stand to wear all those dark clothes in such heat, but he didn't seem to mind. Only a few small drops of sweat dotted his smooth forehead.

He was smiling with self-satisfaction as he reloaded his gun, then placed it down on the wooden stand next to him. Inhaling sharply, he turned to face Sarah directly.

"So, you're sure you want to learn how to handle a gun, huh?" he said, giving her a tight, lopsided grin that made her think that he found all of this slightly amusing.

"Uh-yeah," Sarah said, realizing that she didn't sound at all confident as she took off the ear protectors so she could hear him better.

"Did you bring your piece with you?"

For a second, Sarah had no idea what he meant. Then she got it and, nodding nervously, swung her purse off her shoulder, zipped it open, and withdrew David's revolver. She picked up the gun gingerly by the trigger guard, holding it with her thumb and forefinger like it was a dead fish.

Sy chuckled.

"It's always a good idea to show respect for your weapon, but it ain't a danged rattlesnake. It ain't gonna bite you unless you get on the wrong end of it."

Flustered, Sarah sputtered an apology as she handed the gun to him, being careful to keep it pointed away from both of them.

Sy slid his sunglasses up over his forehead where the short bristles of his sun-bleached hair held them in place. His mouth was a thin, colorless line, and his pale eyes glinted like silver coins in the sunlight as he inspected the gun carefully.

"This here's a .32 Smith and Wesson," he said, barely glancing up at her as he turned the gun over several times in his hand. With a quick flick of his wrist, he raised the gun and sighted down the firing line at the perforated paper figure.

"Not a bad little piece, either. Used to be real popular with the mob, even though it does lack a bit in stopping power."

"Stopping power?"

Sy looked at Sarah with a trace of humor flashing in his eyes.

"Yeah. Power enough to stop a man. You said on the phone this morning that you wanted to learn how to handle a gun for your self-protection, right?"

"That's right," Sarah said, nodding again and feeling like a complete idiot.

"Well, if that's what you want, I would think it'd make sense to get a gun that could really stop someone if you were being attacked, wouldn't it?"

"Yeah, I... guess so," Sarah said, nodding tightly.

Her stomach felt as hollow as a drum. It churned with sour acid at the thought of learning how to handle David's gun just so she could actually *kill* someone with it if she had to.

"Did you buy this?" Sy asked.

Biting her lower lip, Sarah shook her head quickly.

"No, it was—it belongs to my husband. My ex-husband. I just thought, since I'm living alone now, I ought to learn how to use it."

"I see. Mrs.—ah, Robinson, is it?"

Again, Sarah nodded.

"Call me Sarah."

"Sure thing—Sarah. Let me ask you straight out: Are you sure you want to go through with this?"

"I'm sure," Sarah replied, but—not for the first time—she wondered if this was such a great idea. If she was going to back out, now was the time.

But something—she wasn't quite sure what it was—told her to stay. For one thing, although she had no reason to believe that she really was in any kind of danger, she thought that she'd feel more secure, knowing at least the basics of how to handle a gun. Sure, she'd been feeling nervous and uptight lately, and she was convinced it wasn't just because she was edgy following David's death. Although Portland, Maine, wasn't exactly New York City or Chicago, it had its share of street crime. It made sense to have some protection—at least at home, where someone might break into the house at night or something.

"You ever fire a gun before, Mrs. Robinson?" Sy asked, frowning seriously.

The cold pit in Sarah's stomach got worse as she shook her head and said, "Not really."

"Not really," Sy echoed with a half-smile. "Well, you either have or you haven't."

"No, I haven't."

"Lemme tell you something, Mrs. Robinson—"

"Sarah."

"Right. Sarah. The most important thing is that you should never forget that what you're doing here is learning how to kill someone if you have co. There's a big difference—a whole world of difference—between shooting at a paper target like that one and plugging a couple of holes in a living, breathing human being. You shoot at someone, you shoot to kill. Don't you ever forget that, all right?"

All Sarah could do was nod.

"Well, then," Sy said, "there's really not much to it. Here. Lemme give you a couple of pointers first—a few safety tips."

Sarah watched, amazed at how dexterous Sy's thick hands were as he unloaded the bullets from her gun. He passed one of them to her so she could inspect it.

"This is a .32 caliber. Probably eighty-eight grains or so. You can pick up a box of chem at any hardware or sporting goods store. Shouldn't cost you more than ten, fifteen bucks tops for a box of fifty. More than you'll ever need. Just make sure you get the ones for pistols, not rifles. They're a little different."

Sarah nodded her understanding.

"Loading's pretty quick and easy, too," Sy said. "All you do is pop both 'em in here like this."

He slid the six bullets back into the chamber and snapped it shut.

"Contrary to what you might have read in detective novels or whatever, all American revolvers made in this century don't have safety catches, so once this baby's loaded, she's ready to fire."

Sarah found it curious that he referred to the gun as *she* and *baby*.

Being careful to keep the gun pointed away from him, he handed the gun back to Sarah.

"Watch me, first," Sy said.

Picking up his oversized revolver that looked like a cannon compared to Sarah's, Sy quickly reloaded it while giving Sarah a quick run-down on the parts of a gun, the correct way to hold it, the proper stance and posture, and other safety pointers.

When he was done, he slid his ear protectors back on, dropped his sunglasses over his eyes, took a calm, steady aim at the paper target and snapped off six quick shots. Again, Sarah jumped at the sudden report of the gun, but she found herself fascinated as she watched six more holes appear in the center of the human torso.

Moving back, Sy indicated that it was her turn to seep up to the firing line.

"Go ahead and give it a try," he said, shifting behind her. "It's gonna kick a little. Not much, but you have to get a feel for it."

Sarah couldn't stop the cold trembling inside, but her hands were surprisingly steady as she picked up the gun and hefted it. It didn't seem quite so heavy in her hand now. Maybe because it was less threatening, she thought.

"Take aim carefully now," Sy said. "Yeah, that's it."

He moved up close behind her—dose enough for her to catch a strong whiff of his aftershave. Reaching around both sides of her, he steadied her hands until she felt as though she had a good grip. The hard knots of his arm muscles pressed tightly against her arms in an awkward embrace.

"That's it," Sy said. His warm breath blew softly into her ear. "Nice and easy, now. Brace yourself. Steady both hands. Yeah, that's it."

Sarah held her breath as she drew a bead on the paper target.

"Now the most important thing to remember is to *squeeze* the trigger gently," Sy said. "Don't jerk back on it. You do that, and you'll mess up your aim. So squeeze it nice and steady. Go on."

Sarah was feeling all fluttery inside as she sighted down the barrel at the target. She tried to forget about the man standing so close behind her as she squinted her left eye and aimed.

When she let herself realize that she was aiming at the outline of a human being, and that a target had been drawn in the center of its chest, the reality of what she was doing suddenly hie her. A wave of emotion swept through her. Her body started to tremble, and she almost backed down.

"Steady now," Sy said, pressing close against her from behind.

For an instant, Sarah's vision blurred as she recalled last night's dream that she was aiming a gun—not just at Karen and David, but at Tony as well.

Her legs went all rubbery when she remembered pulling the trigger in her dream and shooting first Karen then David, who somehow shifted into an image of Tony before he fell. In her mind, she saw the black hole that had suddenly appeared in the middle of Tony's forehead.

Shaking her head and gritting her teeth, Sarah forced herself to focus as she stared down the line at the paper target wafting gently in the breeze. The blasting heat of the sun rebounded from the ground and danced in wavering lines that distorted her view. For a dizzying instant, Sarah thought she saw a person's face appear in the center of the target. She didn't quite have time to register whether she recognized the features before her finger twitched back and the gun kicked hard in her hands.

The recoil brought her hands up, but she quickly dropped them, adjusted her aim as she exhaled, sucked in and held another breath, and then squeezed the trigger again... and again.

By the fourth shot, the sound of the gun going off wasn't quite so scary.

It almost felt good.

Sarah kept focusing intently on the center of the figure's chest, watching as holes seemed to appear in the paper like magic. Little puffs of dirt jumped into the air behind the target.

It's just paper! she told herself. *This isn't like shooting a real person!*

She was trying to ignore the suggestion of a human face that was superimposed over the paper figure's head; but before she could stop herself, she shifted her focus up and gasped when she clearly saw what looked like Tony Ranieri's features on the target. For an instant, the face on the target took on dimension. Tony seemed to be staring straight at her with wide open, unblinking eyes. His mouth was twisted as if he were laughing at her.

Without even thinking about it, Sarah raised the gun and aimed at the target's forehead. She quickly squeezed off two more shots. With the first shot, a clean, thumb-sized hole appeared dead center in the figure's forehead. The second shot rang out before the echo of the first one had died away, but Sarah couldn't see where—or if—it hit the target.

Realizing that she had been holding her breath, she exhaled noisily as she lowered the gun. Her chest was aching as though she had just been underwater for a little too long. Sweat sprinkled her forehead and was running from her armpits down the inside of her blouse.

Sy cocked one eyebrow as he stepped in front of her and smiled. Stroking his chin, he glanced over his shoulder at the target.

"And you say you've never shot a gun before in your life?" he said.

Sarah took a quick, deep breath and giggled as she shook her head.

"Nope. Never."

"Well, then, I'd have to say you're one helluva natural shooter." Sy nodded his head in appreciation. "You cracked off six shots, and at least five of 'em hit in clean kill zones."

"Kill zones," Sarah echoed.

"Not many people can do that their first time out," Sy said.

"Really," Sarah replied.

She wasn't sure how she was feeling.

It was exhilarating to realize that she had done something she had always despised. And she had done it well.

It also bothered her that here she was, actually feeling a sense of accomplishment for hitting "kill zones" with at least five out of six shots.

"Yeah, really," Sy said." And I'll bee you five to one that last shot of yours went right through the first hole you made in the forehead. As far as I could see, your gun never wavered a damned millimeter. I swear to God, Sarah, you're a regular Annie Oakley."

Sarah shrugged and gave him a tight smile.

"Thanks." Suddenly stiffening, she glanced at her wristwatch and saw the time. "Well, that's probably enough for today," she said shakily. "I–I've got to be at work in less than an hour."

The overcast sky cleared sometime coward morning, but to David the sky above Portland still looked all wrong. Sickly yellow and dull brown light shimmered above the city, casting a muddy, unearthly glow over everything. Distant buildings and trees wavered like mirages in the unearthly haze.

As David walked slowly down the street, heading back to the schoolhouse, his footsteps scuffed loudly on the asphalt, sounding like matches being struck. Although he still had only the slightest sensation of feeling, he could imagine just by looking around how hot the day must be. He was suddenly filled with longing as he remembered how much he missed being able to touch and feel things as simple as the warmth of the sun on his face.

Worse than that, though, was his dread about what he might find when he got back to Pine Knoll Elementary. He held out a slim hope that the Ferryman had been wrong about the wraith who was masquerading as Karen.

What had he called it? A reaper working for the Hierarchy? David wasn't sure what that meant, but it didn't sound very good.

Whatever the case, he was positive that Karen—or the wraith that had assumed her shape—would be gone by the time he got back.

That would be hard enough to deal with, he thought, but worse than that was the possibility that she might not be gone. David seriously doubted that he would have the courage to confront it if that ching was still there.

All he knew for certain was that he wouldn't be able to pretend. He'd had his doubts about Karen before this, but now he was absolutely convinced that something was wrong with her.

He had no idea why the reaper with the limp—or any other wraith, for that matter—would go to all this trouble to assume the shape of his dead daughter.

Was it just to try to fool him?

Try to fool him? David thought, feeling a wave of self-loathing. No, he'd been fooled, all right.

But not any more!

He wasn't sure why he trusted anything the Ferryman said, but it seemed as if the Ferryman was the only person in the Shadowlands willing at least to hint to him as to what was going on. There still was so much for him to learn about existence here, and David had the distinct impression that there was a whole lot more beyond the Shadowlands.

He dreaded every possible scenario he could think of, but worse than all of that—much worse—was the terrible ache of despair and loss he felt because he knew, now, that Karen was lost to him.

Forever... whispered the voice deep inside his mind.

And this loss was more immediate because it threatened even the most remote possibilities or hope he might have had regarding the afterlife. It seemed as though the pain he felt was much sharper and cut much deeper even than when he had lost his daughter five years ago.

Dark despair gripped him, making the walk back to the schoolhouse seem to take forever. With nearly every trudging step, he found himself looking skyward and silently praying that Karen wouldn't be there when he got back. He began to think that, even if this truly were his daughter, he *wanted* her to be gone.

He wanted to be alone with his misery.

Ultimately, it didn't really matter whether or not she was Karen or an impostor. He could feel that he was losing touch with himself. Without the sharp sensory input he'd had when living, he felt as though he were gradually fading away even from this shadowy existence. He couldn't bear the agony of knowing that he was never going to be able to really *feel* his daughter as he held her in his arms. Never again would he be able to comfort her as he had when she was a baby... when they were alive.

His daughter, his baby girl, was dead and gone!

No matter how he looked at it, she was lost to him *forever*, and he was positive that he couldn't stand any more pain or suffering. So if she *was* truly gone, then maybe he should do here, in the Shadowlands, what he had been trying to do but hadn't quite had the courage to follow through with when he was alive. Even though he was already dead, maybe he should truly end his miserable existence.

He knew he could do it.

All he had to do was listen to that dark voice that seemed to be continually whispering inside his mind, telling him how futile all existence was. He would let that voice carry him away and drag him down into total Oblivion.

Isn't that what he had wanted all along?

He would willingly let himself dissolve into Nothingness because at least that way, even though he would lose every shred of his personal identity, the pain and suffering would — finally — be over.

Forever! whispered the voice deep inside his mind.

But this time, David listened to it and nodded his submission. He would go back to the schoolhouse, settle himself in the darkness, and then let this voice carry him away until he finally ceased to exist.

What he *wasn't* ready for was the one thing that he hadn't even considered.

When he got back to the schoolhouse and entered its shadowed, echoing hallway, he was greeted by a voice from the dark that he instantly recognized.

"So, you've finally come back, eh?"

It was too dark inside the schoolhouse to see anything more than a dim silhouette, but David knew immediately that this was the wraith who walked with a limp.

"What the hell do you want?" David shouted as blinding rage gripped him.

"What do *I* want?" the wraith asked. This was followed by a short burst of deep, cackling laughter. "What I *want* is something that I needed help to get. And now, thanks to you, I just might get it."

"Where's my daughter?" David shouted, his voice reverberating with a high, keening wail. "What have you done with her?"

"Done with her?" the wraith replied. He sounded mystified and almost a little insulted by David's outburst. "Why, I've done *nothing* with her. She's right where I left her—in a place *you* will never find! Let's say she's my... my insurance policy to make sure you don't do anything stupid, like try to stop me from finally gaining possession of that knife."

"Haven't you done enough to me already?" David shouted. "I don't give a shit what you want! I just want to see my daughter again! My *real* daughter! "Oh, maybe you will... in due time," the wraith said, its voice almost breaking up with laughter. "But then again, maybe not."

A sudden, blinding rush of anger filled David. He clenched his fists so tightly his hands started to tingle with hoc, throbbing pressure. The hatred raging inside him coalesced into raw, passionate power that made him feel as though he were going to explode. His view of the dark room seemed to be clearing, making it look as though he were seeing the world through a thick, red lens. A deep, resonating vibration spread up his arms and took hold of him. A scream was building inside his chest as he lunged forward at the wraith. He took a single threatening step forward.

"I wouldn't do that if I were you," the wraith said.

He sounded almost casual, but there was an edge of command in his voice that stopped David cold in his tracks.

"Do you really want to spend the rest of eternity—at least eternity as *you* perceive it—a prisoner, locked up in chains?" the wraith asked. "Or perhaps you'd rather I brought you to the smiths and had your corpus forged into Stygian steel. Is that what you want? Your body would be gone, but your spirit, your essence, would still remain, and it would be aware. Oh, yes. Even though you would no longer have a mouth, you would spend the rest of eternity wailing in agony. They say if you listen closely you can hear the screams inside the metal."

"All I want is my *daughter* back!"

David's voice rang with a high, warbling echo throughout the dark building. From somewhere upon the second floor, there came in reply a faint ruffle of laughter.

"Didn't you listen to what I just told you?" the wraith said teasingly. "I'm keeping her where you will never find her. Don't even try to find her. It won't do you any good. I tried to warn you about associating with the Ferrymen. They're dangerous, you know. You can never trust them."

"And I'm supposed to trust you?" David snapped.

He cringed inwardly because he wanted to say or do something to hurt this wraith, but he was too paralyzed by the emotions that gripped him.

"Oh, yes. I have her. The Ferryman knows that. Wouldn't you think, if he knows where she is, that he'd be willing to take you there? That he'd offer to help you?"

"I just want to see her. That's all I ask," David pleaded.

The wraith clicked its tongue as he shook his head from side to side.

"I wish I could feel even a trace of pity for you," he said. "I really do, but that's one thing I never was very good at—feeling pity."

"*Please*," David said. He felt like his insides were being torn into tiny shreds. "I *beg* you. Tell me where she is. Take me to her. That's the least you could do."

The darkness of the room suddenly swelled with the sound of the wraith's twisted laughter.

"What? You mean you want to join her? Why, how noble of you! How-how downright *fatherly!* What a marvelous display of parental love and devotion."

The wraith's laughter rose to a high, keening edge.

"Perhaps you'd even be willing to take her place in my haunt. Is that what you're thinking? Or maybe you want to suffer right there *with* her. I hadn't thought of that. Maybe that would be fun to watch."

"Anything! Just bring me to her! Please!"

"I probably should do just that," the wraith said, sounding almost sympathetic, "but you know what? Even though you've done me a great favor, something for which I'll never truly be able to repay you, I don't think I can do it."

David's fury almost exploded out of him, but he suddenly felt too drained even to stay standing on his feet, much less confront this creature. As surely as if he were being weighed down by Stygian chains, he could feel his strength seeping out of him like air escaping from a punctured tire.

"I'm not an evil being," the wraith said. "Really, I'm not, but I do have to admit that I'm rather enjoying all of this. Working together, you and I, we've set things in motion—momentous things. And I'm sure that very soon, now, I'll be able to get that knife."

"You're doing all of this for a simple knife!" David said, his voice rasping as he trembled with impotent rage.

"Oh, it's not any *ordinary* knife, believe me. This knife is one of three that I've been seeking for a long time. And now—finally—one of them is within my grasp."

"So why don't you just take it and leave my daughter and me alone?"

Waves of exhaustion were sweeping over David, dragging him under. He couldn't help but think the wraith was weakening him somehow. Some kind of unseen magic was draining his strength.

"Look, I'm glad I could help you get it, all right?" David said weakly. "Now maybe you could do me a favor, too. It's not too much to ask, is it?"

"Not really," the wraith said, sounding so condescending it was almost insulting. "But it's just not that easy. And the thing is, if I wanted to cause you *real* suffering, the worst kind of suffering you could *ever* experience in your entire, pathetic existence, all I have to do is… nothing."

Nothing…

The word reverberated inside the schoolhouse and inside David's head with an odd flutter that sounded like wings unseen in the darkness, beating close to his ears.

"Don't you see it? That's the pure beauty of it all," the wraith said, stifling his laughter. "What we have here is a classic approach-avoidance situation. There's someone you love who's still alive, and someone you love who's dead, and there's not a damned thing you can do to help either one of chem. You have to *love* it!"

He's absolutely right, you know, the voice inside David's head whispered harshly. *Haven't I been telling you this all along?… There's no goddamned point in even trying!*

"Then at least let me die."

David wasn't sure if he said this out loud or not. Ultimately, it didn't matter. He knew that the only thing left for him to do was to extinguish himself. He could feel his soul—his life force—whatever the hell he wanted to call it—fading away like a candle that sputtered as it burned itself out.

And that's all he wanted now.

Absolutely drained of all energy and will, David sighed heavily and let himself slump to the hard floor.

"*Die?*" the wraith said.

That single word seemed to resonate in the darkness as though repeated by dozens of other voices.

"You're already dead. What else could happen to you?"

"Okay, fine... You win then," David said, listening to his own voice like it was an oddly detached whisper from the surrounding darkness.

Unable even to sit up straight, he slumped to one side and moaned softly as he watched the wraith turn away from him and, dragging his left foot behind him, start for the door. The wraith's body looked almost transparent as he stepped out into the murky haze of daylight and then, like wind-blown smoke, was gone.

It wasn't until long after the wraith had left, and David realized that he was sobbing softly to himself as he leaned against the wall with his legs drawn up tightly against his chest, that David thought of something.

It wasn't much, but it did give him a slim measure of hope.

He walks with a limp! A subtle rush of excitement filled him at the thought.

So if he walks with a limp, that must mean he's been injured *somehow!*

The rushes of excitement he felt got increasingly stronger as David mulled this over and finally realized something that should have been blatantly obvious—so obvious it was almost ridiculous that he had missed it before now.

If he's been injured once before... even if he carried his injury with him over into death... that must mean that—somehow— he can be hurt!

Long before she was certain of it, Sarah sensed—at least subconsciously—that she was being followed. She was feeling a curious mixture of nervousness and exhilaration when she got into her car and drove away from Sy Warner's firing range, heading back to Portland.

Her first stop was her house, where she quickly showered after hiding David's revolver in the drawer of her bedside stand. Once she was dressed and ready for work, she went outside and walked around the house a few times, all the while calling for Bingley.

She wasn't really surprised when he didn't show up. A lonely ache filled her when she acknowledged that this had to be it. He was either dead or lying injured somewhere, and she was probably never going to see him again. Just in case he did come back while she was gone, she put a bowl of food out on the porch and took one last quick walk around the house, clicking her tongue and calling for him.

When she got to the back steps that led up onto the porch, she stopped short in her tracks. She caught a whiff of something nearby that smelled *terrible!*

She sniffed the humid air and started looking around more carefully. That's when she noticed the high buzzing sound of flies that seemed to be coming from underneath the back porch seeps.

Sarah's heart was pounding hard and fast in her throat as she knelt down on the grass. Bracing herself with one hand on the ground and the other on edge of the stairs, she leaned forward and stared into the cool darkness underneath the steps.

It took a moment for her eyes to adjust to the darkness, but after another moment or two, she saw... something.

A dark, formless lump.

At first she had no idea what it was. It didn't look like anything that had ever been alive, but buzzing flies were circling around it, and it appeared to be seething with a mass of crawling, gray maggots. Sarah's first impression was that someone had spilled an order of fried rice underneath her porch, and it had magically come to life.

It didn't take long for the raw, putrid smell to get to her. Choking down a stomach-tightening wave of nausea, she leaned back on her heels and took a huge gulp of fresh air as she stared up at the heat-hazed sky and tried to collect herself.

She cried desperately to stop thinking what she was thinking. She didn't want to believe it.

It *couldn't* be true, but that rotting, smelly thing *had* to be the one thing she was afraid it was.

What else could it be?

"Oh, Jesus. Oh, no," Sarah whispered.

Another, stronger wave of nausea gripped her. When she burped, her throat and mouth were filled with a sickly, sour taste. A razor-sharp chill of grief filled her chest. Tears began to flood her eyes, blurring her vision. No matter how hard she tried, she couldn't seem to take a deep enough breath. The rotting smell clung to the back of her throat like the stench of burned hair.

There was nothing more she could do.

Sarah's knees popped as she stood up slowly and then, moving like an automaton, walked over to the garage. She went inside, grabbed a shovel, then came back outside. Her legs almost gave out on her as she walked over to the porch. Holding her breath, she go down on her hands and knees and reached into the darkness with the shovel. The flies buzzed angrily, and the putrid smell got so bad she started to dry heave, but she kept at it, working the blade of the shovel under the shapeless lump. Once she had it, she dragged it out into the daylight.

For one, brief instant, hope rekindled inside her. How could this… this terrible *mess* be what she feared it was?

The carcass of dark, rotting flesh and exposed bones was already more than half decomposed. Although it definitely was *some* kind of animal, it looked like a large rat or maybe a gopher, Sarah thought. She could distinguish the animal's head and legs and feet. Two round, bulging, bloodshot eyeballs that stared almost funnily in two different directions glistened like wet bone in the daylight.

The animal—whatever it was—didn't have any fur that Sarah could see, except for on its thin, crooked legs. The rest of the carcass looked like stripped, raw meat. Bones stuck out through the rotting flesh, and there was a black, tangled mass hanging like a pouch from underneath its stomach.

No! This can't be Bingley! It's too small!

But even as Sarah was thinking this, she saw something that made her heart skip a beat or two. Around the animal's scrawny neck was a thin green and black plaid strap.

Bingley's collar!

Trembling wildly, Sarah screamed and dropped the shovel to the ground as she spun around on one foot, dropped to her knees and vomited her breakfast onto the grass. Wave after wave of nausea squeezed her stomach, and her eyes burned with tears as she continued to retch long after her stomach was empty.

It took her several minutes to compose herself. Finally, feeling drained and dizzy, she stood up and commanded herself to stay in control; but seeing what she had feared to be true was too much to handle. Bright, trailing pinpoints of light squiggled like flying sparks across her vision. She felt all feverish and shaky as she picked up the shovel and walked over to the corner of her yard behind the garage, where she dug a shallow hole.

She had to avert her eyes when she went back to the porch and scooped up what was left of Bingley. The flies came along with her as she transported his body to the hole. She cried to shake off the maggots that were crawling all over him, but she knew it was a waste of time. They or something else was going to eat him up as soon as she got him buried. She tried to stop thinking that pretty much the same thing was happening to her ex-husband and her daughter out at Riverside Cemetery.

She hurriedly scooped dirt over Bingley's body and camped it down with the back of the shovel blade. By the time she was finished, she was dripping with sweat. She thought it might be a good idea to go back into the house and take another shower, but she had an errand to run before she went to work.

Leaning on the handle of the shovel, she stared at the small mound of brown dirt that covered Bingley. It looked pitifully small and insignificant. Tears gushed from her eyes as she tried to register that it was really Bingley buried there. Every time she swallowed, she could taste the lingering sourness of vomit.

"I... I'm really sorry, Bing," she said, her voice halting and broken.

Shaking her head sadly, she turned and walked away. She leaned the shovel against the side of the garage, telling herself that she'd have to hose it down before she put it back on the tool rack in the garage. Still crying, she got into her car and started it up, making sure to turn the air conditioner on high before backing out into the street. Tears blurred her vision as she drove away, but she kept telling herself that she shouldn't cry now.

She *couldn't* cry now.

She had cried too much lately. She was all out of tears.

The air conditioner quickly cut the heat in the car as she drove to the Trustworthy Hardware store over on Warren Avenue. Her hair and cloches were damp with sweat, and her eyes were red and raw when she walked into the air conditioned store. She couldn't help but wonder what the salesclerk must be thinking when she asked for a box of .32 caliber bullets. Her hands were clammy, and her insides were all knotted up as she paid for them, but the clerk seemed hardly to notice, much less care what she looked like or what she was buying. He took her money, slid the box of bullets into a bag, handed it to her and barely got off a curt "Thank you" before turning away.

Once she was back in her car, Sarah folded the top of the paper bag down tightly around the box of bullets and slipped it under the front seat before driving our to the university.

When she parked her car in the Bailey Hall parking lot on the Gorham campus, she worried that the hammering summer heat in the closed car might make the bullets explode. Hoping that she was just being overly cautious, she got out, made sure the windows were rolled up and the car doors were locked and then walked up to the library.

Elizabeth, Sarah's boss, seemed surprised to see her. She commented that she thought Sarah looked pale, and asked her if she felt well enough to work. Sarah told her that she not only felt like it, she *had* to work, if only to have one thing in her life that was somewhat normal and stable.

"You know, I had your computer checked out, and everything seems just fine with it," Elizabeth said. "I can't figure out what happened yesterday."

"Must've been a fluke or something, I guess," Sarah said with a shrug. "Maybe the humidity or something got to it."

She wanted to appear unconcerned, but throughout the day she could never quite get rid of the creepy feeling that she was being watched. She tried to concentrate on whatever jobs she was doing; but rime and again, she found herself looking around as though expecting to see a shadowy figure lurking nearby, watching her.

It wasn't until later that afternoon, around six o'clock, when she was driving home from work, that she finally became convinced that she was being followed. As soon as she drove out of the parking lot onto College Avenue, a car she didn't recognize—a light blue Toyota—pulled up close behind her. Sunlight glared from the windshield, so she couldn't see the driver clearly; but she thought she caught a glimpse of a heavy-set man wearing sunglasses.

She couldn't be sure, but her first impression was that maybe it was Sy Warner. Maybe he had taken a little more that a casual interest in her. She tried but couldn't deny the stirring of attraction she'd felt when he stood close behind her to help her aim her gun. She recalled feeling both threatened and comforted, thinking about how his powerful arms could have crushed her with only the slightest bit of effort. She didn't remember seeing a blue Toyota out at his place, but that didn't mean anything.

Her pulse was trip-hammering in her chest and neck, and she had trouble focusing on the road as she drove. She started to worry about having left the gun back at her house, and wondered if she would have felt any safer knowing it was in her purse, loaded and within easy reach.

Calm down... Jesus, you're just overreacting! she told herself, but she couldn't stop glancing at her rearview mirror, watching tensely as the blue Toyota kept pace behind her.

At the traffic light in the center of Gorham, she turned left onto Route 25 and proceeded slowly through the small downtown area. At the fork in the road just past a Mobile station, she veered to the right onto the New Gorham Road. Sure enough, the blue Toyota turned that way, too, dropping back several car-lengths behind her.

"Jesus, it's nothing," Sarah whispered to herself, but her fear spiked every time she glanced at the rearview mirror and saw the reflection of her eyes there. She looked scared to herself, and that only made her think all the more that, whoever this was, he was following her on purpose.

This stretch of road was notorious for its speed traps, so Sarah kept checking her speedometer to make sure she was staying under the speed limit. It seemed as though every time she sped up, the Toyota would speed up. Whenever she slowed down, the Toyota would slow down. And no matter how slow she drove, the driver behind her held back, never getting close enough so she could see who it was.

Even with the air conditioning running at full speed, the car was stuffy and hot. Sarah found it difficult to take deep enough breaths. She felt a slight measure of relief when, up ahead, she saw the wide parking area for Corsetti's, a small "mom and pop" store. Without bothering to use her blinker, and barely slowing down for the turn, she waited until she was almost in front of the parking lot before jerking the steering wheel hard to the right. Her tires skidded on the dirt-covered asphalt as she finished the turn and pulled to a jolting stop between a parked van and a large Pepsi truck.

"You *bastard!*" Sarah hissed as she cocked her right arm over the back of the seat and watched as the Toyota sped past. Its brake lights flickered once quickly, and then the car passed by like a whisper.

Sarah realized that she was breathing much too fast and consciously made herself slow down. Once she was sure that the car had driven on by and probably wasn't coming back, she sagged forward and rested her forehead on the padded steering wheel. Gripping her head with both hands, she closed her eyes for a moment and waited as the watery rushing sound in her ears gradually subsided.

After she was feeling marginally better, she got out of the car and walked on shaky legs into the store where she bought a bottle of iced tea. The clerk at the counter joked with her about how it was as hot as a sauna outside, but she could barely manage to acknowledge him.

Once she was back on the road, she couldn't stop glancing at the rearview mirror from time to time, braced and thoroughly expecting to see the light blue Toyota pull up on her tail again.

She didn't see it and was just starting to tell herself she'd been overreacting when she turned onto Prospect Street, not far from her house, and from the corner of her eye caught a quick glimpse of a light blue car far down the road.

It certainly *looked* like the same car that had been behind her, but a tractor trailer heading in the other direction got between them, and a split second later, the car was out of sight.

"You're really being too paranoid," she whispered to herself, but she still felt all wound up when she pulled into her driveway and parked in front of the garage. She fished the bag of bullets out from under the car seat. Clutching them tightly, she got out of the car and walked over to Bingley's grave.

The dirt had dried out and turned a lighter shade of brown, but the sight—and knowing what was buried there—instantly brought tears to her eyes.

She was hunched over, her body wracked with sobs as she walked up onto the porch. After a quick glance up and down the street to make sure there wasn't a blue Toyota anywhere nearby, she went inside and closed and locked the door. She hurried into the front entryway to make sure the front door was locked and then—even before she poured herself the drink she felt she desperately needed—went upstairs and loaded the revolver.

Wouldn't it be funny, she thought, snickering softly to herself, *if it really was Sy following me, and I ended up shooting him in the middle of the chest, just the way he taught me?*

into the depths.

Chapter Thirteen

The room felt like it suddenly shifted sideways, and then it began to slip away.

A sudden, roaring concussion cracked the gathering darkness, and David felt as though the world had opened up underneath him like a gigantic mouth that was going to swallow him. He let loose a wild, warbling scream as he pitched backward, spinning crazily head over heels into a cold, pitch-black void. Panic gripped him by the throat and squeezed him as he tumbled head over heels into nothingness, twisting and turning in a wild, spastic dance.

After a while, once he realized that he hadn't just fallen over and wasn't going to hit the floor right away, the disorienting sensation of falling passed, and he felt more like he was flying or floating through a dense fog. Wind whistled shrilly in his ears and tugged at him as powerful gusts buffeted him from every side. Seemingly lighter than a feather, his corpus was tossed around like an insignificant mote of dust in the infinite darkness.

This has to be the end! he thought. *It's all over!*

Icy rushes of vertigo and stomach-tightening nausea swept through him as he thrashed about in the dark emptiness. He had no idea whether or not he was still screaming out loud. The wind that shrieked all around him with a thousand voices drowned out even his own thoughts.

All he knew was that he was plunging through a huge, shifting bank of thunderheads. Black, roiling clouds seethed with raw, flickering energy and dark, churning motion.

He lost all sense of time. He could have been falling for a few seconds or for several days.

It didn't matter. Time had no meaning here. All he knew was that he was alone...

Utterly alone...

Just as he had always said he wanted to be.

There was no sense of direction. No up or down. No in or out. Not even an awareness of light or dark, at least as he had understood it before this terrifying, timeless instant. Everything was lost in a spinning chaos that could just as well have been inside him as outside. He was lost... and frightened... and absolutely alone!

... help me...

After a while, the darkness around him seemed to be coalescing into distinct shapes.

Gripped by stark terror, David watched as huge, distorted faces, horribly underlie by flashes of red and purple light, appeared slowly from the churning clouds and then disappeared. Gigantic hands—some of which didn't even look human—reached out for him, raking the air with hooked fingers as huge and terrifying as scythes.

The roaring sound of hurricane winds filled his ears, but beneath it, David thought he could hear something else... indistinct voices that were screaming at him, calling out his name. David couldn't possibly make out anything that was being said. The voices he heard and the panicky thoughts that filled his mind melded into a single, howling cacophony that rose louder and louder with soul-shaking fury.

...Please... make this stop... the voice inside his head whimpered, sounding like a tiny, terrified child.... *just let me disappear... forever....*

And then he noticed something curious. For the first time since he had realized that he truly was dead, physical sensations seemed to be returning. He could actually *feel* the wind, whipping through his hair and slashing at his face and arms like stinging razors. He could imagine thick streamers of bright blood flowing from wounds and snapping like a tangled spider web in the air as he fell.

Unimaginable cold gripped him—a cold like he had never experienced. It numbed his mind, his corpus, his very soul.

But, he thought, *at least I can FEEL it!*

The physical sensation of cold soon became almost indistinguishable from the stark terror he experienced when, suddenly, a face he recognized loomed out of the darkness at him. David screamed and tried to turn away, but no matter where he looked, the face was there, nailing him with a steady, emotionless scare.

It was his father's face! His expression was truly frightening. His brows lowered like dangerous thunderheads. His jaw was set firmly either in anger or pain. Terrifying rage burned in his shadowed eyes.

"You never even liked me, much less loved me, did you, son?" His father's voice boomed like thunder above the shrill screaming of the wind in his ears. The sound of it set David's nerves on fire and made him cringe inwardly.

"I—of course I loved you, Pop," he said in a shattered voice that was instantly whisked away by the shrieking winds. "I—I just-just didn't know how–how co—"

"How to what? How to *say* it?" his father bellowed.

When his face loomed closer to David, a blast of laughter filled the air. The hollow concussion pressed in on David like huge, crushing hands.

"Kind of ironic, wouldn't you say so, Davy? That's a writer's word, isn't it? Ironic? But I would think someone who professes to be a *writer*—if he has any *real* talent at all—would be able to *think* of—and maybe even *say* four simple words like *I love you, Dad.*"

"Even if I had, you-you wouldn't have listened to me!"

Bitter agony and guilt wrung David's heart. He closed his eyes—at least he thought he closed them—but the image of his father's face floated in front of his vision like a bright afterimage burned forever into his retina and memory.

"You drove me to do it," his father said in his deep, all-too-familiar baritone. "Did you know that? I never wanted to do what I did, but I couldn't help it."

"But I never—"

Words failed him, and his father continued speaking as if what he had to say wasn't even worth hearing.

"I realize that I had a family to support—you and your sister and your mother—but I couldn't see any other way out. I suppose it just goes to prove that there's a certain kind of ultimate justice in the universe—the fact that *you* drove me to it, and *you* were the one to find me."

"I–I tried to forget all about that," David shrieked. "I never wanted you to die."

"Oh, I realized that—afterward, anyway," his father said.

For a moment, his voice was almost mild, but there wasn't the slightest trace of forgiveness in it.

"I was there, you see. I was still there in the garage for a couple of days after it happened. I didn't know where else to go. I was there when you came home from school and found me hanging from the rafters. I even tried to break through the Shroud to talk to you, but—well, now you know for yourself just how hard *that* can be."

David couldn't think straight, much less say anything. He watched in mute horror as his father's face suddenly darkened. His cheeks puffed out, and the lighting underneath him turned his face a deep, flushed scarlet that quickly shifted to deep violet. His eyes bulged out of his face so much they looked like poached eggs about to pop. After a terrifying instant, David noticed the knotted rope that was twisted in a single coil around his father's neck. The skin of his father's neck and cheeks swelled with a deep, bruised purple that steadily deepened as the rope pulled tighter and tighter. A watery gagging sound filled the air.

Wailing in utter agony, David reached out and tried to grab the frayed end of the rope that danced and snapped like a whip in the air, but either his fingers or the rope were too insubstantial. He watched helplessly as his father's bulging eyes rolled upward into his head, and his tongue, looking like a bloated, black slug, protruded from his mouth. His father kept making that long, strangled gagging sound as blood gushed from his nose and the corners of his mouth. Then his father's eyes began to bleed red tears as he fixed David with his steady gaze.

"It won't do you any good," his father said in a high, broken voice. "It's all over now... for both of us."

"But I never meant for you to—"

"In the long run, I guess I can't blame you for crying to kill yourself, seeing as how you're the son of a suicide." His father's voice was so distorted David could hardly make out the words. "No, I can't... blame you, but I... sure as hell can't... forgive you... either!"

With those words echoing all around him in the darkness, David's father's face blended back into the darkness, leaving behind a burning afterimage in David's mind that perfectly matched the tortured expression on his father's face that he had carried in his memory ever since that day when he was twelve years old and had found that his father had hanged himself in the garage.

"I–I'm sorry, Dad! Really sorry!" David shouted, but the vision was gone, and the wind whisked his words away the instant they left his mouth.

A sudden, random gust of wind spun him around and upside down, and David continued to fall, screaming, into the dark, endless abyss. As he fell, numerous other faces appeared around him. Sharp voices, ear-piercing screams and bursts of insane laughter trailed out of the darkness.

With a sudden jolt, David realized that another face was moving closer to him. It stood out in sharp detail as though etched from rock. He instantly recognized the thin, handsome features of his literary agent, William Relling.

"That's the best you can do to apologize to your father?" Relling said archly.

His eyes and words drove like red-hot spikes into David's mind.

"Well, I guess you never were all that good with words, were you?"

Relling spoke with that same sophisticated British accent David remembered hearing over the phone so many times over the years, and it immediately reminded him of how, every year, Relling had delivered increasingly worse news about decreasing sales, correspondingly decreasing advances, negative royalty statements, out-of-print books and less than zero prospects for any foreign sales, much less a film deal.

"I–I did the best I could," David replied weakly.

"Oh, sure, I suppose you did," Relling replied smoothly, "but did you ever stop to consider that even your very best perhaps wasn't quite good enough?"

David couldn't speak. All the rage and frustration he had felt about his career over the last fifteen years choked him into silence. The disorienting sensation of falling wouldn't let up.

"I kept trying to tell you," Relling said, sounding almost snide and mocking as he narrowed his gaze at David. "I tried to warn you about how serious the situation really was, but you just wouldn't listen, would you?"

"Sure I listened," David muttered weakly in his own defense.

"Didn't I keep telling you that the boom years of the eighties were over? Over and gone. But you had to keep at it, didn't you? Because you were a writer, you kept telling me, and that's *all* you were. And I suppose, short of pumping gas for minimum wage at the local Sunoco, that was all you ever *could* do, wasn't it?"

"I had to cry," David said, cringing inside. "Jesus! What else could I do?"

"True, true," Relling said, nodding his head as a cold light filled his eyes. "But after a while, one would think that even you would have wised up to what was happening. It was almost as though you were acting out that definition of insanity. You know, the one about doing the same thing over and over again, and expecting different results. You kept hitting the same thing, but for different reasons. After a while, it was rather pathetic."

"That's not true… That's not at all true!" David shouted, but his voice was swept away by the screaming maelstrom that embraced him. He turned away, unable to look his agent straight in the eyes.

Before long, his agent's face faded back into the seething darkness, but then other faces of friends, enemies and business associates resolved out of the darkness and leered at him. Every one of chem taunted him by forcing him to remember all the dark, secret hurts he had thought were safely hidden deep in his heart….

Alan Lindwall, the young, aspiring writer David had introduced to his agent and who had then gone on to sell his first novel for more money than David had earned throughout his entire career. And after all his good fortune, Alan had *never* bothered to thank David for his help. Not even a brief acknowledgment in his book!

George and Ralph Rich, the twin brothers who had made his high school years such an absolute torment because they were always picking on him and threatening to beat him up after school. Sometimes they made good on their threats and pounded the piss out of him.

Hope Parker, his "one true love" throughout all four years of high school, who had broken up with him when he came home from freshman year at college for Christmas vacation, after telling him that she had been seeing Mike Harlow, David's best friend from high school, for the last year or so. She and Mike had gotten married, had three kids and—at least as far as David knew—were still a happily married couple.

Alexander Courtland, the investment counselor who had invested a large portion of David's earnings into a "sure-fire" money-making real estate scheme that was going to be his and Sarah's retirement. The deal had gone bust, and David ended up losing every penny he had contributed. Alex, of course, hadn't lose a dime and walked away clean.

Bernie Ryerson, the principal at Buxton High School who had fired David from his first job right out of college, teaching English. After only six months on the job, Ryerson had informed him that he had decided not to renew his contract. A gentleman's way of saying he was being fired.

Other faces appeared. They whispered or shrieked at him, forcing him to remember all the insults and injuries, all the pain and frustration he had suffered throughout his short, meaningless life.

Is this never going to end? David wondered.

The thought filled him with blinding panic and a fear as stark and painful as anything he had ever experienced before in his life.

Maybe this was what had been waiting for him all along.

Maybe he would *never* find release in Oblivion!

He would spend the rest of eternity plummeting through this dark void, being tormented by all the regrets and losses and fuck-ups he had ever suffered.

If so, then this was Hell, not Heaven. No fiery furnaces. No demons with pitchforks, prodding sinners into the flames. No agonizing tortures on the rack.

This was bad enough. It was just him with his guilt and despair.

And it was just a matter of time, he supposed, before the faces of his dead daughter and his wife appeared, and he had to suffer their bitter recriminations for the sorry, final chapters of his life.

The thought of that was too much to bear.

David was positive that his mind would snap like a dried twig if he had to squarely face his own grief and guilt about Karen's death. He tried to cling to the last, few mutilated shreds of his unraveling sanity, but the icy winds were ripping through him and tearing his mind apart. He knew that before long, there would be nothing left of him except the tiniest core of his being—all that was left of his soul.

And he would have just enough sanity remaining to realize that he had completely lose his mind and would be in utter torment for the rest of eternity! There was no release in Oblivion!

He was going to end up just as the reaper with the limp had said he would—screaming without a mouth… seeing without eyes… conscious and aware without a body… thinking without sanity….

All the while he continued to fall, thrashing and clawing through the dense clouds. After another timeless moment, though, another face resolved out of the darkness.

At first, David didn't recognize it; he saw only the eyes—slit, golden irises, like a cat's that sparkled like coins inside the dense shadows of dark, lowering brows.

As the light increased, the face resolved more clearly, and David felt another powerful shock of fear.

Above and below the eyes, where there was supposed to be flesh, the features looked gray and hard, like old bone. As David's eyesight cleared, he saw a thin, skeletal face, staring at him from underneath the dark folds of a heavy hood. The harsh, angular lines of bone cast deep shadows under the eyes and chin. The lipless mouth appeared to be grinning at him. The only spark of life or intelligence was in the glowing, golden eyes.

When he finally recognized the Ferryman, David wanted to scream but couldn't. The wind was pushing his voice back into his chest. He watched in mute horror as the hideous creature came nearer to him and reached out with a thin, bone-white hand.

"Can you trust me?" the Ferryman said, his teeth clacking like stone against stone as he spoke.

David wondered how such a creature could form words without lips or a tongue. He remembered what the reaper had said something about not trusting the Ferryman; so even though he was still flailing about in freefall, and the Ferryman looked as though he was standing firmly on solid ground, David didn't dare to reach out and grasp the hand that was extended to him.

"*Can you trust me?*" the Ferryman repeated more emphatically. His eyes flashed like gold coins glinting in bright sunlight.

Go away! You're just another illusion to torment me! David either thought or said out loud. *There's nothing more you can do to help! … Go away! Leave me alone!*

"I know many of the byways within the Tempest," the Ferryman said simply. "Not all of them, but many."

David couldn't deny that the Ferryman's voice seemed to have the ring of truth in it. As terrified as he was, he was filled with an intense yearning for safety and release. Like a child who had awakened from a nightmare in the dark, he needed the simple reassurance of someone to touch—a hand to hold.

Do you mean there's really a way out of this?

"A way out ... or a way in." The Ferryman chuckled and shrugged. "Sometimes it's very difficult to distinguish the two, wouldn't you say?"

I don't want to play word games with you! ... Just help me if you can... if you can make this stop!

It took a great deal of effort, but David slowly extended his own hand. The instant he clasped hands with the Ferryman, his arm went numb all the way to his shoulder.

And something else happened.

As soon as their hands touched, the wind died away with a hollow *whoosh.* The shrill, screaming voices immediately subsided, and dim light began to bleed into the darkness like a slow-spreading stain. David could feel something solid under his feet, but he didn't quite dare to believe or trust that he was standing on solid ground. The dark clouds still churned overhead, but they seemed to be dissolving away to nothing.

When he looked down, he was amazed to see that he was standing on a hard-packed earthen surface. As his vision cleared, he saw that he and the Ferryman were standing on a flat, rocky ledge. On one side was a steep, rugged mountainside. On the other was a sheer drop down into a mist-filled abyss that shimmered with dull, gray light.

"Where-where are we?" David asked.

His voice was wrung out with exhaustion. He realized that he was still gripping the Ferryman's hand tightly, and he sensed that, if he were to let go, he would instantly be swept away again into the dark, directionless void.

The Ferryman's face was obscured by the deep shadow of his cowl, and as David watched, the darkness within the cowl deepened and expanded until it appeared to be the opening of a cave in the side of the mountain. With a sudden start, David looked down and saw that he was no longer clinging to the Ferryman's hand. The Ferryman had disappeared, and David was left alone, clasping his own hands tightly together.

"What the—" David called out, but then his voice echoed off. The only reply he heard was a reverberating echo from deep inside the cave in front of him. He shivered when he glanced down over the cliff edge and listened to the shrill hiss of the wind.

I can't take you to her. The Ferryman's voice sounded in David's memory as clearly as if he were still standing beside him on the cliff edge.

You'll have to find her on your own. After that, I'll do whatever I can to help both of you. Then the voice faded away like a low, grumbling roll of thunder.

Ahead of him loomed the cave opening. David knew that, if he was ever going to see Karen again or find any peace within himself, he was going to have to enter that cave.

Maybe, he thought, *just like the Ferryman said, the only way out... was in.*

Cozy little place, Sy thought as he pulled over to the side of the road and parked his car a short distance up the street from Sarah's house. He killed the engine and slipped the keys into his jeans pocket before slumping down in the front seat, carefully positioning himself so he could keep an eye on the front of the house and the side porch.

Daylight was gradually bleeding out of the sky. Thin, purple streaks of cloud stretched like claw marks across the western sky. The air was heavy and warm, but Sy thought he could detect a slight drop in temperature as the sun slowly dipped below the horizon. He sighed as he settled back and listened to the faint whisper of distant traffic. It sounded like there were a lot of cars passing by in the distance, but the road Sarah lived on—Canal Street, the sign had said—seemed perfectly quiet and peaceful. In the first fifteen minutes, only two cars went by.

Nice, quiet street to raise kids, Sy thought.

He chuckled softly to himself because he knew that he would probably never be one to settle down and raise children—not unless he and Dianne decided to adopt. That didn't seem too damned likely, so in the meantime—at least for the next day or two—he had decided to "adopt" Sarah. He wasn't sure what it had been about her that had struck him so deeply, but there had been something in her demeanor that had made him feel protective about her.

He was pretty sure it wasn't just some bullshit macho thing. Sy considered himself a fairly intuitive person, and out at the firing range today, he had sensed that Sarah was in some kind of serious danger. Not too many women who had never handled a gun before showed up at his place so anxious to learn how to shoot—not unless they were feeling threatened by something… or *someone.*

In Sarah's case, Sy had sensed an almost desperate urgency, so he figured it wouldn't be such a bad idea to tail her for a day or two, just to see if there was anything he could do to help her out.

He checked the luminous dial of his watch and saw that it was already a little past eight o'clock. Dianne would have gotten home from work over an hour ago. He'd left a note telling her where he was and not to worry, but he thought maybe he should give her a call. Leaning forward, he started to reach for the cellular phone, but then decided not to and slumped backdown in the seat. He'd wait another half hour or so, maybe just until night had fallen all the way, and then head on home. He cried not to think about it very much, but he had to admit that he found Sarah sexually attractive. It was making him horny, and it might be nice to get home before Dianne was asleep.

As the sky darkened to the color of soot, the streetlights lining the road winked on. One window in Sarah's house—the living room, he figured—lit up with a warm, yellow glow. Through the drawn window shade, he could see the flicker of the television. Just once, he saw Sarah's silhouette move across the window.

Sighing deeply, Sy shifted his gaze over to Sarah's car, which was parked in front of the garage. She didn't have the outside porch light on, so he guessed she wasn't expecting any visitors tonight.

Everything seemed so quiet and peaceful; he began to suspect that he must have overreacted. After taking early retirement from the Portland Police Department, where he'd worked as a detective for the last twenty years, Sy figured he was probably just looking for something to keep himself occupied on the days when it was slow at the firing range. He sure as hell didn't consider himself a super-hero who was out to save the world, but he liked to keep his surveillance skills honed, just in case. You never knew when you might need them.

The air in the car was beginning to feel stuffy, so Sy rolled down the window to let in a breeze, though there wasn't much of one blowing. Beneath the smell of hot asphalt that wafted in, the night air was tinged with the faintly rotten scent of the nearby ocean at low tide.

The steady sound of crickets singing in the gathering darkness began to lull him. He started to consider that maybe he was being foolish. When the gun in the holster he was wearing began to dig painfully into the small of his back, he shifted around in the seat, crying to get comfortable. He was feeling so relaxed that he almost missed it when a dark shadow moved out from the chin stand of shrubbery behind Sarah's garage.

"What the fuck?" Sy said, tensing as he sat up.

His powerful hands gripped the steering wheel tightly as he leaned forward and watched the dark figure that crept along the side of the garage. It looked like a moon-cast shadow moving against the lighter background of the building. Sy had no idea who this might be, but whoever it was, he sure as hell didn't move like someone who belonged here.

Without taking his eyes off the indistinct figure, he leaned forward slightly and withdrew his gun from his holster. He checked to make sure it was fully loaded — as if he'd ever leave the house without checking the load — and slipped it back into the holster.

The figure crouched low by the side of the garage, obviously scanning the house. Then, with a sudden burst, it darted across the narrow strip of lawn and leaped up to the porch. Whoever it was, he moved with a stalking, feline grace that Sy had to admire. Keeping low, the figure shifted over to the side door and stood up to peer cautiously into the house through the door window.

Sy considered calling the Portland police on the cellular, just in case he needed backup, but then decided not to just in case he was misreading the situation. His hand was on the car door handle, all set to snap it open and get out if he felt he had to.

Then things happened too quickly for him even to think about calling the police.

The figure grabbed the doorknob and, twisting his body to one side, rammed his shoulder hard against the door. Sy was far enough away that the sound of shattering wood was almost too faint to hear, but he saw the door swing open. After a quick glance over his shoulder, the figure darted inside.

Sy was out of the car in a flash, drawing his gun as he ran across the street toward the house. His footsteps clicked on the pavement and echoed in the dark. Within seconds, a cool sheen of sweat had broken out across his forehead, and he was trembling with a pure, sweet adrenaline rush. This was the part of his job that he always missed — the thrill of the chase!

As he was crossing the lawn, Sy saw a light wink on upstairs. He hoped that it was Sarah, that she had heard what was going on and was getting her gun out so she'd be ready for the intruder. Jumping up onto the porch, Sy said a silent prayer that Sarah would remember everything he had showed her this morning at the firing range. He sensed that her life depended on it.

It was dark in the cave, but not quite pitch black. A weird blue glow flickered like heat lightning inside the entrance, casting thin, wavering shadows across the hard-packed dirt floor and making the uneven texture of the stone walls stand out in harsh relief. Spills of dirt and small stones littered the floor. From somewhere deep inside the cave, David could hear a low-throated whistle of wind and the steady sound of dripping water that echoed loudly in the dark, sounding like an animal licking a bone.

As he stepped into the cave, sharp, winding tension filled him, compressing his chest so much that he could almost remember the sensation of breathing in and holding his breath until his chest ached. His throat felt tight and dry, and his eyes were fixed wide open, unable to blink.

I could be imagining all of this, he thought, but he pushed the discomforting thought aside, determined to accept the unreality of the situation.

With no idea what else he could do, he took several more steps into the tunnel. The darkness inside seemed to expand like a widening maw about to engulf him.

As he plunged deeper into the cave, the glowing light seemed to withdraw farther into the depths, luring him on while maintaining the same distance ahead of him. After following it for a short while, David paused and looked back, surprised to see that the cave entrance was already out of sight.

How can I see in the dark like this? he wondered as he glanced up at the dense shadows above him. *I was never able to see in the dark before.*

But no matter what doubts assailed him, he knew he had to keep moving forward. He was amazed that the glowing light seemed to be leading him along, and he wondered if he could trust it, or if this was some kind of trap.

The deeper he went, though, the more his apprehension increased. He had no idea what he might find in here or what might happen to him; but as much as he dreaded the prospects, he knew that there was no turning back.

He *had* to keep moving ahead.

The single, fragile hope that the Ferryman had brought him here because Karen was somewhere nearby propelled him forward.

I have to find her myself.

With each step, his feet scraping against the dirt floor made loud tearing sounds that set his teeth on edge. To help keep himself oriented, he ran one hand along the pebbled surface of the wall. Even that little bit of contact seemed remarkably acute, and he was filled with the hopeful notion that he was experiencing physical sensations more the way he had when he was alive. He could almost taste the dense, dank air inside the cave, and he thought he could actually *feel* the cool, almost chilly air against his skin. He had the distinct impression that his forehead and armpits were moist with sweat. If he dared to stop and close his eyes and listen carefully, he thought he might even be able to hear and feel the feathery beat of his pulse in his chest and neck.

No! That's not possible! I'm dead! he told himself, even as the illusion continued to heighten in intensity.

Before long, he found himself thinking and hoping that he might even still be alive.

Maybe that's what's at the other end of this tunnel, he thought with a gathering rush of excitement. *Maybe I'm still alive! Maybe I'll regain consciousness and discover that I'm still lying face-down on the side of the road after being hit by that vehicle!*

The idea sparked a fleeting rush of hope inside him, but he knew that, whatever he discovered or encountered, and whatever was going to happen, first he was going to have to make it out of the darkness of this cave…

—or through it!

There was no turning back.

Every sound inside the cave seemed strangely amplified. Even the slightest hint of noise—his feet scraping on the earthen floor or his hand brushing against the cave wall—set off a chain reaction of echoes that ripped through the silence, first growing steadily louder until they finally faded away to faint whispers.

But the sounds never seemed to be completely gone.

The distant ring of dripping water seemed much louder now, and below that David could heard something else— another sound which, although maddeningly familiar, he couldn't quite identify.

What the hell is *that?* he wondered as a frantic fear blossomed inside him.

The sound teased his ears just at the edge of hearing, like the barely remembered *whoosh* of blood running through his veins.

Filled as he was with fear and faint hope, David forced himself to follow the glowing blue light as it retreated deeper into the cave. He was hoping that it would lead him in the right direction, but the farther he went, the fainter the light became.

Finally, David stopped short, gripped by the panicky thought that, before too long, the light was going to fade away and then be extinguished entirely.

And then where will I be?

He shivered as a crushing sense of claustrophobia gripped him. He didn't like any of the answers he came up with, but he knew that he was going to forge ahead even if the cave were suddenly plunged into the total darkness.

If there was even the slightest chance that Karen was down here somewhere, then he had to find her. He had to cry to save her if he could.

His life might not have had any meaning, but finding his daughter and saving her soul certainly might give his *death* some meaning.

He started walking again, but after only a few paces the scuffing his feet were making in the dirt suddenly drew his attention. He stopped and looked around, absolutely convinced that the sound he'd been trying to get a fix on was getting louder, but it cut off the instant he tried to focus his attention on it.

David cocked his head forward, his eyes wide open as he listened, but now he couldn't hear a thing. Not even his own breaching.

Ahead and behind him, the darkness beyond the faint glow of light was so dense that it seemed to swallow everything, even sound. The silence was so complete that David had the momentary impression that *this* was the silence of the comb — utter and total *dead* silence!

"No," he said in a whispering voice that sounded cracked and ancient in the echoing cave. "No, by Jesus! I still *exist!*"

Even though he said this as softly as he could, his voice resounded like a rumble of thunder in the pressing darkness. His words echoed crazily and blended together until they finally faded away. The cave was perfectly silent except for that elusive sound that he still couldn't identify.

David lost any sense of how long he had been inside the cave. Just as when he had been tumbling through the clouds, time seemed to have stopped. He experienced a momentary dizzying rush of eternity, and was suddenly frightened by the thought that there might be no end to this cave.

He could be trapped here... in the darkness... alone... for the rest of eternity!

But just as he was thinking this, and fear began to sweep him away, he caught a hint of motion up ahead. He saw the distorted shadow of a person shift across the uneven cave wall. It vanished around a corner before he could even begin to react, but he thought he caught a trace of faint, trailing laughter.

Convinced now that there was someone in the cave with him, he cupped his hands to his mouth and shouted.

"Hello."

"... *hello... lo... lo...*"

His voice echoed with an unnerving reverberation that trilled higher and louder before it gradually faded away to nothing.

Nothing... murmured a voice deep inside his head.

"Is anybody there?" David called out.

"... —body there..." the echo repeated.

David had lost any sense of direction, but he was convinced that there was someone there, moving ahead of—or behind— him...someone who was watching every step he took. He clenched his fists, poised and ready either to fight or run if he had to. He tried to push aside the unsettling thought that, all along the walls and the ceiling of the cave, bright shining eyes were opening and staring at him.

He felt suddenly, horribly transparent, almost nonexistent as though whoever—or whatever—was watching him could see right through him and easily read everything that was written in his heart and soul.

"Where am I?" he called out.

"...*am I...*" the echo resounded.

"I'm lost."

"...lost..."

"I'm afraid."

"...afraid..."

"Please."

"...please..."

"Somebody answer me!"

"...answer me..."

David was almost paralyzed with fear. Every muscle and joint in his corpus was frozen in place. He knew that he had neither the courage nor the strength to continue, but he also knew that he couldn't turn back, nor could he couldn't very well stay where he was.

He was paralyzed, his mind almost overwhelmed with dark despair.

The terrible truth was, he had no idea which way to go. The darkness at either end of the tunnel was equally impenetrable, just like the darkness he knew was inside him. Sadness and sour, choking fear twisted within him, filling him with an unspeakable agony.

Although he could no longer detect even the slightest hint of motion beyond the faint glow of blue light, he still felt like he was being watched. The skin on his arms and the back of his neck prickled and crawled with the feeling that cold, steady gazes were fixed on him. He could all too easily imagine that invisible hands were reaching out at him from the darkness and brushing against him with light, feathery couches. Those touches seemed more real, more substantial than anything he had previously experienced in the Shadowlands—if that's where he still was.

He reached out with his right hand and rubbed the rough surface of the wall, amazed by how deadened his sense of couch still seemed. The most real thing—the *only* real thing here for him was his fear, which was as solid and palpable as his living body had once been.

The light up ahead shifted, and once again David thought he caught a fleeting glimpse of a shadow, rippling like dark water across the cave floor and walls. He took a quick step forward, almost calling out again, but then drew back.

"No," he whispered.

Maybe the shadow was trying to lead him in the wrong direction, he thought.

The cold, clutching fear in him spiked stronger.

Maybe he should be going in the other direction.

With a cautious glance over his shoulder, David turned and started walking in the opposite direction. Before he had taken more than three or four steps, a voice whispered softly to him.

No, come this *way.*

The voice hissed in the darkness—or inside his head—like escaping steam.

David gritted his teeth and shook his head, all the more determined to keep moving away from the shadow. After a few more steps, he paused and looked back. The shadow was clearly etched against the stone wall of the cave, and whoever it was had raised one hand and was gesturing to him.

Don't be foolish… You'll be lost forever if you go that way….

David wanted to reply, but his voice was trapped deep inside his chest. The walls of the cave pressed in on him like a vise. His legs felt frail and brittle, as if they were about to collapse underneath him, but he forced himself to walk away from the beckoning shadow.

No! … It's no use! … You can't save her!… Just like everything else in your pitiful life, you may as well give up any hope of helping her... of helping either one of them, Karen or Sarah! ... It's much too late!... Why can't you admit that?...

David thought his eyes must be playing tricks on him, but it appeared as though the blue glow in front of him was getting steadily stronger, while behind him it was fading. The shadow on the cave wall vibrated with a solid, eternal darkness. He kept walking away from the shadow, not at all sure if he was heading in the right direction or not. He couldn't decide which to trust—the shadow or the light.

You're a bigger fool than I thought you were!... You still don't get it, do you?... There's nothing you can do to help them! ... Absolutely nothing! ... Karen's dead! ... And you're dead! ... And pretty soon, once Sarah's dead, it will all be over for everyone you've ever loved! ... You will have lost it all!...

David found it extremely difficult to keep the frantic edge of fear at bay. The rasping voice behind him was growing louder, more demanding, sounding almost angry; but David tried to convince himself that it couldn't hurt him. The shadow kept beckoning to him insistently, but no matter what it said, no matter how badly it taunted him, it was just a shadow.

"And shadows can't hurt you... not unless you listen to them," he muttered to himself, hoping that the sound of his own voice would drown out the other, more insistent voice behind him.

You'll regret it! ... You've already lost them! ... Both of them! ... Karen and Sarah! ... So you have absolutely nothing left to exist for!... No hope! ... No future!... Nothing but Oblivion! ...

"Yes, I do!" David shouted. "I *still* have one thing, dammit! Hope!"

David's voice was strained and tight, not much more than a dry, crackling rustle in the darkness. As it echoed from the cave walls, it sounded like several people, speaking to him all at once.

Turn back now before it's too late!... You'll regret it if you don't! ... I swear by anything and everything you've ever held sacred or holy that you'll regret it! ...

But David was convinced, now, that the shadow was trying to lure him in the wrong direction. The farther he moved away from it, the fainter its voice became until it was replaced by something else—that same indistinct sound he had heard earlier and had not been able to place.

Only this time, as he got closer and listened more carefully, he *was* able to place it.

It was the strained, muffled sound of somebody crying.

Almost unbearable tension coiled inside David.

He had heard that sound before... even after he had died and arrived in the Shadowlands. It was the sound of a little child, sobbing softly to herself in the darkness. David knew that it was absolutely too much to hope for, but he was suddenly convinced that it was Karen.

It *had* to be her!

"Hello?"

He stood tensed after calling out into the darkness, and waited for the echo of his voice to fade into the surrounding shadows.

The sobbing stopped the instant he spoke. The silence was as solid as the wall of darkness around him.

"Is somebody there?" David purposely kept his voice low because he didn't want to frighten whoever it might be.

"Leave me alone... Please... Don't hurt me anymore."

Before the first words had faded, David recognized his daughter's voice. Hope flared within him as he started forward, looking ahead and trying to pierce the dense darkness. The blue light was glowing so dimly now that it was almost impossible to see; but after another few steps forward, David saw up ahead, huddled on the stone floor, a small, dark figure.

"Karen?" David called out, fighting the tortured flutter in his voice. "Is that really you?"

For what seemed like an eternity, he heard nothing in response, not even the reassuring whisper of his long-stilled pulse in his ears. The darkness around him swelled like a hungry beast, and he was suddenly afraid that he might be imagining all of this. This could be another illusion. It might be just a shadow, created by the dimming light against the rocks and his own desperate need.

"It's me, Karen," he whispered brokenly. "It's Daddy, and I–I promise that I won't hurt you. Nobody's going to hurt you *ever* again!" His words echoed and then faded away to total silence.

After what seemed like much too long a time, there came a long, warbling cry from out of the darkness. It built up steadily until it resounded through the cave like the piercing wail of a siren.

"Daddy?... *Daddy!*... Where *are* you?"

"I'm right here, honey," David said, as he rushed toward her and knelt down.

"How come I can't see you?" Karen asked in a voice that was faint and broken with misery. "I'm really scared, Daddy! It's so dark in here. Where am I, Daddy? What's happened to me?"

crossing over.

Chapter Fourteen

Sarah leaped up from the couch and, covering her mouth with both hands, screamed the instant she heard the sudden, loud crashing sound coming from in the kitchen.

The loud bang was followed by the sound of splintering wood and shattering glass falling to the linoleum floor. It made such a loud noise that Sarah's first, wild thought was that a car must have missed the turn onto Canal Street and careened into the side of the house. She held her breath and was keenly aware of her heart slamming heavily inside her chest as she took a few hesitant steps toward the kitchen.

What the hell is happening?

She cringed as she listened to the heavy tread of footsteps crushing broken wood and glass underfoot. She almost fainted when she entered the kitchen and saw Tony Ranieri, standing by the broken door, which was hanging at an odd angle from one twisted hinge.

"What the—" Sarah started to say, but then she stopped herself.

She couldn't believe how Tony looked. His clothes were dirty and disheveled. His sport shirt was torn at the left shoulder. Sweat plastered his dark hair to his forehead, making him look like he'd just stepped out of the shower. He was panting heavily through gritted teeth as he stared at her, his eyes blazing with an insane inner light.

"Just thought I'd step in for a quick visit," Tony said in a low, controlled voice that sent a shiver racing through Sarah.

He chuckled softly to himself as he looked over his shoulder at the shattered remains of the door and then kicked them with his heel. Shards of glass tinkled lightly as they fell to the floor.

"Sorry 'bout the mess," he said, snorting loudly as he wiped his upper lip with the back of his hand and glared at her crazily. "But it's your own damned fault, you know. You never did give me a house key."

"Jesus Christ, Tony! What are you—? What's the matter with you?"

Panic raced like ice water through Sarah's veins. She knew that she should get away from him as quickly as possible, get to a phone and call the police, but fear rooted her to the spot.

Tony sniffed with laughter as he turned to one side and reached behind his back with his right hand. When his hand came back around, Sarah saw that he was holding a knife. The thin, wicked-looking blade gleamed with a dull glint in the kitchen light.

"The matter? With me?" he said, panting heavily as he shifted his focus from the blade to Sarah. "Why, nothing's the matter with me. I just dropped by to fuck with you a little."

His face was flushed, and his eyes were bugging out of his head as he snapped his wrist and flicked the knife back and forth a few times. The blade made a faint whistling sound in the air.

"This has been a long time coming, don't you think?" he said hoarsely.

"I–I don't know what you—what you're—"

Sarah's voice choked off, and then she screamed. Clenching her fists tightly at her side, she turned and ran back into the living room. She almost tripped on the rug in the entryway as she wheeled around the corner and started up the stairs, taking them two at a time. The muscles in her shoulders and the back of her neck were knotted painfully as she cringed, waiting to feel a sudden impact or a sharp pain jab her from behind, but she made it up to the landing safely before daring to stop and look back.

Tony wasn't anywhere in sight.

Not yet, anyway.

But she could hear the heavy clomp of his feet on the kitchen floor as he started after her with strong, measured steps. Sarah's lungs were burning as if she had swallowed fire.

"You can run, but you can't hide," Tony called from downstairs in a teasing, sing-song voice. This was followed by a burst of crazy-sounding laughter that stripped Sarah's nerves raw.

Without waiting for him to appear, she turned and dashed down the hallway to her bedroom. She swatted the overhead light switch on as she spun around and slammed the door shut. She didn't have a lock on the door, but David's old bureau, which she now used for her off-season clothes, stood beside it. Usually she had trouble even budging it, but the adrenaline surging through her system gave her the strength she needed to slide it over in front of the door.

She knew that at best, it would only slow Tony down, and it would probably piss him off all the more; but she told herself that all she needed was a few seconds.

Just long enough to get out her gun!

Her hands were trembling out of control as she dashed around to the other side of the bed and slid open the nightstand drawer. When she pulled out David's revolver, her grip felt too weak to hold it. The gun seemed amazingly heavy in her hand.

Beyond the door, she could hear Tony tromping heavily on the stairs. He was whistling a song. Through her raging panic, Sarah recognized the old standby, "Strangers in the Night."

She whimpered softly when she realized that the gun wasn't loaded. She hadn't bothered to do that after getting home from work with the box of bullets. Skinning her upper lip over her teeth, she fought back her fear as she fumbled open the box of ammunition and grabbed a handful of bullets. They rattled like dice in her hands as she tried to open the gun. A few bullets made dull clicking sounds as they dropped onto the bed.

"Here kitty, kitty, kitty," Tony called out, clicking his tongue and then laughing like a madman. "Have you seen a little kitty around here somewhere?"

Sarah's eyes were watering so badly she could barely see what she was doing as she shoved three bullets into the chamber then clicked the gun shut. A spike of fear shot through her when she heard a light, rapid knocking at her bedroom door.

"Hello-o-o-o in there. Are you hiding from me or something?" Tony called out teasingly. "I know you're around here somewhere"

Gripping the gun with both hands, Sarah raised it and aimed at the door panel just about chest level. Her hands were shaking so badly the gun kept weaving from side to side, but she struggled to bring it back into line.

"Come on, now. Open up the door and let me in," Tony said in the high sing-song voice again. Then, in a low, gravely voice, he chanted, "Not by the hair of my chinny-chin-chin," and then laughed hoarsely.

"*Get away from me!*" Sarah shouted, surprising herself by the strength in her voice. "*I'm warning you! I've got a gun!*"

"Ohhh, so you've got a gun, do you? I'm *so-o-o-o* scared! Listen! Can you hear that? It's the sound of my knees knocking, I'm so scared."

With that, Tony grabbed the doorknob and twisted it viciously from side to side while pushing on the door from behind. The door opened a crack as the heavy bureau started to slide across the floor. Its feet made a harsh scraping sound on the wood. Sarah whimpered again when she saw the expanding darkness at the edge of the door.

"I mean it!" she shouted. "I have a gun, and I'll use it if I have to!"

"Well, I have a knife, and I *sure* as hell plan to use it!" Tony shouted.

The bureau shifted another few inches, and Tony's face appeared in the widening crack. The bedroom light caught and reflected in his left eye, making it gleam brightly.

With a loud grunt and a sudden shove, he pushed against the door. The bureau toppled over and hit the floor with a loud crash. The impact shook the room and rattled Sarah's teeth. Tony was grinning idiotically as he stepped into the room and stared at her. Fury boiled deep in his eyes, and the corners of his mouth were twitching as though he were tasting something terrible.

Sweat broke out on Sarah's brow as she stepped back, being careful to keep the bed between them. She was trying desperately to remember everything Sy had told her today at the firing range, but she was so scared her mind drew a complete blank. Whimpering softly, she squeezed the gun with both hands to steady it. She spread her legs in a firm stance, sucked in a breath and held it until it started to hurt. The aiming bead at the tip of the revolver drifted around until finally she managed to center it in the middle of Tony's forehead.

"I swear to God I'll use it," she said, trying to keep her voice low and measured.

Tony appeared mildly surprised, maybe a little irritated when he saw that she was, indeed, holding a gun. Then his smile widened even more as he raised the knife and twisted it back and forth in front of his face, all the while staring at the blade as though completely mesmerized.

"Frankly, I don't think you have the balls to pull the trigger," he said softly as he took another step closer. "In fact, I *know* you don't have the balls to do it because I've *fucked* you, and you didn't have any balls then!"

He laughed tightly at his own sick joke.

Sarah knew that he'd be able to catch her if he lunged across the bed. She braced herself, trying to control the icy flood of adrenaline that coursed through her body and made her tremble. She remembered what Sy had said, about how much difference there was between shooting at a paper target and a real human being. She knew she shouldn't hesitate. Her life depended on it.

"Fuck you, I don't have the balls!" she shouted.

Her eyes tightly shut, she jerked back on the trigger. The split second before the gun went off, she knew that she had made a crucial mistake.

She hadn't *squeezed* the trigger the way Sy had told her to.

The gun exploded and jumped in her hands like a live animal. The bullet went wide and hit the edge of the door jamb, splintering the wood inches behind Tony's head.

Tony glanced back over his shoulder at the ragged hole the bullet had made, then turned back to her and smiled widely. His wide, white teeth glistened like a wild animal's.

"I'm impressed," he said, nodding subtly, "but you were a little wide of the mark on that one."

He shifted around toward the foot of the bed, closing in on her fast. Sarah backed up against her own bureau, feeling the edge of it dig into her rump.

"Do you wanna try again? Or was that all the bullets you have?"

"I mean it, Tony. I swear to God I'll shoot you," Sarah said, but this time there was less conviction in her voice.

Tears were streaming from her eyes, blurring her vision. The gun in her hand felt suddenly much too heavy for her to hold. The tip started to drop until it was aiming halfway down at the floor.

Tony raised the knife and then snapped it back and forth once, quickly. The blade sliced the air with a soft, whickering sound. Chuckling to himself, he moved within striking distance.

"Get down!"

A different voice suddenly split the tension in the room.

Sarah froze where she was, but Tony reacted quickly. Dropping down into a low crouch, he started to wheel around, but he wasn't quick enough.

The deafening sound of a gun going off split the air.

Sarah screamed and dropped her own gun. She automatically covered her face with her hands but couldn't help but watch between her fingers as Tony's head exploded like a melon dropped from a second story window. A fan-shaped spray of bright red blood shot up to the ceiling. Chunks of pink and gray material flew everywhere, some of the chunks landing on Sarah's chest and face, but she was too stunned to notice them. She watched, petrified, as Tony continued to spin around, looking like he was doing an awkward curtsy. His wide eyes held the glazed look of surprise, but that quickly faded as he crumpled to the floor.

Sarah saw a man's face appear in the doorway.

For a shattering instant, she didn't recognize who it was. Then she started to laugh hysterically when she realized that it was Sy Warner.

"What the hell are you —" was all she managed to say, and then her voice cut off, and all she could do was make a low, whimpering sound.

"I was just in the neighborhood and thought I'd stop by for a visit," Sy replied casually.

He chuckled softly, but then his mouth fixed into a thin, hard line.

"But do you wanna know one thing?" he added. Before Sarah could reply, he said, "I was afraid that would happen."

They both glanced down at Tony's lifeless body.

Most of the top of his head was gone. Dark blood was seeping out of what remained of his head and soaking into the rug. His lifeless eyes were staring up at the ceiling as though he still couldn't quite believe or accept what had just happened to him.

"A–afraid—? Afraid of wh–what?" Sarah said, amazed that she could speak at all.

"Well, at first I was afraid that, like he said, you wouldn't really have the balls to pull the trigger. Then, when you did— You almost hit me, by the way. That was too damned close for comfort. I thought I taught you better."

Sy puffed his cheeks and exaggeratedly wiped his brow with the back of his hand.

"No, I–I didn't even s–see you there. I was—oh, Jesus, Sy!"

"Well it's a damned good thing your aim was off to the left instead of the right. Otherwise, you'd have blown *my* brains out." Sy followed this with another nervous chuckle of relief that seemed totally genuine.

Sarah suddenly felt all woozy inside. She almost fainted when Sy stepped over Tony's body and came up close to her. Her entire body felt numb, and she imagined that she was a useless sack of grain as she slumped forward into his powerful arms. She closed her eyes and let him hold her up.

"He... I didn't know what he was—what was happening," she said in a faint whisper.

She opened her eyes and looked over Sy's shoulder, down at Tony's corpse on the floor. No matter how hard she tried, she couldn't make herself turn away.

"He wanted to—I think he really was going co... to kill me!"

"Yeah, I think he was," Sy said evenly. "Good thing I just happened by, huh?"

He took a shuddering breath and held her close to him, squeezing her tightly. Sarah couldn't believe how secure she felt in his embrace.

"We probably ought to call the police, don't you think?" Sy said after a long moment.

Sarah bit down hard on her lower lip and nodded her head numbly as she clung to him. She was unable to look away from Tony's amazed, lifeless expression. She noticed that he was still holding the knife, his right hand gripping it so tightly the knuckles had turned bone white.

Then, as she was staring at him, something incredible happened.

The knife in his hand seemed to flicker like a strobe light. The blade glowed with a bright, purple radiance; and then, in the blink of an eye, it winked out of existence.

Sarah leaned back and gasped. Breaking the embrace, she looked at Sy and then back at Tony. She wasn't ready to accept what she had just seen.

"What the hell was that?" she whispered.

When David got up close to Karen and looked into her eyes, he saw a deadness there that filled him with terror. Her face was nothing but a gaunt, pale reflection of what it had been in life. The skin, especially on her cheeks and around her mouth, looked as dry as an Egyptian mummy's and was stretched paper-thin. A network of fine, dark lines like hairline cracks in porcelain marked her face. Her lifeless, glazed eyes stared back at him from beneath dark, bone-ridged sockets.

She seemed to register only dim recognition of her father as she slouched forward, her head lolling to one side. She would have toppled over onto the cave floor if her arms and legs hadn't been bound to the wall by heavy, clanking chains. A wave of despair swept through David when he realized that the chains and cuffs on Karen's ankles and wrists were forged from Stygian metal. The heavy links were set with thick concrete into the cave wall.

Trembling violently inside, David knelt down beside Karen and studied the chains. For a dizzying instant, he thought he could hear a faint chorus of shrill screams coming from inside the links. Remembering the pain that he had experienced when the reaper had bound him with similar chains, he didn't dare touch them; but he knew that he was going to have to if he was going to release her.

His mind clouded as the fear inside him intensified.

It isn't going to end like this! he thought as a sudden, savage fury ripped through him.

It can't end like this!

I won't allow it!

He grabbed the chain that bound Karen's legs and squeezed it tightly in spite of the paralyzing cold and excruciating pain that tore through him like a hurricane.

The screams coming from the metal grew louder, almost deafening. David knew that, if the sound continued much longer, it would drive him insane. He wondered why Karen wasn't reacting to the sound. Maybe she had been here for too long and had gotten used to it.

Feeling his strength draining from him by the second, David wrapped a length of the chain around each hand twice and clutched it tightly.

The pain grew unbearably intense. His vision went blank, and he found himself staring into a void of Nothingness as, with a wild cry of rage, he started to pull his hands apart.

His body shuddered from the tremendous effort. He could feel his strength draining away from him like lifeblood flowing from an open artery, but he kept pulling until he felt the metal beginning to yield.

The agonized shrieks coming from inside the chain rose even louder as the links slowly separated. Bright flashes of red filled David's vision; and then, with a final burst of savage energy, he yanked his hands apart, snapping the chain like a whip.

The cave was filled with the sound of clanking metal as the links of the chain separated and fell to the cave floor, scattering like a shower of coins.

No longer conscious of the horrendous pain that seized him, David took hold of the chain that bound Karen's arms and started to pull it apart. His corpus was infused with a violent, insane strength as he concentrated every ounce of his dwindling power on tearing the chain.

The screaming voices from the chain filled the cave as the links slowly pulled apart. The instant the arm cuffs fell away from Karen, David dropped the remnants to the cave floor before he lost any more strength.

He looked down at his hands and moaned softly. Although he experienced the pain only as a distant, throbbing pulse, he could see chick purple welts marking the insides of his palms and the backs of his hands. The skin sizzled like frying bacon. Thin wisps of smoke trailed upward in the still air.

Total exhaustion almost dragged him under, but then, like a cold spring breeze, a measure of relief flowed through him when he realized that Karen was free.

"Can you… Can you get up?" he asked with a strangled gasp, not entirely sure that he could move, either.

Karen looked back at him with a dull, vacant stare, but after a moment she smiled faintly and nodded.

"Yeah—I think—maybe," she answered in a ragged whisper.

"Come on, then," David said, extending his hand to her. "Come with me."

He felt completely dissociated and found it almost impossible to focus on what he was doing as he took his daughter's hand and raised her to her feet. Her body felt as light and hollow as a paper-mâché mask.

Karen seemed terribly unsteady on her feet. David was afraid that he might crush her as he wrapped an arm around her waist to support her.

"I... can't believe I... found you," he said, his voice threatening to break on every syllable.

"Me neither," Karen replied, still looking at him, dazed.

As broken and lifeless as her voice sounded, David was positive that this was *really* his daughter, and not some impostor. Although he suspected that it might be just another illusion, a trick of his emotions, he was positive that he could feel tears—*real* tears!—welling up in his eyes.

He almost jumped when Karen took his hand in hers and squeezed it tightly, almost desperately.

"I know you're scared and... and confused, honey," he said, trying to keep his voice low and even so he wouldn't frighten her any more than she had already been frightened. "But we really do have to hurry."

"Yeah, but I–I feel so... so weak," Karen said brokenly. "I don't have any idea how-how long I've been down here, but it seemed like... like *forever*." She paused and for a moment seemed to be focusing on something far, far away. "And it was *so-o-o* scary!"

"I know it was, but we'll have to talk about it later," David said. He cocked his head to one side, positive that he had heard a sound from deep inside the cave. "Right now we have to get back and cry to help her."

"Help... who?" Karen asked weakly.

The dim light in her eyes seemed to fade. She sagged forward and clutched her forehead with one hand as she shook her head in confusion. She looked as though she could barely stand, much less walk, but David knew that they had to get out of here fast. And he sure as hell wasn't going to leave her behind.

"Your mother," he said, and as soon as he said the word, a powerful wave of emotion filled him. "She—she needs my help."

For an instant, he thought he caught the faintest hint of a glow returning to Karen's eyes.

Side by side, with him supporting her, they started along the narrow, echoing corridor. Up ahead, the faint blue glow lit their way, but David was so exhausted that he had trouble focusing on it. Even as the echoes of their voices were fading away, another voice began to speak softly in his mind.

You're already too late! the inner voice said with a grating whisper that set David's nerves on edge. *You can't help her or anyone else!... Not even yourself! ... Why not just give up! ... You're much wo late! ...*

David thought he heard what sounded like approaching footsteps echoing from deep inside the cave. At first he thought—he hoped that it might be their own footsteps, echoing in the cavern; but once he stopped and listened for a moment, he knew the sound was getting louder.

And closer!

He distinctly heard a rough scraping sound... as though whoever might be following them had a bad leg and was dragging one foot on the ground! The thought filled David with a sudden, blinding panic, but he forced himself to control it.

"We have to hurry," he said, clutching Karen tightly to support her. When he looked down at her, he almost couldn't believe that this *really* was his daughter walking beside him.

She looked so small, so thin, so frightened.

Conflicting emotions twisted like coiling snakes inside him. He didn't even want to try to imagine what the reaper might have done to her while she was his prisoner here in the dark.

Everything that came to mind filled him with hatred and anger. Gripping her tightly, he urged her forward, and somehow they both found the strength to start running.

As they ran, the sound of pursuit behind them grew steadily louder.

David had no idea where they were headed, but he knew that he had no choice but to follow the faint glow of light that kept moving several paces ahead of them. He knew, but didn't dare tell Karen, what might happen if he was wrong—if the light was luring them deeper into the cave instead of out of it.

"Do you *really* think you can get away from me that easily?" a voice suddenly shouted from behind them.

David instantly recognized the shrill voice of the reaper.

He paused just long enough to swing Karen up into his arms and then, clutching her to his chest, redoubled his efforts as he ran through the darkness. The only clear thought in his mind was that, if he was going to cease to exist, then *this* was how he wanted it to be—clinging onto his daughter with every ounce of strength and love that he still had.

He had no idea how long he ran, but he was amazed that he didn't tire. He would have thought that contact with the Stygian chains would have sapped him of all his strength, but he ran knowing that his and Karen's very existence depended on getting away from the reaper.

Their footsteps and the wailing voice of the pursuer echoed wildly in the cave. The corridor twisted and turned like a huge snake, and as they ran, David once again had the distinct impression that he could see eyes opening up in the surrounding darkness. Eyes that watched them with a cold, steady stare. He could feel their piercing gaze like needles, making the back of his neck prickle.

"You'll never get away from me!" the voice shouted. This was followed by high, squealing laughter, but David thought that it sounded much farther behind him. He began to feel a faint hope that they might really make it.

But where would they go?

Where did this cave lead?

Maybe he was going around in circles... or heading right back coward the reaper.

His feet pounded against the hard-packed earth floor. Every impact made his vision jump and his teeth click together. The icy panic inside him was like a huge hand had gotten a tight grip on his heart and was squeezing... squeezing....

He was so lost in the fear of his flight that he didn't at first notice when the glow of light up ahead started to fade away. The cave blended into darkness so gradually that David barely noticed the purple, trailing afterimages that streaked in the corners of his vision.

But then, ever so slowly, the darkness closed in on him.

Once again, he felt a sudden rush of tumbling head over heels as he fell. He clutched Karen close to him as raging winds whistled and shrieked all around them. He could faintly hear someone calling out to him, but he had no idea if it was the reaper who had been pursuing them or Karen or himself.

But then, from out of the swirling darkness, he saw something—a hand, extending coward him. It was thin and bone white, and glowed with a faint iridescence.

Can you trust me?

David was so filled with terror that the voice barely registered in his brain. He saw the bony fingers spread like the framework of a fan as they reached out for him, but he didn't dare grab at them for fear of losing his hold on Karen. He chanced to look at her and saw her ghost-white face, staring up at him.

"I'm... scared... Daddy," she wailed.

He could hardly hear her above the rushing roar of the wind around them, and had to shout even to hear himself.

"I know," he said. "I am too."

Can you trust me? the voice repeated more emphatically as the Ferryman's face resolved out of the darkness. His heavy cloak shadowed his features, but David could see the steady glow in his sunken eyes, and he suddenly realized that he could—he *had to* trust the Ferryman!

He had brought him this far.

He had helped him find Karen.

As far as David could see, he had no other choice.

The fear gripped him that, should he let go of Karen, she would slip away from him and spinoff into the black, bottomless depths of the raging tempest. Clutching her as tightly as he could with one arm, he reached out with the other. His hand looked pale and as insubstantial as smoke as he grabbed for the Ferryman's hand.

The instant they touched, the dizzying sensation of falling stopped.

David looked around, amazed to see that they were standing on the sidewalk of a dark, deserted street. Something made a dull concussion in the air, but when he turned to look, there was nothing there. A vague sense of relief filled David, but he still had no idea where they were or how close the reaper might be. Groaning in pain, he lowered Karen to the ground, but he still held her around the waist until she seemed stable enough to stand on her own.

"Where the heck are we? What was all of that?" Karen asked. Amazement added a faint edge to her dead-sounding voice.

"I–I'm not sure," David replied as he looked around nervously, trying to get his bearings.

The street looked vaguely familiar, but he couldn't quite place it. All around them were ruins of buildings and thin, skeletal trees that looked like hands clawing at the night sky. David could see the abandoned wrecks of a few cars lining both sides of the street. He could also sense other people—other wraiths nearby, even though he couldn't see chem. Some of the densest shadows close to him shifted threateningly. When he turned and looked back at the Ferryman, he was only mildly surprised to see that he had disappeared.

"We-we have to keep going," he said to Karen, cringing inwardly as he tried to hide his own fear from her.

Holding hands, they started to run again. Their footsteps echoed with loud clicks in the silent night. For a fleecing instant, David had the distinct impression that they were still fleeing through the dark cavern.

That's right, said a voice inside his mind, although it sounded much fainter than it had in the cave. *Nothing's changed!* *... No matter where you go or what you do, you aren't going to accomplish a damned thing! ... I'm telling you, you're too late!...*

David tried to push the voice out of his mind, but as soon as it fell silent, he heard something else—a sound that he had heard on his first night in the Shadowlands. This time, however, he knew what it was.

A pack of barghests!

And this time, he knew that they were hunting for him and Karen!

The mournful baying sound filled the still night, broken only by the sound of their footsteps. Karen stumbled and stopped, then cast a terrified glance down the street in the direction they had come.

"What's that?" she asked in a trembling, tight whisper. "I– I've heard it before."

"I'll tell you later," David said. "Come on. Just keep moving as fast as you can."

And so they ran through the night with the howling sounds growing louder and louder behind them, spurring them on.

The night seemed to close down around them, and David had the distinct impression that, no matter how much effort they expended, the darkness was slowing them down, making them drag their feet. Faintly glowing eyes appeared in the dark windows and deeper recesses of the buildings lining the street. Hissing whispers filled the night, and shadows shifted, but nothing could block out the steadily rising sound of the hunting barghests coming closer.

David considered turning and confronting the pursuing beasts, but he was positive that it would mean a final death for him and for Karen—if not something worse, either imprisonment by the reaper or else something that he couldn't even imagine!

They had no choice.

They had to keep running, but David suddenly halted and looked around. Karen jerked to a stop beside him and looked around, bewildered.

Before she could ask him what it was, David said, "I think I recognize where we are!"

Somehow—he had no idea how—they had ended up on Forest Avenue, at the far end of Canal Street, not more than a couple of hundred yards from the house where he, Sarah, and Karen used to live—

Where Sarah still lived!

"We're almost home, honey," he whispered.

His voice was almost drowned out by the piercing howls of the barghests. David looked behind them and saw huge, black silhouettes under the faint glow of distant streetlights.

"Do you know where we are?"

Momentary confusion registered in Karen's eyes. Then a faint smile twitched one corner of her mouth.

"Yeah. Mommy and I used to come this way... on our way to... to that park!"

"You got it," David said.

All the while, he was looking down the street at the rapidly approaching creatures. They appeared to be a variety of shapes and sizes. Some of them ran on four legs, like huge hunting dogs; others walked with an awkward shamble on two legs, their knuckles dragging along the ground.

"We'll be safe at home," David said, not really sure if he believed that himself; but it was the only hope they had.

Taking Karen by the hand, he starred running again, pulling her along with him. The howling beasts pursuing chem must have caught sight of them because they raised a raucous chorus of howls that rang against the night sky. David didn't dare to look back as he ran, but he could feel their terrifying presence bearing down swiftly on them.

Ahead, almost lost in the gloom of the night, he saw the house. A few lights were on downstairs, and there was a light on in the upstairs bedroom windows. The warm, yellow glow was like a beacon that drew him onward.

As they ran, the street seemed to telescope outward. David was thinking that they should have covered the distance easily by now, but they appeared to be no closer to the house, even though the barghests behind them seemed to be closing the distance—fast.

"Please... Hurry," David said, having to shout to be heard about the baying of the beasts.

Somehow, Karen found the strength to scream as she ran. The sound seemed to send the pursuing creatures into a frenzy, spurring them on all the more.

With a sudden rush, the house loomed up close to them as though the ground had suddenly slipped under their feet. David stumbled and almost fell as he rounded the corner and started for the porch. He jerked to a stop when he saw something—a small, dark figure crouching on the top step. Two silver-green circles glared at him. It took David a paralyzing moment to recognize that it was Bingley.

"What's that? Will it hurt us?" Karen asked, cringing away as the cat hunched up its back and hissed viciously at them.

David cast a worried glance over his shoulder and saw that the barghests were quickly closing in on chem.

"Not as much as they will!" he said.

Clasping Karen by the hand, he charged up the steps to the side door. It took him a moment to realize that the door had been broken open and was dangling from one twisted hinge.

Bingley tracked them with his cold, unblinking eyes, but then he turned and looked up the street, past the single parked car, to the approaching beasts. With a loud hiss, he jumped off the porch and darted out into the street.

Just before David and Karen entered the house, he looked back in time to see the barghests turn and chase after the wraith of the dead cat.

"Jesus," David whispered as he watched the dark, seething pack disappear down the street. Their cries and the loud squalling of the cat gradually faded away.

David didn't have very long to appreciate their rescue. For all he knew, the barghests would quickly tire of chasing Bingley and come back looking for them. He was sure that they were implacable, untiring hunters who, once they had a scent, would not give up until they captured their prey.

David looked at the shattered door and instantly realized that Sarah was in danger.

There was no way of knowing when this had happened, but the voice in the back of his mind had been telling him all along that he was too late to save her. It felt to David like he had dived into cold, brackish water as he entered the kitchen. The ceiling light was on, but it seemed hardly bright enough to light the room.

"Sarah," he called out, knowing that she wouldn't be able to hear him... unless she were dead too and had become a wraith.

Side by side, they moved through the kitchen. David glanced at Karen and was deeply saddened to see the wan expression on her face. She looked as though she vaguely remembered this house but couldn't quite place it—as if it was part of a dim memory from long ago and far away.

As they were entering the living room, the muffled sound of an explosion rumbled through the house. It was deep and low, and sounded impossibly far away, but Karen screamed and pitched forward onto the floor. David was also staggered by the sound, but he immediately looked out into the hallway in the direction from which the sound had come.

"Stay right here," he said. "Find someplace to hide, just in case those—those things come back."

Karen looked at him with mounting terror in her eyes. She started to say something, but then another explosion rang out, this one louder. David drifted like wind-blown smoke up the stairs and then down the hallway toward Sarah's bedroom.

Tony was dazed.

For the briefest instant, he felt a sharp, searing pain in his head. This was followed by an abrupt release of pressure. He had a momentary sensation of spinning around and falling down, but then—somehow—he found that he was standing up and feeling unusually buoyant, as though he might float up into the air if he allowed himself to.

The instant the gun went off, the light in the room seemed to dim. It cast a dull, yellow glow that made everything in the room look like an old-fashioned sepia photograph. No matter where he looked, Tony saw tiny spikes and shifting curtains of light dancing and sparkling at the edges of things. He had the frightening impression that he was looking at things through a thick, distorting lens.

Sarah and a heavy-set man who looked like a goddamned weightlifter appeared to Tony as faint, almost transparent shadows. When he realized that he could barely distinguish their faces in the murky light, a bolt of fear shot through him.

What the fuck is going on here? he asked himself, but he didn't have time to wait for an answer.

Another person—someone he didn't recognize—had appeared in the doorway.

For some reason, Tony could see him more clearly than the others, but he could also see by the man's facial expression that this man saw and apparently recognized him.

"You son of a bitch!" the man shouted, his voice booming like a cannon shot in the air as he entered the room. He moved fast coward Tony, who backed up and raised his hands defensively.

That's when Tony realized that he still had the knife in his hand.

He looked at the blade, amazed to see how much it seemed to have changed. Ever since he had found it, he had thought that it seemed to glow with subtle energy, but now it was fairly vibrating with a tangle of interlacing strings of blue and purple light. The blade was humming like a tuning fork in his hand, sending a throbbing, almost painful sensation up the length of his arm.

The man saw the knife and instantly reacted, but he didn't slow down.

He hit Tony, hard and low, like a football tackler. The impact, although strangely muffled, carried them both to the floor. Before he could react, Tony felt the man grab the wrist of the hand that held the knife. By twisting and bending it backward with a quick jerk, he loosened Tony's grip on the rubber handle.

"Oh, no you don't, buddy!" Tony shouted, trying desperately to keep hold of the knife.

He was surprised by how distorted his own voice sounded to him—as if the air had suddenly gotten thicker, or he was talking underwater.

"You rotten son of a *bitch!*" the man growled through gritted teeth.

His face loomed closer to Tony, and what he saw paralyzed him with fear. The man's eyes glistened like dark, wet marbles, but there was an icy, distant glow in them that shook his courage and drained him of all strength.

The man's eyes looked absolutely *dead!* His face was seamed and cracked, and the skin looked pale and dry, like it was ready to slough off in large, flaky chunks.

"*You're not going to have her!*" the man said between clenched teeth as he thrashed viciously from side to side and tried to pry Tony's fingers from the knife handle. "I *won't* let you have her! It's *not* too late!"

Tony was still feeling oddly dissociated from his own body, so it was almost impossible for him to resist the man's savage strength. His hand holding the knife went numb as tingling waves of pins-'n-needles spread like wildfire up to his shoulder.

Tony thrashed from side to side, but it didn't do any good.

All he could do was watch helplessly, as though distantly viewing a movie while the man pried his fingers apart and forced the knife out of his hand.

The blade was shining with such shimmering energy that Tony found it almost impossible to look directly at it. Struck dumb with terror, he watched as the man turned the knife around and, raising it high above his head, prepared for a downward thrust.

Icy numbness filled Tony when he realized what was going to happen next.

He's going to kill me!

This was one of his last clear thoughts. He wished fervently that he could close his eyes, but he couldn't look away as he saw the tip of the knife begin its downward arc.

The motion seemed to take forever.

As the knife descended, it made a dull, rolling concussion in the oddly silent air. Then, like the stinging bite of a snake, an intense pain pierced the center of Tony's chest.

When the man pulled the blade out and raised it again, preparing to strike a second time, Tony looked down to where the knife had entered his body, amazed to see, not gushing blood, but a dull, white glow of light that seemed to be radiating out of the wound.

He was terrified beyond belief.

He tried to scream, but his strength was rapidly draining out of his body. His view of the room dimmed until he and everything else were nothing more than a distorted shadow show. The last thing Tony saw before he plunged into the bottomless, eternal darkness was the looming face of a man that he didn't even know...

The face of the man who had killed him!

bargaining for souls.

Chapter Fifteen

David was feeling utterly exhausted.

Fighting with the wraith for possession of the knife had drained what little strength remained in him. He had watched in absolute amazement and rapidly mounting horror as the glowing knife blade, almost as if moving of its own volition, had penetrated deep into the man's chest. He had felt his own life force dissipating like wind-driven smoke as he watched the man writhe in agony, his corpus slowly dissolving away until there was nothing left except a small, dark smudge on the floor like a pile of wee ashes. After another few seconds, even that disappeared, dissolving like dirty ice melting in the sun.

Filled as he was with anger and hatred and fear, David didn't feel the slightest compunction about destroying the man's corpus. As far as he was concerned, he deserved to die a thousand deaths, if only because he had been trying to hurt Sarah.

The man's physical body still lay sprawled on the bedroom floor at the foot of the bed, but it, too, looked like it was deteriorating much faster than it normally would. Thick, dark droplets of blood and globs of brain fell like rain from the splattered ceiling. The man's face appeared to be bleaching out as it caved in on itself, looking like time-lapse photography of rotting fruit. His eyes looked as cold and dead as scones as he stared sightlessly over at the baseboard beside the closet door.

David reached out helplessly with both arms as he looked over at Sarah, who was still clinging to the muscular man with the close-cropped, blond hair. Neither one of chem appeared to be the slightest bit aware of the terrible struggle that had just occurred in the room, practically at their feet.

As David struggled to stand, still holding the knife in his right hand, a high buzzing sound filled the room—or maybe it was in his head. He wondered if the sound might be coming from the blade itself. The knife in his hand felt as though it must weigh at least ten pounds.

His first impulse was to get rid of the damned thing, but before he even started to do that, he tensed as another thought occurred to him.

It isn't over yet!

Sarah was safe, at least for the time being, but what about Karen?

Trembling violently, David turned toward the bedroom door and stared into the deep darkness that filled the hallway. It looked like a solid wall of black stone. He wanted desperately to go downstairs to his daughter, but he was not sure that he had the strength to move.

"*Karen,*" he whispered, his voice no more than a rattling gasp.

The instant he said his daughter's name out loud, Sarah grunted as she spun around and looked directly at where David was standing. Her eyes were wide and moist with fear. Tears sparkled like diamonds on her cheeks. She licked her upper lip with the tip of her tongue.

"Did—did you just say something?" she asked, frowning as she glanced at the muscular man. Her voice sounded strangely modulated and was almost lost in the dense atmosphere of the room.

The man looked at Sarah quizzically and then slowly shook his head no.

"I thought I heard a—"

Sarah glanced around the room, an expression of absolute bewilderment on her face. She sucked in her breath and held it as she listened for a moment or two, then exhaled noisily. The sound filled David with sadness, reminding him again how much he missed as simple an act as breathing.

"I could have sworn I heard a… no… never mind," she said, gnawing at her lower lip as she narrowed her eyes. She looked like she had a terrible headache. "Must be my imagination, I guess, but I could have sworn I heard someone say—"

"Say what?" the muscular man asked, his eyes softening with sympathy.

"My—No! I'm sure it was nothing," Sarah said emphatically. She sighed and tilted her head to one side as though trying to shake water out of her ear.

David watched as an expression of mixed worry and fear played across his ex-wife's face. He was positive that she had heard him speak but he was also quite sure that, were he to speak again, no matter how loud he shouted, she wouldn't be able to hear him. Perhaps talking to the living was one of those skills the Ferryman had mentioned. If so, it was something David was determined to practice until he learned it.

Right now, though, his sudden fear for Karen's safety overrode any desire to communicate with Sarah.

It took an immense effort of will for him to step over the corrupted corpse of the stranger and move past Sarah and the other stranger to the corridor.

Thick, pulsating darkness filled the hallway.

David could tell that there was a light on downstairs, but the feeble glow seemed dimmer than that of a single match. He suspected that his own vision was fading. He might be so exhausted from everything he had been through recently that he was fading away.

The sound of his feet dragging across the carpet in the hallway echoed in the pressing darkness like long, weary sighs.

It seemed to take him several minutes, if not hours, to move from the bedroom to the head of the stairs. If he hadn't been so concerned about Karen, he was sure he never would have been able to descend the staircase. He would have been content to collapse right there on the hallway floor and let Oblivion sweep him away.

Somehow, though, he dragged himself down the stairs and made it into the living room. The thick, murky light in the room swirled like daylight seen by a diver, looking up from the muddy depths of a lake. Vague, distorted forms appeared at the edges of his vision but disappeared just as quickly when he looked straight at them. He thought he could hear snatches of raw whispering voices, bits of conversations as well as faint laughter, but he couldn't get a fix on any of it.

But suddenly, in the center of his vision, he saw something that filled him with absolute terror.

There wasn't just one but two shadowy figures standing in the center of the living room floor in front of the couch.

David rubbed his face with his hand and shook his head, trying desperately to clear his vision, but the illusion wouldn't go away. What he was seeing didn't seem possible!

There couldn't be two Karens!

His first thought was that he was seeing double, but as his vision cleared, he saw that there really were two figures of his daughter, standing side by side, like twins.

"Daddy?" one of them said in a voice that was low and hollow-sounding.

Before David could respond, the other Karen looked at him intently and said, "I'm *really* scared, Daddy."

David staggered backward, overwhelmed by confusion. His right hand gripped the knife handle so tightly that a dull ache started to throb in the palm of his hand and up his arm. He looked back and forth between the two figures until it finally dawned on him what was going on.

The reaper must have arrived and assumed Karen's shape in order to confuse him. Obviously he was trying to trick David so he could gain possession of the knife.

That's what this was all about, wasn't it?

The knife!

"Please..." David said, groaning softly as another smothering wave of exhaustion swept over him. The image that he was drowning and looking up at the sky got sharper. "No more games. Please!"

David heard his own voice as a low, fluttering whisper. The sound reminded him of the moaning the wind makes, fluting inside a chimney during a blizzard. It sent shivers racing through him. The darkness at the fringes of his vision steadily deepened and began to close in from all sides with vague hints of shifting, swirling motion.

Looking like distorted mirror images, the two Karens regarded each other, then looked back at him. Their postures were as stiff as corpses lying in their coffins. Their faces were thin and pallid, absolutely void of all expression.

"One of you... one of you is an impostor," David whispered, cringing at the weakness he could hear in his own voice.

Exhaustion squeezed in on him like huge hands, crushing his head and chest. He knew that he had to find a safe place to rest—soon!—or else he would slip into Oblivion.

"It's not me," one of the Karens said, stepping closer to David with upraised arms.

"Yes it is!" the other one cried out, sounding almost pitiful. "I'm the real Karen! Can't you see that, Daddy?"

David couldn't help but notice that both of them spoke with a terrible dead-sounding flatness in their voices, as though they were just as exhausted as he was...

Just as dead!

It made sense that Karen would be exhausted, David thought. He knew from experience that being bound by Stygian chains can drain everything out of a corpus.

How was he going to determine which one was the real Karen and which was the reaper?

Squeezing the knife so tightly that his hand trembled, David took a halting step forward, his eyes shifting back and forth between the two images of his daughter as he studied them carefully, looking for some slight difference between them.

But the illusion appeared to be absolutely perfect. There was no way he could tell them apart. If he had enough time, could wait long enough, he guessed that the reaper's illusion would eventually lose strength and fade; but he didn't have much time. He was already well past the point of collapse.

He had to figure out which one of these was really his daughter so he could get her away from the reaper, but how could he decide?

As long as he had the knife, the reaper obviously would be driven to keep pursuing him. And he wouldn't hesitate to capture or harm Karen if he thought he could use her against David to get the knife from him. As long as the reaper had his pack of barghests or whatever other allies he could summon from the Shadowlands to hunt him, David knew that he and Karen would *never* be safe.

And then it hit him.

All the reaper wants is the knife!

So why not give it to him?

What difference would it make?

David no longer had any doubts about what was so special about the knife. He had seen the power it had when it destroyed the wraith's corpus. No wonder the reaper was willing to use any means necessary to get possession of it.

But the Ferryman had said that he would bargain for it too.

"This is what you want, isn't it?" David said as he raised the knife and waved it back and forth in front of his face. He thought he saw one of the Karens flinch away from him while, at the same time, the other Karen twitched and took a tentative step forward.

"Right from the start—it's been about this, hasn't it?" he asked, knowing that the reaper couldn't be tricked so easily to break cover and reply. "You'll do *anything* to get it, won't you? *Won't you?*"

"It's not me, Daddy!" one of the Karens wailed, pointing angrily at her Doppleganger. "It's *him!* He's the reaper! Use the knife on him!"

"No, *I'm* your daughter!" the other Karen replied. "Come on, Daddy! Don't you even *recognize* me?"

David had to admit that whichever one was the reaper, he was playing the masquerade perfectly. There was no way he could determine which was the real Karen. He stumbled backward as heavy waves of exhaustion swept over him, threatening to drag him under.

And that's when he got an idea.

It wasn't much, but it was certainly worth taking a chance. It might be all he had left.

Raising the knife above his head, he stepped forward. His mouth was set, grim and menacing.

"There's only one way out of this for all of us," he said softly.

Both images of his daughter stared at him in amazement.

"Wha–what do you mean?" one of the Karens said.

For the first time, David thought he detected a slight tremor of emotion in the voice.

"I mean," he said, "that I'm going to have to use this knife… on *both* of you."

"But we're already dead," one of the Karens said, sounding nervous and a little mystified.

"Oh, I know that, but I've already seen what kind of power this blade contains," David said. "I know how truly dangerous it is."

"You have no idea," the Karen who had flinched earlier said to David.

"I'm really sorry about this, honey," David said, addressing that one, "but it's the only way I can make sure that, whichever one of you is the reaper, you never get control of it. I can't begin to imagine the misery and pain someone could inflict with this. It has a *terrible* power here in the Shadowlands."

One of the Karens, the one that had flinched, opened her mouth as though about to speak, but then fell silent.

The other Karen slowly lowered her eyes and meekly bowed her head. David thought she looked exactly like a condemned prisoner, preparing herself for execution.

"You're right, Daddy," she said.

And as soon as she said that, David knew.

The other Karen took a quick step away from David and raised her arms as though to ward off a blow.

"It's you!" David shouted at the one who was backing away from him. He almost tripped and fell as he lunged forward at the figure, but before the knife could strike home, the figure of Karen shrieked and darted away from him. Standing with her back pressed against the wall, her body began to shimmer as though the light in the room were flickering rapidly. Her body slowly expanded and then transformed into the slouched figure of the reaper.

"It isn't over yet," the reaper snarled, his eyes gleaming wickedly as he glared at David.

The other Karen — the real one — looked at the creature with a mixture of surprise and fear registering in her expression. Her mouth dropped open, but no sound came out. Her body began to tremble violently as she clung close to her father.

"Don't worry, honey," David said. "He's not going to hurt you anymore. Not as long as I have this." He slashed the knife through the air, satisfied to see the reaper shrink away from him.

"We'll see about that!" the reaper said, his voice rising to a high cackle. "You can run, but you can't hide!"

David lunged at him again and swung the knife, but missed by several inches. The reaper dodged to one side, moving closer to the door that should lead into the kitchen, but David saw something else. A dense, churning black emptiness filled the doorway.

As David watched, absolutely amazed, chick clouds underlie by a fierce red glow that flickered with sharp forks of lightning formed into faces and distinct shapes.

For a dizzying instant, David could feel himself being sucked toward the doorway. He suddenly felt ungrounded... totally off balance... uncentered. The memory of falling and floating in that vast, dark emptiness filled him with terror. It was only by a great effort of will that he focused on where he was standing and what he was doing.

"I tried to work this out with you," the reaper said, all the while edging closer to the doorway, "but now it's too late for that. You're going to be sorry."

David narrowed his eyes, fighting hard against the sense of total disorientation.

"And I swear to you," the reaper cried, "by anything and everything you ever held holy—especially on your daughter's soul—that you'll come to regret this. I'm going to make you suffer like you've never suffered before, and the beautiful thing about it is that you and I both know that it will never end!"

The reaper pointed at David and shook his forefinger angrily.

"I'll be back for you—for the *both* of you! You won't get away with this!"

With a final, nervous glance over his shoulder, the reaper darted through the kitchen door and was swallowed by the swirling clouds.

"Go after him!" Karen shouted, tugging anxiously on David's arm. "You can't let him get away, Daddy! You have to stop him even if you have to use that knife to kill him!"

But David couldn't move. The terror he was feeling, remembering his fall through the directionless void of Oblivion, rooted him to where he stood.

"*Terra firma,*" he whispered, and then chuckled softly when he remembered something his mother used to say. "*Terra firma, and the more firma, the less Terra.*"

He stared helplessly at the empty doorway as the raging tempest subsided, and once again he saw the ordinary reality of Sarah's kitchen.

Shaking his head from side to side, he looked at Karen and said, "I'm sorry, honey, but I can't."

He wondered if his daughter had seen the same thing in the doorway that he had, or if it was something only he was able to perceive. The feeling that such a bottomless, eternal storm was at the heart of everything, just waiting for him to slip into it, filled him with dread.

Pushing aside the dark waves of dizziness and nausea that filled him, he stamped his foot a few times on the floor, grateful to hear and feel the softly resounding impact. It still seemed oddly distanced, but it was real enough for him. He only vaguely sensed that Karen was at his side, hanging onto his hand as she called out his name.

But the dizziness inside him was growing steadily stronger. He knew he was too far gone as he slumped forward, only dimly aware that he was slipping away into a twilight world where everything was muted and quiet and—ultimately— peaceful.

His last thought before he blacked out was—*If this is the end of it all, then I am truly at peace.*

Sarah let out a shrill screech when she finally realized that her face and chest were splattered with blood and wormy-looking bits of Tony's brain. Shrinking inward, she tore herself away from Sy, not even aware that she was whimpering softly as she frantically wiped away the streaks of gore. All she managed to do was smear the mess even more. Her hands slid across her breasts and arms with a sickly greasy feel.

When Sy grabbed her wrists with both hands and held her tightly, she at first cried to resist, but eventually she gave in and let him pull her to his chest. She could feel his large hand cupping the back of her head as he stroked her hair.

"Hey, now. Take it easy Just cake it easy," he whispered.

His voice seemed to be coming from light years away, but—somehow—it cut through Sarah's swelling panic. She sighed and closed her eyes as she nestled against him and let her hot tears course down her cheeks.

"You... you shot him," she said between shuddering moans. "You–you actually *k-k-killed* him."

Sy's hold on her tightened, but it never got painful. His hug was warm and all-encompassing, making her feel totally secure. It was like being smothered by a huge, hard bear.

"Yeah, I had to," Sy whispered, bringing his mouth so close to her ear that she could feel the warmth of his breath against her neck. "It was either him or you. Pretty easy choice, as far as I could see."

"Umm," was all Sarah could say.

A cold, hollow vacuum opened up inside her stomach when she let herself realize just how close she had come to dying. The stark reality of that thought terrified her and made the aching grief she was feeling all the more intense.

Tony's dead! Jesus, he's really dead, and I helped kill him!

To be responsible for the death of another human being — even one as deranged and dangerous as Tony obviously had been — was too much for her to handle. But just as she was considering whether or not she would ever be able to live with herself, another thought hit her. It filled her with an icy dread that sapped all her strength.

This must be how David felt when he saw Karen die!

For the first time in her life, she realized that she had been so blinded by her own grief at the loss of their daughter that she had never truly appreciated or understood how terrible it must have been for David to feel solely responsible for Karen's death.

Until now!

How could she have been so callous, so blind to what he was going through? She knew that she couldn't excuse herself by telling herself that Karen was her only daughter, and that she had suffered the loss just as deeply as he had.

He had *been* there when she died! He had *seen* it all happen!

She had *died* in his arms!

He had watched the light in her eyes dim and go out!

And now both Karen and David were dead… lost to her forever.

She was never going to get the chance to tell him how sorry she was for all the pain and suffering he had gone through, all the heartbreak she had caused him.

"I… I wish I could die," she whispered into the crook of Sy's neck as wrenching sobs choked her. "Right now. I–I wish I could just — just curl up and *die!*"

"Hey, you don't want to be talking like that," Sy said. His voice was edged with firmness as he stood back and held her at arm's length and stared, long and hard, into her eyes. She felt nervous and very small under his steady gaze.

"But I–I *do*!" she said, trying hard to stifle the numbing, gut-twisting rush of emotions that filled her. "I *really* mean it!"

"No, you don't!" Sy snapped. Anger flashed like lightning in his eyes. "Look, I know you're upset right now, okay? And it's understandable. Who wouldn't be upset when some guy breaks into your house and tries to kill you? But you can't let it get to you. Do you hear me? You can't!"

Sy was still holding her tightly by both arms as he glanced over his shoulder, down at Tony's bloody corpse on the bedroom floor. Without blood pressure, the blood was no longer flowing from the gaping head wound. It had pooled on the rug, looking like a huge splash of India ink.

"The scumbag's dead," Sy said, "and I don't feel a single ounce of pity for him. Now, I can't stop you from letting him break your spirit because of what he did—not if you want to let him; but if he does, that means he wins in the end. Is that what you want?"

Sarah closed her eyes, trying to stop the flow of tears. Gritting her teeth hard, she shook her head, rubbing her face against Sy's chest.

"No," she said, so faintly that she could hardly hear herself above the rushing whoosh of her pulse in her ears.

"You're alive, dammit!"

She looked up and saw the bright fire that lit Sy's eyes.

"And as long as you're *alive*, you'd better make *damned* sure you appreciate every second of it, because in the end—it'll be taken away from you just like *that*."

He snapped his fingers loudly in front of her face, but Sarah was too numb to react. She was finding it almost impossible to register what he was saying to her. His voice echoed and modulated so wildly that she thought she might be close to passing out or something. The fringes of her vision were closing in on her like heavy curtains.

Somehow, though, she kept her balance and remained standing.

Her stomach clenched like a fist when she looked past Sy at Tony's body. It was impossible for her to believe that this was the same man she thought she actually might be falling in love with... the same man who had taken her out to eat and out dancing... the same man who had shared her bed with her.

He had seemed so loving, so kind; but tonight he had seemed like an entirely different person.

What could have made him change like that? What could have driven him to such murderous rage?

She wondered again about the knife and where it might have gone. She was positive that she had seen it in his hand, just as she was positive that she had seen it flicker and then fade out of sight.

But that now seemed impossible.

Ridiculous.

A small part of her mind was telling her that it *couldn't* have happened that way. Either the knife had gotten kicked under the bed, or else it was hidden underneath Tony's body. The police would no doubt find it once they investigate.

Or maybe Tony had never even had a knife. She could have imagined him holding one and threatening her with it.

"—to me?" Sy's voice suddenly broke through the spiraling rush of Sarah's thoughts. It took her another moment or two to register that he had just asked her a question.

Feeling dazed and oddly dissociated, she shook her head and looked at him. Her vision was all hazy. Everything—even Sy's head and shoulders—seemed to be edged by a shifting white glow of light. The sensitive, supportive expression she saw on his face helped her ground herself.

"Wha–what did you say?" she asked in a high, twisted voice.

"I asked if you were listening to me?"

Sarah bit down on her lower lip and considered everything he had said for another moment. Then she sucked in a quick breath and held it as she nodded.

"Yeah," she said. "I am."

Looking again at Tony's body, she exhaled slowly, once again feeling herself starting to collapse inward like a deflating balloon. Then she shook her head, squared her shoulders, and forced herself to smile.

"I guess we'd better call the cops now, huh?" she said.

Sy regarded her with a cautious gaze, then smiled as he nodded and said, "Yeah, that would probably be a good next step."

For the longest time—so long, in fact, that he had no idea when he first became consciously aware of it—David realized that he had been listening to two people whispering his name.

The voices blended subtly from one into the other, warbling and fluttering in the darkness like two unseen, hovering birds. Sometimes they were more like colors or smells or feelings than sounds, and before long, such distinctions between any of the senses seemed futile and absolutely meaningless. The voices sounded like high, fast winds, blowing through a pine forest... like the slow, bubbly hiss of air, leaking from a punctured lung... like the soft rush of a fast-flowing river... like the distant buzz of bees in a summer field....

David wasn't sure what—if anything—they were saying, but every now and then the words *David* and *Daddy* seemed to come through like faint radio signals. Before long, every sound merged with the others until they all made a new sound that had no literal meaning, but which seemed to encompass many deep, unspoken meanings.

All David knew for certain was that, for a single, timeless instant, the voices filled him with a deep sense of peace and tranquility. He could feel his corpus getting thinner and lighter than the air as he floated above or beyond everything else. All of his worries and fears seemed to slough away like old, dry skin, and he found himself in a place where everything—even his own thoughts and feelings—were cushioned and comfortable. Rich, deep, wordless concepts formed in his mind like bubbles rising to the surface of a perfectly motionless pond. He was thrilled and almost overwhelmed by a sensation of clear and perfect understanding.

Unfortunately, this feeling of complete well-being didn't last for very long.

In fact, as soon as he became consciously aware of it, he could feel it beginning to crumble.

In his mind an image formed of a huge, elaborate sand castle that was being pulled apart by relentless, rising tides. In the center of his being, he could feel a glowing core that had density... gravity... beginning to grow.

And then it started to pull him downward, back into himself.

No, I want to stay here!

But even as he thought this, David knew that it was too late. He was already no longer in that perfectly tranquil, timeless place, and he despaired of ever finding it again.

Once more, he became acutely aware of his own essential being, of his individuality. That thought or concept or whatever it was filled him with subtle alarm and a deep, nameless anxiety.

No, wait! ... I don't WANT to be ME anymore! he thought, but the voices were drawing him back like fishhooks that had pierced his body and were pulling him down.

After another timeless moment, David heard the soft concussion of an explosion deep inside his head. He opened his eyes and looked around with frantic fear welling up like dark water inside him.

He found himself staring into a solid wall of darkness.

As consciousness returned, gradually and painfully, his vision sharpened. He caught a hint of motion off to one side — something moving against the deep darkness.

He longed to hear the soft, steady pumping of his heart in his chest, to feel the slow, steady expansion of his chest, but there was nothing.

He felt as cold and lifeless as a wet lump of clay.

He realized that he was sitting splay-legged on a hard floor and leaning back against a wall.

Wait a second… This place seems familiar.

Then, with a cold rush, he knew that he was back at the schoolhouse. A hint of hazy gray light filtered like low-hanging smoke through the darkness, but he was able to see clearly enough to recognize the two figures that were standing close beside him.

One was Karen and the other was the Ferryman.

"You gave a good accounting of yourself back there," the Ferryman said in a low voice that had a soothing, vibrant pitch to it.

The darkness filled with the soft sound of rustling cloth as the Ferryman stepped closer to David and held out a skeletal hand, palm up. The hand bones glowed eerily white, like streaks of lightning in the close darkness.

"Now, if you don't mind," the Ferryman said, sounding more demanding, "I can't demand it, but I would like you to give me that knife."

David's mouth dropped open as he looked down at his lap and saw that he still had a firm grip on the hard rubber handle of the knife. He had such a tight grip that his wrist and forearm had gone completely numb. It was like looking at someone else holding something. There wasn't the slightest sense of feeling in his hand. Subtle blue light shimmered along the edge of the blade, and David thought he could hear a faint humming sound coming from it.

"I–I've seen what this knife can do," he said in a dry, shattered whisper. "And I–I'm not so sure I... that you or... anyone should have it."

"Oh, it's not for me," the Ferryman replied solemnly. "Theone who might be able to harness its power and use it is far greater than *I*."

"Really?"

David tried to laugh, but his throat wouldn't make the right sound. He twisted his body to one side, shielding the knife from the Ferryman.

"If it's so damned important," he said, "then why doesn't *he* come here and get it himself?"

"Because—" the Ferryman replied in a voice that sounded like something scraping against hard-packed earth. "Because he may no longer even exist. In any event, I thought we had a bargain—the knife as surety for you and your daughter's eternal salvation."

David glanced over at Karen and once again was pierced by deep regret when he saw the pale, dead look in his daughter's eyes. He wondered how—or if—those eyes would ever sparkle again with any semblance of hope or love. His hand was trembling as he reached out for her and took her hand. It felt like a small, fragile bird. Sadness filled him because their couching hands still felt so far away. He had to accept that death was a chasm that even human love wasn't able to span.

"Where can you take us?" David asked, trying his best to keep the winding fear at bay.

"Someplace safe. To the Far Shores, just as we agreed," the Ferryman replied. "There you will both find eternal peace and tranquility of the soul."

"*It's a lie! It's a bloody, damned lie!*"

The ragged voice that suddenly thundered in the darkness made the air throb with dangerous energy.

Karen squealed and huddled close to her father, hugging him around the neck. David scanned the darkness until he discerned the stooped figure that was moving toward them from the open doorway. The dark silhouette looked like a hole that had been cut out of the night. Only the Ferryman seemed unfazed by the sudden intrusion.

"I warned you, didn't I," the figure said, "about trusting him and his kind?"

The darkness was filled with the sound of approaching footsteps. David had no doubt who it was when he heard the sound of one foot dragging like a dead weight across the old wooden floor.

"And I'm supposed to trust you instead? Is that it?" David asked archly.

The reaper halted and almost responded, then caught himself and took a few steps closer, stopping a short distance away from David.

"No," he said after a long pause. "You should know by now that in the Shadowlands you can only trust yourself and no one else! Haven't you even learned *that* much yet?" The reaper cackled with twisted laughter that set David's nerves on edge.

"What does it take for you to learn such a simple fact as that, huh?"

"I–I'm not sure," David replied edgily, "but I *do* know that I can't trust you—not after what you did to my daughter!"

"Hey, what can I say? She was the bait—just a lowly pawn in this whole foolish game, okay? Do you actually still think that an individual—any individual really matters or counts?" He laughed again, more strongly, and much more darkly. "If you do, then you're an even bigger fool than I suspected."

"We'll see who's the fool," David said softly.

He was trying hard to control the burning rage that filled him, but he couldn't block out his memory of everything this reaper had done to him and his daughter since his arrival in the Shadowlands. Remembering his daughter's imprisonment in that cold, lonely tunnel of the reaper's haunt filled David with blinding anger.

He was tired of being lied to and cricked. He couldn't even be sure if it had been Karen or the reaper impersonating her when he had first seen her that rainy day out at Brighton Avenue Park. He had no idea who or what to trust anymore, but he was positive that *this* reaper had more than earned his eternal hatred.

"Do you actually think that this... this *Ferryman* will do what he *says* he will?" the reaper asked. Another burst of braying laughter sent a horrible chill through David.

Throughout the conversation so far, the Ferryman had remained perfectly motionless and silent, but David could feel his intense gaze from under his hood slicing into him. Once again, just as he had while fleeing the reaper's haunt with Karen, David had the distinct impression that uncountable eyes had opened up in the surrounding darkness and were staring at him with unblinking gazes.

"It–it doesn't really matter what he says or does," David said. Although he still felt totally drained of strength, he heaved himself up off the floor and stood shakily. He knew he would collapse if he didn't lean back against the wall.

"Not as long as I have *this!*" David said. He stepped forward and jabbed the knife at the reaper, satisfied to see the reaper jerk back quickly out of harm's way.

"I saw what it did to that man in my wife's house," David said between clenched teeth, "and I suspect that it would do pretty much the same thing to you or any other wraith. You wouldn't mind if I gave it a try, would you?"

"Don't be a *fool!*" the reaper snarled.

David was pleased to hear a high note of tension in his voice.

"That's exactly what I would be if I gave this to you," he said. "I have a pretty good idea how you would use it."

For emphasis, David cut the air with a few quick flicks of the blade. The reaper ducked back another couple of steps, keeping out of harm's way.

"*He'll* use it for worse purposes," the reaper said, so angry he was trembling as he pointed to the motionless Ferryman, who remained so perfectly motionless that David couldn't dispel the impression that he had turned into a statue. "Do you *really* think that *he* won't be tempted to use a relic with that much power?"

"You have no conception of what I would or would not do with it," the Ferryman said in a low, controlled voice that resonated with strength. Even the reaper seemed cowed by it.

There was a soft rustle of cloth, and David sensed more than saw the Ferryman move closer to him. The darkness behind the Ferryman seemed to be agitated as though churning with dark energy. It looked like a kaleidoscope made of black and smoky gray glass. David had the vague impression that the darkness behind the Ferryman was chinning, as though a doorway was opening up behind him. He gasped when he saw the boiling clouds of the Tempest behind the Ferryman.

"You both may come with me," the Ferryman said. "I gave you my word that I would bring you to the Far Realms. There you will both know peace and true transcendence."

"No, you won't!" the reaper shouted, his voice so shrill it wavered and broke. "What you'll *know* is *Oblivion!*"

He started to take a few steps closer to them, but David raised the knife and fended him off. The shimmering light emanating from the blade pulsated with energy, growing steadily brighter. David could almost sense the knife's need to cut—to *kill!*

"There *are* no *Far Realms!*" the reaper squealed. "They're a myth—a fairy tale—a delusion that exists only in the minds of lunatics, fanatics, and fools. Do you *really* think there's a level of existence where you can be eternally happy and at peace *forever?* A heaven where you will strum on a harp and sing *hallelujah* for the rest of eternity?"

The walls of the schoolhouse resonated with the reaper's derisive laughter.

"Can't you see? It's exactly the same thing as Oblivion! You'll lose yourself. Your entire being—every aspect of your personality that is unique and individual to you—will be completely annihilated! You'll be destroyed—lost forever! The only place where you remain even a shadow of who you were in real life is right here in the Shadowlands! You don't want to lose what little is left of you, do you?"

"I do," Karen said in a frail voice that cut through the darkness. "I want to go there."

David Looked at her and felt his heart shatter into a thousand pieces. She looked so small, so vulnerable, and he knew—as he had always known—that he would make any sacrifice necessary for the love of his child.

"I mean it, Daddy," Karen said, looking up at him with wide, glowing eyes. "I at Least want to try."

David could feel a dull pressure gripping his hand as she took hold of it again and squeezed it tightly.

"So give him the knife if that's what he wants. He'll do what he says. He's given us his word. We should both go, if only so we can get away from... from *him* and all of *this.*"

David didn't have to ask what she meant by 'this.' He knew perfectly well that she meant the darkness and the terror—the loneliness and utter despair of the Shadowlands.

He could feel the allure of wanting to go with the Ferryman to the Far Realms, even if Transcendence and Oblivion *were* the same thing; but deep in his heart, he knew that he couldn't leave the Shadowlands—not just yet, anyway.

Not as long as Sarah was still alive.

He still had at least one fetter binding him here, and if his ex-wife was a strong enough fetter to keep him, then he was more than willing to embrace it.

Powerful emotions unblocked by any physical restrictions choked him as he knelt down and looked deeply into his daughter's eyes. Conflicting thoughts and feelings raged inside him with almost unbearable intensity.

"Honey, I... I'm not sure I know how to say this."

"You mean that you're not gonna come with me?" Karen said.

David wanted to deny it, but more than that, he couldn't lie to her.

"I can't leave your mommy behind. Not just yet, anyway."

He could hear the rough catching in his voice, but he forced himself to continue. "She—I know she still needs me to—to watch over her, to be there for her... to make sure she's still safe."

Karen regarded him with a steady, blank expression, and then nodded her head slowly. He placed the knife down on the floor by his knee as he gripped both of her arms just above the elbow. His chest ached with repressed sobs as he pulled her close to him.

"You understand that, don't you, sweetie?"

Intense surges of emotion swelled like a storm-churned ocean inside him. His vision pulsated with wave after wave of vibrating flashes that made Karen's face waver in and out of focus. Sometimes she appeared so small she was almost lost in the darkness, but an instant later her face would loom close to him, large enough to fill his entire field of vision.

"If you want to go with him... with the Ferryman now, I promise you that I'll come along just as soon as I can, okay?"

Karen said nothing as she continued to stare at him. Her gaze pierced him to the core of his being.

"And do you know what?" David said, choking on his emotion. "I'll bet it won't even feel like more than a couple of minutes before I'm back with you. Do you think you can handle that, honey?"

David glanced over at the Ferryman, hoping to see some sign of reassurance, but the Ferryman's face remained shrouded within the dark folds of his hood.

The emotional torment inside David was becoming unbearable. He knew that he couldn't handle this much longer. If he was going to let the Ferryman take Karen away, then he wanted her to go soon—

Right now!

"It's all right, Daddy," Karen finally said. Her voice wasn't much more than a breathy whisper in the dark, but the reassurance David felt was immeasurable. "You don't have to cry, Daddy."

"But I'm not cr—"

Before he could finish speaking, David became aware of a thin, wet line that tickled him as it slid slowly down his cheek from his left eye. He tried to speak, but his voice choked off when Karen reached out and caressed the side of his face. She wiped the tear away with her finger and held it up to show him. A diamond—bright droplet glistened wetly on the tip of her forefinger.

David was almost overcome with emotion. He was just starting to stand up when the reaper made his move.

As quick as a striking rattlesnake, he darted forward and made a grab for the knife on the floor. David caught only a hint of motion in the darkness, but he sensed the danger immediately. His entire body seemed to prickle as though charged with static electricity. Pushing Karen roughly aside, he picked up the knife and, crouching low, swung it up in a wide arc that slashed across the reaper's face. In spite of the tight grip he had, the impact almost wrenched the knife out of his hand.

The darkness erupted with the creature's agonized wail.

Covering his face with both hands, the reaper staggered backward, tripping over his limp foot. He shambled off into the darkness to the far corner of the room, but David knew that he hadn't left the schoolhouse because he could still hear the creature wailing in pain.

Before he consciously thought about it, David turned and handed the knife to the Ferryman, who solemnly bowed his acceptance as he took it.

With a slow, graceful morion, the Ferryman spun around and tossed the knife into the seething darkness that had opened up like a dark flower behind him. Instead of falling or disappearing from sight, the knife seemed to float, suspended in midair as it spun slowly end over end like a compass needle going haywire.

"You fool!" the reaper shouted.

From deep inside the well of darkness, David heard a faint ruffling sound that immediately made him think of fluttering wings. He watched in utter amazement as a large bird—what looked like an owl—flew out of the maelstrom and clasped the knife with both claws. Wheeling about in a lazy circle, the bird flapped its wings and flew away. Then, with a softly fading *whoosh*, it flew off into the darkness.

"Are you ready to go?" the Ferryman asked, extending one bony hand to Karen.

She turned and looked at her father. For the first time since he had met her here in the Shadowlands, he saw the trace of a smile flit across her mouth.

"Go on," David said, choking with emotion as he motioned her forward. "Don't worry. I'll see you again. Real soon."

Karen looked up at the Ferryman, who was nodding his head gently. "I promise you he will," he said. "Come with me, child."

David almost shouted for her to stop when he saw Karen take the Ferryman's hand. The skeletal fingers closed around her fragile hand, engulfing it. David was burning with the desire to say something more to her. There was still so much in his heart that he had never told her.

But his voice failed him.

Tormented with doubts about his decision, he watched as the Ferryman and Karen turned and walked into the swirling darkness. Their figures wavered for a moment, seeming to swell to gigantic proportions as they rose upward in a lazy spiral. The Ferryman's cloak flapped and snapped in the gentle wind, sounding like a bird's flapping wings. And then the darkness collapsed around chem like heavy, velvet curtains. Once they were gone, the only sound David could hear was the raw, winding moan issuing from deep inside his chest.

"You are a *total idiot!*" the reaper said.

His voice was hard-edged, but it barely cut through to David's awareness.

"And you *will* regret this, I *promise* you that much!"

Shaking his head like a dazed prizefighter, David turned around slowly and faced the reaper. He was still hunched in the far corner of the room with one hand covering the wound on the side of his face. David tried not to imagine the terrible damage the knife might have done to him, but he was satisfied that he had marked the reaper.

"I don't regret it in the least," David said.

He turned and looked longingly at the spot where, moments before, the Ferryman and Karen had disappeared.

"Even if it's like you said," he continued, feeling his strength returning as he spoke. "Even if the Far Realms are the same thing as Oblivion, at least I'll know that she's out of *your* reach."

"Oh, I wouldn't be so sure of that," the reaper replied threateningly, but David realized that the reaper hadn't made a move to attack him, even though he was no longer holding the knife. Either the wound had seriously weakened him, or else he didn't dare attack him because David was somehow under the Ferryman's protection.

It didn't matter.

Whatever else happened, David thought, no matter where Karen may have gone with the Ferryman and no matter what Sarah did or what happened to her next, he was content. He knew that he could have chosen to go with Karen, but he realized that the love he felt for his ex-wife was still powerful, too. He was determined to stay in the Shadowlands, if only so he could study and maybe even master some of those powers the Ferryman had mentioned. Maybe he could even learn to communicate with Sarah and make it so she could see him.

In any event, he was going to keep a watchful eye on her just to make sure she was safe. David was even content to wait even until Sarah died, if he had to, and then... and then he would decide what to do next.

"There are two more of those knives in the Skinlands, you know," the reaper said teasingly.

David saw him as he started moving toward the opened doorway. His foot made a long scraping sound as it dragged across the floor, and he kept his hand clasped over his wounded face.

"As soon as I find another one of them," the reaper said, "if my horde of barghests hasn't already ripped your corpus to shreds by then, you're the *first* wraith I intend to *use* it on."

David heard himself sniff with soft laughter the sound multiplying in the darkness of the schoolhouse, sounding like several other people laughing as well.

Suddenly he felt much less fearful than he had since arriving in the Shadowlands. He watched as the reaper limped out of the schoolhouse. The creature's hunched silhouette looked like an ink stain against the dark background of the night before it disappeared.

"We'll see about that," David shouted after him.

He listened to the hollow reverberation of his voice in the big room. Then he started to laugh. For the first time, David actually enjoyed hearing the soft chuffing sound of his laughter as it blended with the other sounds and voices that were all around him in the dark schoolhouse.

Curious about other Crossroad Press books? Stop by our
website: http://crossroadpress.com
We offer quality writing
in digital, audio, and print formats.

Subscribe to our newsletter on the website homepage and
receive a free eBook.

www.ingramcontent.com/pod-product-compliance
Lightning Source LLC
Chambersburg PA
CBHW021427240626
47153CB00001B/63